The Seven Seals of Agartha

Harley Aguilar

D1527181

The world is not as it seems.

Each hidden truth brought to light reveals further mysteries beyond.

How deep dare we go in search of the final secret?

CHAPTER 1 BATTLE AT SEA

The crew of the pirate ship Luna Triada had been three weeks at sea when the lighthouse came into view. Their merry songs of plunder from faraway lands ended with a call of alarm from the crow's nest.

The one-eyed captain Jofon trained his spyglass on the dark silhouette emerging behind a rocky island. It was an enormous black vessel, with wide sails and hundreds of oars bearing down on them with unnatural speed.

Behind the captain at the bow, the sailors had gathered in ominous silence. They knew what was to come. What they needed was to hear in their commander's voice their chances of survival.

The cabin boy came to stand beside Jofon.

"What is it, Father?"

"A Kinari war ship. Get below deck, Ranser." The old sea captain growled and turned to his men. "It seems our fate has caught up with us. There is *no* escape! Today we *fight*! For our treasure, for our ship, for our lives! These dogs are far from home, let us lay them to rest in the deep!"

The pirates scrambled to their battle stations, preparing to use the powerful weapons they had found on their journey to defend against the ones who had invented them. Two pairs of sailors cranked the windlass on each of the harpoon-ballistae at the bow and stern, while others began climbing the masts with packs of glass bottles.

There was still no sign of movement on the enemy deck as the Kinari warship drew near and the pressure of the sky reversed. Shuddering with the whipping wind, the gigantic black ship lulled side-to-side in a slow, menacing dance.

"Aim for the sails!" Jofon called out to the harpooners, "Hold!" He knew the wind at their stern would limit their range. It seemed to be their only chance of slowing the war ship down, they must not miss. The gap was closed in a few short seconds. "Fire!"

The rope spun in a blur from its coil as the whirling iron bolts flew out over the ocean. A crosswind drifted them to the side, causing one of the shots to miss, but the other tore through two of the great blackened sails.

The sailors began firing arrows from atop the masts and prepared their anti-ship defense. They filled the glass bottles with volatile liquor, plugging them with strips of cloth which they set alight and hurled across onto the enemy vessel's deck, spreading flame along the rigging and sails. But the dark craft charged on them relentlessly as the skies darkened with encroaching storm clouds.

Jofon tried to swing the wheel and turn away but it was too late. The spiked iron body of the massive Kinari war boat rammed into the comparatively delicate Luna Triada, shattering the timbers of her hull like dry twigs underfoot and causing some of the sailors to fall from the masts in the initial impact.

The grizzled captain turned back and drew his cutlass as he watched the landing plank rise up from the enemy stern and drop its spiked end onto his deck. Lightning flashed above as the water and sky churned and darkened, and a line of knights in black armor began crossing the plank.

"Titanos, lord of the sea is with us!" Jofon called above the wind and rain, "Have no fear!"

Charging to the breach point, Jofon picked up a belaying hook and stood on the boarding plank, parrying blows from the invaders' strange swords and spears with the hook, chopping at necks with his cutlass, and kicking the clumsy brutes into the water.

The ballista had readied another shot and fired at the back of the line of soldiers, impaling and knocking many overboard, but they continued to file out of the ship's dark underbelly like ants from a hive.

Valiantly Jofon held them back until the Luna Triada, taking on water in the lower decks, listed low and crashed broadside into the Kinari ship, breaking off the boarding plank and nearly crushing the plummeting captain between the hulls.

Jofon caught hold of a rigging rope and pulled himself back up to see the enemy soldiers jumping down from the deck of the enormous warship whose edge was now directly above their tilted, crippled vessel. The sailors engaged the invaders in a disorganized melee.

The waves swelled and gushed over the combatants and the wind roared in fury. Flashes of light descended from the clouds and lit both enmeshed sets of sails ablaze. A few caught sight of the towering wall of water rising up in the distance, and knew the fight was over.

To the cabin boy Ranser, sequestered in the captain's quarters beneath the bow, the world seemed to heave and crash with ever-intensifying violence. He heard shouting and banging on the door just as he was thrown to the deck and sent rolling across it. He slammed hard to the port wall among a shower of coins which spilled from a jarred-open chest.

Ranser's head came to rest near a shining jewel set into an ornate golden crown. The child had no care for treasure, yet he regarded this gilded headpiece with awe, and reached out to grasp it, but was again hurled across the room and inundated with water as the waves capsized and swallowed the Luna Triada and the Kinari war ship.

Some fools clutched ingots of gold as they sank to their doom. But the crown was unclaimed as it drifted down to bury itself in the silt at the bottom of the ocean, not to be seen again for a very long time.

* * *

Where the sea met the land, a current found a path through a long chain lined up through the endless churning of the sands.

Jolted awake by some inner implosion, Ranser opened his eyes as the surf bubbled up and caressed his twisted and mangled body.

In the sky above, the gulls called out to each other "It is still alive."

The sunlight gleamed from the crests of the waves and crystals of the sand, making them hum with a low-pitched resonance.

As the saltwater poured from Ranser's lungs, a vision came to his blurred eyes of the massive sandaled feet of the Sea God, Titanos, moving across the great waters, the rest of his body hidden high above the clouds.

Ranser had never held true belief in the stories of the old sailors. Even as the giant legs blocked out the sun and its feet tremored the beach on which he lay, Ranser could hardly believe it. The vision of the enormous man, to which the ocean was but a puddle, moved off into distance before the purging finally ended.

The cabin boy collapsed on the warm sand. At such a young age, he had been many places, and suffered many hardships. The life of a boy at sea is not an easy one, but the thrill of adventure and discovery is worth every toss and turn of the keel, so the mariners had said.

Turning over, the waves washing up with his own blood and splinters of wood, Ranser looked up, expecting to be surrounded by the faces he had always known, that were always there. There was no one in sight.

He called out for his adoptive father "Jofon!" But there was no reply.

He felt as if he were sinking as he scanned the coastline, which was unperturbed but for the sparse wreckage of the ship Ranser had sailed in on. The sun was setting, a high tide was moving in.

Ranser pulled himself out of the water with his right arm. His legs and left arm seemed to be numb, as if he had lain asleep on them, and they hummed with a dull warmth.

His wounds were grievous. The femur of his left leg protruded from the middle of his thigh, his left shoulder was dislocated, and his ribs and skull were cracked. Yet all this crushing agony was dammed like a great river by the boy's strength of will, for the moment.

Ranser called out again. "Jofon!"

Again there was no response, and his spirit sank yet further.

Ever since his earliest memory, of being praised by the old one-eyed sea dog Jofon and his shipmates, who were surprised a boy of such a young age could actually help out on the boat, in the time since then he had never once been completely alone. The sailors called out to each other constantly, working together and watching out for each other. If a man went overboard they'd have to rescue him right away.

What is this solitude? What am I to do?

Ranser fell back, sinking into the sand, his eyes shining and clinched shut. The arrows of pain stabbed up his leg and across his back, pouring fire through his nerves. He'd broken a finger before, and by that time had learned not to cry around the sailors, and he held himself together back then.

Now, all alone, critically wounded and nearly drowned, he lost his solidarity. The pain washing over him like an ocean of acid and the despair of being a child lost in a strange land were too much for him. He wept for his own pitiful, helpless state, and for his lost friends. Ranser had thought he would sail to new ports with Jofon and the others forever, now this childhood illusion was quickly and violently shattered, and the tears came ever more uncontrollably.

Why has this happened?

The despair turned to anger, pounding his fist into the sand he cried out a curse to the one he blamed for this calamity, "Titanos!"

Isn't he supposed to be a protector of sailors? Why hadn't he helped?

Ranser's anger turned to determination. He resolved to confront the "Sea God" Titanos, and make him answer for this. Perhaps, he thought, when I grow a bit taller.

Among the wreckage around him, Ranser found some lengths of rope and broken planks of wood from which he fashioned a crude splint as Jofon had shown him when he broke his finger. Then he pulled himself up the beach under a small overhang of rock.

For what seemed an eternity, he sat contemplating his situation, propped up against the weathered stone cove. His stomach clenched and gurgled with hunger. He might have been able to crawl to the nearby forest, and there find some plants or scuttling vermin to eat, but he knew nothing of land survival, and felt the beach a much less hazardous location (which it was; the flora and fauna of this area were none too friendly to humans).

There seemed to be no good options. He could barely move and there appeared to be no signs of civilization anywhere around, although if this was an island, it was a huge one, and most likely inhabited to some extent. Ranser shuddered to think of being hauled away by wild-eyed savages, beaten, clubbed, cut to pieces. A peaceful sinking into the water would be a preferable end. He sighed in defeat.

What woe to be so forsaken!

Just before the sun set and the boy prepared for a grim night of pain, starvation and loneliness, a small shadow came bouncing along the shore. As it came closer, Ranser saw it was a shaggy, floppy-eared little puppy, bounding toward him with a flailing crab in its mouth. To Ranser's amazement, the animal ran up to him with bright eyes and wagging tail, dropping the crab on its back before him with an excited yap. Thanking the dog and the crab, he pulled it apart, enjoying the tender meat and sharing it with his new companion.

The little wolf ran and jumped around him, barking a few times, wondering why he did not get up. Ranser tried to explain that he had hurt his leg, but the young pup did not yet understand. It ran off again, digging in the sand and returning with another succulent shelled creature. They shared the shellfish happily, then Ranser reclined on the sand and the furry little creature snuggled up next to him. He would get some sleep tonight, thanks to this tiny wolf and the food he brought.

The world whispered in his ear.

Ranser, you are not alone. You will not perish before your purpose is fulfilled.

CHAPTER 2 CHILDHOOD DREAMS

Levan awoke from a restless slumber. His dreams had been more vivid than ever.

On a bank of the Velumine River, the wise men and women of the council sat round a campfire in hushed anticipation. Levan was walking along the water's edge when he saw the fire like a mirage in the distance. He was drawn to the circle, and every eye there followed him, waiting for him to sit and speak.

"Hello, friends. A comforting evening isn't it?" The thin, russet-haired boy greeted them.

"It is indeed." One of them replied with a warm smile.

The group sat closely knit, one of the men sitting on a log, a woman reclined against his legs, the other two men and two women in similar proximity, and the fire-maker was adding logs to the flame.

Studying their faces, Levan realized that they were not from this land, but seemed somehow familiar. In fact, each of them seemed to have the distinctly different features of the humans of each of known continents of the world. The prospect of stories from distant lands intrigued Levan immensely.

"Where are you from?"

Their eyes attentive to him and his question, they exchanged knowing glances.

"From all the corners of this world, as you know." A blonde bearded man clad in bear fur answered with an exotic accent.

"Just as you, we are everyone that came before us." Said a comely woman with dark skin as a tiny frog hopped from her shoulder to her lap. "And what has brought you here?"

Levan thought for a moment. "I seek the mysteries and magics of this world."

"Let us show him." A red-haired man turned to one of the women behind him who held a preening insect. Her eyes lit up. "Yes."

The magicians lent him their vision, and Levan was inundated with images, feelings, and sounds. His thoughts and memories melded with those of all the people around him. He lay back on the river bank next to the fire, experiencing all the pleasure and pain of countless lifetimes in a few short moments.

Before his eyes, a vision coalesced of a huge disk of interlocking people with Levan at the center, and a deep, hypnotic drumming seemed to come from everywhere and nowhere. He floated languidly in this bottomless sea of emotion, and had never felt such a sense of belonging, acceptance, unconditional love.

In this circle of humanity, not one of them had he ever met, all eyes seemed to be on him, all hearts beat for him, he was at the center of the universe and yet above it, a light by which his people found the path of harmony with their world and each other. He lived a thousand lives in the next moment, reaching the highest peaks of glory, knowing the most powerful love.

With utmost pity he also delved also into the darkest pits of human experience, lived the torture of those poor souls condemned to a cage or forced to toil their lives away in a mine, denied the life-giving light of the sun, never knowing a moment's peace or happiness in their entire lives, but for the sweet escape of sleep. Some of them came to embody the careless, selfish nature of mankind, those things that make us feel we are separate from the plight of our neighbors. These low spirits, who feed from the sorrow and conflict of the living, and bespoil those things which are sacred, they are to be avoided, but not ignored, lest their fate become your own.

He wished he could share with those people whose hearts were hardened by the pain and injustices of their lives this same sublime knowledge of each soul's endless journey, and the connectedness they share with their world and family, both living and departed.

Somewhere in all these lifetimes of his ancestors, his own story, his origins, the people he knew, even his own name became less relevant as he saw the truth with the eyes of his spirit, that he had had many, many names.

Levan recounted the dream as he took his daily walk to the wizard's academy in the city, and pondered its meaning.

Perhaps my imagination had gone too far. Or could it have been a memory from my ancestors?

He daydreamed his lessons away that day.

The student of magic was supposed to be learning to purify water, but instead heated the flask with the stopper plugged and shattered it. His face flushed in embarrassment as his classmate Sabrena erupted in laughter at his mistake.

His instructor Tosgan shrugged it off with an amused smirk, "Levan's affinity appears not to be with water. No matter, we all have our specialties."

The citadel's tower cast a long shadow across Levan's path homeward.

In the darkened ditch below, two filthy men fought viciously for a moldy rind of bread. When one had rendered the other unconscious, he ate the soggy morsel while grumbling vague insults and threats at the passing onlooker.

There is more than enough food for all. How do we avoid entwining our lives in greed or guile?

A cool breeze followed his walk home that day, and he passed no one else on the road.

He finished the chores just as the sun set, its last fading glow emblazoning a fleet of dark storm clouds sailing in like pyre-boats across the sea of stars. Levan put the animals inside as the raindrops began.

Tomorrow was his last day of magic schooling, and his final test, but there was no time to study.

If we lived in a manor we would have candles to read by at night. Of course if we lived there, we'd have a couple of sweet maids to do the cleaning and the milking.

Levan's mother had already fallen asleep. He wondered if she knew it would be like this when she married a free-spirited adventurer. Now his poor, addled mother's follies and delusions no longer held Levan captive. Though he had never realized it, her humble and pragmatic nature tempered the wild spirit he had inherited from his father, creating in him the best of two very different worlds. It was long since he had appreciated her unconditional love, as is typical of adolescents.

He planned to set out on his own, to know all the world's mysteries, and become the greatest wizard that ever lived. As soon as he'd earned enough gold, he would find a good caretaker to stay with mother.

The rain pattered on the thatched roof, thunder rumbled in the distance and Levan drifted off to sleep, but it would not last for long.

❋ ❋ ❋

A drop of icy water fell from a crystalline stalactite, splitting across the bridge of his cracked, bloody nose to stream into both of his eyes. It took a moment for Avus to remember where he was as he blinked away the haze from his sight.

The high ceilings in this underground cavern were covered in white spires of crystal reaching down to the terraced flowstone floors, and dripping copious amount of water which ran in little channels through the rock to the underground river cutting a path through the middle of the chamber.

The Deepriver Hall.

Avus and his students, twelve in all, had been surrounded by scarlings, the twisted mutations said to have crawled from the Great Scar when it opened a vast rift in the land more than a hundred years ago.

These monsters had jet-black skin, shiny like onyx, with sharp horns protruding from their head and shoulders. They were nearly as tall as a man, hunched over, and carried swords, spears and knives wrought of stone coated in crystal. A formidable enemy, especially that there were at least ten of them, and he the only capable fighter.

Avus was telling the students of the dangers of the swift, freezing current of the Deepriver, and the slippery channels in this particular hall that made caution imperative, when he noticed the swarm of bulging white eyes creeping in on them from the shadowy recesses of the cave.

The stout dwarf cursed under his breath. Scarlings had never been seen in this part of the caves, though he'd encountered them before with hunting parties nearer the Scar. Many of those hunters never returned. Of the few scarlings they killed, none there had dispatched one without injury, including himself. Somehow, in those sickly, gaunt limbs, they possessed an unnatural strength, perhaps the equal of a dwarf, and, he conceded them, a slightly longer reach.

Avus clutched his axe tightly. The dwarf children

had already noted the threat and began to move toward their teacher. He thought the elven young ones perhaps could see something as well, though their vision be a bit different than ours, working best in the starlight. The majority of the spelunking class, being human kids, were mostly oblivious to the movement of the others, and spread out much farther than Avus would have liked them to be.

"What are they, master?" Darius asked. He was a dark haired human youth of thirteen, sharp of mind but slight of build.

"Scarlings, deathly creatures from the deep. Everyone, gather behind me!" His words were spoken in a sharp whisper, reflecting their crucial order at just such an angle to reach the area behind a huge slab of slate where the rest of the class were (a skill the dwarves called Stonespeak, which he had promised to teach them).

The dwarven warrior moved to the front of a semi-circular cavity in the wall, herding the students behind him as they moved up the staircase-like terrace of crystal.

The last two boys jumped down from the precipice they were exploring to the flat expanse before the frozen waterfall staircase. As he followed behind his friend with the torch, some nightmarish black claws reached out from the darkness, ripping at Garico's back. His cry of horror echoed through the cavern.

The boy showed his speed and surefootedness as he dashed off ahead of Deko, leaping across moist, slippery boulders with the tattered remains of his ripped shirt streaming behind him.

Deko was turned around toward the darkness, seemingly in shock from what he had seen receding into the shadows from behind Garico. He was walking backwards, pointing the torch warily, moving far too slowly. The monsters were all around him, just outside the light.

"Deko, run!" Avus called to him emphatically. He tried to move down the staircase to the boy's aid, but the scarlings began to creep up to the edge of the rock face covering the children, and he had to retreat to his former position to ward them away from the small opening at the front.

Garico climbed up and rejoined the group, collapsing in the small cave, his friends helping him to lie down and regain his breath.

The torch in Deko's hand sparked and flared as it fell to the ground, and a flurry of movement snuffed it out. All of his peers saw this, and some of them gasped in fear or broke into tears and wails of despair. But Avus saw that one of the creatures had struck the torch out of the boy's hand and they swarmed on it, giving Deko the chance to run for the frozen waterfall.

Avus had made Deko a Torch Leader because he was strong in spirit and body. He now saw his faith rewarded by Deko's expeditious escape, in the perfectly balanced form of a StoneWalker, seeing the footfalls even without the light on them.

The scarlings moved fast up the waterfall just behind him. Their claws ripped at his back, monstrous arms reaching around to pull him away into the deep dark, never to be seen again. But at the last step, Deko leaped and was caught by Avus' outstretched arm, pulling him up to the ledge with the other students.

Then it began.

With a deafening, stone-shattering crash, colossal sections of the cavern walls splintered and collapsed all around. The children gave a brief wail of alarm, but were unharmed and panic was averted by the presence of their teacher, Avus.

But another, fully terrified cry of distress came from across the chamber. It was a girl's voice.

There were only two girls in this troupe, and Avus had noted the human Alecea's presence in the protected alcove behind him.

That left only NuMoon, one of the four young

elves. She had wandered away from the group, crossing a narrow crystal bridge over the river to study a flower which grew in a tiny patch of sun from a skylight in the cavern ceiling above. Her eyesight was good enough let her wander freely without need of a light source, but not so keen as a dwarf's, who would never be snuck-up-on in the underground. She had realized the danger too late.

The cave rumbled and shook violently, dislodging more rocks and collapsing the small bridge that NuMoon was trying to move back to.

Another great aftershock hit, and a massive boulder shifted from the wall behind Avus, blocking off the front of the alcove where the children huddled. He could see and hear them through a tiny opening near the bottom of the boulder, and knew they were unhurt.

The rock trapped the young ones in and the monsters out, a boon at the moment, giving Avus the opportunity to begin running toward the river and the panicking elf girl on the other side.

The world shook ever more intensely, sending monolithic spears of stone smashing down from above as Avus bounded down the frozen waterfall. He caught sight of the girl for a moment, but she moved behind a rocky outcrop along the steep shore in an attempt to avoid the encroaching fiends. Her arm was bloodied and she was crying.

Come on, Avus! Go!

He heard her scream in pain as the scarlings stabbed and hacked at her exposed fingers with their stone weapons.

"No! Get away from her!" His heart thumping in his chest, Avus threw his hammer from far across the room, knocking one of the scarlings into the river, where it was swiftly sucked under and swept away.

But it was not enough.

A chittering flock of vile creatures pulled the tiny elf girl away from her rocky perch and swarmed around her.

NuMoon was knocked to the ground and crawling toward the river when Avus reached the other side. His gaze met her bloody, tear-streaked face before he leapt into the river, an image which seared forever into his memory.

He knew jumping to the other side was not dwarvenly possible, but he had to try anyway. The frighteningly-fast current sent him careening downstream as he struggled to resurface.

Just when he gained his first breath of air, it was knocked out of him as he slammed into a huge, flat boulder within the stream. His axe dug into his back as the freezing water rushed past him. With a groan he exerted all his strength to stand up and push through the iron wall of water between him and the other side of the river.

Avus hoisted himself up on rocky ledge of the shore and looked to where the girl had fallen. The scarlings were crawling all over like a swarm of insects. Then they noticed him and ceased their frenzy in order to defend their prize.

As the monsters stood and skulked towards him, Avus saw the blood splattered across the rock, the fine golden hair splayed out in a slowly spreading crimson pool, like sunrays in a blood-red sky.

At once he was out of his body, floating above and looking at himself. His wild, primal roar reverberated throughout the cavern as he charged the army of seething scarlings.

Avus, or whoever was controlling his body, waded through the front lines of the black-skinned creatures, heaving his double-bladed battle axe across the uniform level of their throats. A spray of glowing-green blood filled the air as he severed three heads on the first swing, and two on the backswing. While this action would have given most any group of fighters pause, the scarlings were fearless in the dark, and did not relent, but pushed their attack in further, creating a crowded circle around the raging dwarf.

From the small opening in the hidden alcove, the students saw the phosphorescent blood flying from the steel edge like a neon whirlwind on the far side of the underground river. Avus' blade cut through wide swaths of them as they prodded and slashed with their weapons, drawing his blood here and there, which only seemed to further enflame his mad frenzy.

As Avus watched from above, he was astounded at the ferocity with which he fought, and the sheer carnage he was wreaking on his foes.

With a bellow of fury he brought his weapon down in a vicious chop, rending a scarling from shoulder to waist. Sparks flew from the blade as it slammed into the rock, carving out a jagged furrow of sundered stone.

When he lifted the axe again, Avus could see that the haft was badly cracked, and would soon break. He hefted the weapon to swing again, and as he did, the axe head broke off, spinning forward with great force. The whirling missile sliced through many scarlings, killing and lopping off limbs, before it lodged with a shower of sparks in the far cavern wall.

Avus was only a few steps away from the fallen girl. The bloodthirsty wretches still blocked his way and continued to charge toward him. He caught the sword arm of an attacker and, with a beastly roar, stabbed the broken end of the axe haft through its chest and kicked it backward.

The dwarven warrior then dashed forward, his shoulder lowered, and slammed into the next advancing scarling, knocking it down near where NuMoon's body lay. He moved to its head and dug his fingers into the eye sockets, slamming the skull into the ground, screaming with rage. When it would not stop moving, Avus moved to its throat and fiercely, maniacally tore out the vital artery there with his teeth. His head rose up, looking like a lion after a kill, mouth dripping bright-green blood.

Avus was shocked and revolted by this horrific thing he had just done, and the scarlings seemed to have the same reaction; they faltered in their attack.

The ground started quaking again, the magnitude rising in intensity. The walls cracked, ancient supports crumbled and gigantic columns of stone crashed down.

Then it ended.

The Deepriver Hall was deathly silent when the dwarf awoke, pinned to the ground by fallen debris. A dwarf-sized chunk of rock had landed on Avus' head, knocking him unconscious, which was a fortunate respite for a time from the pain of the war-ship-sized stone wall that fell and crushed his right leg.

He threw his voice to the top of the chamber, resonating it within the alcove the children were in, being glad to hear it still mostly intact. "Cave cubs, make a noise if you are in there."

The rapid trickle of the river was the only sound for a moment. Then he heard a stirring of rubble, and a pained chittering below.

Avus looked down from the columns of stones he was wedged in-between, and saw a dark arm and torso rising up from the shattered debris just below him. He took up the nearest large rock and threw it down on the struggling scarling, sinking its head back into the sand. Yet more of its body emerged as it spasmed and convulsed, and Avus threw down more and more stones. After the first few small boulders he threw he was fairly certain it posed no more threat, but he kept tossing them down there anyway as he tried, with great pain and effort, to dig himself out.

What had fate had befallen the children?

The question drove his haste in finding his way out. Dislodging his maimed leg, he dragged himself up higher on the column to survey the cave.

The sun was shining in a newly-collapsed exit across the river. The student's alcove was partially opened, and his hope returned, as he saw a path from there to the exit, flooded with light.

They surely escaped through there.

Avus struggled to the bank of the river. Crossing was his only means of escape, as futile an idea as it was.

I will return for you, NuMoon.

He was just about to hurl himself into the dark rapids and hope for the best when he heard shouts coming from down the hall.

Torchlight entered the cavern as the human boy Deko led a group of armed dwarves and humans to the Deep-river Hall.

"There! At the river! There he is!"

The rescuers used a pair of stilts connected by a span of canvas to cross the river, the same device they would use as a stretcher to carry the wounded.

Brave Deko. He led them to safety and returned with the rescuers to this perilous place.

Avus felt so low, he thought himself unworthy of saving.

I put the children in danger, I was unable to defend them. Poor, sweet, innocent NuMoon is dead and buried somewhere under that rock, and I, the despicable failure of a teacher, still draw unjust breath.

He waved the rescuers off as they tried to get him on the stretcher.

"Not *me*! Go get *her*!" Avus cried, pointing to the rocks behind him.

The rescuers were confused. There was no one else alive here.

Deko reluctantly explained. "It's NuMoon she...was killed by the monsters."

"Avus, we have to get you out of here." One of the armored rescuers with a long spear cajoled.

"We can come back with the right equipment—"

"No!" Avus yelled, getting up on his knees, dragging his crushed foot over to a tremendous slab of stone, as large as a cargo ship. "There will be nothing left by then! You

know elves have something very special in them—just like us
—her remains must be kept in their sacred ways! Erraahh!" He
slammed his palms against the mountainous stone, pushing
with all his might.

Awestruck for a moment as Avus lifted impos-
sibly huge stone column over his head, revealing the place
where the elf girl lay, the rescuers scrambled to duck into the
passage to reach her.

The dwarf's arm muscles quivered and swelled,
his veins bulging with torrents of power, and his skin turning a
darker and deeper shade of red with each passing second.

One of the rescuers pulled the girl's body out,
cradling her as if she were alive. Avus was glad the rescuer gave
this unfamiliar girl that dignity.

Now his work was done. His arms expired into
numbness, the blood drained from his head and his vision
faded out. He was unaware of the rest of his journey out of the
cave and to the nearby village which had no name.

✳ ✳ ✳

The boy and the dog had taken a wrong turn in
the night and were now lost in an unknown land. Icy rain
pelted their faces and thunder rumbled in the distance as they
continued down the muddy road. None of this was trouble-
some to either of them, until Rune tensed and began to stalk,
growling nervously.

The dark thicket to the left of the road bristled
with some menacing predator.

A cloud of ash and ember moved through the
shadows and Ranser lost sight of it until it was among the
canopy and drawing nearer, swirling through the limbs like an
ethereal serpent, its burning eyes fixed upon him.

Rune stood his ground and barked at the creature
which roared and billowed with dense black smoke and flame

as it charged forth from the treetops toward the dog.

The stones on this road were all perfect for throwing. Without hesitation, Ranser picked up one of these fist-sized rocks and flung it forth.

The stone flew perfectly into the monster's eye, but the smoke merely parted into two dragon-like heads, re-coiling to engulf both targets at once.

Just as the fiery jaws sprang forth from the tree-line, a thin tendril of light rose up from the ground, followed by a blinding flash. The searing burst of lightning exploded the creature into a plume of brittle ash, and blasted the boy back onto the the gravelly lane.

Perhaps nature was on my side this time, but I shall not test it further today.

"Rune, let's go!" Ranser shouted as he regained his footing and sprinted down the road.

An eerie fog lingered across the valley despite the driving storm as the boy and his dog raced in any direction far from what ever that thing was. Soon a warm glow flickered in the distance, and they hurried toward it.

A knock at the door was unusual at any time, but especially at this hour, and it awakened the young wizard Levan. The explosion of thunder on the third knock rattled the shutters of the small farm cottage and jarred him out of his bed. The storm had set in fiercely, setting the sky alight with darting webs of electricity.

Levan opened the door to see a rain-drenched, sandy-blonde boy and a shaggy gray dog on his doorstep.

"Um, good evening. I was wondering if you fo—" A crush of thunder drowned out the boy's words.

"What?" Levan did not immediately realize that his visitor was ill-prepared for travel in such a storm, and would surely not be just passing through this obscure lane in the countryside, asking to trade for some milk in the middle of the night. But Levan would have known to let him in, even if he were not shivering in the rain on his doorstep. Something told him that this boy had a powerful fate, a story to tell, and an important one yet to create. He waved him in. "Come in."

The soaking-wet traveler stepped into the cottage with his dog. Thoroughly saturated, the big, smoke-colored canine shook out its fur as soon as it stepped in, and the boy mimicked a similar motion, shaking his head back and forth, slinging droplets of water from his wild mess of sandstone hair. Levan's mother was sound asleep as always when there was noise in the night, almost nothing would wake her.

"We thank you." The traveler said. "Most days we'd just sleep outside but this tempest was way out of control. The sky be angry tonight, huh Rune?" He spoke the last words to the dog, reassuringly scratching its neck.

"It is." Levan noted the unusual accent and manner of his speech, determining him to be a traveler from far away. "Sorry about the weather, we usually keep it mild and calm here."

"Oh, don't worry about me," Said the boy, as a staccato of hailstones pelting the house and barn began, "seems like your crops will suffer the deluge more."

Levan had begun rekindling the fireplace. He winced as the hail smashed down loudly outside among the fields.

"Ha—you're right. That's just our custom in this land. Anything that meets the dissatisfaction of an honored visitor from a distant land is taken as our responsibility to right, or make amends for, as our once great king of old did. Come close to the fire. I, Levan Cloudborne, am pleased to make your acquaintance and bid you welcome to our humble dwelling, may our hospitality leave you wanting for nothing."

"Pleased to meet you as well, I am called Ranser..." He tried to sound proper, but his introduction was not so eloquent as Levan's, who nearly went to the lengths the elves do at greetings, minus the genealogies and family trees. A sailor's greeting was never formal, and they rarely belonged to clans, so they used no surname.

Levan brought Ranser a dry, stone-colored tunic.

"So if I may ask, to what do we owe this pleasure?" Levan was aware this question was most often used sarcastically, and vaguely so did Ranser, but, even though it was very late in the night and he did have a test the next day, he was truly happy to see spend some time outside of school with someone near his age.

"Well, Rune and I were headed to the city, thought we might find some gainful employ in the capital." Ranser said, warming his hands.

"Oh, where were you before?" Levan asked, sitting down by the fire.

"At a farm, like this one, far over the hills to the north, by the seashore where my ship was wrecked..."

The old farmer's wife was gathering shells and driftwood on the beach when she found Ranser in his cave, dying of thirst. She brought her husband and they carried him back to the farmhouse. The puppy he'd named Rune followed. There, he was nursed back to health, and he stayed, helping with the farm. The old farmer and his wife were very glad he was there, as they had no children of their own, and he was a great help to them.

"So why'd you leave?"

"After the fifth harvest I helped with, near the beginning of this year's summer, we woke up one day to find all of our animals slaughtered, their bodies were chewed up, some of 'em carried away, and Rune was gone. I heard him growlin' and barkin' in the night, thought he took off to chase somethin', didn't think anything of it. Later on he came back all slashed up and wobbly. I knew he didn't kill the livestock, but the old farmers wouldn't listen."

Levan looked over at Rune, stretched out and asleep by the fire. There were livestock animals in their pens in the same room to which the dog didn't give a second glance. He believed Ranser was right.

"What did they do?"

"The old man said we'd have to put him down. We couldn't just let him go wander the countryside wild, could attack a person. I begged him, said he wouldn't hurt anyone or anything. But the farmer would not abide."

The farmer's wife was now deathly afraid of Rune, even though she was very fond of Ranser. They gave him the ultimatum: get rid of the dog or both of you must leave.

"So," Ranser continued, "I said, we'll go then. I'd become strong enough to make my own way in the world, thanks to them. I could not ask for more."

The old farmer and his wife hugged him together. She pleaded with Ranser, please, couldn't he just get a sheep dog or a gopher dog, instead of such a big scary one, but it was no use. Rune was Ranser's first and most loyal friend in this entire land.

"And besides, that was no place for either of us to stay." Ranser added, petting Rune.

Levan imagined it was quite a change for him, to have grown up on the sea, literally always moving, then to spend several years not straying far from a single spot.

"I'm going into the city tomorrow." Levan yawned. "We can go together. There is never a dull moment there, always something to get into, perhaps too much. You may take my bed if you wish."

"No, this is fine, thank you." Ranser stretched out on the floor next to Rune in front of the fire, and Levan returned to his bed.

The hypnotic rhythm of the falling raindrops lulled them into a peaceful slumber. They had no way of knowing it would be the last of their carefree days of childhood.

CHAPTER 3
STRANGERS

The next morning, Levan awoke to the smell of bacon cooking. This was usually reserved for special occasions, and the pigs had not littered recently. His mother, Mimora, was chatting and laughing delightedly with Ranser, as he sat before a plate which she kept refilling with bacon, pork roast and vegetables.

Rune was happily wagging his tail and licking Mimora's face, standing up on two legs when she offered him a treat, to her great amusement.

"Look at how he dances for it! Haha! Do you see him? Oh, Levan, honey, do you want some bacon?" She always acted so sweet to him when visitors were around.

"You know I do." Levan replied curtly as he washed his face and hands and prepared his wizard robe and packs. "Ranser will accompany me to Karikoss. We may be home late."

Levan took some strips of bacon and headed out the door. It was a long walk and he didn't want to be late.

"A safe trip to you my son, mind your studies." She recited her daily mantra along with a kiss on the cheek.

Ranser took up his pack and weapon. It was a grain threshing sickle with a short, curved blade. He liked it because it reminded him of the curved sabers of the buccaneers, and the rigging hooks he'd become accustomed to using as a child sailor on the Luna Triada.

"Farewell, Mrs. Cloudborne! Thank you for the breakfast!" Ranser said as he walked out of the cottage. Mimora called back her earnest goodbye.

Two young men and a dog walked down a dusty road, eastward to the rising sun, and toward a fate they could never have imagined.

"There are some strange animals around here." Ranser remarked while chewing a piece of meat. "But you must know that. It was not far from your pasture when it attacked us."

"What animal?"

"Well, it was a...hmm...it put out a lot of soot and smoke, like wet firewood. It almost seemed to be a living flame."

"I protected the house from it one moon ago, but I could not save the herd." Rune barked, but was not understood.

"A living flame? A creature which emits smoke?" Levan rubbed his chin skeptically. "Hmm, no, I've read of no such thing. Nor does anyone ever seem to see anything out of the ordinary beyond the walls of the wizard's academy."

The thought occurred to Ranser that perhaps he had seen an illusion, a trick of the light and shadow. And the lightning bolt would've made the whole story too hard to believe.

"So you're a wizard, huh?" Ranser asked as they turned to the south, and the shining spire of the royal palace in the city of Karikoss came into view.

"That's right. I've studied with the mages of the court six days a week for the past six years." Levan was proud of his dedication to attendance, despite having to make a four hour walk each morning to get there.

"So, what can you do? Could you shoot lightning bolts from your hands, or fly? I guess you can't fly..." Ranser realized he would not walk to school if this was the case.

"No, flight is a very advanced and specialized

magic. Dangerous as well, in my opinion. Perhaps I will learn it later, but now my area of expertise is in manipulating the elements." Levan held his palm upward and uttered a pair of words which made his voice reverberate "**Manus Ignus**", causing a candle-like dancing flame to appear in his hand.

Ranser gave an unimpressed grunt.

Then Levan whispered something and threw the ball of fire upward, while continuing to stroll casually. The tiny flicker from his hand erupted into a huge scorching sphere of flame above their heads.

With a yell of shock and surprise, Ranser recoiled, covering his face in bewilderment and to shield from the radiant heat.

Levan glanced back with a smirk as he walked on. He knew the altitude was fine, that he would be unharmed and still feel the heat.

"What was that!?" Ranser panted.

"I'm working on my fire spells."

"Spells—so magic is real?" He tried to catch the magician's eyes to determine whether he was telling the truth, or merely a trickster.

The two shared a look of affirmation and amazement at the wonder of true magic, and a moment of silence in its profound implications. Though the young wizard Levan had studied for some years at the magic school in Karikoss city, it seemed he had only recently begun to awaken his real powers, and it still gave him pause to awe at the mysteries of what was really possible with enough focus and guidance, or exceptional inborn talent.

"I'm working on a newer spell, but it's not quite mastered yet. I practice it on these roads, since I can't use it in town, or on the farm."

"So you just blow stuff up?" Ranser asked with a grin. He would have been satisfied with a simple "yes".

"Not at all. We learn to brew potions, to imbue inanimate objects with magical power, purify water, and bend the elements to our will. Even the fireball can be put to good use re-seeding the great pine forests, and clearing pest-ridden areas."

Levan was not eager to know the effects of a fireball on a person. He was taught never to use his magic to attack, only defensively, if his or another life was in danger and there was absolutely no other course of action. And there was his belief that all of humanity was connected, able to judge his every move.

"You learn all those things from those books?" Ranser pointed to Levan's book satchel.

"Yes, and from my teachers."

"Do you...think you could teach me to read someday?" Ranser asked bashfully.

"Of course, it would be my pleasure. What is it that you want to read?"

"Well..." Ranser pondered wistfully, "hmm....if there is a map to my destiny, I should like to be able to decipher it."

"The city library has many maps. Perhaps you'd like to read the tale of the legendary ship's captain, Neru."

"That sounds great! What did this Captain Neru do?"

Levan began to relate the adventures of Captain Neru and his quest for his true love and his lost hat, when Rune began barking in alarm and ran to the top of the hill.

Ranser sniffed the air. A tinge of smoke came to his nose. He called Rune to his side with a sharp whisper.

A moment later they felt the ground shaking slightly and heard a rumbling coming from up ahead. A cloud of dust rose up in the distance as the tremorous din grew louder. Moving to the crest of a hill beside the road, they beheld the source of the chaotic clamor.

A massive army of men in dark armor, some riding tall black horses, were marching south-eastward. Their flags were red, black and gold, a banner Levan had never seen before.

"An invading army—I can't believe it!" Levan said, ducking his head down low, a look of grave peril on his face. "We need to hurry and go around them." Levan told Ranser, who was trying to comfort Rune's incessant growling. "Let's go!"

They ran to the south, cutting a path parallel to the road among the softly rolling hills north of Karikoss. They were well ahead of the invading army, who were moving slowly and to a disadvantageous spot for attack, as the city was flanked on two sides by steep cliffs, and the other sides were relatively narrow roads at the north and south exits. Levan could see one of those gates now, and it was opening.

From out of the north gate poured the knights of Karikoss in their glittering polished plate mail, prancing out on powerful armored horses and flying the umber and crimson pennant of king Fahfren III, an eagle talon clutching a serpent. Behind them were hundreds of pikemen, marching out in rows of five abreast across the drawbridge, their towering spears glinting in the early daylight. Masses of archers came out then, followed by a disorganized but enthusiastic throng of the common folk with leather armor at best, wielding pitch forks or other farm implements. Among them, one was mounted on a white stallion, holding a short, recurved bow up in the air with a shout as they charged.

Levan decided to detour to the west entrance instead of moving head-on towards the imperial army. It was a hidden path among the mountains. Ranser and Levan slid down a steep, rocky hillside as the imperial army thundered past them. Making their way across a clifftop, their path left sight of the main road. Ahead was a natural stone bridge spanning the wide canyon on their left which led into the city.

Rounding the narrow ledge along a jagged crag, Levan first came face to face with one of the tall, dark horses they'd seen earlier. Atop it, a fearsome-looking warrior in polished black armor pointed a vicious spear at his chest.

The warrior screamed in some strange language, his mount stamping nervously. "Atzhu zu hak! Zu hak!?" He kept yelling and pointing his spear, poking into Levan's chest.

Levan looked around in desperation. The cliff side was so narrow, he could barely move, and Ranser was right behind him. Neither could the soldier's horse back up, in fact this was no place for a horse at all. He had no idea what this man was saying, which made diplomacy impossible. Reluctantly, he prepared his last resort. A fiery glow sparked up in his hand.

"Wait!" Ranser pushed past Levan, holding out a handful of grain to the horse. The famished animal devoured it in an instant.

The warrior stopped yelling and lowered his weapon, but his face remained twisted in battle-rage, now tinged with confusion.

Ranser then held up his jug of water to the foreign soldier, who took it hesitantly from him, smelled it, sipped it, then poured its entire contents into his mouth. His mask of hatred had calmed, though the lines of it were still deep in his face. He nodded at the two young men for a moment in gratitude which crossed the language barrier and they saw the common humanity among each other.

Suddenly, with a whistling whoosh, a white arrow flew like a ray of light from across the canyon.

The warrior turned just in time to see the arrow enter and pass through his neck, shattering on the rock below him. He held his throat, gurgling up blood, and gazing with horror into Levan's eyes. The black horse reared and neighed, and the rider fell back, dragging the reins so that the horse fell too, and both slipped off the narrow ledge, plummeting to the rocky stream far below.

The mounted bowman on a white horse paused on the rocky precipice across the canyon, watching them for a moment, and performing some gesture with his hands.

Ranser shouted out to him. "Why did you do

that!?"

The archer returned his call across the gorge. "War has come! Get to safety as soon as you can! They must not find this entrance to the city!"

With another of his peculiar salutes, the mounted bowman rode off. A bit further up the mountain they saw him again, along with several other men. They were pushing huge boulders down to block off the far end of the bridge, and the western gate.

"Oh, no." Levan groaned. This meant only the north gate was accessible, as the south was blocked by impassable mountains and ravines on one side and a battlefield about to erupt on the other. "Come on, we have to backtrack."

They moved with haste down the way they came, descending the slopes of the cliffs down to the foothills and returning to the north road.

The imperial army had moved on to intercept the invaders to the east, and the gate was still open, with a few guards standing outside. Levan and Ranser dashed towards it, but saw the drawbridge raising up as they approached.

"Stop! Let us in!" Levan yelled to them, but to no avail. They made it to the closed gate and Levan addressed the guards on the other side of the moat. "I am a member of the court wizards, you must let us enter!"

"Court wizards? Where's ya pointy hat and ya old white beard then, boy?" The crude guard sneered at him and he and his partner shared a chuckle.

"Ahem...I'm not a fully official wizard yet but I have a test today at the Mage's Tower and you *must* let me in!" Levan stomped for emphasis.

"Oh, pardon me, O *great* sorcerer, perhaps you'd like to fly over this wall and see for yourself, everyone's scared outta their wits and locked up in their homes, expectin' enemy soldiers to be crawlin' in the streets by nightfall. Nothing is open today, not the library, the tower or the temple. We can't be lowerin' the drawbridge for two kids, not now." The guard spat crudely.

"Besides," added the other guard, "you could be Kinari spies, paid to get us to lower our defenses, then your army rushes in from the eaves behind you."

The crude guard laughed cruelly.

The paranoid guard glared over at his partner. "I do not jest." The laughing stopped.

"Come on Ranser, let's leave these dolts to their own folly. They are just sore they aren't strong or clever enough to go get some *action* with the *real* army down there."

Levan turned and walked away with a smirk. The crude guard growled in anger and started to stomp towards him.

"Boy, someone's got to teach you when to—" His words were cut short as he was collared by his partner and pulled back from edge of the moat which he nearly walked right into in his blind rage.

"Damn you, little he-witch!" The guard yelled out as Levan walked away with a bemused sneer.

He harbored no ill will toward the guard. He had been resistant to the first push, and, Levan supposed it was commendable that any soldier be staunch in following orders, even if they are to stay and guard the gate and let no one in. But he had fallen (nearly) for the taunt, and if the other one hadn't been there, it might have been fun to watch him try to swim in that armor.

As they walked northward, avoiding the main road, Levan's brow was furrowed with the implications of this war that had just begun.

If I were in the city, I may not be able to get out, and could end up defending it from the attack. What would mother do if I were gone for days? What if they raided the countryside, and our home? Will the instructor delay the test until the end of the siege?

Ranser kicked a rock down the lane. "Well, I guess we can't visit the city today. What shall we do instead?"

The innocent boy who grew up on the sea was

blissfully ignorant of the tumult and suffering these feudal military campaigns wrought. Whether won or lost, a heavy price was paid in order to glorify one supremely greedy and vain person, and this seemed to be an ancient, perpetuating cycle. Ranser was aware of what fighting and killing was, of course, but he did not understand conquering nations and subjugating people.

Levan wanted to omit these dark parts from his teaching when he began tutoring Ranser. Sadly, it seems history cannot be told without the stories of wars, violence and conquests. But his unshaken, unbound sense of carefree adventure was inspiring to Levan, and he put the conflict out of his mind for now.

"Why don't you show me where you saw that monster last night?" Levan suggested.

"Sure, it'll be this way." Ranser began down the hill to the side of the road.

"I've not taken this route before. Usually stick to the road." Levan noted as the footing became rocky.

"It's a straight shot from here, easy to find your way in the daytime."

Rune ran to the top of the ridge in front of Levan and Ranser. He stood there watching, ears perked up.

Friendly people? Food?

Ranser and Levan approached cautiously. There, in a newly tilled field, a woman stood gibbering and convulsing, spouting wails of madness and drooling on herself. There were a few houses in the distance, with more crop fields around them, and a few more people around, also seemingly stricken with the same strange malady.

"What is this? Has everyone here gone mad?" Ranser muttered, mystified.

"Perhaps we shouldn't get too close." Levan cautioned.

Ranser ignored his warning and moved in closer. The quivering woman in the field simply stood there, shaking, her auburn hair mostly covering her face.

"Hello?"

The woman gurgled unintelligibly.

Ranser bent down, attempting to look at her face. For a moment he caught her eyes, as clear as his.

"What is the matter?" Ranser asked.

The woman gnashed her teeth and growled under her breath to him: "Just go away!"

The woman began moving away, teetering and jilting, toward one of the farm houses. Ranser glanced at Levan to confirm they were both perplexed and intrigued. All the other villagers but one had also disappeared into one of the four buildings, three small cottages and a modest round communal building or boarding house.

A middle-aged woman stood near the corner of one of the cottages with a carrot in her hand. She looked at them for a moment, then spasmed toward the door, putting the carrot in her apron.

"See that? She's gathering food from her garden. These people may not be ill or mad at all." Levan said as Ranser followed his nose to the window of the cottage the woman had just entered. He took a long draught of the air.

"She's cooking—baking bread is nearly done." Ranser salivated at the intoxicating aroma. "Perhaps we should see if she needs any help?"

Levan knocked a few times, listening.

"I hear a child's voice inside."

"Should we—?" Levan was hesitant, but Ranser opened the door and walked right in. Rune stayed outside.

The elderly woman they had seen in the field was standing by a fire pit stirring a cauldron filled with delicious-smelling soup. There was indeed a brick oven with risen, browned bread inside. She looked up at them impatiently.

"It took you long enough. When I asked Non for help I didn't think he'd send kids. Oh well, wash up, dinner is ready. The basin is over there." She pointed them to a wash bowl at the side of the kitchen. They went over and began washing their hands.

"Who is Non?" Ranser whispered.

"I don't know." Levan shrugged.

"Let's play along anyway." Ranser said the next part aloud, in compliment to her cooking, "This stew smells great!"

The kind old lady poured bowls of the stew and broke pieces of bread into them.

"This one's for you..." She placed a bowl on the table in front of Levan.

"Levan."

"And for you."

"I am Ranser."

"And for me. My name is Undra." The sensible and efficient woman of about the same age as Levan's mother sat down at the table with them. "Now, I suppose you want to know why everyone in the town is acting mad."

Levan and Ranser exchanged a glance and nodded while sipping their soup (which was even more delicious than it smelled).

"Well, we convinced the king's men that a plague of madness had infected us, and they packed up and left town. All the better for us. If the king does not visit or pass through here, he will not build a road through our village and tax us into poverty. As long as we keep up the ruse to outsiders, we can be free."

Levan paused in eating to respond. "So you do not recognize Fahfren as king? You support the other?"

"We don't fly the flag of the king Fahfren, or that upstart of the Veldgar clan who claims to be the rightful sovereign. We have no wish to be part of a kingdom. But of late I have begun to suspect a spy from the king is in our village. There's these two visitors who've been staying at the boarding house, they know of the plague and aren't willing or able to move on. If it's discovered that our affliction isn't real, the king's wrath will be severe."

"We can go check them out for you." Levan reassured her. "Talking to them should be easier since we are not from this village. I have a very good sense of truth and deceit."

"Good, good. Return to me when you have a report on both of them, and I'll have a reward for you." Undra smiled at them.

They thanked the kind old lady for an excellent meal, and stepped outside. Ahead was the two-story longhouse which rented rooms to travelers, injured people, and refugees, before the plague supposedly came.

Rune, as usual, did not want to enter the building, and Ranser did not make him. He stalked around outside, catching a rat while waiting for them.

The inside of the boarding house was like a spider's web of dark wooden beams interconnected among the ceilings and rafters supporting the second floor balcony. The main hall was deserted and quiet.

Up the stairs on the second floor, a snoozing snore could be heard in one of the rooms, and a grinding, scraping sound like a whetstone on a blade came from the room across from it. At the top of the stairs, they signaled to each other which way they were splitting up: Ranser to the grinding and Levan to the snoring.

Levan opened the door to the contented buzz of a snoring dwarf. His leg was bandaged up and immobilized. The room was a terrible mess. He was surrounded by empty wine bottles, crumpled sheets of paper, and a capsized inkwell which dashed black stains across the desk and floor. Levan picked up a crushed piece of stationary with some writing on it.

"To the parents of NuMoon Aelivestian, my heart cannot express the eternal sorrow it feels for the passing of your daughter, my student and cherished friend. I would understand if you cannot forgive me, for I cannot forgive myself. I want you to know that I did everything I c—"

The note ended with a hole ripped in the page.

Another scrap of paper on the floor read thus:

"I, Avus Deepstone, hereby enter my resignation as cave lore teacher..."

The ink trailed off the page.

The note on the desk, partially smeared in spilled ink, was written quickly and sloppily, as if he had already been drinking copiously.

"My dear friends and family, there are many things I must atone for. I have not reached this decision lightly. The world is unbalanced with me in it, I have failed... (an ink blot obscures this part)....better if I had died. I will cry out my eternal apology as I leap from Boden Rock, and forever in the afterlife. Let my name never be spoken again in this world, please forget I ever existed..."

The poor dwarf had obviously suffered a great loss. A student of his had died, and he had contemplated suicide, written the notes, and drunk himself to sleep. Perhaps he still meant to go through with it, and jump off the high mountain cliff of Boden Rock.

Levan cleared his throat loudly. The dwarf stirred a bit but continued snoring. Levan tapped the bedpost with his foot and Avus moaned, turning over to look at him.

"Huh? What? Are you housekeeping? Not needed, please go." Avus groaned sleepily.

"I am Levan, a wizard and a healer. I can help you if you help me." Levan said, examining the wounded leg.

"What is it that you want?" Asked Avus, as a dog began barking outside.

"My associate and I are charged with keeping this little village safe. A suspicious light has been cast on the patrons of this establishment; it is believed that someone here is gathering information for sale. You know what I mean. A spy."

"Is that so..." Avus lowered his voice and leaned in. "Well I must say that man in the room across the hall is awfully shady. He's got crazy eyes. Two nights ago I thought I saw him dragging two corpses into the woods."

"My associate is over there interrogating him now."

Avus' eyes went wide, and his jaw dropped in a gasp. He tried to get up to move but grimaced in pain as he could not.

"Go! Go now to your friend's aid! He will kill anyone that uncovers him!" Avus cried from the bed as Levan turned to run, slipping slightly in his haste. He threw open the doors and saw a black-haired man crouching over Ranser, pushing a blade down towards his neck.

"Levan!"

The spy glared over his shoulder at Levan. He had a freshly opened laceration down his cheek and collarbone. Ranser tried to push him off then, but the burly man easily overpowered him, attempting to execute the boy before moving on to his friend in the robe.

Avus could see the scene from his bed in the other room, and with an agonized heave he threw himself onto the floor.

"Stop!" Levan magically pushed and taunted him as his hands drew up a powerful primal force in preparation to defend himself. The spy stood up from Ranser (who scrambled frantically to find his dropped weapon) and turned his blade on the new target.

Levan knew the time had come. This was it. Kill or die.

The spy stepped forward in a thrust at his midsection. The blade went by in slow-motion as Levan side-stepped and incanted his spell. But at the last moment a flaming skull flashed before his eyes, and for that instant he was ablaze in hellfire; eternal, unforgivable guilt. Instead of exploding or incinerating the man in a blast of flame, he spoke instead the imperfect words of the air sorcery he was studying.

From Levan's fingers swirled up a sparkling wind,

and two small cyclones blasted out from his palms, hurling the spy out into the hallway at the top of the stairs.

There, Avus had crawled on his stomach to the threshold and constricted his great arms around the covert agent's legs like a python.

Ranser, being unable to find his sickle, went running past Levan, screaming wildly and leaping onto the back of the spy man. He flailed and swatted at Ranser, slamming him into the wall while trying to kick at Avus.

"*Levan*—! Finish him!" Ranser growled like some feral beast as he struggled to hold on to the spy's neck.

Finally, the man got a grip on Ranser's shirt and tore the boy off his back, hoisting Ranser over his head and throwing him into the stairwell. Ranser tumbled down the stairs, striking hard edges in the most unforgiving ways. He crumpled to the landing with a pained moan.

Still struggling with Avus, the spy crouched down and began pounding his fist down like a hammer onto the dwarf's head.

Levan stood frozen for a moment. The cyclones had not enough force to incapacitate him. Though the taunt had worked, his power of suggestion was ineffective, as obviously the king trains his spies to resist pushing, or mind-manipulating magic. He had only just begun to skim the wall spells, and now was no time for experimenting. However tedious and unimpressive those sleep and stun spells he had skipped over seemed to him in his earlier years, he sorely missed them now. He felt cornered, trapped, given no choice. This trained killer was not going to have a problem exterminating two teenagers and a lame dwarf in a few more moments.

Levan now wished he had never learned the fire magic, that ultimate destructive force, so that he would not have to use it. He was terribly afraid to kill.

Avus, under great duress from the hail of blows slamming his head into the floor, any of which would have rendered a normal man unconscious, shouted out, "Levan! Do something!"

The young wizard felt his throat constricting, his muscles tensing. His breath came in short, quick bursts as he looked from the dwarf's now-bleeding head to the crumpled body of his friend Ranser at the bottom of the stairs, then to the evil man who had caused this.

You've given me no choice. I will not flee and trade their lives for mine. I'm so sorry, you don't know how this pains me, but I will free you from this shell that your soul may soar. Do not think ill of me, our lives are but a cycle. May your next turn be a happy and blessed existence.

Levan closed his eyes, pointing his outstretched finger, and spoke the incantation.

"Meld within the crucible, purified with dragon's breath...**Ignus Vureltis**!"

A searing tongue of flame roared out from Levan's fingertip. The spy did not have enough time to scream, for which Levan was grateful. The man's legs, the only part remaining, toppled down the stairs.

Avus lifted his head up from being totally submerged in ash, coughing and spitting. "The boy...how is the boy?" Avus sputtered, straining to maneuver himself to the stairs.

Levan's face was a cold, hardened mask. "He will live. We must go."

As much as he had tried to minimize the fire in this wooden building, nevertheless the twigs and hay used to insulate the roof ignited with fervor from the blazing hot magical fire.

Levan surveyed the area and his repertoire of resources. He could float small objects; this would help somewhat with the limp weight of Ranser. Avus was far too heavy for it to be of use, but he could push with his good leg. He would move them both out at once.

"All right big guy, here we go." Levan grabbed the dwarf's arm and began dragging him down the stairs.

"No, leave me. Help the boy!" Avus pleaded, both angrily and sorrowful.

Levan shot him a stern look. "I'm not leaving you here, Avus. You already saved his life. And there was nothing you could have done to save NuMoon."

Avus ceased his protest and slid down the stairs with a shocked and perplexed expression.

Who is this kid? How does he know my name...and about NuMoon?

The flames spread across the ceiling, licking eagerly at the dusty wooden rafters. Levan hoped there was enough time. Drawing a circle around Ranser, Levan chanted a spell.

"**Optero Nimbus**...beside me floats a tiny cloud."

From the floor beneath Ranser, a fluffy white cloud seeped up and condensed under him, raising him slightly up. Levan took Avus and Ranser's arms and began pulling them toward the doorway.

Avus looked up at Levan. "You're a bag of good tricks, kid."

While Ranser's feet dragged on the floor through the floating cloud, Levan was struggling to pull Avus. "Aye, push with your leg!"

Avus complied, but this only worsened matters, as he jolted into the back of Levan's knee, then fell, and Levan lost his grip.

"Ugh! You're too heavy!" Levan shouted as embers came raining down.

Stay together, building. Just a little longer.

Fire! Abandon ship!

...This could work.

Avus reversed his position, turning over and swiveling around to point his feet toward Levan. He placed his wrapped leg gingerly over his other calf and called out to Levan.

"Let's try this! Grab my leg!"

Levan was going over in his mind what needed to be done after this and in what order. He heard what Avus said, but didn't engage much energy to interpreting what his eyes were telling him. He lifted the white bandaged leg into the air.

"Oww! Wrong leg!" Avus cried agonizingly.

"Sorry, sorry about that!" Levan picked up the dwarf's strong leg, with its intact foot, and Avus held himself up, walking backwards on his arms like a one-handed wheelbarrow. This went surprisingly smoothly, and they quickly made it to the exit of the burning inn.

Undra was watching from her door and witnessed their egress. She immediately came running down and stooped to aid the mangled sailor boy and dwarf.

Levan stood up with grim determination. "Get them to safety." He said, as he walked back into the burning building.

"Wait! What are you doing!? Boy, are you mad!?" Avus called after him.

The boarding house was dripping with flame, billowing smoke from the roof and collapsing some beams on the stairway. A spiteful blaze blocked Levan's path. It seemed to open up in devilish, roaring mouths, laughing balefully at him.

"Water floweth freely here...**Aquos.**"

A stream of shining water spouted forth from his hands. The flames screamed and hissed as they were dissipated and Levan climbed over the debris, rushing upstairs.

When he made it to the spy's room, only his clothing was out in the open. Levan threw the clothes into the fire downstairs. Frantically, he looked for a ledger, a scroll, a paper, anything which proved he was truly a spy with malicious intent. He would not be haunted by this doubt forever.

Under the bed, he found Ranser's sickle, and then in the bottom drawer of the desk he found a single page of paper. On it was a map and description of the village, with the names of everyone living in each house. All sixteen people were described as dissidents, enemies to the throne and tax evaders, with Undra being their "ringleader". Levan knew what fate befell those labeled for such crimes; it would be far worse than a road and a tax.

Are the lives of sixteen plus two worth one evil man's life? It would seem right. But why am I still vexed? If no trace of him is ever found, I cannot be punished for killing one of the king's men. But the ancestors still saw....they see everything...

Levan stashed away the intelligence notes in his pack and was rushing out of the room when he saw the spy's knife in the corner of the room.

Another piece of evidence. One which can't be burned.

The young sorceror had seen personalized weapons before, many warriors, and those who wish to be like them, customized their weapons with their name or unique symbol. And many varying militia groups and secret orders used specific kinds of weapons that identified them. Yet still he argued with himself. He did not want to pick the weapon up.

Perhaps it's just a plain, simple dagger. One which could have come from anywhere.

The blade had a wide bloodletting groove, with a round green jewel in the center of the cross guard and an eagle talon and serpent emblem on the pommel. A drop of blood had fallen on the jewel, likely from gash on the spy's face which Ranser had inflicted with his sickle.

Just grab it.

Levan picked up the blade.

Murderer.

He dropped the dagger in his pack and rushed out of the room. As he was about to go back down the stairs, the scrawled pages in the dwarf's room caught his eye. Levan decided it would save him some face if no one found it, and that he would convince the dwarf it was worth it to go on. He picked up the notes and fed them to the roof flames. If nothing else, he could rewrite it later. He checked the clothing bonfire and it was thoroughly ashen.

Now on the lower floor, he began casting more water at the blaze until it died down and was snuffed to smoking embers in a few moments.

The roof would need repair, but he had saved the greater part of the structure. Outside, some villagers were feebly pouring water-buckets on the walls, but they stopped when they saw him.

"It's the wizard!" exclaimed one of the villagers, "He's extinguished the blaze *and* saved everyone at the inn! Hooray!" The villagers cheered and smiled on him.

Levan wore a blackened-face scowl. He could not accept any praise for what he had done, and he was feeling sickly and weak from the smoke.

"Where are...where are the people I rescued?" Levan coughed.

"Undra has them at her house. They're hurt badly, but still alive."

Levan returned to Undra's house. Ranser and Avus were laid out on a layer of hay on the floor in the front room, sleeping soundly.

"Levan! What has happened!?"

Still catching his breath, the wizard procured the intelligence report and displayed it before Undra.

"Well this is a doozy..." Undra said, reading the page. "Such a good thing this didn't get back to the king!"

Undra tossed the paper into the cooking flame. She made Levan sit down as she readied something in the cauldron for eating. She opened a big spice drawer and ran her finger over the rows of herbs and minerals. Levan moved from his seat and eavesdropped on the contents of the cabinet.

"You have Halivex? Can I see that bottle?" Levan asked Undra, pointing into the spice cabinet.

"This? I don't care for it much, but Imola likes it in her eggs." She said, handing it to him.

Levan held up a vial of the dark green leaf, dried

and brittle. It was half full. "This is great." He said, "Did you know you can make a powerful healing salve from this?"

"Wha?" Her brow raised in disbelief.

"You've never heard of Halivex Healing Salve? There is so much information that should be disseminated to the country folk."

"Hey, little wizard," Undra retorted in mock indignity, "best not insult the person makin your food. I keep the nightshade right next to the salt."

"Ma'am, you just fed us. Do you not remember?"

"Maybe the dwarf will be hungry when he wakes up. You know they eat like dragons, those dwarves. I wonder how they fit all that food in them wee bodies of theirs. Oop!" She lifted her ladle to cover her mouth, as if she'd spoken too loudly. Dwarves were notorious for not taking lightly any humor made of their height. "So how do you administer this stuff? Just put it right on the wound?" Undra inquired curiously.

"Yes it soaks through the skin, but first you must chop it very finely and boil it with clay or preferably milk-cream. Also it is much more effective when catalyzed with Phorm Root, but I doubt you have any of—"

"Phorm Root, right here" She handed him another vial. "And the bucket of milk from this morning is right there."

"You are wonderful, Undra. I shall start preparing the salve right away. It will do both of them a wealth of good."

"You seem to know a lot of medicines and cures. I wonder...how are you at curing nightmares?" Undra looked at him imploringly as he poured some cream into a pot with ground Halivex and hooked it above the fire.

Levan did not know what to say at first. "Who is having nightmares? You?"

"No, it's my daughter, Imola. Come."

Undra led him quietly into the back room, which was mostly bare, but for the child lying on a bed in the corner, an old fireplace with a metal grate underneath, and fuzzy stuffed bear sitting on the mantle. The girl was pale and emaciated. Levan did not know if he could help, but he wished for all the world he could somehow.

He sat down on the bed next to Imola. "Hi, Imola. I'm Levan."

She turned to him, blinking. "Are you the wizard?"

"I told her a bit about you." Undra commented.

"Yes I am, and I want to help you stop having nightmares and get well again." He brushed back the hair matted to her forehead with sweat. "You have to be really strong for me, and think only happy thoughts so the magic will work, understand?" Imola nodded and Levan turned to Undra. "She has a fever. Fevers from sickness can often cause nightmares. If we treat the fever, the nightmares will go away. I can prepare a drink that will help her."

"It's not the fever." Imola spoke weakly.

"What?" Levan turned back to the child.

"It's not the fever that's making my dreams bad, it's the monster from the fire pit." She pointed to the coal trap beneath the fireplace.

Her mother told her, "No, darling, you're just sick with a fever."

Imola reached for her stuffed bear doll across the room.

"No, Imola," Undra cajoled, going over and picking up the bear, "you're too old for these toys. This filthy thing is probably what made you sick. I'm going to use it for kindling tonight."

The sickly child sobbed pitifully.

Levan stood up and went over to Undra. "She needs to be as comforted as possible until she has recovered. Let her have the doll." He took the bear from Undra, held it up to his nose and sniffed it. It actually smelled quite pleasant. "It's fine, it's not infected. Go prepare some tea water for her." He handed the bear to Imola. "There you go."

"Mister wizard, will you kill the monster that

lives under the fire?" Imola said when her mother had left the room.

"Of course I will."

Levan went over to the fireplace and pulled up the metal grate. Below was nothing more than a small stone recess with a few ashes at the bottom. He humored her anyway by sending forth two small, sparking splashes of flame which burst into a shimmering cascade down in the coal trap. A simple pyrotechnic spell, no chance of burning any buildings down. "There now, that took care of him." Imola cheered and clapped in delight.

When Undra returned with the hot water cup, Levan mixed in some Drylazort and a pinch of sugar and asked Imola to please drink it and then get some rest. It must have tasted good, she drank it all quickly.

Levan and Undra left the room as Imola settled in to nap.

"She's been this way for over a year now." Undra said in a hushed tone. "Won't play outside, barely eats. She is the reason the rumor of the plague started here. With all this talk of monsters, I'm afraid her mind's been addled by the plague—er, fever."

"Don't worry, I'm sure she'll be fine, just let her rest and don't cause her any undue distress." Levan said, yawning.

"Thank you so much, Levan." Undra said, her eyes beaming with gratitude, as if her daughter was already recovered. "You poor dear, you look exhausted. Why don't you rest a while too?"

Levan's eyes were burning and his body felt weak. He did need to lie down for a while, but first he had to apply the healing salve to Avus' leg and Ranser's bruises. He took the boiling pot off the fire and ground in the raw Phorm Root, stirring to make a greenish-white paste, and slathering it on the two wounded, sleeping warriors. Ranser's bruises began fading away immediately, and he could feel the bones in Avus' foot reforming themselves. When he was finally done, he lay down on the hay-covered floor, and Undra brought him a big, fluffy feather pillow. His head sank into the pillow like a soft, cool cloud.

What a great alchemist I never knew I was. Ranser and Avus will awake jumping for joy. They will revere me like the villagers did. It felt nice to hear them call me "wizard". Imola is going to be fine, her nightmares will stop now that she thinks the monster is dead. The poor girl will learn someday that monsters don't live in houses.

He was soon to find out how wrong he was.

CHAPTER 4
NIGHTMARES

When they awoke the cottage was dark and empty. Avus, Levan and Ranser were standing in the front room of Undra's house, and saw a fiery glow emanating from the bedroom. They entered the back room. Imola was not in her bed anymore, but her stuffed bear was there, sitting in the same spot.

BOOM! The fireplace rumbled and shook BOOM! Smoke and soot shot upwards from the ash pit as ghostly flames rose up the chimney. BOOOMM!! The fireplace exploded as a flaming monstrosity emerged from the coal trap, roaring with fiery breath. Its ashen, magma-like skin billowed with thick, dark smoke. The eyes flared with fiery malice and when it opened its mouth, a raging inferno burned within.

Avus hefted his old axe, readying it for battle. Ranser readied as well, drawing a glittering golden saber, just like a ship's captain would have. Levan began gathering magical energy for a spell.

The fire pit monster billowed out into the room, a dark, smoldering cloud of ash in the shape of a giant cobra. The body rose and swelled to the appearance of a black molten dragon spreading its wings and filling the room with a vile, noxious fume. From its hazy underside, clawed hands of thick, roiling smoke wafted down towards the three.

As the ghostly arms reached out to strangle them, Avus chopped with his axe, and Ranser slashed with his sword, easily cutting through the smoky tendrils, but the arms moved around them in a wispy haze before reforming in another spot.

Levan blasted away the ashen claws stabbing toward his mouth, nose and throat with his wind spell. It was getting stronger. But the arms widened out, becoming a score of tentacles of dark smoke, winding their way towards him like a barrage of flaming arrows.

They hacked, swatted and blasted at the burning smog as it crept in, barely escaping its grasp as the monster's huge, grotesque head floated around the room, smoldering and flaring with malice.

Levan gusted away another salvo of smoking missiles, and they in turn became ten times as many, regrouping and rushing at him even faster. There was no avoiding it. Despite all his desperate resonant spell-words, the wizard was inundated with suffocating fire and ash.

Avus and Ranser were not faring much better, slowly becoming engulfed in the insidious black fumes.

Levan was pummeled to the floor, burning and choking as the gas seemed to push him down and seep into his nostrils. He held his breath, writhing on the floor as the suffocating soot burned its way into his sinus cavity.

The next lifetime is close at hand.

Then something in the corner of the room moved.

Imola's stuffed bear toy stood up with a small wooden sword in its hand. The furry little creature leapt from the bed and severed the smoking monster's head with the tiny wooden sword, ending its stream of toxic breath.

The house shook with a deafening roar as the fiery monster recoiled itself into the fireplace. The flame in its mouth and eyes intensified as it fixed its fury on the bear.

The choking gas fled from Levan's throat and he stood up, instinctively moving to the side, away from the enemy's frontal attack. This was a fortunate move, for he narrowly escaped the cone of flame that exuded from the monster's reemerging mouth like a dragon's breath, pouring over the corner where the bed and the bear were.

But the fire could not touch the bear. The flames deflected around the surface of a bubble-like sphere surrounding the magical stuffed-animal. The barrier glowed faintly blue and gold as the blaze engulfed it, and the ghostly image of the sleeping girl Imola, stirring restlessly on the bed, faded in and out of view.

"Levan, your robe!" Ranser shouted.

Levan was unaware that the corner of his robe had caught fire in his dive out of the monster's breath weapon. He batted it frantically until it stopped burning and bathed him in smoke.

He looked back at Ranser, noticing he was now wearing an elaborate captain's hat, complete with a long white feather, and was dressed in a fancy gilded breastplate with the trappings of a nobleman or lord.

"How did you do that!?" Levan asked, bewildered.

"I thought it! I just make it happen! Look!" From thin air Ranser's left hand pulled a glittering, steaming sword made of ice. "Let's see how he likes this!"

Ranser threw the icicle sword at the fiery monster and it shattered, puncturing the smoldering carapace and turning those spots dark and brittle. The beast sizzled and steamed, hissing at him.

Levan was trying to put the pieces together, though his mind was not making connections normally at the moment. He was always a practical realist, despite being a wizard. His rational mind was always aware of its limits.

Is this Imola's nightmare? Can I really do anything I imagine?

"Cut it down!" Ranser called out, holding out his golden cutlass as if commanding a charge.

Avus had imagined his axe being greater and

longer, and thus it was, taller and wider than the dwarf himself. He charged in swinging the huge weapon, slashing across the face of the monster, ripping through one of its eyes. The ghostly pit demon bellowed ferociously as lava poured like burning blood from its cleaved head.

The searing hot cinders melted down and caused the ground to quake violently. Molten rock and metal gushed in splintering fracture-lines surrounding them. The three were but moments from being engulfed in flame before a plan came to the wizard.

Well if it's just a dream...it can't hurt to try it.

Levan was told never to recite aloud the passages in the Vimaticon known as the Songs of Destruction. Yet it only fueled his curiosity about these passages, and he skipped ahead to read them. They claimed ten year's practice was needed to even read these pages

If this is truly a dream, I could survive it, right?

As he spoke, his words reverberated around the room with magical power. "Falling crystal light, bring your messengers from the heavens, **Ao Meteo**!"

Outside, the night sky lit up and a fist-sized meteor plummeted from the sky, slamming through the roof of the house, smashing into the fireplace with a bright flash. The ashen demon coiled and hissed as its smoke swirled in to fill the hole punched in it by the shooting star.

The shattered thatched roof revealed the night sky drawn with endlessly circling parallel lines of light, as if the world were moving at great speed and the starlight blurred together. In the darkness between, translucent orbs and sheets of luminscent colors floated past each other. Another meteor came screaming in, blasting rock and thatch all over, shaking the ground and punching another hole in the harried monster. The shooting stars began falling like rain in a downpour, with blinding flashes and explosions of rocky shards.

Ranser and Avus were harried with debris, and

looked over to Levan as wind whipped up around him, tossing his hair and robe.

The young wizard began to rise into the air, chanting another spell. His eyes were as the sky outside, swirling multi-colored nebulas and explosions of light crossed by motion-blurred stars. In that moment he did not look like the kind, humble young man they had met. His eyes were mad with power, and the destruction he was raining from the heavens was frightening in its intensity.

Floating in the air above the ruined cottage, Levan raised his arms to the sky, calling out a magical verse.

"From the call of the abyss…"

More fireballs crashed in, scattering the ashen body of the fire pit monster. Yet again the beast reformed into a snake-like chain of billowing darkness with some of the bricks of the fireplace within it, shooting fire and gnashing its teeth as it flew up to destroy the hovering wizard.

"There can be no escape, farewell, **Ostrium orbis**!" When Levan raised his hand, a huge portal, darker than the night sky, opened up above a furious tornado and the coal-trap beast was hurled by a vacuum upward, disappearing into the Abyssal Gate.

Levan floated back to the ground, his eyes and the sky returning to normal and the furious wind subsiding.

The destroyed cottage around them began fading away.

In the morning, the three all awoke at once, sitting up from the floor in Undra's house, exchanging wide-eyed looks as they caught their breath. Avus and Ranser then stiffened, staring straight forward. In the same moment, their faces contorted in pain, and in unison they cried out.

Avus was clutching his broken foot screaming out "What did you do to me!?"

"It's the healing salve, it's repairing your bones and muscles." Levan explained apologetically.

"It hurts! And it *itches!* Ahhh—!" He growled loudly as he tried to scratch his wrapped foot.

"The itching should subside in a day."

Ranser wriggled on his back, trying to scratch where the worst of his injuries were. "Waahh...damn you, Levan, don't put stuff on me in my sleep again!"

Undra came in the house from outside beaming with joy, bubbling with excitement. "Oh, you're awake. Oh, boys, I just can't believe it! Guess where my little Imola is!"

Avus narrowed his eyes, thinking of where country-folk would find exciting to go. "Karikoss City?"

Undra regarded him quizzically for a moment. "No! She's playing outside with the other children! They are running around playing wizards and pirates or some silly thing, as if her illness never happened! Oh my dear boy, I can never thank you enough." She hugged Levan who stood rather awkwardly with his arms bound by his sides. He looked down at his feet and realized the edge of his robe was burned.

Was it a dream?

The old lady released him at last and said "Now how about some stew?"

Levan acquiesced, and brought Avus and Ranser some water and food. As Levan sat eating, Ranser struggled to his feet and stood, wobbly, gasping in pain, scratching his knee, then his elbows. He headed for the door to the outhouse in the back.

"Do you need some help?" Levan half stood up to help his friend who was having great trouble walking, but Ranser dismissed him.

"No, I can make it."

"You sure? I can do the little cloud thing to carry you again."

"No, I'm good, thanks." Ranser said, exiting the cottage.

"Heheh," Avus chuckled at the boy's peculiar gait and spastic scratching, even as he scratched at his leg himself. "that was a good trick, too bad that little cloud isn't big enough for all of us."

"That's a good idea, Avus, I'll work on it. It seems a far simpler method of aviation than the polarity switching propulsion, sacrificing velocity for surplus cargo capacity." Levan said as if he were talking to a professor at his magic school, but slurping soup between breaths.

Magic School! I should be taking my test right now!

"Wha?...uh huh..." Avus was unable to follow the technical jargon, thus he had no reply, but ate his soup. He thought the boy an interesting well of information and tricks, as well as a loyal friend.

"Has there been any news from the city, Undra?" Levan inquired earnestly.

"Well yes, as a matter of fact, a messenger rode in just before daybreak with a report. He brings it to me and I relate it to the rest of the village at our meetings. I reckon that's why I was pegged as the ringleader in that spy's report."

"What was their word, Undra?" Levan asked as Ranser re-entered the house.

"Well I was just about to read it to ya. Ahem. The foreign invaders known as *Kinari* have begun their siege on Karikoss City. Their initial force consists of roughly half the number of soldiers as Fahfren's standing army in Karikoss. There have been multiple successful campaigns from the king's men, our attack parties, and some members of unidentified groups shoring up our defenses, cutting the enemy's supply lines and harassing their troops. A minor skirmish was fought to the northeast of the city, presuma....presumabobble..." Undra stumbled over a word.

"Presumably?" Levan offered, impatient to hear the rest of the information.

"*Presumably* to test the fighting techniques they are using and the weaponry they have brought. The majority of the forces returned to the city later in the day, with an air of triumph. They are not demons or beasts, they are men and their weapons are the equal of ours. With our defender's advantage, and the weight of numbers on our side, we seem safe for now, but our outposts on the north shore have been overrun, thus we have no means knowing how many more ships are landing. All townships and dwellings north of Karikoss are *presumed* raided and defunct. If citizens need to enter the city while the blockade is in effect, you may do so with the units that return at nightfall. Signed: Lieutenant General Eltas ForgedArm."

"So, men have joined in large groups to fight each other to the death," Avus droned wearily, "this is not news to me." He laid back down.

Lower down on the page a few more notes were written by a different hand.

"And then this...your village is safe. The Kinari have not crossed west of the Northward Imperial Way, and we have no reason to believe they will. If they near, our watchmen will alert you with all haste. You have my word. Jofon." Undra finished the report.

"Did you say Jofon wrote that?" Ranser asked, exasperated.

"Yes, he is a friend of mine in the city. Looks out for us here. That old sea dog may only have one eye, but it sure sees a lot." Undra said fondly.

"It's him!" Ranser exclaimed excitedly, then hissed in pain as his back cracked. "My father from the Luna Triada, Jofon!"

"So you must be the boy he was looking for when he came through our village five years ago!" Undra said in a rising voice that then broke like a wave on a rocky shore. "Oh, a father-son reunion, *how* special. I know he will be *so* glad to see you. Aww..."

"Yes, yes, where do we find him in the city?" Ranser inquired impetuously.

"Well, he works with closely with Tor Veldgar in the resistance army, and most of them are probably busy repelling the foreign enemy in the field by day. But they have a meeting place…I suppose I can tell you, and you can say I sent you…it's in the back room of the Mountain Chalice Tavern, after dark. Tell no one about this! Tor Veldgar is a very secretive and private person, a righteous outlaw. He must not be discovered."

"Thank you, Miss Undra." Ranser said, lying back down. "I'm afraid I can't move yet, though."

"That's fine, hun, you stay and rest as long as you need to."

"Then Tor Veldgar is alive?" Avus sat up and spoke after hearing this. "Everyone thought the Veldgar line was extinguished, or even a myth. My people know that family to be the founders of this kingdom. It is sad what the Fahfren dynasty has done to this land and to Tor's name. And this is the reason the kingdom is falling prey to invasion and strife, a false king sits on the throne. Tor would have it better. I will go to meet with him and do what I can to further his cause….ugh…perhaps tomorrow…" He lay back, wincing in pain.

"Yes, you should both rest the day here," Said Levan, "I must go see to my mother's safety."

"Oh dear, you can't leave your mother out there alone with strange men roving the countryside!" Undra berated him. "You go get her and your stock and bring 'em down here where we've got protection."

"Are you sure? She's old and not good for much."

"Yes, of course, it's no problem, it's the least we can do for you. I'll put her up here or at the inn once we fix the roof. Wonder who was the dimwit using a lamp in the daytime and burning the roof off, should make him fix it. But no matter. You bring your good-for-nothing old mum here and we'll see to her. Fine and dandy."

"Thank you, Undra." Levan smiled. He would finally be leaving home now, out on his own in the wide world. It was both an empowering and daunting thought. On the other hand, he would also he abandoning his land, becoming a vagrant. All the same, he longed for the open road.

As Levan gathered his pack and prepared to leave, Undra protested. "You're leaving right away? Don't you want another bowl of soup?"

"No, thank you. I must get going now if I am to return by sundown. Or perhaps later...my mother walks very slowly."

"You can use Omra, our quarter horse in the stable. She's the black and grey spotted mare."

"Excellent. Thank you again for everything, Undra." Levan said, as he closed the door on his way out.

He went to the horse pen at the back of the house and met Omra. He was good with animals, and she was friendly with him from the start. Without objection she allowed Levan to saddle and rein her, and they set off north out of the village.

Riding through the smooth grassy hills, Levan savored the cool breeze in his hair. The horse was healthy and fast, he was making good time toward his house. He pulled out his spellbook and studied a bit where he left off, memorizing the incantations and symbols of the elemental wall spells.

Descending into a wide meadow surrounded with hills, the sound of another horse's wild, panicked neighing came to his ears. Then he saw it come galloping full-speed over the ridge to his right, a tall, powerful black warhorse.

It had no rider but was harnessed to a wagon-like wheeled structure with four massive sets of bow arms mounted upon it. As it came closer, he could see the horse's tail had been lit on fire, and it ran from this inescapable flame in a bewildered frenzy.

He rode towards it, preparing to douse the flame with a shot of water. When the horse and carriage came near, he sprayed its flanks with water, but the flaming tail was not completely doused, and the horse kept running. Now he could see the great metallic gears inside the wagon turning, pulling taught the giant crossbow arms which were loaded with long spear-like bolts. Just a few more clicks and...

There was no time to move out of the way. The ballista bolts were aimed right at him and Omra, only a brief moment from skewering them both.

Choosing his solution and reacting quickly, Levan took a chance with the only option that seemed viable at the time. His wall spells were amateur and not well-practiced, but he felt his control of fire was sufficient now to try it.

He waved his arm in a wide arc and a wreath of flame fanned out around him. The wall of magical fire spread up and outwards just far enough away from the other horse not to harm it, and just in time to disintegrate the two arrow shafts that came flying out from the crossbows.

The heavy iron arrow heads kept moving however, one tumbling to the ground and the other spinning off and hitting Levan solidly in the shoulder, which threw him from his mount.

The wind blew well in this valley, and with it he was able to cushion his fall, sustaining only a few minor scrapes.

A gust lifted and pushed him forth to gain pace with the panicked burning horse. As its hooves thundered beside him, Levan reached up and grabbed hold of its mane, hoisting himself onto its back. He extinguished the flaming tail with a splash of water, then, finding the metal rivets fastening the carriage to its back, he loosed the bindings and the contraption fell off, releasing the ponderous weight digging into the poor creature's back.

What foul weapon is this? The Kinari invaders must be nearby. There is no time to waste!

The black horse finally calmed down and obeyed his commands. Levan named him FireTail. He strode FireTail over to Omra and switched horses, tying a rope around the other's neck. This would allow both he and his mother to have a steed, and for them both to carry more supplies. It was a fortunate event, he supposed. Though it was very lucky that un-practiced Wall of Flame spell worked.

He rode as swiftly as he could, holding FireTail on the rope. No one was on the road. His home came into view beyond the familiar grassy slope.

Everything appeared normal, and he saw his mother moving around inside. He tied up the horses in the rear of the house and entered the back door, surprising his mother.

"Oh, Levan. Where have you been?" She stopped chasing a chicken around the house."I thought something bad happened to you when you didn't come home. Will you help me catch this darned chicken? I been chasing him around all day!"

"Mother, we have to leave." Levan said, as he slowly and calmly walked over to the corner where the chicken was and picked it up. The hen bocked softly at him, protesting her mistreatment. He put the chicken in the cage with the others. "A big army is invading Lorestian. We need to move closer to the city."

"Levan, you know we can't afford to-" His mother began to protest but he cut her off.

"I have a place arranged to stay that is safe. Pack what you want and let's move *now*. Raiding parties could arrive any minute."

"Why is your face bleeding, son?"

"I came across one of their weapons on the way here." Levan rubbed his aching shoulder. He couldn't see it but he knew it was badly bruised. "You need something to defend yourself with." He opened his pack and handed her the dagger with the green jewel. "Here."

"Alright…" His mother sighed reluctantly.

Levan considered how to transport the chickens, a pair of pigs and goats, along with as many of their tools and other useful items. He cursed himself for not having already fixed the axle on the horse cart, even though they didn't own any horses at the time. But it seemed the only way.

He went out back and looked at the old cart, overgrown with tall weeds. If he were a metal forger he could reconnect the broken axle. He knew the basic steps of creating metal objects from scratch from reading about it.

He thought for a moment. Deciding to take another leap of faith in his own abilities, he moved down the hillside to the creek at the bottom of the ravine behind his house, feeling the minute fluctuations of energy in the ground. A heavy slab of dense earth buzzed below him. There, he washed away the leaves atop the ground to expose and soften a layer of clay with a long red and black vein of iron imbedded within it.

Digging his fingers into the ground, he whispered to the clay. "Thy burden is lifted, **Opteros Neam**."

An arm's-length cube of clay encasing a rich iron vein rose up into the air before the wizard. Moving the cube back toward the house, he hurled blasts of wind and water at it, pulverizing it to an amorphous blob. Then, as he spun his fingers round each other, the wind spiraled into cyclones, whipping the mass of clay outward and isolating the rocky iron blocks within the spinning windstorm. He threw a tree branch up into the mix, as from what he'd picked up of metallurgy, the charcoal made the iron stronger. Still spinning like a lathe, he blasted it with jets of flame and the metal turned white-hot, softening and melding into a long bar. He narrowed the wind tunnel little by little, eyeing the size of the axle he needed. Finally he sprayed the hot metal bar in water and let it drop to the ground. It was slightly narrower than the broken axle bar, which was hollow, allowing his creation to fit snugly within and the wagon to stand up respectably. He hitched both horses to the cart and laid a blanket across FireTail's back, since they had no saddle.

Levan hoped he hadn't used too much time. He kept imagining an army of strange warriors showing up at the last minute and cutting them down just as they were leaving their home for safety. Running to the back door, he entered the house and began loading the chicken cages onto the cart. The two pigs were too heavy to carry by himself, but he found that his tiny floating cloud was a bit less tiny, and he was able to push the cage with the pigs in it along the floor on a pocket of high-pressure air. He picked up the bags of grain and skins of milk and wine and stowed them on the cart. He threw on the moderately expensive metal-headed shovel and harvesting tools. He was ready to leave.

Back inside the house, his mother was filling up a canvas bag with her decorations, but she had stopped to look at a piece of wood on the mantelpiece.

"Do you think we should bring this along? I don't know if I really like it." Mimora said, holding up the oddly-shaped burl.

Levan snatched the gnarled wood piece from her hand and threw it across the room. "We don't have time for this! Bring only what you need!"

Some movement outside caught Levan's eye. Dark shadows were moving down the road.

"Oh no, they've come. Go now!" Levan pulled his mother by the arm to the back door as the squad of mounted Kinari warriors stopped at the front of the farmhouse.

We won't be able to outrun them with two horses pulling a cart.

Levan saw the front door opening as he opened the back door and rushed his mother through. He was about to have a very close encounter with a hulking Kinari warrior when the door skidded to a stop a few inches ajar. The ugly wooden mantelpiece decoration had wedged under the bottom of the front door, preventing its opening. The brute on the other side kept pushing, warping the hinges, but could not yet enter, allowing Levan time to exit through the back door.

The dried, thorny tendrils of the blackberry bramble growing in the backyard caught and tugged at his robe for a moment, which gave him an idea.

His mother was climbing up on Omra and Levan went and mounted FireTail. From the window in the back of the house, Levan saw that all ten men were now inside, and they then noticed him. He heard their shouts and saw them moving toward the back door. He yelled at the horses "ya!" tapping his heels at FireTail's sides, and they embarked.

Moving past the blackberry bramble, Levan willed the vines to grow to fantastic proportions with a magical phrase.

"A wall of wooden daggers blocks your way, **Talos Barius!**"

The bramble stirred and revolved, rustling and shaking as the back door opened. Then it exploded with huge tentacles of wood, as thick as a horse's chest with thorns like swords, wrapping the enormous vines all around the house. As they rode away, Levan and Mimora saw some of the soldiers trying to hack through the wall of thorns, or climb through them in vain. Some of them had tried to climb out the windows and were stuck suspended in the network of spiked vines, yelling for their companions for help.

Levan was supremely relieved as they rode away. He had narrowly escaped death twice as a result of reading the next few pages in his spellbook pertaining to the creation of fire and thorn walls. He hoped that he would not fall behind on his reading, and be bereft of some other ability that he didn't know he needed when he needed it. But right now, he couldn't read, his mind was too scattered, too tired, drained. Magicians were only supposed to practice one new spell a day. Levan's energy was depleted.

He managed to make it to the point just past the crossroads where he told Mimora "From here we go due south. We'll come to the village with four buildings, that's where we stay...and...sleep..."

He could hold his eyelids and his body up no more. He fell off the horse and Mimora stopped them just before the cart ran over his head.

Levan woke up with a sharp pain in his stomach. His mother's face was above him, glowering down at him with a strange glint in her eyes. He looked down at his abdomen and was horrified at what he saw. Mimora, his mother, was pushing the green-jeweled dagger into his belly and upward towards his ribs.

"M-Mother—what are you doing—why—?" He choked up the words with blood.

"I never wanted a child...you took my life away from me you...*murderer*!" Her face twisted into a horrible monstrous one with a huge mouth that opened up and swallowed him head-first.

Levan burst up from his nightmare screaming, but the monster was still there. His mother was leaning over him and he knocked her down, pinning her to the ground, his hands around her throat.

"Levan, no!" Mimora let out a strangled cry.

Levan's grip loosened as he realized what had happened.

I was on a horse. I must have fallen off. Hmm...that wasn't real, was it? I really should take it easy on those new spells.

"Ahh...I'm so sorry, Mother. I've over-exerted myself. Please forgive me." He stood and helped her up. Then, helping her to her horse, he removed the knife he'd loaned her from her bag, without her noticing and returned it to his own.

They remounted their horses and continued to the south, speaking no further of the incident, so Levan did not analyze it too carefully. To him it was an unfortunate result of energy-drain, but he felt very remorseful and shameful for the violent outburst, and could find no suitable way to express it to her. Dreams were a bit too realistic for him lately.

It would be nice if we didn't need sleep. I could get so much more done.

Levan made himself stay awake the rest of the trip. He was supremely grateful for Omra and FireTail, these noble beasts, without which his mother would have to carry him, he was so weak. Mercifully, before long, the little village came into view, nestled among the hillsides.

Back at Undra's house, Avus and Ranser were sitting up at the table chatting with Undra and she, of course, was cooking for them. They cheerfully welcomed Levan back.

"Hey, you made it! Good timing too, food's ready!" Avus bellowed in high spirits.

"Food is always ready here," Levan droned, staggering in, "this is my mother Mimora. Mom, these are my friends."

"It's very nice to meet you. Thank you so much for giving us a safe place to stay during these troubled times." Mimora greeted them cordially.

Levan spoke to Ranser. "I'm glad to see you've recovered. I'm sorry I wasn't there to back you up when you were attacked."

Ranser shrugged nonchalantly. "I got him pretty good before he pinned me down. I wasn't hurt till I got thrown down the stairs."

"Oh, that reminds me, I found your sickle." Levan pulled up his pack to the table and began taking things out to get to it. He placed the spy's dagger on the table in front of Ranser, and then pulled out the rusty old sickle.

Ranser picked up the green-jeweled blade. "I recognize this. Almost went into my neck." He flipped it in his hand, feeling the balance. Scrutinizing the jewel in the hilt, he frowned and wiped the congealed blood droplet off of it. Pressing his finger to the tip of the blade, he said, "This thing is sharp, pretty well-balanced. Can I use it?"

"Yeah, go ahead, it's yours." Levan said dismissively as he turned around. "I need to rest a while. If I fall asleep please wake me before dusk. I head to Karikoss tonight."

Exhausted, Levan went over to the piles of hay and reclined there. His body ached, especially his shoulder and head. He thought of putting some Halivex salve on the wounds too late, his body refused to move any more.

Avus stood up and headed for the door. He was nearly fully recovered, with just a slight limp in his step. He said he was going to help with the inn's roof repair so that Mimora would have a place to stay, and that he'd return later in the afternoon. He exited the cottage.

Mimora was telling Undra what they brought from their farm, about the chickens and pigs, the goats they had to leave behind. They went outside and Mimora showed Undra the cart.

Ranser gazed over at Levan, believing him to be asleep, then followed the women outside. There, by a window they spoke in a hushed tone, but Levan could hear some of what they were saying.

Ranser was speaking to Undra and Mimora in a whisper "It's Levan he's...gone mad...flames from his hands...an innocent man...your son...*murderer*..."

Mimora sobbed quietly.

"Shh.....you know he is....danger to us all..." Undra whispered to them. "...what must be done..."

The door to the cottage creaked open again. Ranser entered alone, creeping silently over to where Levan lay, one hand concealed behind his back.

Levan's eye was ever-so-slightly open, and he could see Ranser approaching him with malicious intent. In the reflection of a glass vase behind Ranser, he could see the green-jeweled dagger held behind his back. He saw all this, and yet he did not move. Perhaps he could not, or did not want to fight back.

Ranser flashed the blade to the sleeping wizard's throat, and a gush of liquid poured down his chest. Levan opened his eyes wide, seeing his life flooding out of his neck in great torrents, and his friend standing over him with the bloody knife in hand. As he felt the last of his vitality slipping away onto the floor, Levan tried to speak, to cast a spell, to gain some retribution or absolution, to proclaim his innocence, or to make his guilt true, but his words were suffocated by the blood draining down his splayed windpipe and his breath came no more.

Levan started awake, gurgling and clutching his throat, rolling around on the ground. Undra and Ranser looked over from the kitchen with surprise, and Ranser rushed over to aid. Levan scrambled to his feet, still holding his neck, backing away in terror from Ranser's approach. He backed into a wall and was frantically searching for an avenue of escape or an object to attack with when Ranser grabbed him around the torso saying "It's alright, buddy, it's alright, calm down."

Struggling and kicking in a panic, Levan's body would not let him breathe. Ranser restrained him and kept him from hurting anyone. Though he was considerably stronger than his studious wizard friend, Levan's flailings were wild and difficult to control, it was the power granted to living things in the moment of their most desperate struggle for life. At last Levan gasped a great breath, the tension left his body and he realized where he was. He looked up into Ranser's concerned eyes.

"My...apologies, my friend."

"It's alright. Everyone has bad dreams now and then." Ranser said, helping Levan to his feet.

The sight of the dagger on Ranser's belt caused Levan to flinch and recoil away from him.

"That thing—I'm sorry, you can't keep that dagger. We have to get rid of it."

"Aww, that's too bad, I kind of liked it." Ranser said in feigned disappointment. To him, an object, even a fine weapon, was just a tool to be used to accomplish a task, and there was always something else around you could use as a substitute. "Oh well, things get lost on ships, sometimes they come back, most times they don't. You can't let your golden finery drag you down to the bottom with it."

Avus returned with sweat on his brow and a wood axe on his shoulder. He had spent the past three hours helping the humans of this village hew beams and re-thatch the burned roof. He was stupendously exhilarated to be back on his feet, swinging his axe again. And these two young men were the reason he did not give up. While at work earlier in the day, he vowed to himself he would help their quests to come to completion as well.

"Ah! He's awake!" Avus said, turning to Levan. "Now I can say thank you, boy, you are a miracle worker with those medicines!" His good-mood voice boomed loudly.

"Oh, nature made those medicines, I just put them on you." Levan remarked humbly.

"You're too modest! You are already a great wizard! Now, what do you say we go get you your staff and hat? I think they owe it to you!"

"Yes. The sun is nearly set. Let's head to Karikoss." Levan said, picking up his bag.

Mimora came back in the house. Some of the villagers had been helping her to unload the horse cart and move her things to the inn. Undra and Mimora stocked their packs with food, and pooled together their tiny nuggets of gold and gave them so they could get food when they ran out. Mimora hugged Levan, telling him to take care, that she loves him and to go become a great wizard. He returned the sentiment and they all thanked Undra again before heading out the door.

Avus, Ranser and Levan set out on the road southward toward the Capitol city of Karikoss. Before they had gone very far, they saw some children playing in a corn field.

"Wait! Wait!" One of them called out to them. The child ran up to Levan and they stopped. It was Imola. "Thank you for helping me! I'm not afraid of monsters any more. Now I can play outside and get strong like you. Will you come back and see me again someday?"

Levan did not know if his travels would bring him back to this tiny village with no name, but he agreed with his most heartfelt, sincere intention to do so. "Of course I will."

"So you don't forget me," Imola said, "I want you to

have this. Mom was right, I don't need it anymore."

Imola handed Levan the stuffed bear doll.

"I won't forget you, Imola. Stay safe and I'll come back and teach you some magic someday."

"Bye Mister Wizard!" Imola waved as they strode off into the hills.

Lost in his thoughts as they traveled down the darkening road, Ranser gazed into the distance, examining the mystery that had vexed him for years since that day. "Do your eyes ever deceive you?"

Avus snorted in amusement. "Heh, more often than they show the truth. Few things are as they appear in this world. But a dwarf keeps his ear to the ground, listens to Nea. Our mother never lies. For you two, though, it would seem a bit more complicated."

"True," Levan nodded, "perception can be a tricky thing. Dreams can seem so real at times. Why do you ask this, Ranser?"

"Ah..." Ranser sighed. "back when our ship wrecked and I woke up on shore, I thought I saw something in the sea...which I could not believe...but since meeting you, anything seems possible. Are there truly giants who stand at the bottom of the sea and rise above the clouds?"

"I should say not!" Avus laughed, "How much seawater did you say you drank?"

"A giant from the sea," Levan's voice rose in fascination, having seen such a painting in a very old book, "taller than the clouds! You have *seen* Titanos?"

"I...I don't know what I saw. To me, the stories of gods were all useless fairy tales, but that vision I had that day." Ranser's brow furrowed as he gazed at the horizon, shaking his head. "If it was real, it does not fit."

Levan blinked. "You do not believe in the gods?"

"I believe in poetry, that the sea can be compared to a man. But not that it *is* a man, taller than the sky! Why do you believe in them?"

"It is the blessing of Agartha that allows us to bend the forces of nature. She is with us in the kingdom, thus our abilities work here, but not elsewhere."

"Yes, but have you ever *seen* the goddess herself?" Ranser pressed him. "With your own eyes?"

Subjectively, Levan knew Agartha was there, he could feel the resonance of her energy source from his tap of it every time he used a spell. But this was difficult to explain to a layperson.

"I have not," Levan replied, "but there are many things that exist which you and I will never see. We will know them by their effects in the world around us."

Ranser's skepticism was giving way to curiosity. "So, if this god Titanos is real, I should like to know more about him, and the others, Nea and Agartha."

Levan recalled his days of schooling, delving into the ancient text known as the Vimanticon.

With years of study, the mysteries contained in the great scroll revealed themselves in poetic parables, songs of rejoice and lament, accounts of historic conflicts and compendiums of magical formulations.

"Before the First Age, Nea and Titanos danced in the endless sea of time. La—"

Avus chuckled to himself. "Funny way of saying it."

"Hm?"

"Nothing. We just say it differently. Go on." The humor in the dwarven translation would be lost on them.

"Land and ocean met, illuminating the world and in their union, giving form to the spirits which would become men, elves and dwarves—"

Avus interrupted Levan again with a correction. "Dwarves came first."

Levan gave him a mirthless grin as his patience eroded. "As you like. You know what—as simply as I can say—Titanos is the father, sea and sky, Nea is the mother land."

"Sure, everyone knows that." Ranser replied.

Levan sighed. "But they haven't been around in a long time, things got bad, everyone lost their magic and started trying to kill each other with sticks and rocks. Then Agartha, the divine and benevolent teacher came down from a cloud, as luminous as the sun."

Avus stifled his laughter, shaking his head but making no further correction.

"She placed a seed in the soil, and with a word it sprouted into a great tree whose branches were laden with the sweetest fruit. She captured the fiercest warthog, and the swiftest stag, and commanded them that they would no longer fight or flee, but humbly feed and clothe their new masters. She spoke to the sky and the winds pushed the thunderstorms back to the sea. The goddess plucked a living branch from the forest and bade it burn eternally, and give everlasting warmth to her people. Even the adamantine stones of this mountainous land knelt down at Agartha's will, and she coaxed the streams to fill the fractured ground with revitalizing, crystalline waters. The divine teacher has revived the ancient words of magic and guided our kingdom toward the light ever since."

"So then," Ranser spoke hopefully, "it seems we've set a favorable course. If this divine teacher is to be found in the city ahead, she will know where my father and crew is, and perhaps where my destiny is to be found."

"Halt here." Avus stopped them, scanning the horizon.

"What is it?" Ranser squinted, unable to see what the dwarf did.

A beastly gray figure approached them from the tree line. A few steps into the field, Rune broke into a run towards them. Avus grunted in alarm, readying his axe to fend off a wolf attack.

Rune dashed across the plain and tackled Ranser, licking his face.

"What? Oh, that's your dog?" Avus lowered his

axe, and Rune came over to him, wagging his tail. Avus scratched his neck a bit. "What a nice boy." Rune pawed his chest and licked his face. "Haha…"

Rune also greeted Levan. They nodded to each other, and the four companions continued on.

They came upon a hole in the ground at the top of a mound. It seemed to have a deep cavern below it. Levan paused. It appeared to be about the right size. Looking up at Ranser, he said "Come over here. Drop that knife down there."

Ranser held the spy's green-jeweled dagger over the hole and dropped it in. They tried to watch it fall but it disappeared into the darkness. Rune stuck his head inbetween theirs, pushing against them, trying to see what the excitement was all about. A few seconds later a metal clink on rock signaled the end of its fall.

"That's deep enough. That thing will never be seen again. Good riddance." Levan said, standing up. Avus was transfixed with a vacant stare into the distance. "Everything all right, Avus?"

"…Yes, all is well." Avus replied unwaveringly, but he held back tears. He could see perfectly down into the darkness in that hole, to the cavern floor, where a single flower grew among the stony wreckage.

Farewell, NuMoon.

CHAPTER 5 QUEST

The companions arrived at the north city gate as the sun began to set. Various military units from Karikoss were gathering before the drawbridge. They blended in with the crowd as the bridge lowered and the soldiers filed across. They were tired, having fought hard today, and their chatter bespoke a rumor that the Kinari army had nearly doubled in size since their last engagement, and that their weapons were so very strange.

Ranser gaped upward as they passed through the tall stone gate and the palace came into view with its towering spires and glowing chamber of light on top. He had never seen buildings so big.

The city sprawled out below. Avus had worked in the mine at Karikoss many years ago, but had not entered the city since then. He was surprised at how many more buildings there were, and the castle seemed to have gotten even taller and more extravagant. The opulence of the city was overt here at the top.

A beggar, shrouded in dull blue cloth, beckoned to them with his cup. A tattoo of a shield with a dragon crest could briefly be seen on his wrist.

"Alms for the poor?" Asked the leper or whatever he was, his ice-blue eyes glinting beneath the veil.

Levan picked from his pouch a small gold nugget, about a tenth of their pool. He was always a friend to the less fortunate. It tinked into the cup with a particular sound which Avus picked up. Gold on silver. The cup he carried, though heavily burnished, was solid silver.

Even the beggars have silver cups here.

Avus kept this thought to himself.

"Thank you, kind sir," the panhandler said as he walked away, "may your path be ever well-lit."

The gate closed behind them, and the mass of warriors moved southward toward the road junction at the north end of the palace. There, at a courtyard square, the mob slowed to a stop to witness a ceremony taking place in front of the castle. A crowd of townsfolk gathered around as well.

A crier announced the spectacle. "On this day, five hundred and fourteen years ago, the great king Fosfaro Fahfren, who drove the demons from this land, sank his sword Mountain Maker into the ground at this very spot, declaring this his capital, to be watched over only by the one who can pull this blade from the ground, the leader of his bloodline. Behold, your king, now and forevermore!"

A crowned man with red hair reached down and lifted the sword from the hole in the ground. Levan heard a mechanical clicking sound as this happened.

The crowd cheered. In the din, a man pushed past Ranser to the front of the group. He extended his arm to point at the king and a lethal poisoned dart flew from a tube concealed beneath his sleeve.

The projectile was perfectly aimed, but just before reaching the monarch's neck, the bolt halted in midair and dissolved as a wisp of ethereal fog rose up from the ground and engulfed it.

Levan percieved a slight movement from the shrouded figure standing beside Fahfren as this happened, and the would-be assassin froze with a gape of horror.

The assasin's skin withered, showing the bones beneath, and his oaken hair turned to gray, as if he had aged 50 years in an instant. By the time the guards accosted him and drew him away, the assailant was reduced to a shriveled, lifeless cadaver. The king then returned the sword to the ground, turned and disappeared with his entourage back into the castle.

The crowd began to disperse, some were very excited and stayed to chant "long live the king!"

A hooded man standing near Avus scoffed. "You know this is a farce, right?"

"Hm." Avus stroked his beard. "I've heard such, but I don't know if I believe it."

"What do you mean—"

"No." The man cut Levan's inquiry short with a stern look. "Come have a drink with me. We can discuss this further. Elsewhere." He turned and beckoned them to follow him to the tavern.

The city was built on a mountainous cliff side, terraced into long landings connected by sloping pathways cascading down from the summit upon which was built the towering spires of the Imperial Palace. Further down, the great structures of the Temple of Agartha and the Imperial Library connected to the Mage's Tower and the Alchemist's Apothecary. Below this were many of the houses of the nobles, fountains and gardens with many trees. The next level down was a long marketplace thoroughfare, culminating in craftsman's shops, blacksmith and armory at one end, and a large hall used for auctions and various venues at the other. A raised causeway draped with tapestries continued from this level to the south gate, rising above two more terraces crowded with dwellings below.

They continued down through the city, walking along the building that was the brewery, just behind the Mountain's Chalice Tavern. To their right, the sheer rock wall soared high above, and a cascade of water shimmered in the setting sun as it took flight down the cliff beside the lowest path leading into a mine shaft at the bottom. A muddy road beneath the causeway led to the stables on the other side. Most of the fighting men went directly to the tavern.

They entered the Mountain's Chalice Tavern as the first star appeared in the night sky, and Rune left on his own adventure. The main room was filled with many humans, and some elves and dwarves. Many of them were just back from the hunting and scouting parties, and were relating their stories of valorous combat with the Kinari.

The sweet, lilting voice of a bard wafted over the bustle of the tavern goers, singing a rousing ballad of an ancient king and his sword of the mountain. It was a thinly veiled homage to Ussar Veldgar, the true founder of the kingdom of Lorestian.

The hooded man sat at a table that conveniently opened up, and removed his hood. He was a dark-haired middle-aged man with strong features, and a fierce and righteous fire in his eyes. Leaning in, his voice was deep and quiet, inaudible to any not meant to hear.

"No doubt you've already guessed, I work for an organization in support of Tor Veldgar. Undra told me you were coming, my name is Erevor."

"Do you know where Jofon is?" Ranser inquired immediately.

"Before we ask anything of each other, you must know the truth. Anderjor Veldgar, father of Tor Veldgar, had declared that he had proof of the royal family's lineage in an ancestral scroll handed down for countless generations, and that Veldgar should rightly be king. He was ridiculed, and his scroll confiscated, probably destroyed. But the scroll told also of an ancient sword, the Mountain Maker, and of the king Ussar Veldgar driving it into the ground at the center of his kingdom. So this so-called 'king' Fahfren opened up that side of the palace walls and had his craftsmen build a hollow stone, which locks the sword in place until they release it when Fahfren pulls it, and they have been putting on this disgusting little show here for over 20 years to capture the hearts and minds of the poor, hoodwinked people of this land. I can show you the metallic teeth that anchor the blade inside the rock if you need proof."

"Any dwarf could see that stone was crafted." Avus

commented.

Ranser had wandered off.

"I suspected the sword was connected to a machine." Levan said triumphantly. "What of that assassin? Was that part of the show?"

"No. A vain attempt to end this tyranny, but the dark magic of his sorcerers will not allow him to fall so easily. So, after being publicly ostracized, Anderjor Veldgar, insisting that the king's sword, the Mountain Maker, was real, and not stuck in a fake stone in the palace courtyard, he went off in search of it…and never returned. Tor, my master, has gone into hiding, but he still searches for his father and the lost sword that would prove his rightful place on the throne. With the power of the Mountain Maker and the kingdom reunited under Veldgar, we can drive out the monsters and men that seek to tear us apart."

"What monsters?" Levan had seen them in his dreams, and the lore books, but he thought them only myth.

"I would that you should not need to know of them…" Erevor muttered grimly, frowning enigmatically as he drank his wine.

"I have seen the things that crawl from the under ground, with blood like a pyrefly's tail." Said Avus, his eyes shining with vengeful malice. "They broke through into the Deepriver Hall, just beneath the Corhasan Hills, attacking me and my students. Perhaps it is the Mountain Maker that draws them here. If Tor Veldgar can rid us of this scourge, then my allegiance is with him."

Erevor paused a moment, looking at Avus. "I think you could be of aid to us. But if it is truly your wish to join the court of Tor Veldgar, you'll have to get another recommendation. Come to think of it, our friend Latus at the brewery could use a hand or two. It seems he's having a problem with some sort of 'infestation' in his basement. Tell him that Erevor sent you and he'll fill you in on how to join us."

"Our thanks to you, Erevor. Our cause is yours, you

will find no more loyal comrades than us." Avus saluted him with his tankard.

A moment later, a tall, muscular man came from the back of the tavern, holding Ranser by the back of his shirt. The bouncer walked the sailor boy across the tavern, to the laughing and jeering of the drunkards, took him by the back of the trousers and tossed him out of the tavern like a sack of wet trash. Ranser shouted back a furious insult.

Avus and Levan met him outside.

"What happened?" Levan asked.

"Undra said Jofon would be in the back room of the tavern after dark. I tried to go in there and they threw me out!" Ranser exclaimed annoyedly, brushing the pebbles from the front of his clothes.

"Haha...my friend, a secret meeting calls for an invitation." Avus laughed.

"We have a mission," Levan explained, "a show of good faith it seems, so that we may be given a chance to meet with Tor Veldgar and his clandestine royal court."

"Ohhh." Ranser grasped the significance of their conversation with Erevor now.

Levan thought to try to impose on Ranser the importance of sitting still and listening sometimes, but he thought it rather futile, and, perhaps, his wandering spirit was just the thing they needed to find the Mountain Maker and rid this land of the encroaching darkness.

They spoke mirthfully as they walked up towards the darkened brewery to meet Latus.

"Good job back there anyway," Levan praised him, "one can never dismiss the straight-forward approach."

"Ha!" Avus snorted, "Get this sailor boy some spirits he'll get in that back room! Right!?" He had had a taste of them himself somewhere in the interim.

"Spirits?" Ranser retorted, "Like rum? Nah, I hate rum. It's all rum to me. It just makes adults easy to fool at night."

"Of course, a sailor does not a drunkard make, though it can bring balance to his world." Said Avus, thoughtfully. "But it is so for them because it was so for their fathers, and grandfathers. It seems each man has his purpose and his poison in his blood, which he passes to his sons. Was your father fond of drink?"

Ranser was indecisive on how to answer this. In his mind and his memories, his father was Jofon, the old sailor with the eye-patch, who drank as much as any salty old mariner. But Jofon had told him that he was not his true father by blood when he was about nine years old, just before the shipwreck.

"My father...my father is Jofon, the man we are going to meet in this town. My blood father is someone I do not know. He said he would tell me some day." Ranser's voice trailed off as they reached the brewery door, and Avus began knocking.

The shadows of the cliffs made this side of the city dark and foreboding. Pungent fumes wafted from the vents near the roofline.

Avus noted a small hole in the ground outside the door, the cavern below it was probably fairly large. He thought it must be the cellar where they age their wines. He knocked again.

A voice came from inside, acknowledging their arrival, then footsteps echoed across the floor to the large wooden doors.

A bald man with an amiable countenance appeared in the threshold, holding a candle. Smiling, he appeared happy to see them.

"Hi there, I'm Latus. You must be the help Erevor was sending. Marvelous, I'm glad that you've arrived. We can speak inside."

They walked in onto a small wooden platform landing high above the floor below, with two staircases of dubious structural integrity leading down to the basement and up to Latus' living chamber. The rest of the large two-story building was occupied by massive vats in which some dark liquid bubbled. The strong, acrid aroma here singed Ranser's and Levan's nostrils.

"What can you tell us about Tor Veldgar?" Levan asked before their feet stopped moving.

"Whoa, whoa, slow down there. I only talk about such matters with friends. I'm only friends with people I trust. Maybe I'd trust you more if you listened to my proposal and agreed?" Latus raised his eyebrows, a slight grin on his lips.

"Yes, what can we help you with?" Ranser asked him.

"You've heard about the pest problem in my basement there, right?" Latus pointed to the round door at the bottom of the stair. They nodded. "Well, I've always dealt with rats and giant cockroaches, no problem, I'm not squeamish. But no, there is something else down there now. When I saw long fangs and claws I ran and sealed the cellar door. I think I saw two of them…I don't know what—shadows with teeth—two, maybe more. What do you say, will you clear it out for me? I'll pay you some gold and tell you what you want to know."

"Sounds like a good deal. Let's go." Ranser started down the steps.

"Here, I have two extra candles for light." Latus said, offering a pair of unburned candles. "It's impossible to see down there. Except for you, I guess." He said, indicating Avus.

Ranser lit both ends of the candle from the candle Latus held, blew one end out, drew his sickle and stuck the melted end in the bend of the blade, creating a sort of macabre lantern, casting a great hooked shadow.

Levan lit his own candle and held it forth. Not that he needed the candle for light, he could create a flame of nearly any size he wished, given the time and energy. But this little flickering heartbeat in his hand represented "the hard part" in fire magic: getting the air to ignite. With this active flame, he could bend the fire to his will without a word and with little effort. Having a pure, natural source of the element you wish to manipulate nearby always made the magic more potent and quickly-evoked.

Unbolting the door, they descended into the dark, musty undercroft. A preponderance of spiders, moths and other insects and arthropods crept and fluttered all along the earthen walls and stone floors. They felt a chill in the air as they crossed the last few steps down and entered the cellar chamber. Huge barrels as tall as a man were stacked up in rows on the floor and along the walls, creating perforated barriers they could see in-between at intervals, but not over.

Slowly, cautiously they entered into the labyrinth of kegs. A skittering, scratching sound was heard, followed by a gasping, echoing hiss. An icy breeze wafted past them, on which Avus could smell the deep caves.

Through one of the diamond-shaped spaces in the barrel walls Levan saw something bright orange move along the floor in the next row, its many tiny legs moving in synchronized waves. A bug. It wasn't what they were here for.

Then Avus saw it. A ribbon of dull, black shadow, its body paper-thin, covered in tiny black scales which perfectly absorb light, crawling along the ceiling of stone and sod with its vicious-looking claws.

"Heads up! There, on the ceiling!" Avus shouted, pointing out the creature coming towards them.

Ranser was moving to the side to get more room, and trying to see what Avus had warned about, when his foot bumped into a loose piece of stone. When he looked back up, he saw the movement, the four sets of claws outlining a target on the ceiling. His aim was honed to perfection hunting ship rats. He picked up the rock and threw it, hitting the creature and knocking it off the ceiling. It fell on the top of the row of barrels just in front of them. Its mouthful of spiky fangs showed as it hissed down at them.

Avus and Ranser moved to the barrels.

"I'm going up there!" Ranser pointed up.

"Jump on my back!" Avus called as he braced himself against the rack of brewing barrels.

Ranser ran at full speed toward Avus and made a flying leap, landing with both feet in the center of Avus shoulder blades.

The dwarf had miscalculated the weight of the boy, or the height of the ceiling, for when he stood up, he boosted Ranser at an alarming speed toward the stone roof.

Ranser flew up past the barrels, flipping around and catching the ceiling with his feet, then pushed off from there, plummeting down right onto the clawed shadow. His candle had unstuck from his sickle when he reversed direction, and it continued to fly upward, sticking with a splat of wax to the ceiling and continuing to burn. Ranser wrestled with the wild, flailing creature, bashing and hacking at it with his sickle, while Avus attempted to scale the barrel wall yelling "I'm comin'! Hang on!"

Levan shot a few pyrotechnics around the room and saw the other shadow moving along floor, approaching from a far corner in attempt to ambush them from the rear. He moved around the wall where he would be able to cut it off as it came into the intersecting pathways. There on the corner, beneath the edge of a wine barrel, was a bucket of water.

Good.

Shielding his candle, he willed the water to rise up and saturate the air, creating a shower of cold mist across the barrels and wooden support beams.

The dark shape of the clawed shadow appeared in the crossway, its body waving like a flag in the wind. Menacingly, it bared its claws wide, preparing to pounce. As it leapt into the air with a rasping snarl, Levan pushed his hand forward behind the candle and the tiny light erupted in a cloud of orange, gold and blue flame. The conflagration lasted but an instant. The body of the creature was vaporized and only its fourteen claws and 60 needle-like teeth remained, blown back and scattered across the floor by the explosion. The dampened timbers sizzled and steamed, but did not ignite.

Avus had struggled up to the top of the barrels with great effort as Ranser dodged the clawing swipes at his legs. He and the creature were both standing on the same barrel when Avus came up behind the shadowy monster and sent his axe crashing down through its body, and the wooden slats of the barrel below. The vessel shattered and Ranser fell into it, taking a great gulp and breath of wine while the other barrels rolled out of their housing, tumbling and smashing Avus between the massive drums of wood.

As Ranser knelt on his hands in a pool of wine, coughing more of it up from his lungs, he saw something approaching him from the shadows. He reached for his sickle on the ground nearby and whipped it across his body just in time to skewer the last clawed shadow, pinning it to the ground. It squirmed and thrashed as he stood on it, pulled the blade up and severed its top from bottom with a quick slash.

Levan walked over to see Ranser soaked and dripping with wine, and Avus crawling out of the toppled barrels. The dwarf stood up, grunting in relief, then the candle stuck to the ceiling fell with a splash in the wine-puddle in front of him and startled him nearly out of his boots. With a shouted curse, Avus jumped backwards, slipping and falling on the wet floor.

Levan snickered slightly but Ranser burst into laughter seemingly so uncontrollable that it brought him to his knees.

"Hehe..." Avus laughed feebly as he regained his footing. "Well, let's hope that was the cheap wine...hey look." He approached the far wall of the cellar which bore a crack about the width of a hand, through which a cold breeze flowed strongly. "This is how the creatures got in here. We should plug it up with something."

Levan took some of the stones lying around and

dipped them in the bucket of water. The stones became malleable as clay and he packed the paste into the crevasse. It dried in seconds and the wall was sealed.

Avus looked on it with approval. "Nice job. *Ow!*" He grimaced in pain as he looked down at his feet. Attached to the back of his foot at his ankle were the fang-like antennae of a giant, bright orange millipede. "Ahh!" Avus screamed as he hacked at the creature with his axe, chopping its body into smaller and smaller sections, but the sharp-horned head still did not release. Ranser went to pry the fangs off with his hands, but Levan stopped him.

"No, don't touch its stingers, it is very poisonous. Use your blade." Levan cautioned.

Ranser pushed the sickle blade in between the serrated fangs of the millipede and Avus' leg, and pried until they separated from the head. Levan wrapped his hand in his robe and carefully removed the broken teeth stuck in the dwarf's flesh.

"Ugh...poisonous you say?" Avus grumbled. He took off his boot and surveyed the puncture wounds. They were swelling and darkening. "Well, we dwarves are resistant to these kinds of toxins from cave creatures, though I've never had the misfortune of being bitten by one. It sure hurts."

"Yes," said Levan, remembering his studies of venomous creatures, "it's a very good thing it wasn't one of us bitten by it. If we weren't killed by the toxin, we would be bedridden in agony for weeks, and likely lose the use of a limb. There is nothing I can do to help you, but the venom should run its course in you within a few days."

"Well that's nice to know." Avus said, putting back on his boot.

"Alright, let's go talk to Latus."

They went back up the stairs to the round cellar door. It was locked.

Bang! Bang! Bang! "Open up!" Avus shouted, pounding on the door. Even in the dim candlelight, Levan could see the hue of the dwarf's skin reddening as the anger boiled up in him. Ranser leaned against the wall a few steps down, giggling to himself.

"Let us out, damn it!" Avus yelled at the door, continuing to slam it with his fist.

"You should probably keep your blood slow and stay calm." Levan gave the suggestion that is rarely ever heeded when spoken.

"I am calm!" Avus growled indignantly.

Luckily, they heard Latus' apologetic voice on the other side "Coming."

The bolt slid open and they exited the cellar.

"Hey, what's the deal with locking us in there!?" Avus shouted into the brewmaster's face.

"I'm very sorry about that," Latus explained, "those things have hands that can open doors. I saw them turning the handle. So I couldn't keep it unlocked. You understand. So I take it you've cleared the cellar of the infestation?"

"Yeah!" Ranser exclaimed with excitement, "We killed three little shadow things and a centipede, and patched up the hole in your wall down there!"

Latus assessed the soaking wet boy. "And went for a swim in the wine there as well?" He sniffed at Ranser once. "Ah yes, the 497 vintage—not our best year. You didn't break any *more* barrels, did you?"

"No, just that one." Ranser giggled.

"Haha, well it's an acceptable loss. Thank you so much for helping me out with that. Now that I know we can trust you, I invite you to join our meeting with Tor Veldgar tonight in the back room of the tavern. Take this." He handed Avus (since he was closest) a ring, which was too small for any of his fingers, so he handed it to Levan. It had a small oval opal set in the top, and hidden on the bottom was a triangular shield with a coiled dragon on it. "On the bottom of that ring there is the signet of the court of Veldgar. Do not show it openly in town. The meeting starts in about an hour. Show it at the tavern back room and say 'Veldgar is King', and you will be granted entrance to the meeting. I'll see you there. Thank you again, friends."

They headed back down the hill to the Mountain's Chalice Tavern. Latus had given them a small sack of gold coins, and they used one coin each to order food and drink. Levan had milk, Ranser wanted water.

"No more wine for you, boy?" Avus laughed as he drank his mead.

"No, and I hope I never taste the stuff again." Ranser retched and sniffled as the wine burned his throat and nose.

Avus snorted and choked as he laughed.

They ate and talked a bit about their past. Ranser spoke enthusiastically about his life at sea; he was still a bit tipsy from the wine. Levan talked of when he was recruited for the magic school by Tosgan the wizard when he'd finished his normal schooling at the age of twelve. Avus spoke of when he was a boy, how he used to love riding the water tunnel tubes in the caves, telling them they must try it someday.

They noticed a person disappear behind the bar. Then another. The meeting was starting.

They went to the back of the tavern, behind a wall concealing the door to the hidden room. A metallic peephole slid open when they knocked and a pair of eyes peered out from the other side.

"Veldgar is King." Levan said, holding up his palm to show the underside of the ring.

The door opened up to them.

Ranser eyed the bouncer spitefully as they walked in.

"Leave your weapons at the door here, please." The muscular man at the door pointed to the weapons leaned against the wall, as a precaution against assassination attempts.

Ranser narrowed his eyes to the man who had

thrown him out earlier, saying, "I'm watchin' you." But he complied with the rule, setting his sickle down next to the door. Avus propped his axe there also.

They entered a medium-sized room with a long table in the middle displaying maps of the kingdom, the city and the mines. Two scores of people were gathered around, about as many women as men, among them Latus and Erevor, listening to the man at the head of the table.

It was Tor Veldgar. He was tall and powerfully built, with long chestnut hair, ice-blue eyes and a dragon-crested shield tattoo on his wrist.

"My friends," Tor said, holding up a scrap of blue cloth."Danatar has brought me this emblem of my family, taken from an old burial mound to the south. She says a giant has made its lair near there, and guards the mound fiercely. Tomorrow, we will go there and investigate the mound. If the giant attacks us, we will defeat it."

The conspirators seemed to relish in this plan of action, and stirred in hushed enthusiasm as he went on, un-rolling a map of the kingdom upon the table.

"As you know, our kingdom is under attack. The Kinari invaders camped *here* have the army ranks swelled and at their defenses. We have shored up the city's fortifications and the outlying settlements are protected by our scouts, I feel there is no need to keep killing these soldiers, but evade them until they run out of supplies or the will to fight. We can move refugees along a network of safe-houses to the west of the city, moving south. We have seen some raiding in this area, but it will get much worse when they begin to run out of ra-tions. What think you of the visitors, Oslan?"

An old wizard seated at the table near him spoke. "So little is known of these foreigners that war between our peoples is inevitable. I believe we must come to learn their language, understand and develop trade between our nations. I submit to your consideration, my lord, that this is the only way to make peace with them, since there seems to be no end to their numbers."

Levan recognized Oslan, he was an instructor at the Magic School.

"If someone captures one of their troops," A silky voice came from a slender female wrapped in black suede, her head concealed in a wide-brimmed tricorn hat, reclining her chair on two legs. "perhaps in time we can come to learn more about them. Though abducting and smuggling a Kinari into the city would be something of a delicate task."

"Thus," Tor said, "it should be entrusted to none but you, Unadel. Oslan and Rotocles, the linguist, will take charge of him at the library vault. I have also this report to convey: the guards are not patrolling the city through the night. There have been far too many robberies and murders of late. I need some of you to stay in the city with your squads, sentries at Water Street and Garden Street. One of the recent murders has brought dark tidings—a corpse removed of its eyes and its heart. We believe this to be the work of a necromancer in our city. This dark cultist must be discovered and purged from our midst."

The mention of the necromancer sent an anxious murmur through the small crowd.

"Finally, I would like for you to keep an eye on the items turning up for sale at the auction house and the black markets. The recent quake has uncovered lost sections of the catacombs which are bearing many artifacts of significance. We may find some clue therein to the whereabouts of my father or, who knows, perhaps the Mountain Maker itself. That is all for now, rest well my friends, tomorrow we go giant hunting!"

The attendees gave a whoop and began to disperse. Levan moved to the front of the table.

"Master Oslan, it is fortunate to see you."

"Oh, Levan, so you've joined the cause." Oslan patted him on the shoulder."You seem to have proven yourself well. Haven't you attained your staff yet?"

"Well, no, that's kind of what I wanted to talk to you about."

Oslan sighed. "The Mage's Guild is in disarray at the moment. Tosgan has been summoned to aid the king's army, so he cannot administer the final test for your class. It's really only a walking stick anyway...helps to focus some spells..."

Levan was crestfallen. "Just my luck."

Oslan wanted to cheer him up. "All right, I can give you a task that I will recommend to suffice as your final test. You may still have to wait till this war is over to get your full accoutrements. Come meet me at the library first thing in the morning. And study your spellbook before you sleep tonight."

"Certainly." Levan affirmed.

Avus askied Tor a question. "Where did you say the body was found which was harvested by the necromancer?"

"No one seemed keen enough on that to ask," Tor replied, "but it was found here." He pointed to a spot just beside the south gate of the city where a small stream ran.

"Sir," Ranser interjected, "can you tell me where to find Jofon?"

"Jofon?" Tor contemplated, "The sailor with the eye patch? I suppose he wasn't here tonight. Last we knew he was operating covertly in the city, left a message saying he was worried his cover may have been compromised by a double agent."

"I sincerely hope he is not imprisoned in the dungeon. Jofon's a good man." Erevor commented.

"A city watchman would know," Tor offered, "if he could be interrogated, but finding your way into jail may be much easier, though I wouldn't wish that on you, my new friends. So these are your companions?"

Avus and Levan nodded.

"It's an honor to meet you, Sir Tor."

"And an honor to have you with us, brave heroes." Tor smiled on them. "I hope you'll join me tomorrow for the burial mound investigation."

"Yes, sir." Avus said, saluting.

"Can't wait." Ranser chimed as Tor turned to leave.

Levan said nothing. He had other plans tomorrow.

There probably won't be a real giant anyway.

"Rest well, then." Tor bid them farewell, donned his hood and exited through the back door.

They reclaimed their weapons and left. The hour was late, their day was long, and they were very tired. They each paid a gold piece to rent a separate room for the night, and settled in to bed.

Levan stayed up studying his spellbook. The next page was jumbled with unintelligible figures, diagrams, a branching tree of many nodes, and faint images of obscured creatures phasing in an out of sight. He traced his finger across the snaking line and the first node lit up. A gust of leaves and birds flittered across the page, revealing the hidden inscriptions around the first spell. On the second, the book pulsed with a ripple as if it were made of water and a fish jumped from one page to the next. The third spell was invisible until he held it away from the light, and it opened with a swarm of bats and other shadowy creatures that lurked in the dark. The fourth node did not activate for him, but he knew he was close to unlocking its secret.

Summoning gates were tricky and sometimes dangerous spells to use. You never quite knew what would emerge from them. He decided to wait until tomorrow to try putting any of the spells into practice.

CHAPTER 6 KNOW THY ENEMY

From a distance, a cow-farmer saw a silent, shadowy mirage dart down from the crenellations at the top of city wall while holding a rope fastened at the top in a backwards rappel, which transferred her downward momentum into forward speed. As she reached the edge of the moat, her body bent and whirled around, spinning and accelerating in several round-offs, the last of which vaulted her high into the air. Eclipsing the full moon for a moment at the height of a long back flip, her flying, inverted shape silhouetted against the bright white disk like a fire brand on a cheese wheel.

Unadel landed smoothly and silently on the other side of the castle moat, falling like a feather, touching down one toe at a time. She vanished from the moonlight within the line of trees and moved swiftly through the forest toward her objective.

As torchlight appeared in the distance, Unadel sprang to the top of the trees for concealment. Moving through the canopy like some arboreal creature of the night, she approached the Kinari war camp.

Among rows of tents and campfires, dark-haired warriors milled about the clearing. Tethered all around the camp were an army of tall black steeds, nearly as many horses as there were men.

Unadel moved around the perimeter, surveilling the soldiers. She was not looking for just any sword-swinger.

The fate of the kingdom may rest on the enemy soldier she chose.

After a long while of watching patiently, moving ever so slowly, she came upon a group of Kinari sitting around a fire talking. One of them seemed to be telling a story, gesturing with his hands. The others who were gathered around seemed riveted. Now and then they laughed. It seemed to be a good story, and a good storyteller. Unadel lay across a tree limb, watching, waiting, like a suede-suited panther. At last came the opportunity she was waiting for. The storyteller left his group to relieve himself, wandering into the woods to her right.

Unadel slithered across the branches without rustling a leaf, and perched above him. As the soldier passed below, the lithe elf dropped down behind him and pulled a fragrant white cloth from her wrist. The alchemist had told her one breath of the perfume she sprayed on this cloth would put a man into a deep sleep, and it did its job well. She wrapped the soldier's face in the cloth and he fell to the ground like a log of timber.

Just then, someone shouted from the camp. They wanted the man Unadel had just incapacitated to finish his story, and were impatient for his return. She pulled the ponderous weight of the soldier behind a tree out of the light, and covered him with leaves as one of the other soldiers from the campfire came into the woods, calling "Wrexon. Wrexon!"

The man began wandering toward her. He had an odd-looking sword on his belt, with a circular blade at the end. Unadel slipped back into the treetops, unraveling a long, thin chain from her hip. The soldier caught sight of the unusual lump at the base of the tree, and headed over to investigate it.

"Wrexon?"

Unadel linked the chain to itself, making a loop at the end, and dropped it down over the soldier's head. He had enough time to look up and see the her in the tree at the other end of the chain before it went taut as she fell from the limb, creating a pulley over the tree branch that hoisted him into the air. She dropped down to the next branch and hooked the chain to itself again, suspending the muted, struggling warrior a few feet off the ground.

When Unadel released the branch and landed on the forest floor, she was surrounded by five armed, angry Kinari soldiers. They moved in on her with swords drawn, and she took a few steps back, pulling another chain out from her side. One of the warriors charged forward with an overhead slash, attempting to cleave Unadel's slender elven neck. She stepped slightly to the side, tossing the bunched-up chain, which tangled around the soldier's sword. She flipped a loop around his leg as well and pulled the cord, forcefully ripping the sword out of his grasp and sweeping him from his feet.

The other four assailants spread out and rushed in from all sides. Unadel crouched down, reaching to her side to grasp another chain, and then spun into the air in a sideways cartwheel. The cable whirled out from her hand with a black, snowflake-shaped blade at the end, howling as it cut through the air in a lethal spiral around her.

All four were hit and staggered backward. The first slice's deadly accuracy cleaved an unprotected soldier's throat, and he quickly collapsed. The enemy to her right was slashed across the neck and chest, and he dropped a few seconds later into a pool of his own blood. The man behind her was cut across the ribs, and though he would live, his lacerated pectoral muscles would not allow him to wield a sword again. Beside him, the man who lost his sword was getting up and his head entered the arc of the whirling chain as the blade whizzed by and shaved off his ear. The man to her left dropped in a spray of blood as the black snowflake blade glided across his legs.

The soldiers' tortured cries rang out through the forest.

Unadel flicked her wrist and the chain recoiled in her hand. She attached two lines to the unconscious storyteller and began pulling him off into the forest.

She reached into her pouches and produced several strings of small incendiaries and a little metallic box. While pulling the Kinari warrior across the forest floor, Unadel placed the fuses of the bomb strings into the top of the metallic box and squeezed it. The strings erupted in flame and she began throwing them in a long line separating herself from the small army now pursuing her. The tiny bombs popped and shrieked, drowning out the wails of the wounded men, and spewed a thick smokescreen across the forest. Unadel stalked off into the night, towing her prisoner on a pair of bloody chains.

At the forest's edge, within sight of the north gate, she took from her pack an off-white padded cotton vest, of the sort worn by the king's soldiers beneath their plate mail. Before the mission she had added a puncture and blood stain for authenticity. She strapped the padded outfit onto the Kinari soldier and unwound the chains from his body.

The torchlight of Imperial troops scattered across the woods as Unadel reached to her shoulder and pulled her sleeve down, reversing it to reveal the white and red badge of a battlefield medic. She reversed her other sleeve, tunic, pants and hat, and nearly instantly transformed her all-black stealth suit into the pure white habit of the medic.

Unadel emerged from the forest like a ghost, with wisps of pearly hair streaming from her cap, waving and calling to some soldiers as she dragged the unconscious man out, still with the cloth over his face.

The eager soldiers ran over to her and helped pick the wounded man up.

The elf began to sweat as she held his shoulders and head, making sure the cloth stayed on his face. She and her captive were well-disguised, she thought. But as they approached the tall torches along the road into city, the revealing light and her proximity to the two men helping her made her fear that they might see through it. Medic's outfits are made of linen, not suede, and they were not so tight-fitting. She feared the men might also notice that the captured soldier was wearing a type of sandal that wasn't made on this continent. And Unadel realized she could now literally see through the wet cloth on the soldier's face, which further made obvious that he was a foreigner— and these men should recognize it too, if they'd been fighting them all day.

But they were young human men. So easily distracted from important details by a pretty face. One of them gazed at her, and blushed when she met his eyes. She gave a slight smile.

"We, uh, really appreciate what you do. The um, medics." The young soldier stammered.

"Yeah," The other one smiled dumbly, "you're ah....you're just great...you're fantastic...wonderful..."

"O no, it is you brave souls who fight to protect us, the delicate and defenseless. Praise be to *you* heroes of Lorestian." Unadel played her part flawlessly, even though she meant the opposite, and wished she could turn them into a rope swing off the drawbridge as they walked across it.

As they entered the city, Unadel went left and the guards started to go right, almost causing them to drop the Kinari. When they did, the small white cloth covering his face slid off. Unadel dropped the soldier's head and arm on the stone street to snatch the cloth up and cover up his face again.

As the Karikoss soldiers looked at her questioningly, Unadel said "It is...very important that he breathe these vapors. Come, we must get him to the library."

"The library? Why aren't we taking him to the temple with the other wounded? Agartha's grace returns our finest fighters to the battlefield, if they are worthy." He sounded like he was reciting a tired old military adage, but with the enthusiasm of a greenhorn.

"*Because*" Unadel improvised, "this man has Spiral Ornigyrus it's highly contagious, that's why we have to isolate him."

"Oh, right...did you say Spiral Orni...ja...contagious, is that, like, spreadable?" The young soldier inquired with growing dread. He thought he had heard the word before.

They were already inside the gates, it didn't matter anymore. "Yes, it's a horrible disease that spreads with close physical contact, such as touching the afflicted's skin with yours, oh..." Unadel looked down at their bare hands. Hers were gloved.

One of them was holding his ankles, the other had the Kinari's hand touching his wrist. They both dropped him on the spot and backed away.

"Uh, we have to go now." The soldiers said nervously as they moved backwards.

"Thanks for the help, I can take it from here. Bye, now." She winked at them. They left grinning, hoping to be wounded on the battlefield so they could be cared for by this enchanting medic. Of course, they never would be. She was Tor Veldgar's best covert operative, not a medic. Nor a linguist.

The tall marble pillars of the library were a few steps away. Unadel dragged the sleeping Kinari to the side of the library and entered a door there. The small passageway led to the stairs descending to the vault beneath the building. There, the linguist Rotocles was waiting for them.

"His name seems to be Wrexon." Unadel smirked as Rotocles gaped with joy and fascination.

He would work with the Kinari man to learn their ways and their language. A victory had been won, in secret for now, for Veldgar and the people of the kingdom.

❊ ❊ ❊

Avus was in the cave again. NuMoon's eyes screamed silently, begging him to hurry to her, to help. He tried to run but his feet were slowed, as if treading a thick mire. He felt a jolt up his leg and saw the massive millipede clamped on to his ankle again, its carapace pulsated with vibrant, expanding bands of fluorescing colors, glowing and revolving in a sheen around it as it spread up his leg.

He gasped as he felt the first spear point enter her back, the sword blades puncturing her organs. Avus became NuMoon as the giant, crystallized rock club fell on her skull, distorting her vision, then more pressure and hot blood until the final crushing blow faded them out.

Floating above, he saw the world change many times over the ages, while his body became a vein of gold riddled with gemstones, at the base of the tall, magnificent Luuvitas tree which NuMoon had become, whose fruit cured all ills.

There they stood and watched for an eternity. The living world was sad for a moment, because they did not remember what it was like, for an age, to sit still and be a rock, or a tree.

Before he knew it he had forgotten why or how he arrived there, and it ceased to matter anyway. He transcended biological emotions in his spirit form, as he had done when he watched himself slaughter a pack of scarlings, at least one with his bare hands, and thus transcended his limitations.

Of course, this grisly, haunting memory of NuMoon's physical death would return as soon as he re-entered his dwarf body, but as a cold, uncaring mineral deposit, set to witness the eons of time pass before becoming something else, immortal as the tree whose roots cradled him, he could hear her voice, and he knew she had forgiven him. She told him he could come back to this place any time he wanted, that it was not a sad place.

"Let my memory bring you strength, let your soul become golden wings to dance among the stars."

Avus awoke with his ankle swollen and throbbing, wishing he was still made of stone.

Levan woke up feeling very refreshed. His dreams were pleasant and unmemorable, for once. Imola's stuffed bear was sitting on the dresser next to his bed. He hadn't remembered taking it out of his pack.

Ranser was still sleeping and Avus had gone to get some water.

Levan packed his book and the bear in his bag and left for the library to meet Oslan. The hour was very early, the sun had not yet risen, but the stars had mostly disappeared.

Passing beneath the pillars of the library's front entrance, he pushed open the tall door and entered the large hall filled with rows of books, scrolls, maps and artifacts. It was a museum, a research lab, and a library in one. Over in one of the sitting areas, the only person around was the elderly sage Oslan, who sat comfortably reading a book. He looked up as Levan entered.

"Good morning, young apprentice." Oslan greeted him. "Glad to see you so quick to your task. What I will ask of you will be an unusual final test, but its success is of great importance in the service of our king, as you will see."

"I am honored to be entrusted with a mission of significance, rather than that boring old obstacle course. I will make the Mage's Guild proud." Levan stated confidently.

"Of course you will. All of us, your instructors, knew you were special. It wouldn't be prudent to say it in public, but you must know you are. Not just a person of extraordinary gifts, but possessed of a powerful destiny, an indicator of all, a beacon for your world." He closed his book and took off his reading spectacles. "Come, meet our new friend."

Oslan led Levan to a small passageway and a set of stairs which descended to the basement. The heavy wooden door swung open and they entered a large stone room.

The chamber was well-lit and filled around the edges with all manner of bushes, flowers, small trees and hedges. In the center of the room was a transparent cage, with long bars made of glass or some other hard, clear substance. Within it, a dark-haired man sat on a cushioned, upholstered chair, opposite a scholar who was showing the captive pictures of objects and writing down the phonetics of the words he said. The cell was lavish with comforts, despite being inescapable, and the prisoner seemed calm and cooperative.

"This is our Kinari friend, his name is Wrexon." Oslan said to Levan as they walked closer.

Wrexon looked over at them for a moment as they approached. Levan had seen his kind without armor before. Even though she was a woman spirit traveler sitting around that fire, he could easily see the features which defined their race. She had spoken to him, but only through telepathy.

"Good morning, Rotocles. How goes the study of the Kinari language?" Asked Oslan.

Rotocles sighed. "I've only just begun. The task is daunting. But the subject is compliant at least. I understand he was a gifted storyteller, but, being a soldier, I doubt his education is very substantial. Even with years of work, it may be impossible to grasp their syntax, their grammar, their number system, or any of the more complex ideas that could be communicated."

"I've anticipated this problem," Oslan said, "and it is my belief we can remedy it with the help of our young friend here. What we need is a written text of Kinari language."

"How would we get that?" Levan asked, wondering what he was getting himself in to. "Their lands are somewhere across the sea far to the north."

"There is a way we might acquire some of their literature." Oslan told him. "Here in this very library there is a magical book, the Tome of Records. This log book was created over two hundred years ago by a wizard who ran an international merchant fleet. Within it magically appeared the inventory and descriptions written down by all his customers, in their language and in ours. Perhaps, if he did business with the Kinari, the records would be there. I am not entirely sure how it will work, no one here has been allowed to touch the book for a very long time. But now the fate of the kingdom may rest on its contents. This is the like of the symbols you will be looking for." Oslan showed Levan some plates on which Kinari words in dots and slashes of interconnected lines had been painted by Wrexon. "Come, the book is kept in a locked case upstairs."

As they walked up the stairs to the library's first floor, then up another flight to the second, Levan pondered the task given to him.

"Master Oslan," Levan asked as they walked, "why is no one allowed to touch the Tome of Records?"

"Oh, you know, my boy, old books fall apart when they're handled too much. That's thing's a relic." This was true, but Oslan was withholding some information. He knew Levan could do it, despite the risk.

They reached the upper floor, and the resting place of a bronze and glass display case holding a very old book. Oslan produced a key and unlocked it, stepping back toward the stairway.

"Good luck now. I know you can do it." Oslan said, taking his first step down the stairs.

Levan wondered what was so difficult about opening a book and finding some trade records. As he lifted the cover of the tome, a light wind picked up and a few pages flew out. He looked up as the pages covered in writing and numbers fluttered down through the air, then more and more began flying up the book until he was blinded in a blizzard of paper. The wind blew around him with great force, gusting the pages away and covering the floor.

The library was gone around him. Levan now stood in a seemingly endless landscape of reams and heaps of writing paper. Tall, orderly stacks of stationary were being tossed and scattered by the terrible wind blowing through.

What a mess! It could take longer than my lifetime to find a page with Kinari writing on it in this place.

No sooner had he thought this, when a blonde-haired man with bright blue eyes wearing a green robe ran out from behind a mound of papers, coming to a stop before him.

"You!" The spectacled, but rather young man exclaimed, pointing at Levan. "This is your doing! Careless brute, you've scattered years of work, you bumbling fool! **Ah**! That look in your eyes—this was no accident! You've come to destroy my records! I will not abide thee, **Def**iler of kn**ua**lledge!"

A twirling bolt of energy shot from the wizard's finger, knocking Levan back before he had chance to react.

As he fell, Levan realized that the enemy wizard had included the same syllables he knew for the incantation of the air magic Force Bolt, Ah De Fua, within the words of his vengeance, but spoke the spell in a different way than he was taught. A cunning way of concealing one's casting, and catching adversaries off-guard. Levan tucked this lesson away in his mind as he hit the ground.

The book wizard then touched his hands together above his head and traced a circle around himself while chanting in the casting of a more elaborate spell. When his hands met at the bottom, his fingers became the flailing heads of vipers baring their fangs. The flesh and robes on his arms gradually transformed into many more serpentine coils, and it moved through his whole body, until the entire man became a mass of hundreds of venomous snakes spreading across the floor.

Levan sprang to his feet and drew an oval portal in the air, saying, "Creatures of the forest, make your hunting grounds here! **Sylvanofaun Ostrum!**"

He completed the summoning gate just as the foremost handful of snakes reached striking distance of his legs and lower torso. Levan retreated to a safer distance as the portal opened and a breeze laden with leaves blew out from it.

Then, a small white rabbit appeared.

Levan sighed with dismay. He hoped it would get better fast. The serpents flooded in around the furry mammal, and he perceived that they all had red eyes, except for one, which appeared only rarely amongst the tangle of viper tails, which had blue eyes. The bunny sniffed the ground for a moment, then it became aware of the snakes all around it. It bolted off but was punctured by many fangs and did not make it to the edge of the circle of serpents before it was smothered by the slithering, green tentacles. Surprisingly, the little beast kept moving, jumping and kicking through and atop the scaly entanglement, drawing all the snakes to it. Somehow the rabbit kept hopping about, with some difficulty, as the snakes swarmed upon it. It was obviously immune to the venom they had, but seemed also impervious to the hundreds of long, needle-like fangs. These creatures were said to appear as familiar beasts, but from a perfect forest world in another plane of existence. Levan now saw the efficacy of this simple creature.

All of the snakes were jumbled up in a feeding frenzy on the hopping rabbit. Then, the outlying throng of green vipers slithered away, and regrouped, emitting a hazy cloud.

The mist cleared, and the fifty snakes had become a ferocious red crocodile, snapping its great jaws after Levan. These little dragons were rarely seen out of the water. He had only seen these creatures in paintings, and thought it the wrong color, but he knew its jaws were quick and lethal, and its legs short with limited turning ability. He leapt to the right side, then reversed direction as the hissing croc gaped its huge mouth that way. It could not follow him quickly enough and he had time to back away and prepare another summoning portal.

"Congeal from utter darkness... " Levan began, but the whirling winds and hissing snakes were distracting his focus on the spell, and he nearly did not finish it. He was loathe to imagine what creatures might emerge from the caves of the mountains. "Come forth creatures of the deep, **Vallis ostrum!**"

The gray, swirling portal opened, wafting out cool air, but nothing of aid emerged. Levan had to dodge away from the crocodile's jaws again, and as his hand fell on the ground, a stray viper sank its fangs into his thumb. He shook the snake off his hand and felt its searing venom spreading up his arm. His hand swelled and became unresponsive.

It's okay, calm down. You know the words to the Antivenom spell. Breathe.

"Nullify this foul poison...**Purifira aphilos**." Levan whispered, and the pain began to subside.

Then the forest portal, still flitting flying leaves out, emitted a huge, furiously enraged brown bear. Its sharp, fearsome arsenal of teeth slung saliva as it roared in challenge at the massive red crocodile. The reptile's blue eyes flashed in malice at Levan.

"He's come to eat your cubs! Get him!" Levan commanded the bear, and she charged with a furious snarl.

The hulking bear dashed past the young wizard and pounced on the crimson crocodile that the enemy wizard was embodying. The two monstrous beasts went rolling across the floor, tossing up pages of paper as they chomped and clawed at each other. Finally, the bear regained its feet, holding the crocodile's limp neck in its teeth. She thrashed the reptile's lifeless body again for good measure, then dropped it, and plodded off, stomping and pulling the meat out of the sides of the snakes that approached her.

Then a deep, rasping, terrifying voice came from the cave portal, gloating in some vile tongue. Out stepped a gaggle of long, thin green limbs, covered in warts and welts. The troll's head, mottled and spotted with tufts of white hair on top and around its shiny black eyes, rose ten feet tall as it stepped out of the gate. In each of its hands, wielded as weapons, were long, twisted and jagged scraps of rusty metal.

In this endless landscape of paper, which even covered the sky, the bear saw no other substantial targets. The caster appeared as a friendly tree to her, and the snakes were no more than a nuisance. The female bear charged the tall, spindly troll, tackling it to the ground.

"No, don't fight each other!" Levan shouted at his summons, but to no avail. They would not obey his commands.

The snakes and crocodile had disappeared, and though Levan could sense the green mage's presence nearby, he could not pinpoint a target. He stood helplessly for a moment while the creatures that were meant to be aiding him were locked in a battle to the death.

Perhaps this was his plan, to befuddle my allies into fighting by disappearing, or shapeshifting into something else. He must be here somewhere.

The bear tore off the troll's right arm and tossed it to the side as its claws ripped into the splotchy green torso. As the bear bit into its neck, the troll pulled its left arm out from under its body and shoved the huge jagged piece of metal through the bear's midsection. Both creatures dissipated into wisps of light, floating back to their native dimensions through the wood and stone portals. The gates were still open but Levan stood alone. His opponent was unseen.

The strange scribings of countless far-flung, lost civilizations filled every plane of view. Levan's eyes followed a dot flying off a page. It was a tiny gnat flitting around in the air above him. The little insect hovered still and then spread out into a massive swarm of unusually large bees.

As Levan attempted to move away from the cloud of stinging insects, a musky-smelling drop of liquid fell from above onto his head.

Oh, no.

The bees dived in at their desperate defense pheromone reeking from Levan's scalp. He had encountered smaller bees on the farm which swelled their stings for weeks and generally made life miserable. It would take but a small contingent of this massive horde of chicken-egg-sized, black and yellow flying poisoned needles to kill a man.

Levan held a hand above his head and drew a portal directly above himself. "The sea come to land, **Aquos Ostrum**." He chanted the words then held his breath. As the giant bees drew in, a torrent of water gushed down from above, washing away many of them, and the water sprayed out, dampening their wings, making it impossible to fly. The bees were immobilized by the water portal, and they poured across the ground in the stream.

The few insects that were still flying drew together and transformed into a pair of giant scorpions the size of a large dog. They approached Levan from both sides, clamping with their pincers and coiling their tails to sting. They would not be hindered by the rush of water.

Then, from the forest portal, another small creature emerged. It was a squirrel with a tiny bow and a quiver of arrows. The little squirrel moved to the top of a pile of paper, notched an arrow and let it fly. The miniature missile came down and pierced the body of the left scorpion. It was wounded, and slowed, but kept moving toward Levan, dripping a yellowish-green fluid.

As the scorpion on his right neared striking-distance of Levan, a thin, clear strand of silk shot out of the cave portal, and down it moved a massive, hairy black spider, its body the size of Levan's head. It moved with monstrous speed toward the scorpions, baring its dagger-like fangs and spreading its sticky webs everywhere it went.

The scorpion's tail reared up, the barbed end a split-second away from impaling Levan and liquefying his insides.

Just then, a wad of glue-like spidersilk sprayed forth from behind it, enveloping the scorpion in a tangled web. It slashed and tore away the webbing, turning back to face the spider that had now gained on it.

The two arachnids clashed, stabbing each other with their venomous spears. The scorpion's pincers grasped for and controlled two of the spider's front legs, then one of them snapped off, and the other wrenched free. The cave spider skittered across the scorpion's back, attaching lines at each end. The scorpion continued to fight back, but as it did it became more and more entangled in the sticky webs. At last it could only weakly squirm within its constricting cocoon, as the spider siphoned out its blood and organs.

The other scorpion was hit again by one of the squirrel's tiny arrows, which stuck in its tail. The creature stopped moving for a moment and began emitting a white fog. When the smoke cleared, there stood a tall, green insect with huge eyes, and several large, transparent wings that laid down under a hard shell on its long back. The mantis stood nearly twice as tall as Levan, and the sharp, serrated blades on its arms were as long as one of his legs.

The squirrel archer fired another arrow, and it glanced off the hard carapace of the mantis. The huge green monster turned to the squirrel and swiped with its great slashing blades, but the squirrel leapt and scurried out of the way, darting back to the portal and disappearing.

The praying mantis slashed its huge arm at Levan, and he narrowly ducked under it as the air whooshed by his head. The mantis took a step and landed one of its legs onto the spider with a crunch, then brought the sharp tip of its arm blade down and tore the spider apart in a spray of green ochre.

Levan moved past the gates he created earlier, anticipating the next creature's appearance, and trying to gain some distance from the huge swiping blades. The giant mantis pursued him with frightening speed, moving twenty paces in a single step.

The forest portal shined and a sweet aroma blew in from it as thick tree roots meandered out. A walking birch tree as tall as a castle stepped forth from the gate, stretching out its massive limbs, and catching numerous paper pages as they blew by.

The giant mantis took flight with its clear wings, attempting to move past the treant to attack the wizard. An enormous tree limb bent down and swatted it out of the air.

The mantis fell to the array of gently waving roots, a few of which tensed into action, wrapping the insect's legs in a vice-like grip. The mantis slashed ineffectively at the tough white wood as it tried to pull its legs free. The treant leaned over and brought down the sharp end of an ancient dead limb like a giant wooden fist, smashing the insect into the ground.

Both creatures began to dissipate and the blonde-haired wizard in green robes stood before Levan again. He was haggard, sweating and struggling to catch his breath.

"Oh...I can see you're no defiler of knowledge. You must be very gifted to command those creatures." Said the mage.

"I don't have much control of them yet...I sort of just set them loose. But you could *become* them. I have never met a master shapeshifter." Levan was intrigued by this animalistic magic. The snakes went instinctually after the rabbit, so his actions seemed to not be fully under control when in animal form. The volatile nature of this magic, he guessed, was the reason it was not taught at the magic school, and why he'd never met one. "I am Levan Cloudborne. Who are you?"

"Hmm...they called me...Merton. I'm sorry I attacked you, it's just that...it gets very windy in here when people open the cover, and...there was one elderly fellow, not young like you, a wizard of some renown, who got lost in here. He went mad after running aimlessly for some years. He would come across me and attack me, but instead of killing him, I was able to shrink him and seal him away in this vial." Merton showed him a small glass vial with a tiny, writhing, drooling, flailing lunatic inside. "It seems the minds of those who enter this place are challenged, and the old, slow, disorganized brain cannot handle the overflow of information. I suppose they've figured out now they can access my records by sending a strong young wizard like yourself in. This poor soul fell victim to that unfortunate effect of my realm. I would like you take him back w—"

"Wait a minute," Levan cut him off. "I came here

to find a script of Kinari writing, not to help some poor lost soul. This is more important!" Levan was not unsympathetic, but Merton seemed the kind of person to follow his train of thought to places far from the priorities of here and now, and this matter could bear no delay.

"Oh, yes, of course, the Kinari were good business partners when I lived back in your world. I know I have the page with their records around here somewhere..." Merton began thumbing through the nearest stack of papers, picking up random ones on the ground. He seemed to be becoming somewhat flustered at the chaotic clutter the battle had caused. "Ah, this is going to take me years to put back in order again, and I haven't even begun to catalog them. After that I'll build some shelves or cabinets or something to put them in."

The endeavor seemed futile to Levan. To find a single page in this snowglobe of papers still fluttering and falling from the air seemed impossible.

Then Merton stood up and caught a flying page from the countless thousands blowing all around them. "Here it is!"

He handed Levan the page with lists of goods stocked and sold, along with their prices and descriptions in both languages.

"Great! This is perfect! Thank you so much, Merton. And sorry for wrecking your place." Levan thanked him graciously.

"It's no problem, I've got all the time in the world to organize it. You should probably be getting back to your library now." Merton replied, turning to walk away.

"About that..." Levan said, "how exactly do I get out of here?"

Merton turned around. "Oops, I almost forgot. I can show you the way to the exit. But..."

"Forgive me," Levan realized he was asking two favors in exchange for nothing but a beating, and he didn't want to be a bully. "I'll take the old wizard back with me."

"Wonderful!" Merton's face lit up happily. "The

priest at the temple should be able to restore him to his faculties. Follow me, right this way."

He walked amongst towering mountains of papers and walls of text, through a seemingly endless blizzard of pages. At last a small wooden door appeared before them, standing on its own among the swirling pages in the otherwise desolate book world.

"There it is," Merton said, pointing to the door, "the portal back to your world. Good luck in your quest, and let us both hope for the best for the poor lost wizard."

"Thank you again, Merton. I shall have to come visit you again someday." Levan said, grasping the doorknob.

"It better be someday soon!" Merton chuckled as he waved goodbye.

Levan opened the door and stepped through. He was back in the library, standing in front of the Tome of Universal Records as its cover slammed shut with a puff of dust. In his hand he held the key to the Kinari language.

Walking in an exhausted daze downstairs, he found the linguist and gave the page to him. Oslan was there and he congratulated Levan, and said something about sending his recommendation for Levan's completion of the course and that he'd receive his rewards from Tosgan when he saw him. Levan excused himself to go get some food and recoup at the tavern. The scholars eagerly went to work laying out the Kinari alphabet.

CHAPTER 7 GIANTS AND FIERY-HAIRED MAIDENS

The small band of warriors met up at a sheltered cove in the woods just outside the city walls, a place they called the Fox Hole. There were six of them in all, including Avus, Tor, Erevor, two more men and a tall, silvery-white-haired elf. She wore a form-fitting black suit, her pointy tricorn hat tilted down, half-concealing her eyes, and appeared to carry no weaponry. Tor, decked out in his royal full plate armor and longsword, introduced Avus to the party, and they to him.

"Avus, this is Unadel, Wesker, and Saemon." He said, gesturing to the elven rogue, the brown-haired man with a spear in his hand and several more strapped to his back, and the young man with short hair dyed green from the Verden Berries of this forest, who wielded a thin, curved scimitar in each hand.

"Hail and welcome, it is a fortunate to have a — strong axe on our side" Said Wesker.

"Well met, I shall see to your back when the fighting begins." Avus raised his axe in salute to them.

"The burial mound is just to the southeast of our location." Tor told the group. "Unadel will scout ahead and notify us of danger. Is everyone ready?"

They all affirmed and followed behind Unadel as

she slinked ahead through the woods.

Towering spikes of stone jutted from the land like islands in the sea of conifers as they gained altitude. Within the faces of the exposed rock slabs, a myriad of gemstones sparkled and glinted.

Unadel returned to the group and told them the way was clear to the burial mound. They hurried to the site of the clearing where the smooth mound of grass rose the height of three horses, and a stone-lined open tunnel led inward from the side.

Tor pointed out the carved inscription of his family's clan as they moved into the spillway-like tunnel which appeared to go right into the burial chamber. But just beyond the shadow's line where the tunnel ceiling began, Tor's passage was blocked. There was a well-concealed door which, due to its orientation, would never have sunlight directly on it, but just in front of it. He tried to push, then kick it in, but the door and hinges were wrought of steel. Avus recognized the craftsmanship of the door, and the differing lock on the latch.

"That's dwarven forged steel. Not even a giant could bash it in. But that lock is not. Take that off and unlatch the door from this side." Avus offered, though he had no skill with lockpicking.

"Unadel, can you open this?" Tor motioned to Unadel to come to the front.

"Given a moment's peace and quiet, of course." She said as she crouched down to insert a pair of long, thin strips of metal into the keyhole.

Tor gave everyone a hushing gesture so that Unadel could concentrate as she fiddled with the lock. But then she startled and snapped her head back to look out of the end of the tunnel, and up. Avus heard it too. A tumbling of pebbles, a shifting of strata.

Half of the fifty-foot-high, crystal-studded rock face behind the entrance to the tomb shifted position and a tremor shook the ground. The giant turned away from the mantler-ock spire crystals he was eating (which his back-skin mimicked, camouflaging him) and stomped to the narrow exit of the tunnel, blocking it off.

They were trapped in single file in the narrow stone spillway, which perhaps only Unadel could climb out of, but she would have to make her way past Tor, Avus, and Wesker to get back to the open section.

Saemon was at the rear, and he stood his ground against the huge, rocky-skinned stone giant.

The towering colossus brought down a stony foot in a quaking stomp, smashing down the wall at the end of the tunnel as Saemon hopped backwards with a flying slash of his scimitars, to little effect.

The giant then dragged its great foot forward in a kicking motion, and several large boulders went flying down the tunnel. Saemon could not avoid them at this range, and was bashed and wedged into the wall by the landslide of stones. He groaned in agony as he tried to struggle out, but the giant kicked again and sent that dam of rubble flying down into the tunnel. The group was pelted with rocks as Saemon's unconscious body flew to the back of the tunnel, hit the door and fell there.

Tor had been knocked down by a huge flying boulder, and was coughing up dust. Unadel had been bruised and cut in several places as the sharp stones pierced her soft armor. Avus was already half-buried in loose rocks and could barely move.

They were trapped like fish in a barrel. Another small, effortless movement from the giant and they would all be buried alive here. They felt the ground rumble again and thought the end had come for them all, but fate then took an unexpected turn.

* * *

That morning, Ranser had decided to follow the lead given to him by Tor, and check to see if Jofon was in the dungeon. He had seen from the city map that the guardhouses along the walls connected by tunnels to the dungeon beneath the castle. So any of them would do. He purchased a piece of bread before leaving the tavern, and ate it as he strolled down the street toward the city wall.

At the end of the road, set into the stone fortification, was the door to one of the guard stations. Rune ran off as he entered to a damp, rank-smelling room with a few chains and manacles attached to the walls at the far end. Just before that area was a stairwell leading down into the stone floor. Beside the stairway was a man sitting at a desk with some papers and stamps on it. Ranser approached him and knocked on the desk.

"Hey, I want to see the prisoner Jofon."

The record-keeper looked up annoyedly at him. "You can't see him. No one is allowed visitation to spies and traitors."

"So he *is* here. I'm going in there." Ranser said stubbornly, walking past the guard's desk and down the stairwell where a long brick tunnel led down to the dungeon.

"No you are not!" The guard yelled angrily, getting up from his chair. "Who do you think you are, boy? Get out of there!"

Ranser tried running down the stairs, but he was caught by the hair on the top of his head. He pulled and struggled at the guard's arm, but he reached his other arm down and grabbed Ranser's shirt, ripping it as he pulled him up by it. Another guard came in and rushed to the other's aid, restraining and tying up Ranser's arms and legs.

"Should we lock him up?" The guard that just entered asked.

"Nah, he's just confused about visitation rights. Just throw him out." The weary record-keeper sat back at his desk, and the soldier hoisted Ranser over his shoulder.

He was taken not just out of the guardhouse, but to the closed south gate, where the guard walked him up the scaffolding scaling the wall to the very top. There, a soldier at the gatehouse turned to him.

"What have we got here?" The gate house soldier asked.

"Special delivery." The guardsman replied with a mischievous grin.

"Haha, great, I've been needing a good distraction."

The soldier wrapped Ranser's feet in a rope, intertwining it with the binds already there.

They used this rope connected to a metallic pulley wheel to lower down messages or small items without opening the gate. And the soldiers also occasionally used it to lower exiles out when the gate needed to stay shut, or they wanted to have a laugh.

King Fahfren himself had done this personally to an old woman once, when he was touring his city, and found her appearance to be unfavorable. When they had strung her up on the wall, the king asked to take the rope from the soldiers. Instead of lowering the old woman down slowly, as the soldiers tried to do, Fahfren let the rope slide through his hands and she plummeted with a terrified scream headfirst to the bottom of the city wall. The poor old woman crumpled to the ground and was silent, and moved no more. This Fahfren found wonderfully humorous, and he snorted and guffawed as the soldiers pretended to laugh with him. Now this was one of many cruel and immoral techniques encouraged in King Fahfren's army.

They lifted Ranser over the edge of the wall and he hung there, suspended upside down for a moment, and then began to descend. Thankfully, they did not drop him, nor did they take his weapon which would allow him to escape the cord bindings. But as he looked down he could see what was "special" about this delivery. The soldiers had poured several buckets of horse and goat dung down at the base of the wall, at the spot where he was about to land. The rope went slack and Ranser fell to the ground with a foul splash.

Ranser plummeted face-first into the offal and rolled up out of it like a caterpillar, spitting the putrid filth from his mouth as the guards laughed riotously from above. He shouted curses to them and condemnations to their graves when he returned as he squirmed around and jostled free his sickle. He gripped the sickle with his bound hands and sawed through the foot bindings, then holding the blade with his feet, he cut through the lashings on his wrists.

Ranser stood outside the wall and thought of what to do next. Rune was stuck inside the city somewhere, he would have to return for him later. Then he remembered that Avus was going with Tor to the burial mound to the south east. He was good with maps, and remembered where it had been pointed out. He thought perhaps he could still catch up to them. And then, he hoped, Tor and his network could get him access to the dungeon when they returned. Soiled and pungent, he sprinted off into the forested foothills to the south.

The land was scattered with rock formations as it climbed into the mountains. There were so many towering crags and outcroppings, he hardly took note of the low, ashen cone surrounded by dark streams of rock in fractured tributaries as he ran past it. His right foot fell on one of these lava veins and sank in. He could feel the intense heat radiating from it as his shoe rubbed off the dark outer layer, revealing flowing molten rock beneath, glowing faintly red. Ranser tried to pull his foot out, but his shoe was stuck, and beginning to catch flame. He quickly reached down and unlatched his shoe, pulling his foot out as the lava engulfed it. His toes were burned and he poured some water on them, some of which spilled onto the lava flow, causing it to hiss and sputter.

Ranser took a drink of the water, then spit some out on the lava, yelling "Damn volcano! Ate my shoe!"

Then the ground began to rumble violently. A huge pair of enraged, bloodshot red eyes opened up in the ground right in front of him, at the base of what had appeared to be a small volcano. It was, in fact, the head of a sleeping fire giant. The giant stood up, taller than a ship's mast, its skin ashen gray and black, and bright orange lava spewed from the top of its head.

The fire giant resembled a huge statue of a dwarven female, carved in obsidian, with flowing red hair erupting from her crown. She roared with a bone-rattling, bestial fury as a huge axe of dripping molten rock formed in her hand.

Ranser knew one should not wake sleeping giants, and he had always tried to avoid doing so. It was gigantic and awesome, but very angry, and in a very advantageous spot to turn him to cinders if it so pleased. So he ran, not in fear, but in search of a more level playing field. The furious fire giant screamed after him, setting the forest ablaze as it hurled swaths of lava down at him.

Avus and the others should be right around—what the—

The trees opened up before a gently sloping mound, and there Ranser saw another gargantuan figure moving around it.

Another giant. Great. I hope my allies are faring better than me.

He sprinted into the clearing and past the stone giant's legs, the still-pursuing fire giant right behind him. The fire giant bounded over the mound and trampled over the smaller stone giant, sending it crashing into the forest. As it moved to get back up, Avus, Tor, Unadel and Wesker climbed out of the stony rubble piled at the tomb entrance.

Ranser saw a black-clothed figure dart past him in the woods. The agile elf circled around two distant trees, drawing a line between them with a long chain. She dashed to another set of trees and strung more trip-lines between them like a ghostly black widow. The thundering footfalls of the fire giant came in, and became tangled in chains. The trees or the chains snapped, but it was enough to throw the fire giantess off balance and send her toppling to the ground.

Tor Veldgar appeared on the hilltop, running down at full speed. his longsword held skyward. With a fierce battle-cry, he leapt onto the reeling stone giant's left arm with a forceful downward smash, breaking and separating the stone bone inside. Sand poured from the wound instead of blood.

Avus came up to its other side as the giant attempted to regain stance. He swung and his axe dug deeply into the outside of the giant's wrist, and it fell back with a roar.

Ranser moved forward to try to disable the fire giant while it was down, but he had a treacherous time navigating the rivers of flame. He got as close as he could. It wasn't the target area he'd hoped for, but it was safe from lava. He reached out as far as he could with the sickle, and scratched the end of the rusty blade across the fire giant's ribs.

The huge, blackened face turned with an enraged snarl at him, bright white lava surging from the crater on her head.

Unadel tethered the giant hands to the biggest trees around with double chains in a blur of motion.

Giants had a very difficult time getting up if they fell down. This one's struggle was further impeded by the tangle of chains Unadel had lashed her in, which would slow, but by no means immobilize her.

Finally when the fire giant did make it to its feet, Unadel stood on its shoulders, swinging a bladed chain in each hand. She vaulted in a handless cartwheel over the head, wrapping a line around the giant's skull that met under the chin. The giantess tried in vain to swat Unadel off her shoulders, but her hands were held by the chains to the trees.

As Ranser watched in awe, Unadel swung across the giant's chest, flying by a line connected to her belt and the giant's head, spinning in all directions as her dual bladed chains made the illusion of a flickering sphere around her, and tore a jagged wound across the giant's midsection. Lava poured out onto the ground from the hundreds of cuts. Unadel landed back on the giant's shoulder and swung down her backside, slicing it to ribbons to match the front.

Wesker continued thrusting his spearblades into the fallen stone giant's sides, now and then pulling out a new one when the hafts would break off.

Erevor had given up shooting arrows which only bounced off its hard skin, and came forward with his sword to pierce the tough shell and spill the sandy blood.

Unexpectedly, while still flat on its back, the stone giant raised its great arm and dropped it with a crash, flattening someone. When the arm moved again, they could see It was Erevor. He lay there crippled and smashed, but still conscious, weakly groaning in pain. His darkened eyes darted around in agony, the whites of them having turned deep red from the crushing impact.

Avus' eyes went wide. This was the man that first helped them when they came to the city. The first one to give them a chance. He felt that frightening, alien yet familiar tide of rage swelling up again. NuMoon's voice returned, assuring him it was alright, to let it wash over him. To let her memory bring him...

Strength.

He jolted out of his body and watched himself as he let out an atrocious roar, a sound he wasn't sure he could make voluntarily. His arms bulged and flushed crimson, bringing the axe down in an unstoppable chop. It cleaved through the giant's arm, severing it and the lower part quickly decayed into dust, blown away by the wind.

The giant roared and rumbled on the ground. Tor and Wesker had already stabbed and slashed all through the head and neck, so there seemed to be no use attacking there, Avus thought his body had reasoned, or it had just began attacking the nearest target. Reasoning or not, Avus hacked into the giant's side repeatedly, where the bottom of the ribcage should be, screaming maniacally. He marched relentlessly forward as he chopped and slashed in a shower of sand, carving the stone giant's body out through the abdomen.

There were organs analogous to humans, but they were all made of rock or crystal. A cage of crystalline bones was uncovered as Avus kept swinging, and inside it was a glassy, faceted gemstone, through which could be seen the stream of sand blood it pumped.

Smashing through the ribs, Avus brought his axe down on the gemstone heart and was thrown back, along with the others around it, as the heart shattered with a sonic boom and the rest of the stone giant turned to dust.

Meanwhile, Unadel was running and swinging across the gargantuan body of the fire giant, shredding its dark flesh as she went, when it pulled free from the chains and reached up and grabbed her in its massive hand. As it squeezed, Unadel stabbed two blades into the giant's wrist, causing it to release her from its grip, and she fell fast and hard from above treetops.

The crushing grasp had fractured her ribs and one of her vertebrae. The impact with the ground ripped a tendon in her knee and caused something to crack in her lower leg. With an anguished moan, Unadel looked up to see a rod of lava growing in the giant's hand above her. She did not have time to stand up and run far enough to avoid the attack.

Ranser saw the lava axe forming and falling toward the helpless elf. He ran toward the giant, leaping off a fallen log and throwing his sickle with a valorous yell. The blade spun through the air, sticking deep in the giant's back.

The giantess roared and turned toward him, sparing Unadel for now. It threw the lava axe in Ranser's direction and he dived out of the way, but was surrounded by flames. The roaring fire also blocked the advance of Avus, Tor and Wesker.

Unadel limped through the forest behind the giant, who had lost track of her. She had seen something in the distance when she was high up on the giant's shoulders, perhaps the only hope of extinguishing this monster. Hobbling to the east, the elven rogue lit several of her smoke bombs and threw them high up into the trees.

The giantess stomped toward the noise, crashing down trees and enflaming the woods wherever she stepped. She had broken into a run toward the disturbance, and was moving too fast to stop when her foot caught on a chain Unadel was holding and she fell through the wall of smoke. On the other side was the steep drop into a great crater filled with water known as Lake Kiva. The giantess screamed as the horrible blue liquid rushed up and engulfed her in a cloud of hissing steam.

From a distance Ranser saw Unadel pulling tight with all her strength a chain across two trees, and the giant came and fell through the smoke. Unadel lurched forward as if she were connected to the chain which was tangled up on the plummeting fire giant at the other end. She was pulled away swiftly, following the giant through the hazy cloud and down the edge of the cliff.

Rushing to the crater's rim, Ranser and the others looked down and could see no living thing amongst the bubbling, boiling water and mist.

"Oh no....who was she?" Ranser asked Tor in wonder. "She was amazing."

"That's Unadel," Tor replied, "And yes, she *is* amazing. I know this looks bad for her, but worry not, she always comes back." He walked away from the edge of Lake Kiva unconcerned for her safety. He knew she was alive and well enough, but he could scarcely understand her propensity to take such daring risks. At least she's on our side, Tor thought. "Let's get into this tomb and see what's there."

※ ※ ※

Levan shambled into the Mountain's Chalice tavern in the mid-morning, exhausted from his magic battle. He ordered one of Karikoss' delicacies, blueberry ice cream. It was expensive, but extremely refreshing and delicious. He felt a twinge of guilt at spending two gold pieces (enough for a meal and a room) of the group's money for the dessert, but this was a celebration of his graduation. Most of the other new wizards had lavish parties and were showered with gifts on this day. His little bit of happiness melted away and disappeared all too soon at the bottom of the bowl.

The tavern door opened. In walked a young human female wizard with long flowing hair the color of the sunset. She carried an elaborate single-handed silvery birch staff, and wore a green and white half-robe, the skirt fluttering across the bottoms of her long alabaster thighs.

It was Sabrena Fahfren, his classmate, newly-graduated wizard, and the object of Levan's infatuation for the past few years. She knew nothing of Levan but his name, and he knew little of her, but that she was the only girl he'd ever met who could match him in magical prowess. Her fiery red hair told of her royal breeding, she was in fact a niece of the Fahfren dynasty of throne-holders, and thus technically a princess. But almost no one ever called her that to her face, for her retribution would be swift and painful.

Her high-heeled, soft leather boots clopped across the wooden floor like a horse's hooves as she moved to a table and took a seat. The barmaid went over to take her order but she waved her off. She was waiting for someone.

Sabrena didn't seem to notice Levan, or anyone else in the tavern. She sat alone and waited.

To Levan this seemed peculiar, to see her sit there, idle. She was always doing something in school, whether active or reading, so it always seemed hard to find a moment to talk to her. What could make her spirit tame like this? He wanted to go ask her. Still, he hesitated. Confronting her with his observation of her mannerisms and asking her why she was acting differently seemed not a good way to enter an agreeable conversation.

Sabrena had placed her staff on the table. Levan was curious what the process was of awarding or choosing these items, and how the other students fared in their tests. That would be his topic of conversation.

Levan walked over to the table where Sabrena sat.

"Hey Sabrena, how's—" Levan began, but his throat caught and he realized he started the question with the wrong word. Then she looked up at him and he forgot what he was going to say. "ah—how are you? Is everything all right?"

Her vibrant green eyes seemed to peer through him and all of his thoughts.

"Oh, hello." She recognized him from the magic school, but didn't immediately remember his name. "Yes, all is well. I'm just waiting for my companion."

"Your companion?" Levan was sidetracked.

"We've been going out hunting since winter. His name is Cray, he's really tall, with big muscles, and a huge sword. You'll know him when you see him, hehe..."

"So...what are you hunting today?" Levan asked, trying to keep the discussion flowing.

Sabrena leaned in to whisper. "He says we're going to find a dragon."

"Wow, just the two of you? I hope you're very careful." Levan cautioned, in slight disbelief. No one had seen a real dragon in recent generations. "Shouldn't you be brushing up on your spells before you go?"

"I would be, but I haven't been able to find my spellbook since my graduation party yesterday. I think someone took it from my home as a cruel joke. You know it would take years to make a new one, I'd basically have to restart magic school from day one." Her brow furrowed slightly in anxiety. Levan grasped for the words of the solution that would comfort her, whatever the cost. Then she looked up at him again, her eyes brightening. "*You* know....hey—you have a spellbook. Can I read it for a while until Cray gets here?"

"Sure, of course." Levan happily opened his pack and removed his spellbook, his most valued possession representing six years of diligent study of magic, and tossed it on the table in front of the red-haired girl.

Her face lit up. "Oh, thank you so much!" Levan felt a rush of warmth as she smiled at him, imagining her eyes were telling him more, that they were choosing him.

Sabrena opened the book, flipping through years at a time. They had all taken mostly the same classes for the first four years. She slowed down when she came to the sixth year, and looked slightly puzzled as she skimmed through, flipping back and forth. His bookmark was at Planar Portals.

"What's this? You're studying Summoning Gates? Where is the water magic?" Sabrena inquired, flipping through more pages, until she got to the end of year six, and the conclusion of formal schooling. "This looks like mostly fire magic. Your book is much different than mine."

Levan took the opportunity to sit down next to her. He turned the pages back to year five, where the elemental magics were.

"We had a water magic course, if you remember, we were in the same class." Levan said, as Sabrena stared at the book vacantly.

"This is kid stuff. I don't need to study making a little spray of water." Sabrena sighed. "What I need is my healing rain spell. There's not even one healing spell in here."

"Isn't it a combination of healing and water spells? Couldn't you reconstruct the formula?" Levan suggested, though it seemed a long-shot.

"Hmm...let's see...I think I remember the Healing Hands spell well enough to write down....but I'd need to combine it with the water magic..."

Levan produced a quill and ink, saying "You can use the blank pages in my book to formulate it."

"So then," Sabrena began writing and dictating,

"for healing hands...the hands are rubbed together in tiny circles, the right hand spinning forward and away, the left hand, backward and inward...there are many incantations that can be used but we used to say 'care of blessed hands, bring forth rejuvenation, Cura u Manos.' Umm...a sprig of mint or...aloe improves the spell. Now I must study the water fountain spell, copy it here, and intertwine the two down at the bottom...then practice and refine it—this could take some time."

"That's fine. I don't mind." Levan said, thinking he could be happy spending the rest of his life helping her. He turned to the water magic page and began reading it to her as she wrote on the other side of the paper wall between their hands. "The fingers are wiggled in a waving motion—"

She stopped writing. Sabrena had turned her head as a tall warrior entered the tavern.

"Cray!" She called out to him, waving her arm. "Cray!"

The hulking brute with an almost comically-oversized sword on his back turned and moved toward them across the room.

"It seems our journey is about to begin. Can I bring this back to you tonight when I return?" Sabrena looked imploringly at Levan, hastily pleading to borrow the spellbook for the day.

"Yeah, I suppose you can use it for the day. I could come along with you if you want..." Levan's voice trailed off. She wasn't looking at him.

Cray walked up to the table. He was wearing a suit of banded mail, an embossed breastplate and pauldrons of nicked, battle-scarred steel, connected by bands of leather and chainmail. His face was sun-baked, ruddy and scarred like his armor, worn with grooves, though he was not much older than Levan and Sabrena. He was even taller and more muscular than Levan expected, despite being told of his immense stature.

"Hey, you ready?" Cray spoke in a deep, rough

voice.

Sabrena stood up and gathered the book and her staff. "Yes."

Cray looked with disdain at Levan. "Who's this baboon in the bath robe? He botherin' you?"

"Oh, no, he's just a classmate from school." Sabrena said dismissively as they turned and walked away.

Sabrena asked Cray a question and he was answering as they walked out of the tavern, something about where they were going and where he was. Levan could find no words to say as he watched the fiery-maned girl holding his spellbook leave without looking back.

❊ ❊ ❊

The group made their way back to the burial mound, and Avus volunteered to break the lock on the metal door.

His axe sparked off the dwarf-made lock's bar, rendering a deep nick in the blade. Tor told him not to worry about it, they'd get him a new one back in the city. Avus smashed down again on the man-forged iron lock box. The bar separated and the lock fell to the floor. He unlatched the bolt and pulled open the door.

Wesker lit a torch. Inside the burial mound was an oblong oval chamber with an ornate sarcophagus at its center. Spread out all around the coffin were statues, shields and ancient weaponry. At the far wall of the tomb was a coiled scroll, with dusty old purple candles melted into the earthen shelves on either side of it. Avus entered as the others filed in behind him, leaving the door open.

Tor doted over the coffin in wondrous amazement. He read carefully the inscription carved into the stone sarcophagus.

"Here lies Ussar...Veldgar, king of Lorestian...!" A

spot was marred where Tor's last name should have been, so he added it in. The old stories remembered his name, even if this stone did not.

The group pored over the chamber, searching for more clues. "His sword!"

Tor rushed over to a broadsword propped against the wall. The blade crumbled when he picked it up. He examined the old, corroded hilt.

"So it is not the Mountain Maker."

"Look." Wesker showed them the scroll painted with a map with a smudge that could be a sword in the middle. It had water damage at the bottom which obscured some crucial landmarks and legends which would have given it a more comprehensible context, as they could not decipher it.

"Sequester it for our sage Oslan, at any rate, this is most fortunate!" Tor was ecstatic nonetheless. "We have found a clue to my father's line and perhaps the location of the hidden sword. But these markings are worn and archaic, I would like to have this map reviewed by our scholars back in the city. Come, we must return, Saemon and Erevor need healing, and you all look like you could use some rest."

Just then, Ranser saw a shadow move at the end of the tunnel, and a few pebbles tumbled down. "Someone is coming!"

Ranser picked up a rock, Wesker snuffed the torch and they spread out along the walls just inside the door, preparing to ambush the intruders if they were hostile.

A dilapidated figure staggered down the stone tunnel and into the room. It was dark, and Wesker and Ranser nearly attacked with spear and rock before they recognized her.

"Unadel!"

She was hunched over, holding her bleeding knee, her suit was ripped and charred. There was something else unusual about her, but it wasn't obvious until she spoke.

"Glad to see you made it inside. Ah....that giant won't be bothering us anymore." Her voice was muffled by something on her face. "Hey, thanks for your help back there, kid, whoever you are, I thought my goose was cooked."

"You're welcome, ma'am, but you fought incredibly. It's great that you've came back. Oh, my name's Ranser." He held out his hand but it was covered in filth and she could barely stand, so he lowered it again.

"Hah—" She started to laugh, but coughed and groaned in pain. "Just call me Unadel, please. A pleasure to make your acquaintance as well, my smelly little friend. I shall shake your hand when you have a bath, eh?"

Wesker had a laugh at this, and Ranser took a moment to survey himself. His shirt was torn and hanging awkwardly off his shoulder, he was missing a shoe, and all of him was covered in manure. Which wasn't so bad, he had been dirtier and smelled worse before, but never in the presence of a lady.

Unadel faltered, and Tor went to her and helped prop her up. "Unadel...I wish you were not so bold. We can't afford to lose you."

Muted and pained she replied, "To restore this land to its rightful harmony, my life would be a small price to pay."

Tor put his hand to her face. "What is this?" Normally, her hat was low and concealed the upper part of her face, but now it was all dark. She was wearing some sort of black stone mask.

"It is...to commemorate this battle. A souvenir." Something in her voice wavered.

Tor studied her for a moment with concern. Then he turned to the others. "Come! We return to the city with all haste!"

CHAPTER 8
ATROCITY

It was strange being without his spellbook, and waiting. Levan now sat in the inn with the same blank stare Sabrena had. Wizards should keep to their duties through the day, and read when they are idle, or risk losing their mastery of the magic arts. He decided to go back to the library.

He was going to write a note to leave for Ranser and Avus, telling them where he had gone, and he looked through his entire pack before remembering he had given his pen and ink to Sabrena, and writing materials were even scarcer than writers in this city. He instead relied on the innkeeper to pass the word along, which probably would work out better. The old man agreed to tell them if he saw them.

Levan walked out of the tavern into the afternoon sun and down a few steps into the street. A hooded pauper girl a few years younger than Levan greeted him. She held a basket of white flowers, and one in her thin, pale hand.

"Good day, would you like to buy a flower? It's just one copper piece." Her voice and demeanor were very meek. She did not look up at him.

"Oh, those are fine lilies—it's too bad I didn't meet you earlier—yes I'll take one, but I haven't any copper. Will this do?" Levan dropped a tiny gold nugget into the girl's hand.

She handed him the flower and looked up at him timidly. "Do you...want them all?"

The peasant girl was very unusual-looking. Pale white, with vaguely elvish features, Levan thought, but her hair and eyes were a deep shade of purple, and the flesh around them and her lips were dark blue. He had never seen the like of this girl, (there were many races he hadn't, but soon would see) and to a layperson or an incompetent physician, she might appear diseased or hypothermic. She was perhaps malnourished, but otherwise in a healthy norm.

"No, thank you very much, this will do." Levan held the lily to his nose. The sweet aroma was cleansing and calming, yet invigorating.

"I'd like you to have three of them. Mother says they make the loveliest perfume in bunches of threes." She handed him two more flowers. "Thank you very graciously, kind sir." The blue-haired girl gave him a weak smile and hurried onward down the street toward the south end of the city.

Levan smiled to himself as he continued up the road toward the library. He felt glad to have to opportunity to accrue some positive potential energy.

That nugget will feed her and her mother for a week. It seems it is easiest to help those at the bottom and thereby make us all wealthier and happier as a whole. Instead of paying taxes to a lord to keep the town safe, I would give the orphans of his land, young and old, the bread they need, that they will not have to become the thieves and cutpurses that make people afraid of one another. That girl had a spark of magical talent. These perfect flowers attest to her green thumb. She could become a wizard someday, like me, if she did not have to walk around this city all day trying to sell a few flowers to buy some food.

The young wizard entered the library. The sun cast long parallelograms of light across the stone floors from the skylights above. He meandered among the bookshelves in shadowy corners of the first floor. A tome about dragons caught his eye and he flipped through it.

The contemporary author noted that a dragon hadn't been seen in the continent of Lorestian in a very long time, thus, much of the information was over 100 years old. They came in all different colors and types, from the soaring, fire-breathing red dragons of the mountaintops to the icy-breathed whites of the far north, and the vile black and greens of the swamps and lowlands, whose breath was a lethal, toxic poison cloud. The metallics, gold, silver, copper, bronze and the like, were said to be enlightened dragons, very powerful, and friends to those who do good.

There listed also the lesser dragons, from the alligator to the tyrannosaur. He hoped Sabrena was hunting one of the smaller ones. One can still claim to have killed a dragon, if he bears an alligator pelt, he thought. He flipped through more pages and began reading the section on sea dragons, when a hand clasped his shoulder.

"Back already?" It was Oslan, his old teacher. "You did a fine job this morning."

"Thank you. I trust the Kinari record was adequate for your needs?" Levan replied, closing the book and fixing Oslan's stare, no longer as a student, but as a fellow wizard; almost as if he were challenging the old sage to continue to treat him as a child. Instead, Oslan's words were surprisingly deferential and grateful.

"It was, the whole kingdom should thank you, and it shall, in time. To learn the language of a foreign nation, as we are doing now, or perhaps re-learning it, is to gain the ability to trade with them. They shall send what we lack, and we shall send what they lack, and both will be enriched ever so much more."

"What were they trading?"

"The record has shown us they traded not only in tin and silver, ores which have run dry in Lorestian, but their land is also abundant with reeds from which they make the fantastic papyrus on which it was written. To them, through Merton, we sent our meats and stock, the pig, sheep and goat, for which they apparently would pay exorbitant amounts. We are currently arranging a shipment of livestock to trade.

Thanks to you, we have already learned the basic words for parley. No doubt it favors peace, and the profits will exceed our wildest dreams, and you will have a part of it. For now, the mage's guild would like to show our gratitude with this small stipend."

Oslan pulled a large bag of coins from his cloak. Levan took the sack and was surprised by its weight.

"This should be enough to get you something nice." Oslan wrinkled white face smiled amicably at him. "Perhaps you could get your lady friend something more than just a bouquet of flowers."

Levan looked down at the flowers he had set on the table behind him. He looked back at Oslan without a word but with a smile.

Oslan arched his eyebrows knowingly. "It is miss Sabrena Fahfren you favor, is it not?"

"Ah," Levan fidgeted, slightly embarrassed, "she is favorable, but I should keep to my studies."

Oslan shook his head. "Poor boy...I could tell you to save yourself the trouble, but I remember what it was to be young and in love, chasing after fiery-haired maidens. Though I never aspired to wed a princess..."

"So then," Levan was eager to change the subject. He did not want to reveal that he had loaned out his spellbook. "is there any way I can be of further aid to the cause?"

"In fact, there is a small favor I would ask. We need to get these preliminary translations to the cattle master Havien, he will be our primary tradesman on the sea journey so it is imperative he know how to communicate with them. He is meeting with the farmers at the trade post near the south gate, he should be there to receive our letters. Can you do this for us?"

"Yes, I will deliver the papers to Havien at the trade post." Levan agreed. He needed something to do anyway.

"Excellent, thank you again, Levan. You are truly on the path of a great wizard." Oslan dropped an envelope on the table and wandered away.

Levan replaced the dragon lore book, took the note and the flowers and exited the library.

Happily down the sloped paths he went, greeting a few peasants along the road. This would seem to be one of the easier, less-dangerous sorts of missions that would bring the kingdom to peace, he thought to himself. At the end of the southward road, the path split, to the right were the deep, dark mines, and the on his left was the trading post.

The trading post was a bewildering labyrinth of widely varied goods piled haphazardly throughout a fenced-in yard and spacious shack. The baying and bleating sounds of animals all around garbled the air, along with their musty scent.

A man with a quill and paper was speaking to a shepherd, writing a figure down, and showing him to an appropriate pen. More herders were bringing in a few goats and sheep in at a time in a line behind him. Between customers, Levan was able to have a word with the cattle master.

"Greetings!" Levan had to shout above the blaring goats next to him. "Are you Havien?"

"Am." The gaunt, tanned man affirmed while filling a bucket with grain feed.

"I have this letter for you from Oslan!" Levan handed him the envelope.

"Good, am glad it got 'ere so fast. You're Levan right?" Havien asked, and Levan nodded. "Well, heard about what you got done this morning with the Tome of Records. Course, it's all thanks to you, this—" The white-robed man at the front of the growing line tugged on Havien's sleeve and he brushed him off. "just wait a second will ya! So's thanks to you they said to sail to Kinari-Land or whatever it's called. This is best gig what's come along in....ever. Figure some of the spillin' o'er of my cup should fall to yours, us bein' under budget an' all."

Havien walked away to his little enclosed office

at the side of the shack.

"Hello! We're still waiting here!" The impatient shepherd raised his arms in frustration, but was ignored.

Havien returned with a sack of coin and handed it to Levan. Somewhere between 100 and 150 gold pieces. He put it in his other coin bag on his belt, which was getting rather weighed down now.

"All right, got to get the rest of these critters marked up for the boat," Havien sighed wearily. His passion was obviously elsewhere. "You take care now, and tell Oslan he picked the right men for the job, us two."

"Right. I will. Thank you, Havien, and farewell."

Levan left with a wave and back out into the muddy road darkened in the shadow of the tall causeway above him. The line of sheep, pig and goat herders was lengthening outside the trade post. He saw them continuing to file in, and wondered why for some reason they all had only four animals at most. Some only had one. And many of them were wearing the same white robes.

It must be common garb for those that spend all day in the fields.

They all had the same dark skin and eyes, the look of the nomads, said to be from the far south, who owed no allegiance but to the universal currency: gold.

Perhaps they are all one clan of herders, coming to sell their stock at the same time for this request.

Levan's eyes followed the incoming line from the south gate. They seemed to just keep arriving. He was about to step back up the hillside and cross under the causeway to return to the tavern when a stray white dot moved in from out of the line of others at the edge of his vision. He watched as a herder with a single sheep emerged from a recessed pathway down the road from which a meager stream of liquid trickled out.

Maybe it is some sort of shortcut.

He decided to walk across that muddy way to

have a look down the tunnel, instead of crossing the underpass on the next level up, which was more solid. A few feet in, the pathway cut into the stone was sealed off by a metal grate. The tunnel beyond it was a circular brick tube, just tall enough to walk in upright. This seemed to be a storm drain, and perhaps a sewer for the wealthy at the high end of the city. The smell was most unpleasant. The metal gate was slightly open still, and he approached it. The bricks lining the drain pipe were stained with droplets of blood.

Probably from the animals, perhaps they brushed the metal and scraped themselves.

Levan thought he saw a light from the end of the tunnel, shining on the sloping, turning path from above. He thought he would go in and take a quick peek around that corner, and see what was there. If it was a shortcut outside the city, it could be a potential invasion point for the Kinari. The dark, rank-smelling drain tunnel made a stark contrast with the bright white, deliciously fragrant flowers in his hand.

This is no place for flowers, nor for sheep.

Levan propped the bouquet up in the shadow on the brick wall out of the water before crossing the rusted metal threshold. He would return for them in a moment. He entered the tunnel, walking along the side of the circular wall, trying to keep from stepping in the putrid water flowing down the center. There was light coming from in there, and some sounds too.

When he turned the corner, a flickering torch-light came into view from a chamber down the hall and a low deep chanting could be heard. Through the opening in the wall, he could see hooked chains hanging from the ceiling, and a hooded figure in a black robe standing before an altar with a goat spread out on it. Levan moved to the edge of the doorway to watch, and he saw another altar, there with a blood-chilling visage was an amalgamation of a man, its pale skin lined with seams where its various parts had been sewn together.

Then he saw three other bodies chained up on the

wall behind, with various limbs severed and facial features removed. Two of them hung limply from the hooks in their backs, the one in the middle was twitching its head. Levan watched in horror as the necromancer pulled the frayed, umber cord from a human spine hanging from one of the hooks and brought it to the altar, cut the goat's back open with a long, wavy knife, and grafted it there. The dark wizard then went to the twitching prisoner and plucked out his one remaining eye. The body convulsed violently and foam dripped from its mouth, then it was still like the others. The necromancer placed the freshly cut, living eyeball into the goat's gaping wound, then took up a pitcher of foul black liquid and poured some of it into the goat's body.

What is he doing to our animals? He means to poison the Kinari with them? The eye and the spinal cord, perhaps he is making them into scryers, spies. This would not be the plot of a single evil person. Something tells me it's politically motivated...one of King Fahfren's men? Doesn't matter, it has to stop.

He was just about to step in and command the necromancer to cease and desist when he realized he couldn't think of a spell to cast should he need to defend himself. His mind was full of garbles, blueberry ice cream and crimson waterfalls flowing around a porcelain face. He had rested somewhat, but he needed to study his spells after using them so much in a day, for his mind was frazzled. It was the path of madness for some wizards who did not practice restraint, like foregoing sleep and using magic beyond their limits. Levan decided to quietly exit and return with backup.

As he stepped away as silently as he could, the necromancer had sealed the incision and pulled the goat off the altar. Levan had not seen the other man in the room, one of the white-robed nomads, all but his dark eyes covered, until he stepped out into the tunnel with the goat on a leash.

"Ah! Intruder!" The man yelled and pointed as he ran off toward the exit, the goat keeping pace with him.

Inside the chamber, Levan could hear the necromancer's sinister chanting. He moved to block the entrance and saw the black-robed figure turned toward the sewn-together corpse.

"...your master beckons you, rise and feast on the flesh of the living!" The necromancer finished his spell and shot a quick glance back at Levan who stood in the doorway. His face was covered by an expressionless mask fashioned of ceramic.

"Stop!" Levan shouted, pulling the flame from the two torches at the sides of the room into a wall of fire in front of him, covering the doorway. "You will face justi—"

BAM! He could not finish his ultimatum as he was knocked down into the sewage.

The monstrous white zombie had stood up in the chamber, then bent over and strode through the wall of flames, its long, clawed arms nearly reaching to the ground, and the dark wizard running just behind it. The creature was set ablaze. Flames erupted and spilled across the ceiling from the seams that held it together and the decaying patches of skin which melted off it.

The necromancer seemed mostly unscathed, and he continued running toward the tunnel exit.

Levan directed a whirlwind spell in front of him but was interrupted again. With unholy speed and strength, the sickly, pale and burning arms snatched him up, pulling him toward the giant zombie's mouthful of implanted shark teeth. He went in head-first and the loathsome, unnatural maw of this twisted abomination opened up wide enough to swallow him whole, though it seemed it would first shred him into many small pieces with its saw-mill of long, serrated fangs.

There was no time to cast a spell, and his arms were immobilized anyway. He had less than a second before being ripped apart.

This is bad.

The monster had knocked one of the torches off

the wall upon its exit. It rolled out into the cylindrical tunnel, slowly creeping into the water at the bottom and it (like Levan) was about to be extinguished. At the last possible moment he drew the final wisp of flame up from the torch and puffed it into a rapidly expanding explosion around him. Just as the vicious shark teeth bit into him, the thunderous pressure wave blasted away the zombie's arms and lower jaw, and he fell to the ground.

The zombie still stood over him, its arms completely severed, jaws ripped apart, the flesh and tubes of its throat lay bare and its long pointed tongue hung down into the filthy sewage stream. Levan crawled backwards as the monster brought its head down to chop him with its mostly intact upper jaw, and stepped forward to crush him underfoot.

The wizard got to his feet, whipping up the water to creating a ball that surrounded the creature's head. The undead do not breathe, thus the water would not drown it, but the murky bubble of liquid obscured its vision almost completely. It could still follow the light in front of which Levan stood, and it charged toward him. A cool breeze blew in the tunnel, and Levan captured it, spinning it into a concentrated vortex and pushing it down the corridor. The zombie went hurtling down the spillway, its back twisted and inverted as it slammed into the wall.

Levan returned to the necromancer's chamber, and, finding no one alive, grabbed the other torch off the wall in order to incinerate the zombie quickly.

He had only looked away for a few seconds, but when he returned to the hall, the giant zombie was not crumpled up at the end where it had been. The torch and his vision darted around warily. He felt himself growing weak, the cuts on his torso stung and bled.

He took a step toward the exit and the huge white figure appeared behind him, its mangled, armless body running out from the darkness with a horrifying roar. Levan focused the torchlight into four searing jets of fire, one spouting from each of the fingers of his outstretched left hand. As he waved the flames across its body, the zombie was reduced to a smoldering cinder, rolling to the ground and crumbling into blackened, smoking embers.

Smoke filled the tunnel and the smell of burned, rotten flesh was overpowering, almost unbearable. Levan ran down the sloped pathway to the exit of the sewer. Before exiting the metal gate he saw a loose brick in the ceiling.

He stopped and began clapping his hands together, saying "Stone shudders before me, **Nea Tremora.**"

With a momentary vibration, the loose stone in the ceiling fell through, followed by a cave-in of bricks and rocks, making the tunnel impassable, but still allowing the water to flow through. This abominable sewer was sealed that it may not be used again for such nefarious deeds.

Exiting the metal grate, Levan expected to find his bunch of lilies sitting there in the shadow where he had left them, but they were gone.

What's this? A necromancer who appreciates flowers?

The wounds in his side festered and burned.

I need to get somewhere and treat these cuts. I still have some healing salve left. I'll go meet with the others at the tavern and do it there. But first, I must warn Havien that some of the livestock are tainted.

Levan hurried back to the trade post, clutching the weeping cuts across his trunk, which were deepest and most painful at his left hip. He rushed in and Havien came over to him.

"Ma boy, what's happened to you?" Havien held his shoulder and inspected the wounds.

"I was attacked..." Levan wheezed, short of breath. "...in the sewer...a necromancer was...doing something to the cattle...he sent them here. The ones with the line on their back...these ones have been tampered."

He showed Havien the faint surgery scars on the

backs of every one in five goats and sheep (for some reason none of the pigs were affected).

"Yes, yes, alright then," Havien dismissed him with concern for his health, "you need to go get yourself fixed up right away. Ol' Havien can see which of the flock's ailin' or been cut on, and won't let none of them on the boat. You done good, boy. Go on now."

Levan was grimacing in pain when he walked out of the trade post again, and up the road.

That thing was a nightmare. It must have taken many months and many bodies to make it. It almost had me as a snack. If that torch hadn't been there, I would have died today...and the necromancer got away. Why didn't I have my spells ready? Oh, yeah...no spellbook...

Levan sighed. He hoped the book he loaned Sabrena was helping her, and that she appreciated it, though she probably would never have known if he had died down there in that sewer.

* * *

Supreme Commander Eltas ForgedArm reached the top of the lightly-wooded ridge above a bend in the river which spread out into a traversable swath of shallows. The water trickling across the rock face echoed with a hollow hum as it flowed over the submerged cave entrance.

A charge in the air, a subtle tremor in the ground, or perhaps just his instincts told the grizzled old veteran that the enemy was near, and the battle was about to begin.

The commander halted the phalanx behind him on the high ground as a row of tall tents came into view, their tops crested with long, fluttering pennants.

From beyond the far hill, a long-armed catapult launched a hefty urn in a high arc into the sky. The smoldering tinder in the upper portion met the sticky, volatile tar below as the vessel shattered and exploded upon landing in the midst of a tightly-packed formation of spearmen. Knife-like shards of ceramic blasted out with lethal force in all directions, catching several soldiers beneath their helmets and swiftly ending their campaigns. The black tar bubbled and spat flame through the ranks and across the ground, causing screams of pain and chaotic disarray.

General Eltas called for archers to the top of the hill as a white warhorse strode up beside him, a mane of crimson flowing from beneath its rider's helm.

"Sir, we are out of range, we must close the gap." The mounted officer Belina had also been caught off-guard by the attack, but was primed to retaliate. "Our cavalry are ready to charge."

"It was a lucky shot. They will have to move up —" The general went silent as he watched the second fire urn fly up and then fall directly in the center of another group of foot soldiers with the same demoralizing effect. "Gah...prepare to advance! Horsemen to the eastern flank! Swords to the front! Hold your shields high!"

The general's war cry was followed by the sounding of horns as he charged down the rise and the infantry fell in behind him. The cavalry contingent rushed past them on the right, splashing through the river and climbing the hill on the other side. They charged toward the eastern ridge, the high point on the enemy's side of the river, where it was presumed their ranged units would be gathered.

Having seen no enemy scouts, Eltas was correct in assuming there was no cavalry charge or arrow barrage coming from the Kinari to hold the river crossing, and that there were either pikemen or siege weapons at their front, which the heavy swordsmen would do best at destroying. But he was wrong in assuming the enemy was unprepared, and he could not have known what he and his troops were about to encounter as they approached the towering white pavilions which seemed to be growing taller and creeping toward them.

Belina rode at the head of the mounted knights as they pushed their warhorses to full speed, altering her course slightly as she caught sight of the enormous catapult behind the tent row. Strangely, there were still no enemy troops to be seen.

The sound of clanking metallic gears was heard just before a large, iron-spiked orb rolled out of each of the tents. As Belina rode past, she glanced back to see some of the horses collide with the spiked balls and tumble down. Then, when the projectiles stopped rolling, a mechanism inside released its springs, propelling the spikes out in all directions. The thorny spheres were sprung into the air and fired another harrying burst of iron bolts, ripping into nearly every inch of unarmored flesh in a wide area.

A rider who was fond of horses saw another knight nearby hurtle from his stricken steed and tumble head-first down the rocky embankment. He was conceptualizing a type of horse armor that would protect them both when he was also thrown forward as his mount stopped short, and he was trampled beneath the iron-clad hooves of those that were behind him.

Eltas was aghast to see his cavalry charge effectively nullified in a single brief counterattack, as the strange spiked weapons maimed or killed nearly every horse on the field. But they did not pierce armor at any significant range.

The infantry fared better, losing only a handful of the front-liners to the spike-balls as they made their approach in testudo, shields upheld.

The general and another veteran swordsman were the first to reach the tall tents. They first plunged their swords into it, then took hold of the corners and pulled the canvas away. Inside, a wood and iron matrix on wheels contained a stack of springs and gears operating the various contraptions which began to spin and shake violently.

Belina reached the giant catapult alone and severed its throwing arm with a heavy stroke of her blade, causing the self-loading mechanism to drop the ammunition and enflame the catapult.

The nearest ally was now General Eltas who had just revealed some peculiar siege weapon within the tent. As Belina rode toward them, the machine jerked and flashed out a set of long, curved, spinning blades from its underside. She and the others that saw it gaped in horror as their leader was caught by the sickle-like blades and pulled in to the thick wooden crossbar, then dragged beneath the undercarriage and shredded to pieces by the merciless machine.

A mournful and enraged cry rose up from the soldiers as they charged forward at with vengeful fury.

Then all of the tents lurched and rolled back, their veils fluttering as they buzzed with a roaring mechanical furor. Just as the first wave of Lorestian soldiers reached the Kinari siege weapons they were cut down by a whirling chain connecting two heavy iron spheres which flew out of the bottoms of the tents with blinding speed. Columns of armored men were bashed and hurled like pebbles across the river bank as the spinning cannonballs tore through their ranks.

Belina could see from the uncovered tent the next shot drop down to a metal peg on the siege machine's platform where it began revolving rapidly, and was drawn back to be fired again.

More brave soldiers fell as they swarmed on the bloodied machine that had consumed the general, finally disabling it by jamming the gears with their swords. It was a small, short-lived victory, as the structure and men were smashed into oblivion by the next shot.

A rider named Gerod rode up near Belina, tugging at the reins as his spooked horse fidgeted. "The general is dead! Our units are nearly all out of the fight! We should move the men back and target our archers to enflame these things!"

It seemed a reasonable idea. The siege weapons were stacked to the height of three men with ammunition and would keep firing. The ground charge was disastrously ineffective.

But the soldiers had broken ranks and were scrambling all over, the heralds and standard bearers all dead. In the blood and confusion, Belina may have been the only one on that side of the river to notice a glimpse of the ebony-armored Kinari soldiers as they snuck in behind their army to trample down the vulnerable archer corps. An archer's body tumbled down the ravine as dark shadows of enemy troops arose from the horizon around them.

"It's no use!" Belina called out, "Full retreat! Bring what's left of the general back with us!"

As the remains of the Lorestian army withdrew, the Kinari soldiers poured down into the valley from all sides. Belina broke her lance on one of them, and cut down another with her sword as she fought her way down to the river.

Nearby, Gerod was pulled down from his mount by a hooked pole-axe and consumed by the mob of beetle-like invaders. Belina rode to his horse, fighting off a few more attackers, and took from its saddle the plated arm of general Eltas, which still held his sword, and was lashed to his shield.

The Kinari cheered in victory as the lone survivor Belina rode away through the winding ravine. Part of her wanted to go back and fight to the end with her fallen comrades there. But to leave this threat unchecked would doom the rest of the army, and their kingdom. They must be warned. For the sake of the greater war at hand, she fled, but vowed that retribution would come another day.

CHAPTER 9
EXPELLED,
INVITED IN

Levan made his way back to the tavern and collapsed into a chair. There were only a few people spread out around the room. His pain was beyond modesty anyway, and he pulled up his robe to reveal the gruesome tears in his flesh, which were seeping blood and a clear liquid. With a groan he retrieved the healing salve from his pack and poured some on his hand. Then, the innkeeper came over to his table.

"What will you have?" The bartender asked, peering around the table nosily, trying to see what Levan was doing.

"Nothing, please just leave me be." Levan said through clenched teeth.

"Sir, you need to buy something, you can't come in here and just hang around, doing whatever--what *are* you doing over there?" The nosy old innkeeper moved around the table to see his other side, and Levan covered his injuries back up.

"Fine! Just give me a plate of meat and a cup of brandy!" Levan slammed three coins down on the table, an ample tip to not be disturbed. The innkeeper grabbed the coins hurried off to get his order.

The salve stung as he applied it. The bleeding stopped, though the scabbed wounds were still discolored and tender, and it was painful to sit there, but he needed to get his spellbook back. He hoped Sabrena would return soon.

The innkeeper brought his meat and brandy. The plate was covered with three slabs of meat: pork, mutton and goat. Normally he'd eat any or all of them. Today he only took a few bites of the pork. He hated the taste of liquor and had never ordered it, but an old medical sage had told him once that it was a good thing for you when you've lost a tankard of blood or more, or were healing from surgery. He tried a sip, and his face soured in distaste and he drank no more.

A minstrel began humming and strumming a many-stringed instrument akin to a small handheld harp.

The door swung open at the tavern and in walked the young sailor boy Ranser, beaming with excitement, his hand on the hilt of a shiny new cutlass like real mariners used, and a few new daggers on his belt.

Behind him was the stout, muscular dwarf Avus, with his long oaken beard and mass of hair that flowed into it. He looked also to be in high spirits, and was likewise carrying a polished new axe with a wide blade that reflected like a silver mirror.

There also entered a tall, white-haired female elf who seemed to be in a fairly significant state of disrepair, but walked on her own. Levan had seen her face the night before, and now noticed her peculiar black mask as she moved to the innkeeper, ordered a room and retired immediately to it.

Ranser and Avus found Levan sitting near the back corner of the room.

"Hey! So you made it!" Ranser strode over to Levan. "Oh—your hat and staff—you didn't pass your test?"

"Oh, I passed it," Levan replied wearily, "I just won't get those things until later. They are merely a formality anyway...how was the burial mound? I assume there were no real giants today?"

"You assume wrongly, my friend!" Avus chuckled heartily. "A falsehood twofold, for it were a pair, two of the mighty things, would you believe it?"

"I accidentally woke up a fire giant," Ranser explained, "our friend Unadel killed it. She's really an awesome fighter. But she got hurt today, and I was wonderin' if you had any more of that healin' goo you used on us..."

"Yeah, it's right there." Levan pointed to the jar next to his plate and cup.

"What's in the cup?" Avus inquired innocently. "Not thirsty?"

"No, I was waiting for you to arrive to treat you to it." Levan pushed him the cup.

"Thanks I could use a drink!" Avus swallowed the brandy in one gulp, slammed the tankard down and burped. "Another drink!"

"Oh yeah, I made a few coin today. I'll pay." Levan poured out his coin sack on the table. The mass of around 300 gold coins spilled out everywhere in a glittering pile of treasure.

"A few coin eh!? Sheesh, put that away, people are looking." Avus helped him slide the coins back into the bag as eyes studied and murmurs spoke of them from all over the room.

"You guys seemed to have gotten some new gear." Levan noted their new weapons, and Ranser's new black and blue tunic with a chain shirt underneath which showed at the edges of his sleeves and collar. Ranser was walking away to Unadel's room with the jar of healing salve.

"Yes, his majesty was most gracious on our return with an artifact which may lead us to the Mountain Maker." Avus told Levan.

"That is good to know." Levan said. "We are making progress on learning the Kinari language and...I encountered the necromancer Tor spoke of last night. I fought with one of his creations, a horrible monstrosity made of corpses, and he escaped in the fray. I was bitten by it..." He revealed his shredded and bloody robe. "But I've treated myself and it should be a distant memory by tomorrow morning. I cannot rest just yet, though. Tonight I must wait up to meet a friend here and get my book back."

"Well," Avus stretched and yawned, "sounds good. I will be heading upstairs with a bottle of wine to sing me a lullaby. It has been a long day."

"It has indeed. See you tomorrow, my friend." Levan wished him goodnight.

Avus acquired his bottle of dark wine and retired to his room.

Ranser climbed the stairs and walked down the second floor hall. From the third of the five rooms on each side, he heard a woman sobbing. The door was not fully latched, and the hinges must have been recently oiled, for they did not squeak at all as he pushed it open and looked inside.

There was Unadel, sitting on a chair facing away toward the window. The black stone mask lay on the desk beside her. In her hand she held a small mirror.

Ranser stepped inside and approached her, saying, "Una—oh my—" His words cut short as he caught a glimpse of Unadel's right eye. Her eyeball was torn open in a fleshy mess, and discolored yellowish-black with dots of stone burned into her cheek like fiery teardrops.

She dropped the mirror and it shattered on the floor. *"Go away!"* Her snarling yell startled Ranser and he nearly dropped the jar of healing salve. The left side of her face glared back at him, unblemished and beautiful even in its anger.

"I-I-brought this healing salve for your—" Ranser began, but was shouted out.

"GET OUT!" Unadel screamed, picking up the flower pot on the desk and hurling it backwards over her shoulder at him.

Ranser narrowly ducked the flying pottery as it smashed on the wall behind him, set the healing salve jar down next to the door, and slipped out before any other projectiles came flying at him.

Ranser walked back down the stairs, wracked with sorrow and weighed down with dismay, as if this awful trauma had happened to him.

That could have happened to any of us, or worse. She saved us all. If only I could have done something more.

As he walked through the tavern toward the back room where they had hot baths for those who were permitted entry, a group of four adventurers stepped in from the front door. His path nearly crossed that of a tall, barrel-chested brute with an equally-massive two-handed sword on his back and an unusual hairstyle.

The giant of a man traveled ahead of three companions, a heavily armored pikeman in plate mail with a tattered banner hanging from his battle-scarred halberd, an archer whose bow was covered in cobwebs, the earthen leather mesh of his tunic mimicking a forest floor, and finally, a short, slender figure in a white and green hood and riding cloak. Ranser navigated around behind them, and over to Levan, who looked like he was about to get up.

"Hey, there's free baths in the back room if you want to take one after me, not that you'd need anything for free, Mister Moneybags! Haha!" Ranser tapped Levan on the arm. He looked distracted, trying to see past him.

"It's not really that much money, Ranser." Levan was craning his neck to see over Ranser's shoulder. He was almost certain the person in the white skirt that just entered with the other adventurers was Sabrena, though he still couldn't see her face.

"Well, take care, I'll see ya later on or tomorrow." Ranser went off toward the back room.

Ranser took a long, warm bath with soap, and smiled to himself as he recounted the events of the day while he worked his new knife on a piece of cloth. When he finally reemerged, skin cleansed and hair fluffed up, he went back upstairs again.

He returned to Unadel's room, and knocked on

the door. "Unadel?"

"...yes, come in." Her voice came quietly from inside.

Ranser opened the door and stepped inside. Unadel turned in the chair toward him. She had tied the volcanic rock mask back on, hiding her face.

"I'm sorry I threw the pot at you, Ranser. That was unkind of me." She murmured, her words muffled by the mask.

"I should not have walked in like that. I'm not used to knocking on doors. It was not my purpose to see...ah...I mean, if I were not meant to see...I—" Ranser's tongue stumbled over the thought he was trying to convey.

"I am an atrocity to look upon," Unadel wept sorrowfully, "I must hide my face with this mask forevermore. I would rather it be you, who fought the fiery giant alongside me, that see my disfigurement, than even another friend."

"Unadel..." Ranser moved closer to her, pulling a long strip of cloth from his pocket. "you are still so beautiful. Please don't hide your face. When I was a child, I would make a new eyepatch for my father every year for his birthday. I got fairly good at it. I made this one for you. I thought it would suit you better than the mask..." He handed her the eyepatch he'd fashioned from the fabric of his new tunic.

She held up the patch in her hand. "It's black. I like it, heh."

Unadel paused for a moment, then stood up and untied the straps of the mask, slowly lowering it from her face. The eye on her right was a darkened crater. Her anguished, tearful left eye looked at him, then to the mask she held in her hands. She let it drop and break into several pieces among the scatter already on the floor. Then she raised the eyepatch up and slid it down over her right eye.

Ranser was comforted that it fit perfectly, and covered the damage. To him, she now looked even more intriguing than before, with the black eyepatch and the single teardrop-shaped diamond that had melted and fused into the skin on her cheek. He picked up the shattered mirror and showed her, in her fractured reflection, the beauty she still possessed. Unadel's eye welled with tears that spilled over as she hugged him.

"My spirit is lifted, though my body is still broken...that a world of darkness can be made light, my sea of despair washed away by as simple a thing as a strip of cloth. Thank you for showing me this." Unadel gazed into Ranser's sky-blue eyes.

He wanted very much to kiss her then, he hugged her tightly and she whimpered. Ranser released her as she held her collarbone, gasping in pain.

"You are hurt badly, you should use some of this healing salve my friend made." Ranser picked up the jar by the door.

"What's in it?" Unadel inquired skeptically, sitting back in the chair. "Most human medicine is rubbish."

"Well it's made with cream and umm...Halivex...some other kind of root." Ranser didn't remember the extra ingredient.

"Oh, he knows some elven cures then." Unadel sighed in relief. "Lucky that I need not seek out my kin in the forests for this medicine. I'll need to fall asleep before the major repairs kick in, otherwise it will be a bad night."

"Yes, I'd had that problem, being awake during its effects—gosh, was it only yesterday? Seems like ages ago. I think every bone in my body was broken. Levan mixed the stuff up perfectly, he was just a bit off on the timing of its use I guess."

Smooth white shoulders came into Ranser's view as Unadel pulled her coat down her arms and gathered her locks of silvery hair to the side.

"Are you going to help me apply it then?" She asked his reflection in the glass of the dark window. "We're different but much the same, humans and elves, you and I, we have no tail to scratch our backs."

"Haha, right." Ranser rubbed the healing salve down her spine and felt the crushed vertebrae twisted and jutting sideways in the middle of her back. He winced in empathetic pain. He could almost feel it wrenching in his own spine.

She beckoned for the jar and applied the salve to her collarbone and leg. Then Ranser helped her up to the bed. He sat on the chair beside her.

"Unadel?" Ranser had many questions he wanted to ask, but he did not want to bother her now, most of all he wanted her to be comfortable and rest. "Ah, should I leave you to rest?"

"No, stay and talk with me for a while. What is it you wanted to ask?"

"Why do you help the humans?" Was Ranser's simple question to an all-encompassing conundrum for her, which to fully explain would be the very long story of her life.

"You think it not worth it, what I've sacrificed?"

"No, of course I think it is. But you seem to take all the risks and none of the glory. Men do not appreciate the feats of heroic elves. They are suspicious of your kind, and yet you are the one silently protecting them."

"My kin prefer to stay in the forest. 'We are at peace and in harmony with the land, why should we help the humans in their endless wars?' they say. For me there are as many reasons as stars in the sky...the cries of the tortured lovers of life...it was not enough for me to pity you...our poor, hot-headed, short-lived cousins who wandered from the forest so long ago and forgot how to listen to the world. I fought alongside Tor's father, and then there were still men who remembered the times when you could walk down the road to the community feast, stopping at each house along the way, into a complete stranger's house, elf, dwarf, man, even the lion men were still present, and would welcome you into their home to fill you with desserts and drink."

"That sounds very different from this place."

Ranser remarked. "Everyone is suspicious of each other here."

"It *was* this place, not so long ago, before these stone walls and fortress were here, and all the doors tightly shut and locked. In those times, our doors were open for everyone. And each passer on the way was sure to bring something delightful, food, gifts or stories." Unadel yawned. "This was the custom of the Veldgar kingdom, and the reason there was no fighting or stealing and everyone was made happy. It took a long time to build that kingdom of love and trust, only to be wiped away in a moment by a vile usurper. How soon the people forgot the good king when spies terrorized them at night. How easily they were deceived and lined up to move within these protected walls, and under the iron fist of a tyrant. It is not...the way of nature. These injustices...will not stand...'"

Unadel was drifting off to sleep, having given Ranser much to think about.

Can one man truly hold the fate of his entire world in his hands, to bring misery or joy like some wanton god to every person he would ever meet? Is this man who wears the crown any different from me? I doubt it. How is it he has this power? The army he commands. Why do they listen to him? Is it really all based on a cleverly concealed lie?

"I'm with you, Unadel." Ranser whispered as he stood and walked out of the room, shutting the door quietly behind him.

Levan had been sitting and listening to the warriors boasting their exploits of the day to the cranky old innkeeper who was only interested in getting a good tip, and making sure they all paid for being in his establishment. Apparently, the four of them had killed a fire dragon in the mountains to the east. Levan now recognized Cray, the large, rude man he had encountered that morning. He continued to wait and listen, mostly to observe the interaction between Sabrena and Cray and deduce the nature of their relationship while he still went unnoticed with his back turned and in the shadow of a vertical wooden beam.

The bulky warrior ordered a drink and sat on one of the wooden stools and the legs of it broke underneath him, but he caught himself on the bar before hitting the floor.

A young farmhand sitting at a table nearby looked up at him with a half-smile. He was a soft, peaceful soul that was merely slightly amused, but even a bit concerned the swordsman didn't hurt himself falling. It always seemed to go that way, great warriors felled and crippled by a seemingly minor slip. His eye-contact provoked a violent response from the muscle-bound brute.

Cray kicked the chair out from under the farmboy, and pulled him up by his collar, yelling into his face. "Is something funny to you, little man?" He dropped his frightened victim and spat on him, commanding him to "Get out of my tavern!"

The young farmer hurried out of the inn, leaving his food and drink unfinished. Cray grabbed an empty chair and sat back at the bar, turning to his companions.

"You see that? Nothing but cowards in this town! None of these bumpkins ever even met a dragon slayer!" Cray shouted boastfully, drawing his sword from his back. "And this, the very sword that dealt the deathblow to that wyrm!"

The heavily-armored spearman shook his head. "I don't know, you fought well though, of course."

"Who doesn't believe I fought a dragon!?" Cray yelled, pointing his sword around the room.

"No, we believe you..." An anonymous voice chimed in.

The innkeeper stirred nervously behind the bar. "Sir, please put your weapon away, you're scaring the customers."

The girl in the white riding-cloak sighed, handing him a small, flat, square object.

"My hair!" Cray gasped as he looked into the little mirror and put his hand up to the singed-bald half of his head.

The whole left half of his head was blackened with soot and his hair and eyebrows burned off.

"No one disbelieves you fought a dragon, Cray. But it was the arrow from the bow of Garath that killed it." Sabrena motioned to the hooded archer sitting beside her.

"A lucky shot I guess." Cray conceded, finishing another tankard of spirits.

"It took a lot of stabbing to break the scale open for him to get that shot, though." The spearman added.

Sabrena praised his valor as well. "Your spear struck true, Dane. Maybe the next one will have a decent treasure horde, huh?"

"It is the scaly hide that is the true treasure." Commented Dane.

"And the ridding of that scourge of the local farmers, as well." Garath added. "But let us not forget your part in the battle, young wizard. It was only by the mercy of your healing rain that we were spared when the fire came."

A bard nearby shook his head and laughed to himself while writing. Then he called out "Hooray for the pretty wizard and the dragon-slayers!"

The merry tavern folk cheered and clinked their cups.

"Thank you, good sir," Sabrena saluted him with her cup. "I am very glad we all walked away from that, Cray took quite a beating..." She looked over her right shoulder to see the tall warrior who had wandered across the room. "What is he—*doing*?"

The big brute with the half-charred head had gotten staggeringly drunk in no time and followed a pair of newlyweds to the stairway that went up to the second floor where they were trying to hurry to their room. He had stopped them at the foot of the stair and appeared to be harassing the fair golden-haired bride. Her husband, a young merchant slight of build, but with brave eyes, attempted to stand between them. Cray pushed him away easily, yelling "Get lost!"

"Please sir, do not hurt my wife, we've just been married, we're only stopping by on the way to the sea." His voice quavered.

"Corvin!" The woman screamed, trying to get away. But Cray pulled her closer.

Corvin moved in and tried to pry his huge arms away, shouting "Get off my wife!"

"Didn't I tell you to go away!?" The giant warrior punched the husband, more like a swat to bat him away, but it knocked him to the ground and bloodied his nose.

Levan pushed back his chair and stood to intervene, but as he did, a wave of nauseating pressure seemed to fall on him, his vision went dim and he fought to stay conscious as his lifeless limbs dropped him back in his seat. His face drained of color and the wound in his side seared in shocking pain.

Corvin turned over and began to get back up, reaching for his belt with a grim look on his face. He meant to be true to his vows, to die fighting for her, he just hadn't expected it to be so soon, the day after the marriage. The small man pulled out a short dagger and stood to face his opponent.

"Come on, boy." Cray laughed, pulling his giant broadsword from his back.

"*Cray!!*" Sabrena's voice shrieked across the room, not magically, just extremely loud and high-pitched.

Dane was startled by the sudden outburst and spilled his drink.

The drunken warrior (along with most of the others in the tavern) paused to look up at Sabrena after the ear-piercing scream, and watched her as she moved across the room. "Leave those people *alone!*"

While brandishing his sword, Cray relinquished his hold on the blonde woman. She ran to her husband who grabbed her hand and they hastily moved toward the exit.

"Cray! Go sit down and eat, stop bothering married people! Is nothing sacred to you!?" Sabrena berated him, and a pained, despondent look wiped across his face as he lowered his sword.

"I didn't know they were married, Sabrena." Cray blubbered.

"Imbecile." She muttered a word he didn't understand as she walked away.

"I just wanted to talk to her!" He yelled back toward the bar, where the girl wizard was now reluctantly listening to the innkeeper's explanation of how this kind of activity hurts business and that he should really just leave.

Sabrena placated and cajoled him in return, explaining that this was the only place to rent a room in town.

To which the innkeep returned "You can set up tents at the end of Garden Street, or outside of town..."

"Oh, right," Sabrena quipped sarcastically, "Garden Street? Don't you mean Garbage Street? The place is a damned open sewer."

The spearman, Dane, tried to help. "Look, we killed a dragon today, doesn't that warrant some respect?"

Cray was walking back to the bar, and they watched him warily as he took his seat facing outwards, his elbows on the bar behind him.

"See?" Sabrena indicated the big warrior. "He'll be fine."

"Well," The innkeeper sounded unconvinced, "if you can get him to bed..."

"Hey, it's not like that, buddy." Sabrena shot the old man a withering glare.

The drunken warrior pounded on the bar, yelling "Another tankard of spirits!"

The bartender walked over and timidly said "I'm not sure you should—"

Cray turned around and crashed his fist onto the bar again, cracking it, and bellowing "The spirits! NOW!"

The innkeeper brought up a jug, and Cray grabbed

it from his hand, guzzling it.

"Sir, you'll have to pay for that…"

"Better shut up, old man," Cray said, slamming his sword on the counter, "I just killed a dragon today, an old man ain't much."

The bowman from the end of the bar spoke to the innkeeper who was gaping in exasperation and fear. "Don't worry, he doesn't kill townspeople, he just…"

"Sir, I am going to call the guards if you do not leave."

"Guards! HA!" Cray laughed as his massive fist flew into the old man's face.

Garath finished his sentence just after Cray blackened the innkeeper's eye. "…he just punches them."

Levan watched as the old man went running out the door. He had thought to confront the drunken lout, but, though he didn't like Cray and thought he went too far, he also felt the innkeeper deserved a little payback for being so snooty and snouty to him earlier. And it really wasn't his problem. Now the guards would deal with the oaf. He thought this would be an amusing scene as well, but it went differently than he expected.

Cray handed the jug of spirits to his dark-skinned companion Dane, saying "Watch this. Have some of this." The spearman looked at the jug for a moment, shrugged, then drank some, and passed it along to Garath, who set the jug down on the bar without drinking any. People had started clearing out of the tavern all around.

A moment later, the innkeeper brought back a young guard captain and pointed out the offender. As the guard stepped into the light, it became visible that he was missing his front teeth. His hand touched his bruised jaw and he winced, and backed out of the tavern. The innkeeper could be heard out in the street yelling after him "Where are you going!? You coward!"

Cray was laughing madly as Sabrena shook her head

and told them "We have to leave now."

"Bah, they ain't nothin'!" Cray swung his arm dismissively. "If that was one of their captains, I could take a whole roomful of them myself."

Ranser appeared at the bottom of the stairs and witnessed an incredible scene.

Cray picked up his sword as a hooded man walked up from some corner of the tavern and stood in front of him.

"You shouldn't do that." The mysterious, cloaked figure said.

"What!? Who the hell—!?" Cray's face was flushing with rage as he looked down at this average-sized man, probably thinking he could crush him like a bug.

"Don't get yourself killed here." Came the deep, serene voice from beneath the hood. "You don't want to fight with the guards. Remember, you are no careless killer."

"Try to stop me then!" Cray shouted as he readied his greatsword to cleave the man before him from skull to groin.

The shrouded figure stood unmoving. "I mean to."

As the blade fell toward the man's head, his arms flashed out of the robe sleeves above his head, briefly revealing a bejeweled armlet, as he grasped the blade in the air and turned it away. The tip of the sword smashed into the wooden planks of the floor, and the robed figure gave a quick kick to the crossbar to send the oversized weapon spinning out of Cray's hand. The hooded man caught the great sword somehow, and, still without moving from the same spot, hurled it upwards with great force, sending the weapon crashing up into the roof, where it sunk to the hilt in a thick wooden beam and stuck there. He put his hands together in the same gesture as Levan and Ranser had seen the archer do when he shot the Kinari soldier from across the canyon outside the city, hand over hand.

The enigmatic cloaked figure turned to leave the tavern without another word, as the lot of them stood speechless and stunned, especially Cray. You can't throw a sword like that, he thought, the thing probably weighed more than that man did, he shouldn't have been able to even lift it, much less send it flying skyward like a throwing knife.

Ranser had followed the edge of the room and exited to get some air, and some serenity, since that confounding move the anonymous man executed seemed to put an end to the action, and the words they were having.

Before stepping out into the night, the hooded figure glanced over at Levan. His eyes were stark white but for two pairs of bright, wavy green rings, like jagged circular arcs of emerald electricity where irises normally were. Dark cords of hair sprouted in bunches across his head, and blue tattoos streaked in slashes and swirls across his face. His gaze was powerful and seemingly all-knowing, at once both sublimely benign and frighteningly sinister, seeming to assay Levan's capabilities and demeanor for a moment, but said nothing more and walked out the door.

"Hey—!" Cray looked around at his companions, dumbfounded. "What'd he do that for!?"

Garath stood up. "It's time to go. The guards are coming. The strong ones."

They began to leave and Sabrena grabbed Cray's arm. "Come on, Cray, let's *go*!"

"I have to get my sword!" He protested, looking up to it as she kept dragging him toward the door.

"We'll get you a new one with the dragon copper." She annoyedly promised him.

"But it's only a few hundred pieces." He complained.

"The skin will be worth more, now come *on*!" She went behind him and gave him a stiff push.

Levan stifled a laugh as the giant swordsman was sent reeling across the room by a frail girl. Cray's level of inebriation rendered him barely able to stand anyway, and he stumbled several steps, nearly falling down, but catching himself by his forearm on a vertical wooden beam.

"Augh!" He scowled back at her, rubbing his elbow, and finally relented, heading toward the door.

Levan stood up to follow them. He would try to catch Sabrena before she went outside and have a word with her. As he moved around the tables and chairs to come up behind her, the old innkeeper with the left side of his face turned purple from bruising stopped in front of him, blocking his way momentarily.

The innkeeper addressed the few remaining people in the room. "The tavern is closed until further notice for repairs, everyone must leave."

Avus had been jarred from his sleep by the giant sword crashing through the roof and smashing a hole in the wall near his bed. He stood groggily at the bottom of the stairs. Luckily he never went anywhere without his axe, because the innkeeper went over and herded him out, saying "Go on now, out. Everyone must leave."

Grumbling unhappily, his eyes squinted nearly shut, Avus shambled out of the threshold and toward the exit, meeting up with Levan at the middle of the room.

"Where did Ranser go?" Avus yawned sleepily.

"I don't know, he left. I have to catch up with Sabrena and get my book back." Levan hurried to the door.

Outside, there was a commotion in the street. The small crowd from the tavern was loitering in the road as Cray and Sabrena argued over where they were going.

"...why would anyone want to sleep there!? I don't care if it has music and drink!" Cray was yelling at her.

"You are free to sleep outside down on Garden Street, but you won't survive the night!" Sabrena shouted back, though they were right next to each other.

"Sabrena!" Levan called from the tavern step, but Cray yelled again at the same time and drowned his call out.

"If you hadn't run away from those rich parents of yours, we'd all be sleeping in the mansions up on the top of the hill!"

"Don't you ever talk about my family! You don't know—!" Her screaming fit was interrupted by a torrent of armored soldiers flowing through, filling the streets and surrounding them.

Levan tried to move in closer but was pushed back. "Sabrena!" He could no longer see her, and he didn't know if she could hear him over the stomping of boots and the clanging of mail. He tried desperately to push through the pack of guardsmen, but they violently repulsed him again and again.

"Go away now, or you will be arrested!" The soldiers dispersed the crowd in all directions.

Levan had lost sight of Avus and Sabrena, the only people he could see were the mail-shirted guards as he walked away.

The night's breath overtook the warmth of the ground, rising up to jostle the mists above, setting off a cascade of condensation which drizzled down to darken the cobblestone streets as a wintry chill breeze descended on the city.

Levan reached the first crossroads at the middle of town, where the causeway began. He and Avus saw each other from a block away. When they met back up, Avus asked Levan "Did you get your book back?"

"No," Levan replied, "I need to track down Sabrena, wherever she went."

"Wasn't that guy with the sword saying something about a place with music and drink?" Avus offered.

"Hmm...The Mountain Chalice is the only place I know of like that in the city. We need to let Ranser know where we are too, it is dangerous to be alone here at night. Let's head down this way and see if we can find them." Levan started walking to the west, and turned left to walk down the descending path on the other side of the tavern, where Sabrena and her group seemed to have headed. They looked up and down the next road between the lines of buildings, and saw no one. The streets were empty in all directions.

Levan and Avus wandered in the rain.

* * *

Ranser had gone outside after the noisy altercation, which he thought might have dampened his mood had he stayed in there any longer. The night air was cool and refreshing, and the stars twinkled brightly. He sighed, putting out his arms to lean against the railing, and just as he did a gray blur bolted from the shadows to his side and knocked him over. Rune pinned him down on the ground and licked his face. Ranser tried to admonish the big dog, and tell him not to jump on him like that, but he was laughing and being licked in the face too much. He got up still chuckling.

"All right, boy, I'm happy to see you too. What are you so excited about?"

Rune was running in circles, his tail pointed straight, then stopping, leaning down on his front paws, looking up at Ranser and barking imperatively. He began to scamper off down the road, and then returned and barked again.

"Alright, I'm coming. This better be good, Rune." Ranser reluctantly followed the rambunctious canine down the nearest alley. He had to run to keep up, wherever Rune was going, he was in a hurry.

The dog led him down the muddy roads toward the low end of town as the drizzle turned to a light rain. The road ended at the far southern edge of Karikoss in a sheer drop with cascades of water falling all across it. Rune, with a quick glance back at Ranser, turned right, his ears pricked up, and dashed off toward the tall cave entrance which housed the gold and iron mine at the southwest quadrant of the city.

The waterfall roared on his left, echoing on the chiseled stone walls of the gently sloping entrance shaft. There were two entrances here, and Rune lowered his head to the ground and sniffed. The fresh mud of the shoes of his target played up his nose as he inhaled, and blew out the sides of his nostrils as he exhaled and took a few steps forward, readying his senses for the next swath of trail leavings. The tiny particles of mud continued down the path to the left. They turned a corner and it became dark and quiet. Standing in the last weak bit of reflected moonlight from the outside, Ranser could just barely see Rune in front of him as he paused, listening.

And then he heard it too. "Help!" It was a young boy's sobbing, hopeless voice from deep in the dark. "Help me, someone please!"

Rune took off ahead, navigating by the sound of the boy's cries. Ranser stepped into the darkness to follow.

Suddenly, a something hit Ranser in the face and he let out a startled cry. Big leathery wings flapped across his ears and little claws scratched the top of his head as the bat regained its flight.

Irritated, but unharmed, Ranser called out down the mine shaft. "Hello!"

"Hello? I'm over here!" The tortured voice called back.

Ranser found the wall with his hand and followed its rough surface as the path sloped steeply down.

"I'm coming to get you!"

Rune's bark echoed through the corridor. A large spider, or some other creeping creature, crawled across Ranser's arm and he shook it off. His hand brushed across slimy, gelatinous surfaces which seemed to quiver and retreat when he touched them. Ranser reached blindly for the next hold and he tripped over a rock at his foot, causing his arm to lodge in crack in the wall. He could feel several tiny legs crawling up his wrist, into his sleeve, half-expecting something with big jaws to come along and chomp the arm off, or give him a deadly poison sting. He was at the mercy of the creatures of the dark for a moment. Fortunately they spared him, and with only a few more trips and stumbles, Ranser finally brushed past the furry tail of the dog in the dark and knelt beside him.

Ranser felt along the ground. Just in front of Rune's paws, the floor dropped off into a wide, unfinished vertical shaft. He reached his arm down as far as he could, then his sword, and could touch no floor.

He could hear the boy's voice, as if it were right next to him. "Hello? Are you there? I'm down here. I been down here since daytime. I could almost get back up if someone reached down to grab my hand...and if I jumped...now I can't see nothing."

"Where are you? Come to the wall below me." Ranser said, reaching down.

"I can't see you." The boy said from somewhere below. "I'm at the wall."

"Look—do you know your left from your right? Ranser asked. The child sounded somewhat matured, but he wanted to be sure.

"Yes."

"Go to the far right wall and reach up from there —I mean, my right, your left." Ranser jumbled the command and confused the poor boy.

"I go left, you go right?" The uncertain voice resonated up.

"No, no. Follow this wall all the way to the end on *your left*. I will meet you there and pull you up." Ranser explained.

"Very well."

Ranser moved to the wall on his right where the part of the vertical tunnel open to the shaft he was in ended. However, it did not end for the trapped boy below. Apparently, there was a sideways tunnel dug at the bottom of the vertical shaft for some distance on either side of the opening in which Ranser stood. When the boy called back, he was deeper in the tunnel and would not have been visible, if there were any light. He had made it to the far wall, but when Ranser returned his call, he realized he had gone too far. He returned to where he could hear Ranser clearly.

Rune barked impatiently. "He's right there!"

"Ugh, maybe if I reach my sword down you can feel for it." Ranser suggested half-heartedly, trying to think of something better, but beginning to try it anyway.

"Th-that sounds kind of dangerous." The voice from the dark stammered with uncertainty. "I think I might rather wait for someone with a rope and a torch."

Ranser started to pull his sword back up, when its blade caught an edge of stone and a tiny orange spark fell from it.

"Hey, what was that? I saw some light." The boy's voice called up to him.

"Sparks! When I do it again, come to the sparks!" Ranser tapped his new sword on the stone wall and a small shower of luminescent stone fragments scattered out.

"I see them! I'm here!"

Ranser laid down on the ground and reached his arm down where his sword had been. He could hear the boy leaping in the air. Finally he felt the brush of his hand and on the next jump, caught him in his grip and pulled him up.

"Hold on to Rune's fur. He'll guide us to the exit." Ranser instructed him, and he did.

Rune led them out of the mine and into the rainy night.

As they walked out of the muddy road leading into the mine, they introduced themselves. The boy was called Cent. He was a light-haired youth, about ten years old, a pauper living on the low end of town whose only form of entertainment in the city was playing in the mine. He looked in awe at Ranser's weapons and armor.

"Wow, your sword is so shiny and curvy. Where did you get it?" The boy asked, staring at the blade in wonder.

"Well, I helped Tor Veldgar defeat some giants today, and he bought this for me upon our return." Ranser replied proudly.

"Wow...the real Tor Veldgar? That's amazing! You must be a great warrior!" Cent's face beamed with excitement.

"I suppose you could say that." Ranser enjoyed being fawned over, and looked forward to the thanks he would no doubt receive upon returning this child safely to his home. "Now where do you live?"

"It's just over here, on the other side of the causeway." He pointed down the road to the east and they continued onward.

From one of the side roads, a pair of guards stepped into the junction before them, blocking their way.

"What are you kids doing out at this time of the night? You should be at home in bed." One of the soldiers said in a calm, non-threatening tone.

"I was escorting this young man home, he had a bit of a fall in the mines and got stuck." Ranser explained.

"Yeah, he saved me! This guy is a hero, you should give him a medal." The boy spouted joyously to the guards. "He even killed a giant with Tor Veldgar today!"

"Ah, no that's not true." Ranser tried to cover himself as the guards exchanged glances. "Silly kid, making up stories.."

The two armed men stepped forward and accosted Ranser, grabbing him by his arms, and telling Cent to "Go on home."

They carried Ranser toward the nearby causeway pillar as he flailed and struggled to no avail.

"What did I do!? What did I do wrong!? Let go of me!" Ranser snarled and kicked but could not escape their grasp.

The two soldiers brought him to a heavy wooden door in the tall pylon of the causeway, which led into the only guard station that was not positioned along the outer wall. They dragged him into the musty stone chamber where a tired-looking man at a desk looked up at them.

"What have we got?" The dungeon master inquired apathetically.

"Conspirator. One of Veldgar's spies." The guard spat contemptuously.

"Very well, Brelec will make him sing. Put him in block B, cell 10."

The guards took Ranser's weapons and hauled him down the steps behind the desk and beyond the same type of metal gate he had been excluded entry from this morning.

It was not so bad that he was being taken here, it was his destination when he was free anyway. Perhaps he would get to see Jofon again, after so many years.

CHAPTER 10
UNDERWORLD

The rain poured down heavily, soaking Levan and Avus through.

"Ugh," Levan shivered, his teeth chattering, "it's really cold. We should find a place to stay for the night."

"Alright, but where?" Avus replied normally. He was accustomed and adapted to even colder temperatures.

"I don't know...the little village outside of town is a long walk, and we don't have a tent. Let's stop over here and think for a moment."

Levan and Avus moved under the eave of a building, behind a wall of water falling from the roof.

After a moment, a voice came from the shadows of the nearby alleyway.

"So..." The voice assessed them from the dark. "you search for someone on this cold, dreadful night? Your friends? Your loved ones? A warm, dry bed, a place to belong? Pitiful souls, lost in the downpour, we will help you." The gray-robed figure stepped from seemingly nowhere into the light under the awning next to them, his cloak and hood somehow completely dry.

"You..." Levan warily analyzed the stranger. "...you're the one from the tavern. You can help us? Why do you say 'we'? Are you not alone?"

"I am Non, leader of The Hidden Hand." He spoke without showing his eyes. "We strive to maintain a balance between good and evil, and thus sustain life. All the colors that make our world exist only by the communion of light and dark. The Hidden Hand is at work in every happening in this land. We have seen your deeds on this day, and deemed you both worthy to be shown the path to join our group. The way of true knowledge is open to you, if you can pass our test."

"A test of strength, I hope." Avus commented.

"Can you help us find Ranser and Sabrena?" Levan asked.

"Your friends are within our care. If their fortune is with them, they will be unharmed." Non replied enigmatically. The words sounded menacing to Levan. "You will be reunited with them this night, if you are able to join our guild."

"What must be done?" Levan asked leerily.

"From darkness, one rises to the light. Fallen starlight illuminates the shadows." Non pointed to the glowing chamber atop the castle. "The Chamber of Light. There are kept the spirits of heroes called pyreflies for the king's amusement. One of these must be acquired. It is a small space to fit through, and a difficult climb."

"That leaves me out." Avus grunted his interjection. "No one should be that far off the ground. Unnatural."

"Then you will face the darkness. But only If you have utmost faith that your friend will return with the starlight." Non warned him. "Only he can save you once you are in the Chamber of Darkness."

Levan looked uncertain, but Avus was confident. "The dark is my domain. I'm in." The dwarf accepted whatever was to come, and this helped Levan's determination to be set as well.

"Agreed, then. How am I to get into the palace, though?" Levan questioned the white-eyed man.

"The changing of the guard happens soon. The gate sentry will not stop you if you discretely place your right hand over your left like this." Non showed him the sign of the Hidden Hand, which he'd seen before. "Beyond the great doors, the spiral stair winds skyward. When you reach the peak with the light, follow the setting sun. A red stone will mark our meeting place. Go now, waste no time in bringing the light to the darkness."

Before Levan could ask any more details, Non and Avus had turned the corner were gone.

The wizard headed north toward the massive spires of the royal palace. He had walked by it every day for years and, as most everyone in the city, had never been inside.

Nervously, Levan approached the outer wall. The watchman eyed him intently as he walked up the path. The palace guards wore different armor than the city guards, theirs was lined in gold and etchings and they wore fanciful helmets with narrow, T-shaped open faces, and red-plumed crests. The extravagant attire made the confrontation all the more intimidating.

Levan was aware that his robe was quite dirty and burned, he hadn't had time to get a new one, and hadn't expected to be coming to the castle. His mind was inventing short excuses for his presence, that he was just delivering a message, that he would be very quick, in and out.

The sentry looked utterly malicious standing at the spiked iron gate with his ornate poleaxe and crested head. These were the guards that could have you thrown in the dungeon or executed without blinking an eye.

As Levan got closer he almost turned back and aborted the mission.

What am I doing? They're not just going to let me walk in here. A total stranger asks you to walk into a dragon's mouth, that a hand sign will stop it from closing its jaws on you. I must be stupid. Gullible. This isn't going to work.

The palace guard took a step forward and Levan quickly put up his hands, right over left, accidentally getting it right. The guard stepped back to the gate and opened it for him. He beckoned Levan through without a word, but the same intimidating, irritated look remained on his face.

Of course, he was tired, he had been standing at this gate for half a day. Just as Levan crossed through, the changing of the guard happened, and the gate watchman's relief was walking up along the inner wall.

"You're just gonna let him through?" The newcomer whispered.

"He's on the list. You're up." The gate guard said tiredly, and walked away along the wall, back to the barracks.

Levan hurried through the courtyard. He hoped his haste wasn't suspicious, but he wanted to be as quick as possible, and he thought it may appear as if he were headed somewhere important and shouldn't be disturbed.

Okay, that worked, but Non said the gate guard would let me pass, he didn't say anything about the other soldiers in the palace. Best to try to avoid them.

Levan passed through an open pair of tall iron doors into an opulent entry hall, decked with tapestries hanging from its soaring arched ceilings. Ahead he could see an intersecting hallway and the beginning of a climbing spiral staircase beyond. As he approached the opening at the crossing of the halls, a guard was walking up from the side. He slipped into a recess and pressed against the wall. There was a sentry at the middle of the crossing, and his counterpart for the next shift had just arrived.

"You're relieved, soldier."

"Thank you, soldier."

The sentry who had been standing there all day began to walk away. To Levan's alarm, he came down the hall he was crouched hiding in.

He was certain to be seen.

But the guard opened a door in the wall just before passing by Levan's hiding spot, set something down outside, and went in. Outside the latrine was a small bench on which the guard had placed his helmet and codpiece.

Those helmets. You can't see a thing in them. They don't even know who they are talking to if they are wearing one.

This just might work...

Levan picked up the helmet and placed it on his head. He had never worn armor before. It was surprisingly comfortable and light, though he found the narrowing of his field of view to be somewhat disconcerting. Then he picked up the codpiece, unaware of its function, and used it as a reverse door-stopper, wedging underneath the door to buy himself some more time after the guard was done in there.

He walked into the hallway crossing and was greeted by the newly posted watchman. "Hey, you forget something?"

"Uh, yeah, I've got to go upstairs, and get something that I forgot. You need anything?" Levan slowed, but kept walking as he talked.

"No, I meant your armor! Hah." The palace guard mock-laughed at his absentmindedness.

"It...needs repairs. I'll be back for it." Levan said finally as he reached the spiral stair at the end of the hall.

He ran up the revolving stair, which had a series of oil lamps fed by gravity through a tube that lined the wall. Rushing past the second floor landing, a guard standing there tried to get him to stop. "Hey you! Wait!" He heard distant voices shouting, echoing in the stairwell as he ran faster. "Intruder, alert! Raise the alarm!"

He had no magic prepared, and he didn't want to cause any deaths, but he did need to create an obstacle behind him. The lamps on the wall seemed to provide a solution. Levan pulled the squishy, liquid-filled tube from the bottom of the nearest lamp, and let the oil from the end drip on the flame of the lamp below it. The flaws in the inventor's design became evident as the enflamed oil traveled down the tube and began bursting the wells at the bottom of the lamps, scattering broken glass and sticky pools of flame across the stairs. The lamp he had pulled one end of the tube from was sputtering out as its well emptied and continued pouring out a river of dark oil.

Levan could hear several palace guards crowding the stairwell, their armor heavy and slowing their movement, they were mostly shouting to each other to "Go!" and "Move out of the way!" Then, as the combusting fuel line reached them, they were yelling in distress as the exploding lamps spewed flaming oil everywhere. A few suffered some minor burns, and the flame sufficiently did its job of slowing them down.

He made it to the top of the stairs, and the highest ceiling of the castle. The helical stone hall ended in a rudimentary ladder of ten wooden planks bolted into the wall at the top of which was a painted-red iron trap door. Levan dropped the helmet and climbed up the ladder.

Pushing open the heavy metal door, the frigid, misty air of the mountains enveloped his face in its chilly touch. Above him was the light chamber, an elongated decahedron made of huge panes of glass fused together by heat, and suspended high in the air by four stone pillars surrounding the open trap door. But as he climbed out he realized there was no place to stand but the edge of the hatch on the roof, with a precarious drop in all directions around. The pillars rose up from the steep, wet and slippery angled roof about the length of a tall man away from the roof hatch. Levan heard the shouting of the soldiers getting closer, and as he looked down he caught a dizzying glimpse of the sheer drop-off all around him which would take several seconds to impact him if he were to fall.

He hesitated as his pursuers drew even nearer. There was courage and there was knowing your limits. If he had spent his youth climbing trees and mountains, he probably would not have read half the books he did, and may not have been a wizard at all. But then he would have a much better chance of surviving this jump. He procrastinated and analyzed the best course of action until the troops arrived at the ladder below him and forced him to act.

Levan jumped and dived forward as far as he could, slamming into the stone pillar and wrapping his arms around it with all his strength. His hands slipped and slid down the wet stone surface until they finally grasped a set of metal rungs on the outside of the pillar, and he was able to pull himself up and begin climbing toward the Light Chamber.

The first guard emerged from the hatch and stepped up onto the edge. The one behind him came up too quickly after and bumped against the first, causing him to teeter off balance and fall to the steeply sloped rooftop below. Levan winced as he heard the man's diminishing cry. He slammed down onto the roof, shattering a section of stone tiles, bouncing, sliding and rolling off the rain soaked eave and disappearing to the ground below. It was a tremendous height to fall from, but he was wearing good armor, and would soon be treated by a healer, awarded a medal, and be back to patrolling the palace halls in less than a fortnight.

Carefully Levan climbed the slippery rungs on the pillar as the wind howled and battered him with rain. At the top he passed between the sheets of glass where a wall of wind kept the tiny pyreflies imprisoned, yet supplied with fresh air.

The piercing sapphire lights of the tails of the pyreflies sparked and flared excitedly all around him as he stepped out onto a narrow glass walkway with a platform at the center. The open air and a long drop below were all around him still. Levan pulled out an empty vial and captured one of the pyreflies within it.

Standing at the highest point in the city where night had fallen hours before, he looked out over the mountains, beyond the dark clouds over Lorestian to see the last light of the sun disappearing below the western sea.

Non's words returned to him.

When you reach the peak with the light, follow the setting sun.

On the west side of the tower the wall passed very close the castle, and just on the other side of it was a large cart filled with hay. Around it was a rough square of gray bricks in the ground, seeming to depict a diagram of the city, with one red brick at the northeast corner. Just before the leading guard reached his sword up to stab at him, Levan took a deep breath and jumped.

He had never fallen from a height this great, and the sensation of freefall for several seconds was frightfully unsettling to his body and mind. But he imagined, as if he were in a dream again, that he could not be harmed.

This is just Non's little game to test our loyalty. He wouldn't let me die during the initiation ritual. I'm sure this jump is survivable.

Levan landed with a crash in the haycart. His body was cushioned reasonably, but his head hit the wooden railing and smashed through one of the planks.

He sat up, groaning in pain and rubbing the back of his head. His hand came back covered in blood and wood splinters and his skull rang like a stricken bell as a bulbous knot began to swell in the back. But he was out. Free and clear, as long as he didn't hang around here too much longer. He shuffled out of the cart and headed toward the northeast corner of town to find Avus and Non.

* * *

Avus walked alongside the strange robed man, who kept perfectly still but for his smooth forward motion, as if he were floating rather than walking. It was difficult to ascertain if his feet touched the ground as he went, since they were concealed beneath the robe. Non was silent as he glided toward the northeast part of the city. Avus followed along, open-minded but not yet trustful of his peculiar new acquaintance. He disliked manipulative people.

"So, do you make everyone break into the palace to join your little club?" Avus inquired facetiously as they made their way up the street.

"No, usually the light-bearer brings a torch or candle." Non replied simply.

"Ah, you just felt like giving the palace guards a headache, at Levan's expense. Maybe you're trying to get the young wizard killed?"

"Certainly not." Non retorted. "There are reasons for everything I ask. You are both very capable are you not? I would be sure of it. If you must know, the royal guards have been severely slacking in their protective duties of late. It is not safe for a monarch in these times of war. Their vigilance is so lacking that even an inept assassin could cut off the blood-line in a single stroke."

"Bloodline! Pah!" Avus snorted. "That red-headed fiend should claim no part of this land but the grave I would put him in myself. And you as well if you're one of his cronies!"

"I do not work for the king." Non responded as always in his deep monotone, bereft of emotion, impossible to read.

Avus yelled his disapproval of Fahfren. "He is a mad tyrant, squandering the wealth of the people on his gluttonous luxuries, sending young men to die in hopeless battles without care. You don't work for Fahfren, why would you care if he were assassinated?"

"That regime may come to an end, but it must not be through subterfuge. Each moment of history must unfold in perfect order, each character must play their part flawlessly. Without the guiding hand of balance, chaos is inevitable."

To Avus this sounded like self-righteous nonsense. How could be so sure his way was the only right one?

Who is he to think he knows what's best, that he should shape the fate of so many? Why should evil not be done away with?

Avus disagreed with and disliked Non even more as they talked, and he thought if it were up to him he would not have any dealings with this man who thought he had everything figured out. But he did not want to jeopardize Levan's mission, so he went along with the leader of the Hidden Hand despite his misgivings.

As they approached the wall and the edge of the city, Non stopped before an uncovered stone water well. The rain fell ever faster as they faced each other, a barrage of droplets shattering the mirrory puddles all around.

"We are much the same, you and I." Non said to Avus, as though sensing his apprehension. "We have dedicated our lives to altruism, that others may find their true path and complete their life's quest. The Hidden Hand has already begun to work toward a cause that I believe is dearest to *your* heart. You know of the darkness that pours from the great scar in the land. It is not checked by flourishing growth or quite enough righteous champions. Humankind creates ample chaos without the scarling hordes. We mean to seal the Great Rift and banish the dark ones from our land."

Avus paused, absorbing this. If he allowed himself a personal goal, it would be to eliminate the subterranean scourge that had ended his previous life, and that of his student. Yet somehow they knew. They must know everything about what happened that day. Though his natural state of mind avoided it like a spiny cactus, there was something tantalizing about the steadfast, infallible absoluteness of Non's speech. He could see why people listened to and followed this man, but he would not be so easily swayed into committing acts of evil in the name of "balance" or "the greater good".

"I would also see it done." Avus finally responded.

"Then do as I do." Non stepped up onto the side of the well, then into the large wooden water bucket. He held the thick rope as the spring-coiled crankshaft lowered him slowly down.

When the bucket returned to the surface, Avus stepped into it and began his descent. A cloud of steam enveloped him as he passed underground into a large brick chamber. The mist was so dense it obscured even the powerful vision of the dwarf Avus. When he reached the floor, he stepped out of the bucket and peered wide-eyed through the smoky haze.

"Hello!" Avus called out, carefully listening to the reflected sound of his voice and building a mental picture of the chamber he was in, and the possible escape routes. The reverberations diffused on some fuzzy figures around him. He was not alone.

The mist was too thick. He needed light to see through it. Avus pulled out a small oiled stick he used as a match to start fires, and lit it with a spark from his flint box. The little torch sputtered to life and illuminated the foggy cloud around him, casting the shadows of a crowd of furry creatures surrounding him, which receded back from the light. Avus grunted in surprise and readied his axe to swing. From behind him, one of the creatures swooped in and blew out his match with a puff of breath and quickly disappeared back into the mist with a mischievous laugh that echoed in the well chamber.

They were men in animal furs. He could hear them rustling about, giggling menacingly here and there. The dense fog billowed and wafted before him as one of them darted in and kicked his left leg out from under him.

Avus leapt back to his feet, whirling around in a wide arc with his axe. The blade caught and stuck fast in a log which fell from the hands of the concealed assailants. Then they rushed him and tackled him to the ground and he lost hold of his weapon.

Only the combined weight of several of these men could hold Avus down, thrashing and wrapping about his limbs as he threw them off here and there. A few of them seemed to be expert wrestlers, grappling his arms, legs and neck. But Avus showed them why humans and dwarves do not wrestle in the same divisions. His limbs were too short and powerful to be barred or locked, and he turned their techniques against them, rolling up someone who was trying to extend his arm and clenching him within the vice-like coil of his bulging bicep and forearm. He squeezed until he felt the exhale of his attacker and the body go limp, then released him and grabbed hold of the next, pulling him to the ground and dropping an elbow into the solar plexus.

The shadows from the dark swarmed in on him again, and Avus fought on.

❊ ❊ ❊

The solid iron gate clanged shut with a jarring reverberation. This foreboding crash startled Ranser free from the hold of his captors, and with his feet shackled, he fell forward, toppling down the stone steps.

When Ranser stood up, he found himself in the dark and foul-smelling subterranean dungeon. The walls echoed with despairing wails, weak, starving moans, and periodic tortured screams. The edges of the shadowy corridor were faintly lit with a wavering ambience from distant torches, giving no hint as to which direction Ranser should run, but for a slightly greater light off to the right. So he shuffled toward it as fast as his manacled ankles would go as the guards clamored down the stairs, shouting "Brelec, Brelec!"

Ranser's heart fluttered in half-beats just as his feet shambled in half-steps, falling here and there on corroded chains and dry old bones which crumbled to dust underfoot. Passing the central cell block, he looked back over his shoulder as he neared the end of the hallway. The guards that brought him down had lost sight of him, and went searching in other directions. The way appeared open both forward and behind for him to look for his adoptive father Jofon. But in that moment when he glanced away, he ran headfirst into some bulging, rounded obstacle, bounced back and fell to the ground.

When he looked up, he saw that his path was blocked by a massive, corpulent monstrosity of a man, nearly twice Ranser's height and wider than his arm span. The Inquisitor Brelec's skin was a sickening white pallor, spattered and stained with fresh blood, and from his grotesque bald head protruded a swine-like snout with filthy, broken tusks.

A shocked gasp escaped with Ranser's breath as he slid backward on the floor, attempting to escape the torturer's grasp, but with his legs shackled he could not move fast enough. Brelec reached down with one of his huge pale arms and lifted Ranser by his collar high off the ground, bringing him up to inspect with his beady black eyes and a drooling, sharp-toothed grin.

The sailor boy flailed and kicked to no avail as he was carried past rows of cells to an open one and thrown with incredible force to the back wall. His head hit the bare stone and his vision faded.

* * *

The armored guardsmen, in groups of three, marched in and out of sight between the buildings as Levan rushed through the rain-soaked streets, his strides falling here and there in puddles which splashed and drenched his robes.

Reaching a crossroad, he peeked around the edge of a manor house near the northern end of town. To his left, on the next street, a guard captain was shouting some emphatic commands to two squads of soldiers who ran to meet him, then affirmed their orders and ran off in different directions. One of these groups headed toward Levan, and he slipped back behind the building as they approached.

Pressing himself against the wall, searching in vain for a hiding spot, Levan began to feel very exposed as the soldiers' boot-falls clopped ever nearer. Then he saw the other group of guards heading up the road behind him, converging with the ones just ahead of him.

In a brief, shocked glance, Levan's eyes met with the squad captain's and they both paused for that tiny moment when hunter and quarry take measure of one another, accept the preordained challenge, and begin to anticipate the other's course of action.

Across the street the young wizard sprang, his limbs suddenly charged with energy, the pain in his head gone. As the guards shouts echoed off the buildings and rock faces all around, Levan dashed into an alleyway between the double-storied estates across the street, his pursuers nearly nipping at his heels. Sprinting down the shady corridor with mounting despair, his heart clenched and pounded ever harder as each avenue of escape seemed to be blocked. By the time he reached the end of the alleyway, Levan had already begun to consider the terrible fate that awaited him upon being captured.

The road terminated in a loop rounding a circular garden, within which stood a statue of the winged goddess Agartha. The face of the monument was shaded from the moonlight and from a distance her somber expression seemed to look down on Levan with utter pity, and deep, silent sorrow, the rain trickling down her ashen cheek like an endless stream of tears. As he looked upon it, a thunderbolt flashed across the sky, illuminating the statue's face and the stone monument seemed to come alive and speak.

"My faithful servant, soon shalt thou bring about my return."

The enthralling voice froze the lightning streak in the sky and suspended the raindrops in the air all around.

"Salvation lies in deepest darkness."

When the voice spoke its final word, time unfroze, the rain fell to the ground again, the lightning flashed out and a roar of thunder followed in its wake.

From the waters of the canal behind where Levan was standing, murky tendrils rose up, grasping like icy fingertips and pulling him downward. He had just enough time to form a bubble of air around his face before falling into the darkened stream.

A squadron of soldiers filled the circle, their heads swiveling around in confusion.

Through the haze of the water Levan could see a dim, wavering figure appear above him wearing a crested helmet. The guard captain seemed to be looking right at him as Levan lay still at the bottom of the shallow canal, his feet wedged along the angled sides to keep from drifting in the current.

"Use your blades! Check the canals!" The muted voice called out to the others who began stabbing their swords into the muddy rain channels encircling the statue garden.

The sky illuminated and fractured with searing, branching strands of electricity. A gleam caught the guard captain's eye. Just as he raised his sword and plunged it into the water at his hiding spot, Levan's feet released their grip and the dark, frigid current carried him away downstream. The guards did not pursue and he floated serenely in the ambling stream until slipping around a corner where the road and canal began a steep descent.

Now he was sliding down the trench at an alarming velocity which promised to inflict crushing injury wherever he was to come to a stop. So Levan attempted to slow himself by pressing against the walls, but his foot caught a protruding stone and sent him spinning, jarring loose from his pack the two small vials he was carrying. As he tumbled and fell down the slope, he caught sight of the blue glow of the pyrefly in the vial, and he reached and struggled to grasp it. He would not lose this thing he'd come so far and braved such perils for. So it was to the negligence of all else he turned and dived to clutch his pilfered prize, unaware at first that he and the stream had entered a tunnel which sloped ever steeper downward.

Freefalling in darkness, Levan tried frantically to

slow his descent to no avail. After a few terrifying moments, the drainage tunnel came to a sudden end and the young wizard went hurtling out into the open space of the subterranean cistern.

Avus, clenching one man in a headlock under each arm, kicking and head-butting at the others, looked up from the melee as a shining blue light flew out from one of the drainage streams pouring down from the top of the high brick walls.

With a shout of alarm as he cleared the falling stream into open air, Levan plummeted into the deep pool encircling the platform on which Avus stood. From the same gushing portal, two glass containers fell and shattered on the stone floor near the water's edge, and a tiny blue light flew up near the ceiling, bathing the underground waterway in a cool blue glow. The fray of fighting halted immediately as everyone turned to watch the pyrefly rise up and hover around, its light fluttering and winking enthusiastically.

The still waters had slowed his fall, to Levan's great relief. His feet touched down gently on the bottom and pushed back up, resurfacing and pulling himself up on the stone landing. As he hoisted his leg up, it landed on a shard of broken glass which sliced and stuck into his flesh, and it was at this point he realized he had dropped the pyrefly. His right hand bled from striking the mossy metallic rim of the tunnel, which had caused him to lose his grip on the vial.

A mirthful cheer rang out. "A toast to the soggy sorcerer!" The fur-clad men's laughter echoed through the chamber as they dispersed and filed out through a walkway. "A fine idea! And another for the tiny titan! Here, here!"

As Levan stooped down and removed the broken glass from his leg with a hiss, a robed figure stepped out from behind the stone column nearby. Levan stood up to face him. It was Non.

"Non!" Levan's exasperated gasp was both surprised and contemptuous.

"You have done well, Levan Cloudborne, you have brought light to the darkness. I knew you would arrive precisely on time."

Non's back was turned to the still-raging dwarf, who now saw the one that had led him into this ambush as he stepped into the open before his poor young wizard friend, who had been lucky to survive his ordeal as well.

Test me!? Now I will test you!

Avus broke into a bounding sprint across the platform and leapt onto the back of the seemingly unprepared leader of the Hidden Hand, wrapping his legs around the torso and locking his arms around the neck in a vicious chokehold. But something was not right. The man was unyielding like a pillar of marble, a statue of forged steel. And Non stood perfectly still.

As Avus reared back for a crushing head-butt to the base of his skull, Non reached up, wrenching the dwarf's arms from his neck and flinging him over his head. Held fast by his wrists, Avus dangled at arm's length from his target, flailing feebly until being dropped to his feet.

Furious, Avus growled ferociously and charged again at the stoic robed figure.

"Avus, that's enough!" Levan shouted, but was unheeded.

The dwarf went barreling into the still master headfirst, attempting to take him down, but was lifted by a perfectly timed knee strike to his gut, caught by the rear of his pants and hurled back to the place he'd began.

Non turned his head to speak to Avus, who was kneeling, wheezing to catch his breath. "And you held the darkness at bay, brave Avus of Deepstone. Your efforts will not be forgotten. The Hidden Hand has seen your worthiness proven, and celebrate in welcoming its two newest members into the fold. Join us for the toast in your honor."

Avus stood with an unhappy grunt, and stepped over to recover his axe, but ceased his aggression as the robed figure turned to exit.

They followed Non into one of the tunnels, and Levan evoked a small torchlight floating above his palm to light the way.

Non had disappeared into the shadow and was gone, but a low drumming sound and faint blue light came from further down the corridor. The echoing rhythmic pulse beckoned them deeper into the underground.

❊ ❊ ❊

Ranser's head pounded with a dull ache as he awakened. Darkness surrounded him and the only sound was a dripping of water. His eyes blinked into focus on a big mangy rat sniffing at his face, which scurried away as he sat up. His head spinning with vertigo, he still thought he was on a ship until a tortured cry of agony echoed from the mossy stone walls in the distance.

The dungeon.

He hated the place immediately. The air was stagnant and foul, the floor was scattered in unspeakable filth, and the dank old walls seemed to crush in and suffocate him. Even the rats seemed destitute and discontent.

Such a place should not exist. No living thing should be here, criminal or madman or scavenging beast.

He moved to the barred gate at the front of the cell. Across the hall were more barred cells, and along the floor lay a row of sickly, emaciated wretches, barely able to move but held to the floor by a chain looped through the shackles on their wrists and ankles. He grasped and tugged at the rusty iron bars, but they would not budge.

"That is not the exit." A deep, gravelly voice came from the opposite cell. There, half-concealed in shadow, sat a man with long black hair and a powerful muscular frame.

"Huh? Who are you?" Ranser peered across the

hall. This man did not appear as the other prisoners. He was obviously well-fed, and oddly serene. "What are you here for?"

"I am Mezerek, the bard. I come here from time to time to clear my thoughts, and gain inspiration. I've found my solace in every cell of this dungeon. You seem to have a purpose for being here as well, and perhaps ability and luck enough to escape. In fact—your face and voice—they seem familiar."

"I am Ranser of the Luna Triada. I have come to find my father, Jofon."

"Hmm…" Mezerek stood up. He had heard something in the distance. "I suppose it is nearly time for our performances. Look to the wall at your feet. There is your exit."

Ranser noticed some loose rubble at the corner of the cell. A line of bricks blocked a tiny recess in the wall. Having no mortar, they were easily dislodged, revealing a narrow tunnel out into the hallway. He lay flat on the floor and squirmed into it. As he struggled to make his way out, a shout echoed from the front of the corridor, followed by the sound of someone running toward him.

A tiny old man in a wizard's robe, no taller than a finger, went running past his face, squeaking in a fit of mad laughter. Just behind him, the night watch guard strode past their cells and dived to the floor, catching the little figure in his hands. The miniature wizard, still laughing, uttered some magical phrase.

Ranser saw Mezerek turn away, cover his ears and hum to himself. He hadn't enough time or freedom of movement to do the same as an irresistible wave of drowsiness overcame him, and he lost consciousness.

"Ranser…Ranser!" Mezerek's voice called to him in his dream, and he awoke. He seemed to have only been asleep for a few moments, as the scene was the same, only lacking the tiny wizard. The guard lay prone on the floor nearby. "Get the key!"

Ranser pulled himself out of the tunnel and stood

up. A cacophony of snoring buzzed around him. Everyone but he and Mezerek were in a deep sleep. He stooped to the fallen guardsman and removed the ring from his belt which held the master key for all the cells. There also on the man's belt were the three new daggers he'd gotten that day, and he retrieved those as well. Now he could find and free Jofon. First, he unlocked his own shackles, then the cell of Mezerek, his ally who had helped him thus far.

"Thanks, kid. Even if you aren't his son, you'll be a great hero in your own right."

"Jofon, is he here?" Ranser implored.

"The old sailor? Yeah, just down the hall. Wake him by calling his name. I have an engagement to attend now. Farewell and good luck." Mezerek stepped off into the darkness.

Ranser moved to the next cell and unlocked it, swinging open the door. But it was empty. In the hall, he crouched over the sleeping prisoners, calling out "Jofon?" At the end of the row of them, there was a lock binding the chain that held them. He unsealed it and pulled the long chain, freeing a score of still-slumbering inmates, but none stirred as he called out for his father. He opened more cells, and his call became louder as his desperation mounted. "Father? Jofon!?" At last, a familiar, groggy voice came from a cell further down.

"Ranser?" It was the old sailor Jofon. Ranser hurried to the gate and unlocked it, though it would not fully open. "Boy! What are you doin' here!?"

"I came to get you out of this place!" Ranser exclaimed as he kicked the bars and its rusty hinges finally gave way.

"You get yourself out..." Jofon sighed. When Ranser moved closer he could see Jofon crammed into a small iron cage suspended by a chain at the center of the room. "My time is at an end."

"No! There must be a way!" Ranser scrambled frantically trying to find a latch or keyhole.

"It's no use...the bottom's a one-way porthole. Nothing's getting in or out til I'm flat as a flounder. Only Brelec the torturer can release me now."

"Shh...don't say his name—!" Ranser gasped as the caged rattled and began rising upward.

He held onto the bottom rim as they were pulled up through a metallic grate on the ceiling which swiveled open, then slammed shut below them. They continued to rise at increasing speed, and a forest of rusty iron bars, chains and spikes came into view. It appeared they would be impaled on the grid of long sharp spikes as they neared the top, but the chain they were on was looped over a rod, and when the cage rounded it, they went swinging at great speed down and across into an expansive circular chamber. The cage swung low and Ranser lost his grip, tumbling as he struck the metallic floor.

From the ceiling hung an array of chains, cages and hooks like vines in a jungle. The chains connected to various crankshafts along the walls, one of which was being turned by the massive hulking figure of the Inquisitor Brelec. The brute seemed not to notice Ranser as he continued to crank the chain, hoisting Jofon's cage up again, toward the spiked ceiling.

Ranser broke into a sprint toward Brelec, leaping over a round hole at the center of the room. From below, a mess of slimy tentacles sprang up, snatching at his legs. Fortunately, he moved too quickly past them and glanced back in disgust as he kept running. Jofon's cage had nearly reached the dark spears above and there was still a moderate distance to span. In desperation, at the last second, Ranser hurled one of his knives toward Brelec. The blade flew past him and lodged in the crank's inner gear, halting the chain.

As Brelec tugged on the frozen handle, Ranser reached his position and sank his second dagger to the hilt into the half-ogre's back. The blade stuck there and could not be pulled out.

The monstrous torturer bellowed in rage as he wheeled around, swiping one of his great arms out to put a death grip on the young escapee. Ranser narrowly avoided his crushing grasp by leaping backward, and lost his footing. He then had to quickly roll to the side as Brelec hefted a massive meat cleaver in a ferocious chop which threw up a shower of sparks as it dented the iron floor.

From high above, Jofon called out "Ranser, mind the rigging!"

The sailors would often call this out to him when a strong wind picked up or lines needed to be replaced on the upper masts of the ship. Though he was the youngest, he had proven to be the most agile and fearless of climbers, and his acrobatics on the rigging lines had earned him praise and notoriety among the mariners.

He took a few strides and leapt up to catch hold of a hanging chain nearby, lifting his legs just out of reach as the huge blade swung across, then pulled himself higher, well out of range.

Brelec moved back to the wall, heaving his giant blade to strike the line which held Jofon's cage aloft. The chain and blade grinded hard and sparked against the wall, rending a link half-open. Another well-placed slash would sever it.

Needing to create a momentary distraction, Ranser took a bone from a nearby cage and tossed it down to bounce off Brelec's head as he taunted and laughed.

The immense white ogre roared, taking hold of a cage and throwing it with incredible force. Ranser swung and leapt to another chain, then another, avoiding the heavy mass of metal flying in his direction.

Turning back to the chain on the wall, Brelec finished cutting the line with another great blow from his cleaver and Jofon began to drop toward the center of the room, into the lair of whatever that foul creature was that lurked down there.

In that moment, Ranser saw a chain nearby with

a hook on the end and he recalled having saved one of the sailors who fell from the crow's nest with a hooked rope. He had called it luck, but his aim had always been quite astounding.

He wrapped his leg in the chain he was suspended on, swung the hooked line around in his hand, gauging the distance, then released it. The cage was easier to catch than a man's belt in a tumbling freefall. The hook snagged the side of the metallic assembly, flipping it sideways, and sending it swinging in a wide arc across the room. Ranser leapt to Jofon's new line and slid down to him.

"Still with me, Dad? How goes it?"

"Aye, I've had better days, son!"

Brelec moved to another crankshaft at the apex of the room, across from the barred ground-floor entrance. He pushed at the disused stop-latch on the side but its corroded hinge did not yet give way.

"Look! Those latches are our key to victory!" Jofon had been eyeing the workings of the torture room since he'd entered it. Now all the pieces fell into place and he knew what to do. His hope rested on Ranser's remembrance of his compass lessons. "Brelec is to the north! Strike the latches at the corners from southeast moving westward!"

Ranser reached out to take hold of a chain near the southwest corner as the cage swung that way, and held it as he leapt toward the southeast. When he reached the edge he slid down the line and kicked the latch on the crank, freeing the wedge from the ratchet wheel and releasing the tension from one of the four chains connected to the floor. The iron plate comprising the southeast quadrant fell away, partially revealing the huge tentacled monstrosity below, akin to a gigantic sea anemone.

Ranser released the chain in his right hand and grasped the one he had pulled from the other side with both hands. His feet pushed off the eastern wall to swing back over to the southwest.

In transit, he saw Brelec use his heavy weapon to smash open the rusty latch at the head of the room. All of the hanging chains shook as they rattled through the holes in the spiked ceiling, which had begun falling and would soon skewer and crush them.

With increased urgency, Ranser kicked the next latch, dropping the southwest floor panel and took hold of a chain on the western wall. This allowed him to run along the wall to reach and release the northwest crank as the spikes from above neared Jofon's cage.

Now he had to do something about the falling ceiling. Ranser climbed high as fast as he could, just below the rusty spines where he wedged his last dagger into a link in the chain above. To his great relief the chain and knife did not break but lodged at the edge of the opening, halting the descent of the ceiling grid just before the spikes reached Jofon.

But he had taken his eyes off Brelec and did not notice the brute hurl the giant cleaver in his direction. He had just enough time to duck under it by quickly sliding down the rusted chain, shredding the flesh of his hands in doing so. The blade crashed into the wall in a shower of sparks, severing the chain and sending Ranser plummeting toward the pit and the devouring abomination below.

He fell, grasping at the sheer stone wall, finding no handholds. At last he met the narrow edge of the northwest floor panel which had swiveled downward when released, leaving half a hand's-length of ledge on which Ranser was able to take hold and save himself.

Hanging on the precipice, he shuffled to the end and grabbed on to the last standing floor panel. There, Brelec stood above him, bringing a massive foot down to stomp at his exposed fingers. Ranser moved quickly hand over hand to avoid it, but he could not evade the Inquisitor long enough to pull himself up onto the ledge.

He reached down to the underside and felt a small lip there, just enough to hang on to. Brelec lost sight of his quarry as it lowered out of view, but did not fall. Ranser dropped down slightly and turned outward, moving to the other side while kicking away the long, slimy tentacles reaching up toward him as he swung his legs back and forth until he had enough momentum to vault up onto the platform.

As Brelec came charging toward him, Ranser somersaulted beneath his legs and sprang up onto the crankshaft housing.

"You let yourself become a monster." He uttered with contempt. Crouching down, he pulled back the lever, glaring into Brelec's widened eyes as the floor dropped away and the cruel torturer fell. "Now meet your end!" Ranser shouted down at him with ire.

The corpulent white blob tumbled down the pit, but, to Ranser's surprise, caught himself by one arm on the fallen chain from the floor panel. Brelec dangled there feebly as the grimy tentacles gravitated to and entwined around his limbs, the anemone's thrashing, razor-toothed mouth rippling hungrily at him.

"Ranser, this is it! Drop now!" Jofon shouted out as he reached his fingers through the cage, unhooked himself from the line and fell.

Ranser did not hesitate, his trust was absolute and unquestioning. He jumped out into the open air toward where his father had fallen.

Above, a sharp ping echoed off the wall as the dagger dislodged and went whirling out of the chain link.

Ranser hadn't a moment of fear or doubt in Jofon's fall-into-the-pit plan, it merely took him a moment to deduce how he meant them to survive it. The giant anemone at the bottom of the pit was similar to the ones on many warm shores, though the ones he'd seen as a boy were not even large enough to consume a foot. Only when you'd tempt it with something to eat would it reveal its spongy, fleshy trunk.

All of the pit cleaner's hundreds of tentacles swarmed on Brelec, still holding the chain, and pulled at him with such force that it lifted the huge iron floor plate and slammed it against the wall. But the brute's grip would not relent.

Ranser and Jofon landed on the trunk of the anemone and sunk in a bit then bounced back out, softer than a water landing, rolling off and into a sloping drainage tunnel.

Before sliding away into the darkness of the sewers, Ranser witnessed the ceiling spikes fall just far enough to impale Brelec, and then the pit-cleaner take him as its meal. The water flowing beneath them turned to red.

CHAPTER 11 THE SHADOW'S REST

Traversing the odious sewer tunnel, Levan and Avus were startled by a metallic clang as something fell from the drainage hole in the wall nearby. A moment later a body splashed into the shallow channel from the same portal, choking and sputtering. Levan peered around his torch curiously but Avus needed no light.

"Hey, look who it is!" The dwarf chuckled jovially as he pulled Ranser up from the muck.

"Ugh...father!" Ranser coughed, reaching down to tug at the half-submerged cage, but failing to move its ponderous weight. "Help!"

Avus took hold of the cage with the man inside and hoisted it up onto the walkway.

When he had finished coughing and hacking Jofon thanked him. "My thanks to you, good dwarf. These lungs aint what they used to be. Thought I'd taken my last drink there."

"Father," Ranser said as he knelt beside the cage, "these are my trusted friends Avus and Levan. We have joined the cause of Tor Veldgar."

"I see," Jofon replied, "a wild turn of luck to meet them in such a place as this."

Levan crouched beside Ranser, placing a hand on his back. "I am glad to see you again, my friend, and that you have found your father."

"As am I. Can we get him out of this thing?" Ranser asked hopefully.

"Yes, I believe so. Leave it to me."

The wizard cupped a bit of water from the stream into his hand and clasped it onto one of the bars at the top and bottom, creating two lingering sheaths of liquid around it. He then pinched the space between and a piercing light turned the small section of iron white-hot. That piece of the cage melted away without harm to its occupant, and Levan repeated the process on the next bar.

"I am not your true father, you know…" Jofon spoke to Ranser as Levan worked at the cage.

"I know. I don't care about that." Ranser replied, worriedly.

"But you must." Jofon continued. "Before anything else happens…the time has come for you to know who you really are. Your mother brought you to me twelve years ago, to take you out to the high seas where they would not find you."

"Where who wouldn't find me?"

"The men who sought to cut off your bloodline. Your father had gone missing by then on his quest for your family's redemption. Likewise, your elder brother Tor had not been heard from in many months after he left to find your father, Anderjar."

"Wait, so…" Ranser shook his head in disbelief, and could not finish his sentence.

"You are Ander Veldgar, prince of Lorestian and brother of the true king."

Ranser was speechless at the realization.

Levan, astonished, glanced agape from Jofon to Avus to Ranser, blinking back to Jofon and to all of them again, failing to find words.

"Ho ho!" Avus snorted, genuinely impressed. "Companions with royalty, I am honored, Prince Ander!" He said as he knelt and bowed.

"Stop that. I am still Ranser, the same as ever. What is so special about a lineage anyway?"

"In your case, very much." Jofon explained. "There is something in your blood which allows your family to use the artifact that can rid our land of all these vile invaders. That is why you must find it. Any others that touch it will be immediately stricken dead. These days it is called the Mountain Maker. But in ancient times it was known as The Heart of the Life Stone."

"That simple sword?" Ranser shook his head in doubt.

"Before your father made it his life's quest to find, and disappeared, he had said that it bears the same shape but it is no mere sword. That it was not crafted by mortal hands, and its powers were not only destructive, but preserved life and shaped the world for good as its user would have it. That is all I know."

Jofon sighed in relief as Levan melted the last bar and opened the cage.

"I owe each of you my life now. I only wish I could repay you with more than just my gratitude." The old sailor tried to stand and walk, but faltered and Ranser caught him.

"Let us go take a room at the Shadow's Rest." Jofon said, being propped up by Ranser. "It is not far this way."

Avus, Levan, Ranser and Jofon entered the massive cavern from which the deep rhythm and cool blue light radiated. The terraced floor was decked with revelers of all shapes and sizes, from a tiny gnome frantically weaving through the crowd, only half the height of Avus the dwarf, to a hulking, long-furred warrior of the Ivru race, resembling a tiger, chatting and laughing with a group of adventuring humans, dwarves, and pale elves. Below and to the right, the throng of people was mashed together and thrashing around before a stone platform stage upon which a troupe of costumed drummers pounded away the hypnotic beat and a burly, dark-haired man howled some mesmerizing song.

A pale-skinned female elf with dark blue hair and lips carrying a tray of drinks and colorful appetizers asked if they needed anything.

"A room for the night, please." Ranser replied.

"Ask Roogin, he's the gnome at the bar."

They approached the circular glass bar at the center of the room which twinkled like the stars from the pyreflies within. There, a willow tree with faces on each side used them and its many arms to take orders, collect coins, dispense food and drinks and cook various dishes.

On the other side of the bar was an old gnome standing on a pedestal with a ramp which boosted him to the height of the counter. Behind him stood a towering rack with keys hanging inside individually-labeled cubical enclosures.

"You must be Roogin." Levan greeted him.

"Indeed, what size room you want?" The gnome looked up briefly at them, adjusting his spectacles.

"The smallest, closest one." Jofon said. "No rats."

"Got it. Let's see…" Roogin studied the ledger on the counter for a moment. "Mmhm…erm, no rats…" He murmured to himself as he ran his finger down the page. "Ah, here we are, C-13. The customary donation is one gold piece if you can, or you can pay in the morning if you'll be acquiring it during your stay."

Levan dropped three gold coins on the counter and requested food and water be brought to the room later.

The gnome rang a bell and a tiny door on the key rack swung open. From it emerged a devilish little yellow creature which ran swiftly on two legs through the holes in the sides of the cubicles on row C, its long pointed tail streaming in waves behind it. It retrieved the C-13 key and hopped out of the rack onto the floor, then emerged from another tiny door at their feet beneath the bar.

"Follow him, he'll lead you to your room." The gnome pointed the direction and turned to his ledger to record their presence in it.

"I've still got to get my spellbook back," Levan said wearily as they walked away, "I will meet up with you later or in the morning."

"And I was promised a toast in our honor. I'll be at the bar." Avus excused himself and went to take a spot at the bar.

Ranser, propping Jofon up as they walked, followed the little demon with the key hung on its neck into one of the arched tunnel exits and up a slight incline. In the shadows the little creature lit up with a golden glow, lighting the way. After a short walk they reached the room. The little guide turned and held up the key. Ranser took it and thanked him.

"Heh, you're welcome, pal." The tiny creature replied, amused. Almost no one ever spoke to him. "Rest well." It said, and dashed off down the hall.

Jofon's breathing was hoarse and labored as they entered the domed enclosure. The room's only feature was a small drainage grate at the middle of the floor that sloped gently toward it. Jofon collapsed in a fit of coughing.

"Please, let me rest now." The old sailor rasped. "Go get yourself some food."

"Yes, father." He stood and headed toward the door.

"I'm proud of you, son. You've become a great man, Ranser. Someday the whole world will know of your heroism."

"It was your teaching that made me who I am today. I would not have changed a thing."

"Nor I. Goodnight, my son."

"Goodnight, Father."

Ranser shut the door and headed back down to the bustling, booming central meeting room. His stomach rumbled with hunger and his throat was parched with thirst.

Across the room he saw the bard Mezerek on stage, howling a song as dark and deep as these caverns, and hovering his hands out over the wildly dancing crowd like some mad puppeteer. He noticed Ranser as well, pointing to him and pumping his fist a few times in the air. Ranser smirked and waved back, making his way to the bar.

The willow tree bartender greeted him as he sat down. "How may I serve you, young lad?"

Ranser was craving a seafood dish, but was considering being frugal and conserving the gold as he fumbled for his coin bag and realized he had none.

Just then a tiny little fairy with purple wings floated up and whispered something to the tree.

"Whatever you'd like, it's free of charge." The willow's wooden face warped into a kind smile.

"Oh, great. I'll have a sea bass filet, with butter and lemon if you have it." It was an expensive dish, but he felt he'd earned it, and didn't know when he'd get to eat this good again, and for free no less.

"Coming right up!" The tree's limbs on the other side pulled up the fish from a chest of ice and prepared to cook it on one of the grills. "And to drink?"

This was a choice he rarely, if ever, made himself. He hesitated, looking around at what others were drinking. His eyes met with the striking and strangely beautiful appearance of a fish-woman seated next to him. Though he had never seen one of the merfolk before, he pretended as if he had, masking his fascination. She could almost pass as a human or elf, but for the finned ears, the gill slits on her slender neck, and the iridescent white scales which at a close distance could be seen to make up her skin. Cradled in her delicate, webbed fingers was a conical glass with some clear, shimmery liquid inside.

"What's that you're drinking?" Ranser asked, pointing to the glass.

The sea-woman handed the drink to him with a slight smile. Ranser took a gulp and his face contorted in disgust.

"Augh—yuck! It's sea water!" He retched and grimaced as he placed the glass back in front of her.

The fish girl laughed and took a drink. "Sorry, little sailor," she could smell the ocean on him, "I forgot your kind do not enjoy this drink like we do. The spirits in there are too small to be seen, but add such a delicious crunch. Mmm…" She sipped some more. "The land-dwellers here seem to be fond of the strawberry glacier. Perhaps it would be more to your liking."

"Sounds good. I'll try that then." Ranser said to the willow.

"Ah, a fine choice. There you are." One of the graceful, vine-like branches placed a frosty glass before him.

Ranser sampled the red drink and found it incredibly refreshing and delicious. He nodded in approval to the aquatic lady as he drank it. Her eyes followed the plate of fish as the tree placed it in front of him. There was an awkward pause as he looked from the cooked, filleted fish on the plate to the fish-woman sitting beside him.

"Umm…" Ranser did not know what to say or do, though he did not want to offend her.

"His name was Tom." She mourned, biting her lip.

Ranser's jaw dropped and he pushed the plate away.

The fish lady had another outburst of laughter. "Haha, I was kidding! I didn't know him. That is something we both love to eat. Go ahead."

Ranser giggled sheepishly and began to eat.

"It's really good," he said, chewing a mouthful, "want some?"

"Ah, I would, but you land folk always seem to ruin good food by heating it in the fire."

Ranser smiled, enjoying the meal and the amusing company of his new sea-folk friend, Felegrin. They laughed and chatted on as the night progressed.

Across the room, Avus was drinking merrily with the same men he had been brawling with earlier. They raised their mugs in salute to him. "Cheers for the tiny titan! Hurray!" The group lifted the dwarf in his chair with frothy mug in hand, and paraded him to the dance floor. Avus was laughing uncontrollably and greatly enjoying himself.

Levan had meandered about the room looking for Sabrena among the crowd without success. But when he went back to the bar he saw the fair-skinned girl perched on a stool at the other end, daintily sipping a luminescent sapphire drink. She looked different than he had ever seen which was why he did not recognize her at first. As Levan approached, he saw her hair was gathered in a bun on her head and she wore what appeared to be leaves encased in ice strung about her hips and chest in some scant sort of undergarment. His spell book sat on the bar in front of her.

"We meet again." He said, standing beside her.

"Oh! I didn't expect to see you here." Sabrena stood and held the tome. "My thanks for lending me your book. It was a great help."

"You're welcome, of course." Levan smiled. "I hardly recognized you. Where is your robe?"

"Oh, I'm having it washed. This is a bathing suit I made with leaves and magic. What do you think of it?"

"It is—interesting. Like a wood elf fashion." Levan remarked with feigned nonchalance.

"Yes, I saw one of the wild elves wearing something like this and decided to try to make my own. But I could not weave the leaves together, so I used ice spells."

"A garment of ice magic?" Levan's intrigue overcame his reticence, and it was like they were back in school again. "How does it not melt?"

"The permanence magic. A friend, a servant in my father's house taught me the permanence modifier about a year ago. He had read it in a very old book." Sabrena sighed, trudging up that tragic memory. "My uncle had him executed the next day. And my father did nothing. That was the day I left home and have not spoken to them since."

"I'm sorry for your loss, Sabrena." He replied sympathetically.

She shook her head. "It opened my eyes. I wish it had not taken his life to show me what monsters I had called my family, those who would ignore injustice, sacrifice innocence, do anything to preserve their wealth and power. I will show them that there are things greater than gold."

Levan admired the fire in her eyes for a moment before replying. "I believe you will. We wizards really can change the world. And that I will do, but I feel there are many more secrets and mysteries yet to uncover. I must know where I am to know which direction I should be going."

"Well, here's another for your collection of secrets," Sabrena said, opening the spell book, "I've written the formula for permanence in your book." She pointed to the page where a circular symbol was inscribed. "This sigil is drawn during the incantation. It makes the spell last as long as the caster's life. But be careful, it seems to take a great deal of energy to use."

"So add this word per-pat-two-uh to the spell—"

"Per-pechu-ah." She corrected his pronunciation.

"Perpetua, while drawing this symbol—" He stopped as someone pushed the book off the counter and it splayed out on the floor, scattering several loose pages.

"Always got your nose in a book!" Cray sneered with contempt at Sabrena.

"Cray!" Sabrena stood to rebuke the drunken oaf. "You don't just throw people's things like that! You need to go to bed!"

"Fine, let's go!" Cray barked in response.

"Just get yourself a room from the gnome over there!" Sabrena snapped at him fiercely.

To which Cray replied in a hesitant whisper, "I can't talk to those things. They freak me out…"

Sabrena was incredulous. "Gnomes? Really? Some brave warrior you are." She scoffed at Cray then moved around him to speak to Levan, who was gathering up the scattered pages. "Sorry about that. I hope it's not too bad of a mess. Thanks again for your help."

"No problem." Levan's unfazed reply belied the thoughts he was having of revenge but was unheard as Sabrena had already walked down to the innkeeper and was asking about a room for that big bumbling fool over there.

As Levan gathered the last of his pages, Sabrena and Cray left the hall trailing the scampering little guide creature.

Levan followed them into the shady tunnel, staying clear of the light from the torch Cray had lit. At the arched wooden door of the chamber, Sabrena took the key and unlocked it. Cray entered and set the torch into a sconce on the wall.

"Ugh, what a filthy—Hey!" She startled as Cray pulled her into the room and slammed the door.

Moving to the door, Levan could hear her shout in annoyance, "What the—? Hey, back up you pig! What are you doing?"

Levan readied his hands to incinerate the door and make his entrance, but, before he could speak the second syllable, his mouth was covered as he was accosted by the robed man standing in the shadows behind him. He was dragged a few steps back to the middle of the hallway where the two dropped down the drainage grate to just below floor level.

"Do not be afraid." Non whispered, carrying the uselessly struggling wizard across to the grate beneath Cray's room. "Everyone is being tested this night. Fate will run its course. You know he is no match for her."

Cray was advancing on Sabrena, saying "I've slayed a dragon today, now you will be my prize."

He reached out to wrangle the young woman and

she struck him across the face, the hand imprint sizzling and steaming in a freezing burn.

"I am no one's prize!" Sabrena roared furiously. Her body began to turn a frosty white hue and layers of shining ice crept up from her feet. She stomped Cray's toes with one of her glassy feet and the ice spread, freezing his leg to the ground and immobilizing him.

Enraged, Sabrena took a step back as the frost climbed across her face and she raised her hand to strike with the spear of ice forming there. Cray had fallen back and his arms and legs froze to the ground, rendering him helpless.

"Ugh, you aren't worth it." Sabrena muttered in disgust, turning away to leave as she gradually reverted to her normal form.

As Cray squirmed and pulled at his frozen bonds, a mischievous snicker came from the shadows.

"Who's there?" His voice shuddered, his eyes darting about the shadowy chamber.

"Our guests have arrived!" The small voice giggled as the door crept open.

The starving prisoners had huddled together, wandering in the dark underground, seeking a way out after being freed from their chains. The last thing they expected was to turn a corner and find a warmly lit room with a plump, freshly-roasted pig on the floor. Yet there it was, fruits piled up around it and smelling irresistibly delicious. If any of them had any suspicion about the reality of this situation it did not stop them from ravenously pouncing on the opulent pork roast and zealously ripping off chunks with their teeth.

The tiny illusionist squealed with maniacal laughter as he danced around the macabre feast, then fell into a stream of blood and was being carried down toward the drain hole. It was then that Levan realized he had dropped the vial containing the mad wizard.

Non released his hold and, with a gasp, Levan hurriedly searched his pack. He found his last unbroken vial, dumped the herbs out and held it up just in time to catch the tiny wizard within.

Replacing the glass jar in his bag, he turned away from the grisly scene as Cray's choked screams finally died out. Non stood there looking at him and Levan glared back.

"How could you just stand there and watch something like that?" Levan questioned in horrified exasperation, trying to shake the morbid scene from his head. "It is—inhuman."

"How could I?" Non inquired in return, "It was you who released the mad wizard and brought him down here. But it is neither our place nor ability to alter fate. A bit of chaos can bring us to meet our destiny. For some it is not a fortunate one, but without entropy there would be only silence."

"Nonsense," Levan growled, "this was a terrible mistake, he didn't have to die like that. You let it happen and made me watch!"

"You meant him harm yourself, did you not? He would have pushed you to it. We all are here for a reason, and will all meet a perfect end, exactly as it should be. Do not feel regret, the world is a better place without one such as him."

Levan was outraged. "I say it would be better off without you!" He snarled back.

"Opinions differ on that, little wizard," Non's voice seemed to have a hint of amusement, "but perhaps that will be your decision to make someday. I live for such fateful moments."

Levan fumed with anger but argued no further. They both knew that in this small tunnel he would have the life snatched from him long before he could finish casting a spell. He stepped cautiously past Non to the opening beneath the hall, looking up at it then back to the placid, robed figure.

"If you are done with your games, I would like to go to sleep now."

"Of course, your test was done as soon as you came down here. You've bottled the chaos and retrieved your magic. No one would ask any more of you. And the protector of dreams is with you. You will sleep soundly."

Levan leapt up to push open the grate above and prepared to hoist himself out.

"Need a lift my friend?" Non offered an outstretched hand.

"No, I've got it. And we are not friends." Levan grumbled as he hopped up to grab the ledge and pull himself out with a strained effort.

Somehow Non was already standing above him. "I call those who are working with us friends."

"Friendship is a bond of trust and love, things you would know nothing about." Levan returned gruffly.

"Everyone has their own definitions of such ephemeral ideas." Non said dismissively. "Not friends, but neither are we enemies. Have I not kept all my promises to you?"

"Hm...I suppose you have." Levan conceded him that, but he still did not trust him. "But I do not need your help."

"I know you will find the answers you seek, Levan. But when the time comes, will you be prepared to accept them? Let us face the mysteries tomorrow brings with open eyes. Farewell."

✳ ✳ ✳

Oslan pored over the documents with a furrowed brow. The dusty old maps, frayed scraps of parchment and archaic tomes seemed to only give hints about the locations of the events of which the ancient histories spoke. The candles burned low and wax crept across the table as he worked through the night, gradually refining a theory on where the boundaries of the ancient city were. A worn and faded ancient manuscript spoke of the ancestors and their forbidden magics.

The seven seals...circle of ancestors...the first to be given the seven sacred words...their souls imbued into talismans passed down to their descendants...

"What were they used for?" Oslan murmured to himself. He was so engrossed in his work that he did not notice the two figures slip into the shadowy library basement.

Only when Tor spoke did he look up with a startled flinch. "Greetings Oslan." Tor greeted him with a smile.

"Oh, hello my lord, and lady, so good to see you."

Unadel responded only with a raised an eyebrow at the foggy-headed old sage. She moved to lean against the wall near the doorway with folded arms, becoming bored enough to wish someone would try to come through that threshold uninvited.

"You as well, as always. Have you news for me?" Tor inquired, noticing the page he had brought back from the burial mound. "What have we learned?"

"Ah, so here we have a map from the earliest times on record," Oslan pointed to the sword icon and arcane symbol on the ancient parchment, "it shows the location of the sword, but the land was much different in that time."

"And where is this place today?" Tor indicated the sword on the map.

"In that time it was near the confluence of the Ir and Velumine Rivers." Oslan continued. "The Velumine has changed course since then, and we no longer see the Ir river, but, I found some dwarven survey maps that chart the underground river flowing north of the city, which I believe is what the ancients called Ir, and which still meets the Velumine at the top of Karikoss, underground. It appears there were no mountains here then, the ground seems to have greatly risen in our time. I believe the sword to be beneath the city, almost directly below the castle."

"The underground is a maze of tunnels. An old map will be of no use." Unadel commented from the shadows.

"Ah, I have the dwarves' map of the mine, sewer

and caves, it should show a way to the old city, but..." Oslan produced the scroll covered in a mess of multicolored lines and blobs, "I reached a dead end trying to decipher it."

"Hmm..." Tor studied the strange map for a moment, then looked to Unadel. "Where is that dwarf that went with us to burial mound? Perhaps he can make sense of this."

Unadel shrugged. "He went with that wizard kid."

"Ooh, umm..." Oslan scratched his head. "You might find him at the Shadow's Rest, from the central sewer tunnel, left then—"

Unadel cut him off. "We know the way."

"Oh, good luck then, and please proceed with caution." Oslan bid them farewell with concern. He did not feel they had enough information to go searching yet, but there was no slowing down the headstrong Veldgar heir.

"Thank you, Oslan, and we certainly will." Tor said as he turned to leave. "Your contribution will not be forgotten."

❋ ❋ ❋

In the morning, Ranser went to check on Jofon.

"Father?" He called, opening the door, but there was no reply. Jofon lay on his back, eyes shut and motionless. "Oh no...no!"

Ranser rushed to Jofon's side in despair and tried to shake him awake. "Jofon...father..." He wept as he realized Jofon was finally gone.

Why didn't I stay with him? Why? Goodbye father...

Levan was standing at the door when Ranser opened it. He did not need to see in the dark to know what had happened. He noticed the blood and shredded flesh on Ranser's hands as he shut the door.

"Your hands are wounded." Levan said as he knelt beside Ranser.

The young sailor looked down at his palms, calloused from years of life at sea, torn and bloodied from sliding on those rusty chains. "Jofon's hands would not have bled."

Levan produced a dab of healing salve and shared it with Ranser. As he rubbed it in his hands he spoke solemnly.

"He would say: I won't always be here to do this for you. He knew he was dying. That's why he spoke to me that way last night. We had only just found each other…and he's already gone."

Levan placed a reassuring hand on Ranser's shoulder. "He is still with you. He *is* you, and you are him, and everyone else. Our lives are all connected in an eternal cycle, like the turning of night and day. It is not an end, but a new beginning."

"If so, it is a comforting thought." Ranser said morosely. "I was lost until I found him. Now I must find my own way. What a terrible place to spend your last day. I must get him out of here."

"I can pay for the burial." Levan offered, but Ranser declined.

"No. Sailors must return to the sea. I have to find a way."

"I have an idea," Levan assured him, "we will get him back on the sea."

When they reached the main hall of the Shadow's Rest, Levan requested a burial shroud and some dried rations which he gave to Ranser. They returned to Jofon's room and wrapped him in the white cloth.

"Now," said Levan, "let's see how this works."

He opened his spell book and referred to it while he used his finger to draw the circular sigil on the floor around Jofon.

"**Optero Nimbus Perpetua**…A tiny cloud floats beside me, *forever*." He chanted the magical words and felt the powerful jolt of energy surge through him as the magical diagram flashed into sight with an ethereal glow.

From the floor condensed a thick, billowing white cloud which raised the fallen sailor to shoulder level and allowed his body to be easily floated through the air.

A stinging pain buzzed like a roused hornet's nest in Levan's head as he caught his breath at length.

Sabrena was right. It was an incredible energy draw. Almost too much. Could this be forbidden magic?

"This cloud will take him to the sea," the wizard panted breathlessly, "and beyond. As far as it goes, it will persist."

"I will take him to the north shore and set him out to sea. Thank you, Levan. Will you be all right?"

"Yes, we'll be fine," Levan replied quickly with mutual concern, "but do you realize we're being invaded from the north coast? An enemy army is there."

"I know. Whatever happens it will be all the same."

"What about our quest? And your brother?"

"Don't tell him who I am." Ranser whispered grimly. "If I return I will tell him myself."

"*If* you return? Since when does Ranser have any doubt in himself?"

"I will make my way to the sea," Ranser sighed, "but if then the tides of fate draw me in...perhaps we will meet again in the next cycle." He moved to the door and gently pushed the cloud through it.

Levan hated to see his friend so sad and was worried for his safety, but knew Ranser was very capable, and would not be dissuaded. "Good luck, my friend." He said as they exited the room.

Avus met Levan standing in the hall as Ranser walked away.

"Where's he going? Aren't we going with him?" Avus yawned and stretched.

"To the sea. He goes alone." Levan's troubled gaze followed Ranser to the end of the hall.

"Oh, have fun out there, brother!" Avus shouted, waving to him. Ranser returned a slight wave as he passed out of sight.

Levan sighed to himself, shaking his head. Ranser was determined to go alone, thus it was not imperative that Avus know his true purpose and worry himself over it. Levan decided to let the dwarf's blissful ignorance live on, and spoke no more of it to him.

Back at the Shadow's rest, Levan and Avus conferred over a plate of the tavern's specialty, brazed potatoes and glowshrooms.

"I must bring the mad wizard to the priest at the temple." Levan raised an eyebrow at Avus who was biting into one of the luminous fungi. He had never eaten anything glowing and it seemed strange, but Avus appeared to enjoy it.

"Mm? You seem all right to me." The dwarf replied while chewing.

"Not *me*." Levan took out the vial containing the tiny, flailing madman and placed it on the table. "*This* wizard."

CHAPTER 12 INTO THE BELLY OF THE BEAST

The wind was whispering in his ear again. It always spoke about him. As if two or more invisible beings were analyzing his every action. Their voices were so quiet he could barely hear them, muffled so that he could only make out the tone and inflections. He could hear them when he lay down to sleep in a dark, quiet place, though no one was nearby. Perhaps it was the cold, grey isolation of the plateau that let his mind drift away and hear them, or imagine them whispering.

"He's come back...just for that old sailor..."

"...just going to let him go? What if he doesn't come back?"

"...does he remember nothing...can he not hear us...?"

Ranser stopped walking and scanned the horizon in all directions.

"...see? I knew it...can hear us..."

Jofon's cloud kept drifting forward slowly. He was alone, of course. The mountains behind him still obscured the morning sun and the foothills were far ahead, their sparse conifers lightly dusted with snow. There was no place to hide.

"Ander..."

He continued walking on toward the end of the plateau where he could see the north shore in the distance, and determined to let nothing change his course there. Least of all some tricks his ears were playing on him.

"...leave his people...the end of our kingdom?"

"...What am I supposed to do?"

"...the sea...must send him back...nothing can save the king...Ander is our last hope."

The voices were lost in a roaring gust.

❊ ❊ ❊

A pale, copper-haired woman clad in scarred battle armor related the previous day's crushing news in desperation to the king's council. "General Eltas is dead. Our Wolf Brigade has been wiped out at Hollow Dale. We no longer hold any ground north of the city. The enemy's new weaponry is devastating! Where are our mages? Can they not be brought out from their studies to defend our people?"

"The new recruits aren't ready." Vixor, one of the elder sages pleaded, shaking his head.

"Rest assured all of our practitioners are busy at work in the protection of our kingdom." Oslan cajoled her half-heartedly.

"We need more than horses and bows now..." Belina's voice rose as she spoke. "I am telling you the Kinari are far more powerful than we thought! We cannot let them overrun our lands!"

From the shadows beside the king's throne, a man wearing a porcelain mask spoke in a low rasp. "Powerful forces *are* at work against us, my lord. We must awaken Agartha before it is too late."

Belina was incredulous, "Who is this masked man? I will not have council with him!"

"Belina..." The king pleaded apologetically for her silence.

"I have found the seventh seal." Said the masked man. "In the tunnels beneath the city. We need only send a team to retrieve it."

"Let it be done." Decreed the king.

"What!? You'd leave our troops in the field to their doom chasing fairy tales! This is unthinkable!" Belina pulled her sword and pointed it at the man in the mask, and the guards brandished their weapons nervously. "You will show your face!"

The king stood, raising his hands to pacify his enraged niece and the bristling palace guards. "Enough. Please stop this."

Belina's fist clenched and quivered on her weapon, unable to find the words for this outrage, but lowered her sword and stomped out of the room.

Back at her chamber, Belina slammed the door and began unlacing her blood-streaked bracers, grumbling in frustration to herself.

From the antechamber, two frail servant girls quietly slipped into the room, one starting to heat water for a bath, the other began to unclasp Belina's pauldrons. But she was in no mood to be coddled, nor for anyone to witness her frustration, so she snapped at her handmaids to leave her and after a moment's hesitation and an apprehensive glance, they departed without a word.

A knock came from the door. Reluctantly Belina answered and curtly received the letter from the king's courier. Scorn twisted her face as she read it.

"To my trusted subject Belina Fahfren, this imperial writ signifies your promotion to Supreme Commander of the Army. With the fall of General ForgedArm and your valor on the battlefield at Hollow Dale, the troops would follow none but you. I will have the sub-commanders notified immediately. You may pick up your inheritance, Sir Eltas' battle gear at the armory. And as my personal congratulations on your new post, I have commissioned a fine suit of crimson battle plate for your campaigns as supreme commander of our forces. The first of these missions should be our top priority, to find the one called Non. He is known to associate with the group known as the Hidden Hand which haunts the sewer system. Once again I grant my utmost praise—"

Before finishing, Belina whipped the scroll across the floor with sneer of disdain. For a moment she sat on her bunk, head in hands, torn between loyalty to her kingdom and her family, and a growing uncertainty about where it all was heading.

Does my station truly require me to put the word of the king before the lives of those brave souls who shed their blood on the battlefield beside me?

Trust in, and duty to her kingdom had always been the driving force in her life, as dependable as the sun's light. But now, to have it flicker and waver was the most unsettling feeling she had ever had. She would not be able to rest.

"A man-hunt. Is this truly a task worthy of the new commander of the army? He still thinks of me as a child…" Belina continued to mutter annoyedly to herself as she strode down the castle corridor toward the armory.

The second division was arming up for their mid-day campaigns, and some of the wounded from the morning's battle were being tended to by the medics. She was vaguely aware of many eyes tracking her across the room, and murmurs of uncertainty tinged with despair at the loss of their fallen hero.

"Ah, you're here." The quartermaster hailed her from within the storage cage.

"I was told you have something for me." Belina droned, still struggling with the idea of carrying out royal orders which she thought were unnecessary, and being expected to inspire morale in the troops.

"Yes, we mourn the loss of our commander Forgedarm, and pass his battle gear on to you. May it bear you many victories." The quartermaster handed over the battle-scarred and bloody but still-shining sword and shield which had led them into so many battles.

She found the shield to be as light as a feather, though it was thicker than her arm, encrusted with a sapphire phoenix within an etched-gold border.

The wide-bladed long sword was perfectly weighted to deliver a vicious hack or stab, yet light enough to swing in wide arcs more than twice as fast as her old blade, and sharp enough to shave with. Ripples of dark metal which snaked down the edge from the jeweled pommel radiated with many colors in the light.

There was more buzz from the troops as she held these legendary armaments.

A fair-haired young armored man wearing the badge of a lieutenant came over and saluted her. "We've received the mission plan from the king's courier. I am to bring my platoon under your command to the sewer to apprehend the fugitive. My men are ready at your will."

Belina scowled. "Lieutenant Kaden, right? There must be some mistake—you mean to bring your *entire* unit? Perhaps just a single squadron?"

"No ma'am. Our orders are clear. We are to back you with our full contingent."

"Ugh..." Belina shook her head in disgust. "What is he thinking? Sending one hundred of our fighting men into the sewers when an army is at our doorstep!"

Kaden looked around nervously, but said nothing. He had his own doubts but would never risk his promising military career on being accused of insubordination. It was the reason he was chosen for this mission.

"Let's just get this over with quickly." Belina turned and proceeded outdoors as Kaden signaled his unit and the soldiers scrambled to gather their gear and fall in line.

Outside in the courtyard, the passing armed host stirred a hawk from its nest, and it flew up over the city walls and beyond the north gate, across the great plateau where a strange cloud floated low to the ground.

* * *

Ranser's feet propelled him in single-minded determination, north toward the distant sea. The wind swept the tall grasses on this vast plain, featureless but for some smooth rounded red shapes up ahead.

As he stepped toward the clearing, something stirred in the scrub below, and a fleet of grasshoppers flittered across his path. Nearly too small to see were the tiny sprites that had leapt onto the insects' backs and fired their bows at the towering giant at the height of their leap. Ranser felt a light prickling on his forearm as the tiny arrows tipped with speckled blue mushroom caps flew up and stuck like splinters in the unprotected skin.

The hunting party of sprites cheered, catching hold of the long blades of grass as they flew by, and sliding down to the ground while watching their catch shrink and fall. But this was not their typical quarry. The hunters approached with cautious excitement.

"A man-giant!" They exclaimed in wonder.

"Quick, bring Yagi to see!"

"It looks like us! But BIG!"

"It looks dangerous. Let's bind it before it wakes up."

The tiny creatures had just finished wrapping his hands and feet in vines when Ranser awakened, sat up with a yawn and found himself in a startling new place, like a primeval jungle, its strange flat trees towering to immense heights all around and swaying in the breeze. He was then surprised by the appearance of a tiny quizzical face just before his. The little sprite, about half his size, hung from a blade of grass above his head and greeted him enthusiastically.

"Hio!"

Ranser found his hands and feet were bound by

some strong cordage. "Ah—where am I? Who are you?"

At this the sprites erupted in laughter. "It talks so strangely! *Where am I?*" They giggled mischievously as they mocked his slower, deeper tone.

"Who are you? Where am I? Hahaha!"

Some of the sprites began laughing and dancing around him, repeating his words until a distant voice halted them and commanded their attention.

"Silence!" A winged, wild-haired old sprite adorned with a feather headdress and assorted bone and fur trinkets emerged from the grass forest ahead of a large group of common sprites. "Where are the huntsmen? What have you captured?"

"Master Yagi, we've shrunk a man-giant!" The hunter took the old sprite's arm and led him to a rise in the clearing beside Ranser.

"Hail, giant." Yagi called to Ranser. "Whence came you? What sort of giant are you?"

"I am not a giant." Ranser replied. "I have departed Karikoss city to bring my father to the sea."

"The see? See what?" One of the young, brash hunters interjected. "This guy's story does not take root. I don't trust him, Yagi! I say we throw him to the toads!"

"To the sea…" Yagi beckoned to hush his child-like subjects, though their energy could only be contained for fleeting moments. "the great waters beyond the Dark Lands…"

At this point one of the sprites mistakenly though he heard the great waters were returning, and rejoiced jubilantly at the prospect of swimming, which was overheard by another sprite nearby who wanted to be sure and called out about who was going swimming, to which his wife assured him it would not be him while there was moss to be harvested and toads out there gobbling folks up. The subject of discussion branched and mutated into entirely unrelated and irrelevant subjects as it spread and rose to a cacophony of hundreds of little voices until they were again quieted by the old one raising his hand.

"You say your father is with you. There is but one man here. Are there more of you?" The elder's skeptical scrutiny was turned to wistful intrigue.

"My father is..." Ranser's voice trailed off as he realized what was missing. Then, with frantic urgency, and still in his bonds, he stood up and began hopping around, searching for his father on the floating cloud. "where is he!?"

There were gasps of astonishment from the crowd as he hopped here and there and they moved out of his way. He had looked in all directions before finally looking up to see the magical cloud floating far above, its shadow obscuring the small clearing, and realized with amazement how small he had become. He was somewhat outraged, but greatly relieved he hadn't lost Jofon.

"Oh..." Looking up, Ranser breathed a sigh of relief. "There you are, father."

The sprites exchanged bewildered glances and whispers. "His father is the cloud?"

Ranser struggled at his bonds. "Unbind me. I mean you no harm. I must continue my journey."

"Hmm..." Yagi stroked his beard thoughtfully. "I am inclined to do so, of course, we will set you free, we are not savages. But we are in great peril here and I believe you are the one who can save us at long last. It was thirty years ago that the rivers changed course and the Toad King came to take over our ancestral home in the Bloodshroom Forest." One of the sprite children cowered behind his mother at the mention of that dreaded monster.

"Our warriors fought valiantly, yet our arrows could not pierce their armored hide, and many were lost. The Bloodshrooms were our food, our shelter, our very lifeblood, the source of our strength, and are only to be found in what is now the Toad King's domain. Before the last of us had starved, I found a way to use the little poisonous blue Skyshrooms to hunt the great beasts of the plain. Thus we survived by eating what was never meant for us. But we found that defying nature had its own terrible consequences. Lost in the new generation were our survival instincts, the strength and cleverness of our ancestors, and our wings."

One of the sprites had approached Ranser in fascination and cooed in awe at the dagger hanging from his belt.

"Whoa, look at this weapon! Surely this can kill the Toad King!" The little creature raised his palm to the blade's tip and recoiled as it drew blood. "Ow!"

"Yes, Grundit," Yagi continued, "thanks to the hunters and our new guest, our salvation may finally be at hand."

"If I agree to help you, you'll release me?" Ranser asked skeptically.

"Yes."

"And if I decide to depart and continue my own quest?"

Yagi smiled and shook his head. "Be assured, you will never reach the sea at your present stature. Even if there were no dangers between here and there, you will have walked a hundred years before ever leaving this valley, and yet more lifetimes to traverse the Dark Lands of the forest beyond. Only the power of the Bloodshrooms can return you to your original size. So you see, all of our fates rest on the hope of reclaiming the Bloodshroom Forest. Will you help us?"

"Fine," Ranser sighed, "show me to this frog you want dealt with."

Yagi called out to his subjects. "Peblin, Reed, Jaeger, to the lookout point! The rest of you, go back to the village and make ready for war!"

The sprites released Ranser's bindings and headed off to follow the Yagi.

As the crowd dispersed, one young sprite maiden inquired of a nearby mother carrying a child. "What is war?"

"Just a game the boys play."

"A game huh..." Jade's eyes sparkled with intrigue.

"Our place is to look after the babies." The sprite mother hefted her child and walked on through the grassy forest. "Come along Jade, dearie."

Ugh, babies, I hope I never have one attached to me. I want to go to this 'war'. I'll beat the boys at their own game!

❅ ❅ ❅

Levan had studied healing arts at the temple, thus he did not share Avus' reaction of surprise at the temple grounds and the building itself.

"Whaaat...in hells is this place?" Asked Avus as they strolled past rows of graves toward a great stone cathedral, its flying buttress arms splayed out like a massive petrified squid, crowned with sharp spires jabbing skyward.

"Temple of Agartha. Never been?" Levan gestured ahead nonchalantly.

"No," Avus frowned, "no, but somehow it seems familiar. What a strange sensation."

"It is meant to be awe-inspiring," Levan said, "Agartha's grace fills our world with magnificent and wondrous magic."

"To me it's just creepy..." Avus could not shake the feeling that something was wrong about this place. "these stones...they don't want to be here. The worms, they do not consume the soil. The spiders...won't climb on the walls, nor crows roost at the roof. These *stones*..."

They reached a set of tall doors beneath a pair of twin spires that Avus thought were entirely too tall and seemed to glare threateningly down at him. The feeling of dread repulsed him and he could go no further. The walls were dripping blood.

"Well, you don't need me here, I'll wait for you back at the uh..." Avus was sweating anxiously as he pointed downward, "Tavern."

"Very well, I'll get back to you. See if you can find someone from the Hidden Hand, I'm sure they know more than we do, but don't trust them for one moment." Levan bid Avus farewell.

The dwarf could not contain his haste to depart. He had witnessed the eternal mourning of those ancient stones, they wept with the blood of his ancestors. Avus ran out of that place of death as quickly as he could.

The young acolyte entered the temple. He made his way down the dark, cool hall toward the transept as he had done many times before, his footsteps echoing off the polished stone as they traversed the long bands of light and shadow cast from the tall windows.

Two priests in white and gold robes appeared to be praying at a statue of Agartha, one of several in the vicinity which they regularly spent a few moments anointing. They exchanged a few imperceptible syllables as Levan approached, unaware they were talking about him. The sage Herodus finished his ritual and turned to greet the new arrivals. The other robed figure continued his ceremony in a whisper.

"This man is cursed." Levan held up the bottle. "I've recovered him from the wizard Merton in the tome of records."

"So," The old cleric named Herodus scrutinized him, "you've killed this wizard, Merton?"

"No, he asked me to find a priest to help lift the curse. So, here."

Levan held out the vial with the mad, shrunken wizard inside, but Herodus recoiled and did not take it.

"An infernal aura surrounds you," the old man said. "It must be dispersed with care. I am long beyond my years of demon-banishing. But fortune seems to favor you this day, Sage Tosgan is with us. If he can spare a moment, you may see miracles happen."

Tosgan turned from the statue and spoke with a

bemused grin. "It is only by the grace of Agartha can we be cleansed and resurrected. I am merely a messenger."

"Good day, Master Tosgan!" Levan was shocked to see his teacher, the de facto leader of the wizardry college and perhaps the strongest magic user alive suddenly wearing the robes of the priesthood.

To the common folk the two groups seemed to work hand in hand, the wizardry and the temple order both use the powers they gain from their connection to the goddess. But the insider knows the two have fundamentally differing views about how magic should be used, and thus an intense rivalry. Tosgan had always been outspoken about the corruption and deception of the temple of Agartha. Perhaps they had finally bridged the divide.

"Levan, my brightest star. Of course I will help you. A dark spirit is upon your back. Let me make you rid of it." His gaunt-faced, dark-eyed teacher offered a handshake, and grasped the vial.

As he grasped Levan's hand, Tosgan stepped into a prism of memories, floating through a gallery of crystals which reflected the young wizard's experiences, feelings and thoughts. The haunted jewel was easy to spot, not two days hence, it fumed with a foreign energy. As he approached it, a fluorescent fog spewed out, flashing with green and violet flares, and materialized into the form of the impoverished family man turned spy cutthroat who was disintegrated after attacking the wizard that day.

"I've failed." The apparition moaned. "My report and I were turned to ash before I could deliver it. Please say you'll send the payment to my family anyway. My poor starving children..."

"You have served your purpose." Tosgan spoke in finality to the spirit. "As for your family, they will never know you relinquished your humanity and your life for them. I hope that they will not meet with the same fate as you." The enraged spirit lunged toward him, roaring and grasping at his throat. "Keep moving down until you see the light, from there Agartha will take you." Tosgan reached up to make contact with the ghostly haze and a blinding flash erupted from it, blasting away the spirit into a shower of shimmering particles which fell down and seeped out of Levan's psyche.

He moved past the foggy, crystallizing scenes of memory until another captured his attention. His eyes darkened, and the wrinkles in his face grew deeper as the old wizard stopped to view the nomadic teachers at the campfire.

Could they be…the ancestors?

The man in furs reversed his gaze from the tree line and seemed to look directly at Tosgan. But that could not be. He was merely observing a memory of the past.

Among the trees in the distant night, a beastly shadow stalked with a snort.

Tosgan's intrigued gaze became a gape of shocked horror as the gigantic brown bear had seen him, and came charging at him with a harrowing roar. Before he could react, the beast was upon him, felling him under one of its claws and gaping to finish him with a bite to the neck. But just before the bear's fangs pierced him, Tosgan raised his arm holding a lustrous orb of obsidian which pulsed with energy and enveloped him, transporting him instantly out of the memory warp.

Could this be the protector dreams?

"The restless spirit connected to you has been released." Tosgan declared, slightly out of breath. "We thank you for your service to the Goddess…by the Queen of Heaven's grace, this old one will be restored."

Levan felt a peculiar sense of indulgence in the recognition by this most esteemed of wizards, and the bishop who commended him, and for the first time seriously envisioned himself as one of these highest order of spiritual and magical leaders. Someone everyone looked up to for answers, whose wisdom was without question. "I consider it among my duties. What are the wizards doing next?"

"Your classmates are preparing for the defense of

our kingdom," Tosgan placed a hand at his back to usher Levan to the exit, "I was just on my way to check on their progress, shall we?"

Levan nodded and was hurried toward the door. The old man had a surprisingly fast walking pace.

The priest Herodus called out as they left. "Try to bring them back in one piece next time."

✳ ✳ ✳

The sprites' lookout point was a dirt mound at the top of a ridge overlooking a clearing dominated by some huge, blood-red mushrooms. The giant, crimson-capped spires of the Bloodshroom thicket loomed in the distance, a towering fortress of fungus. On their wide red brims, dark green blobs hopped in and out of sight.

"The Kingdom of the Toads." Yagi presented, but Ranser's attention had turned to the horde of ants that emerged from the ant hill they stood on.

They were the biggest bugs he had ever seen and their numbers were beginning to be alarming as they poured out of the top of the mound. Ranser pulled his blade as they closed in but Yagi stopped him.

"Don't be alarmed." The old sprite pulled a wad of moss from his pouch and granted it to the eager mandibles of a nearby ant who scurried away with it. "The ants are good people. Ones with respect for other sentient creatures. They are our friends."

"Not like those ugly green croakers that ate my dad!" Jaeger fired an arrow toward the toads in anger. It disappeared in the distance.

Ranser turned back to the Bloodshroom Forest. "How many toads are there?"

"At least one hundred." Yagi replied gravely.

"And how many fighters can you gather among the

sprites?"

"Perhaps one-hundred and forty, it is not enough to...but perhaps with you—"

"TOAD!"

Reed was caught off guard and nearly crushed as the massive creature bounded to the top of the hill. The toad stood as tall as Ranser and twice as wide as that.

The ants immediately swarmed in on the hulking creature, covering it in a crawling, furious mass of individuals who behaved like one, stabbing and ripping with their rock-crushing mandibles. But their teeth could not pierce its glistening, leathery hide, those that crawled under it were crushed, and only caused a slight irritation around the eyes.

Almost too fast to be seen, the toad's long sticky tongue lashed out, sticking to the ant biting at its eyelid and swallowing it. It took several more of the frantic insects into its over-sized mouth with the next lash and hopped again, making a ground-shaking thump and flattening several ants.

The sprite hunters came in from the sides shouting their war cries. Reed and Peblin ran as fast as they could, jabbing their thorn spears into the toad's flanks, while Jaeger swung in from above, landing on its back, and trying to make his way to the head and eyes. But he was flung off and landed just in front of the toad. Its eyes tracked the annoying little bug as it fell and mouth crept open to devour it as it pounced among the chaotic throng of ants.

Ranser noticed Jaeger about to be swallowed up and shouted "Look out!" as he sprinted a few paces and launched himself into a tackle to narrowly avoid the giant pink tongue that would whisk them off to a swift death.

Jaeger tumbled and fell near a patch of the blue skyshrooms that the sprites used for shrinking prey, and clutched them as the next tongue strike came before he could even get up. Ranser tried to dive and grab his hand was too late. Jaeger's wide-eyed gaze met Ranser's just before he was flung into the creature's mouth holding the armful of mushrooms.

The toad squinted, gnashed and spat out the poisonous blue fungus in disgust, along with the sprite Jaeger, and soon began shrinking to about half of its original size.

Now the sprites were able to flip the creature over onto its back and attempt to make a wound in its somewhat less durable underside. This was accomplished with ease by Ranser's knife. He cut deeply into its neck and at last the creature lay still. The sprites cheered exuberantly, dancing on the overturned toad's belly.

Yagi returned to the top of the mound. "Well, that was easy enough, right?" He chuckled in amusement.

"Saved only thanks to our overwhelming numbers, and those blue mushrooms." Ranser replied, considering the daunting task ahead.

"We can beat them." Yagi was self-assured, perhaps only to keep the others from despair.

"It will not be easy," Ranser spoke apprehensively, "but I think I have a plan."

❉ ❉ ❉

Belina led her troops through the main sewer entrance, splitting the rest of the group among the four other exits. They met around the circular cistern known as the Shadow's Rest, covering all of its entryways with tightly-packed rows of armored knights.

At first Avus did not see the commanders and their entourage enter from either side. The man sitting next to him at the bar had said to wait here, that someone wanted to meet with him. Since then, he had been loudly relating his disdainful views on the city guards to that man and whoever else would listen while quaffing an ale, when he realized the man had left in the middle of his speech.

"Hello? Where's everybody going?"

He saw the host of armed troops then, and was certain they had come for him. He figured he had just enough time to finish his tankard while the rest of the tavern-goers buzzed about trying to escape the guards.

The soldiers gathered around the exits, stopping just before the narrow stone bridges leading to the inner platforms.

"We come for the one known as Non!" The female commander at the front shouted with wrathful authority. "By order of the King, surrender yourself immediately!"

A gaunt, wild-eyed man in rags took off running and met the tall, armored woman at the end of the bridge. She slammed her shield across the man's nose, dropping him to his knees.

"Is that him?" Belina indicated the kneeling man with the bloodied face.

"No." The armored informant pointed to the lower platform where a robed figure stood still among the commotion. "There."

As she passed, Belina elbowed the kneeling man, her bracer slicing his head again. Though she was barely controlling her rage, it was a merciful move, as a pommel strike to an unprotected skull, especially with this sword, would have been a deathblow. The man toppled into the dark stream of rainwater and sewage below, but would survive.

Some of the tavern-goers leapt into the water to swim away. Others tried to run past the guards and were wrestled to the ground. The rest of the crowd parted and moved back as the soldiers advanced into the Shadow's Rest.

A few men near Non drew daggers and attacked the contingent that entered nearest them. One soldier was knocked to the ground and his attacker pressed a blade beneath his helmet before he was cut down by the others.

Non stood still as a statue even as the fighting was so close that his robe was splattered with blood.

A burly soldier fought off two attackers and was heaving his claymore wildly in a blind rage. His final swing was caught just short of cutting into Non, and his sword and arm were jerked downward with a bone-snapping crunch before the massive armored hulk was hurled overhead like a rag doll, splashing into the water. The troops nearby saw this and rushed in on him. Despite the calls of their commanders not to kill him, they meant to stop this fugitive immediately.

Belina was still crossing the middle of the room as she witnessed the chaotic mob attack.

Surrounded by armored knights intent on ending his life, somehow this man was unassailable. Non turned their own blades against them, sidestepping almost imperceptibly to cause one soldier to hack into another, catching the next sword and hurling it out in a deadly spinning arc. The robed figure caught hold of an arm and swung its owner around, knocking back the others before releasing him to fly across the room and slam into the stone wall. Another rushed in to tackle him but was also caught and thrown to the high cistern ceiling. He landed in the water after a long fall, but the impact had knocked him unconscious, thus it was his final battle.

The soldiers then kept a cautious distance around Non, realizing the necessity to respect his bewildering power.

Avus, still seated at the bar, was cheering at first for the king's men, since he wanted to see Non beaten. Yet he couldn't help but laugh at their feeble attempts to subdue him. He was thoroughly entertained with the spectacle, but it ended unexpectedly.

Non faced Belina as she approached. "Ah, Belina. My, how you've grown up."

"I do not know you, or why the King requests your presence." Belina sneered with indignation. "Perhaps you can beg a pardon for killing his men. I am here to bring you in, let there be no more bloodshed."

"Of course, my lady." Non replied calmly. "If only they had not attacked me, they would have come to no harm.

I have a proposition for our liege as well, let us go then."

Non held out his wrists willingly to be shackled. Belina nodded to a nearby soldier who had brought chains. He approached hesitantly, and latched the cuffs on the dangerous fugitive. Belina took hold of the trailing chain with a stern gaze at Non.

"Move out!" Belina's order echoed across the high stone walls and the armed force drained out of the subterranean cavern with a clamor, their prisoner in tow. She made her way swiftly back toward the castle, finally understanding why the entire unit was needed for this capture, and hoping Non would not have a change of heart about being taken in willingly.

When the last of the troops passed overhead and left the tunnel, Unadel pushed back the metal grate and climbed out of the recess in the floor. Tor, disguised in a cloak and hood, followed behind her. At the threshold of the tavern they scanned the nearly empty room.

"Huh, he's still here." Unadel smirked in mock suprise, nodding toward the dwarf still seated at the bar.

They rolled the parchment out before Avus who immediately recognized it.

"Ah yes, a survey map." The dwarf examined the map. "This looks like Brimwald's version but...what is this down here?" Avus lifted the transparent pages layered atop it which showed the various descending levels of the caverns to the lowest chamber beneath the city. A large red blob of fluctuated shades indicated a huge uneven chamber at the bottom, bifurcated by a subterranean river at an average depth of 300 dwarves' height. "How can I not have known of this chamber? It is enormous..." His brow furled in puzzlement as he flipped the previous page down. "But the level above does not connect. How is it accessed?"

"Perhaps this can help?" Tor produced the tattered page from the burial mound. The outline of the old city on it matched the shape of the cavern, and showed the location of the river's confluence, down from the DeepRiver Hall, allowing Avus to infer the connection point as he placed it over the dwarven map.

"Yes. I know this tributary, beyond the DeepRiver Hall." Avus could see the stone crevasse into which the stream disappeared. "I thought it impassable. It is a narrow gap. Flooded, caved in, crawling with scarlings. If you even make it that deep, there lies certain death."

"We didn't expect it to be easy." Tor replied with a smile.

"Well," Avus sighed, rolling up the map as he stood, "can't have you going and getting yourself killed with no chance of success. You wouldn't make it far without a dwarf. Let's go get this sword of yours."

"I am perfectly capable of keeping him safe." Unadel retorted disdainfully. "Now that we know how the map works, you may be on your way to your next drink."

"Of course you are." Tor said to Unadel before Avus could respond. "But there is someone else I want you to look after now. The linguist Rotocles needs an escort to the lighthouse cove near Agypto on the northern shore. He has learned the Kinari language and will be our translator and emissary. The ship awaits your arrival to depart. Make sure no harm comes to him on the way, Avus and I will find the Mountain Maker."

Unadel was speechless in incredulity for a moment as she voiced a weak protest. "But…"

"Please, don't worry about me." Tor embraced her shoulder. "We do what must be done."

"Yes…be careful." Unadel held back tears she did not fully understand.

"I will. You do the same. Farewell."

CHAPTER 13 THE WAY TO WAR

Tosgan led Levan through the laboratory and spiral stairway climbing to his darkened chamber. A white light faded in around the top of its walls which were lined with bookshelves, upholstered couches, tapestries painted with mystical symbols, and polished oak root tables with various glassware, one of which held a bouquet of white flowers.

"We knew you were a descendant the day you were found," Tosgan diverted Levan's attention with his commendation, "how you have mastered so many schools of magic so quickly is still a matter of some debate."

"I dunno, heh…" Levan chuckled sheepishly, "I just feel the words."

"Of course there's more to it than that." Tosgan replied, bemused. "Your teachers have helped to hone your skills, as well as your access to the Vimanticon."

"Certainly, I am eternally grateful for your mentorship, master, and all the teachers. Even I can hardly believe my own capabilities."

"This will project your power even further." Tosgan approached the bookcase on the left wall and pulled back a tome there, which unlocked a hidden latch. A secret door opened up to a wardrobe stocked with hats, robes, staffs, and wands. "I've saved these for you."

He handed Levan a blue hooded robe, a pointed,

wide-brimmed leather hat and a carved staff of dark, fragrant cedar with a clear jewel set into the top. The crystal seemed to cloud with a smoky bluish haze as he took the staff.

"These trappings are but aesthetics, the hat, robe, stick." Tosgan explained. "The tears of Agartha we hold in our staves are what draw out and focus our powers. I know you will use it for great works in the service of the Goddess and our kingdom."

Donning the new garb, Levan felt invincible, powerful, respected. "I am ready."

The two made their way downstairs to the court-yard behind the tower. There, a strong gust of air and a crackling boom signaled the beginning of a battle between two young wizards Levan had known from school, Kalvas and Umber.

Kalvas unleashed a cold whirlwind which sucked the heat from the air, creating sparks along the wall of the vortex and scattering the rocks and earth which Umber was drawing up around him.

Umber shielded his face from the blast and again called up his protective shell from the ground. Packed soil and stones crept up from the ground, covering his body with a rocky armor.

Kalvas summoned up a current of dense, rising air beneath him, and began to float just as Umber slammed his fists down, quaking and sundering the ground beneath him, which spread forth in a wide, jagged fault-line, jutting a swath of sharp stones upward, but crested short of reaching and crushing his levitating adversary.

A few muffled words were spoken as Umber beck-oned the ground to rise up and form an earthen golem twice his height. Kalvas flew higher to avoid its grasp and swirled his staff above him, building the intensity of the growing storm. The golem hoisted a massive boulder from the ground and hurled it at the hovering wizard which would have hit and knocked him out of the sky if Kalvas had not made a quick altitude adjustment.

The clouds he had summoned turned dark, churning and pulsing with energy. Turning his staff downward, a tendril of lightning blasted down onto the golem, exploding it with a brilliant flash and a shower of glassy pebbles.

Umber brought up four huge pillars of stone around him which channeled the subsequent lightning bolts harmlessly into the ground. The wind continued to rise into a ferocious tornado with his classmate floating at the center, tearing away at his rocky shell.

A few of the elder sages were also nearby spectating.

"Keep going, Kalvas!" Vixor yelled to him. "Show us your full power!"

The storm roared ever louder. Umber struggled to hold fast in the relentless tempest tearing up the ground around him and scattering it in the air as his armor continued to disintegrate. He fired more stone spears up but they were shattered and deflected away. At last the fierce winds overpowered Umber and he was flung up into the vortex, flailing and screaming as he was electrocuted and battered by flying debris.

The winds calmed and both wizards returned to the ground, Kalvas with an expression of shock and worry as he looked to where Umber fell. The other boy was face-down on the ground, his limbs twisted and crumpled, unmoving.

Tosgan approached, turned him over, and placed his hands across his chest. He whispered a blessing and touched the fallen sorcerer's forehead. Umber awoke with a gasp, then quickly passed out again as a pair of priest acolytes carried him off.

"Fantastic!" Vixor applauded his apprentice Kalvas as he made his way to the sidelines.

"Bah, bad matchup, hardly a fair fight." Umber's mentor Oslan scowled.

"Oh ho, the prodigy arrives," Vixor smirked as he saw Levan, "late, as usual. Well, let's see what you've learned."

"He will be alright?" Levan was fairly sure his teachers would not risk their deaths in training, but he wanted to be sure. "The healers will revive him, right?"

"Yes, of course." Tosgan assured him, ushering Levan forth to the dueling area, saying "Now it's your turn. Prove yourself, don't hold back."

A herald with a brass bugle called out "No casting until the sounding of the horn. You are responsible for any and all collateral damage! Bring forth the next challenger!"

Levan was surprised and dismayed when his opponent appeared.

"Ah...I can't." He sighed anxiously as they faced each other.

"Just do it," Sabrena growled irritably, "don't make us both look bad."

"I don't want to hurt you." Levan pleaded.

"What makes you think you can?" Sabrena's eyes gleamed as the horn sounded.

Before Levan could react, she blasted him with a globe of frigid water which quickly froze as it spread across his hands and arms, locking them together.

The air around Sabrena began to cool and water vapor condensed into a glimmering sheen across her skin, solidifying into layer upon layer of icy armor.

Levan ignited his hands and shattered the ice on them, then evoked a wall of flame around him just as Sabrena hurled a rippled scatter of icy missiles. A cloud of hot steam blasted through the wall and seemed to linger in the increasingly foggy air.

She charged forward, encased in ice, pushing a shield of water in front and barreling through the wall of intensely hot flames. It melted her frozen shell so that instead of a rock-hard maul of ice, Levan was hit with only a warm wall of water.

"I wish you wouldn't test yourself this way." Levan said, as he puffed a gust of air upward beneath himself and vaulted high into the air, to the gasps and cheers of some of the spectators. Kalvas rolled his eyes and cooed in mocked amazement.

The gust pushed Sabrena at the back and she tumbled forward into her own wave. Again they were both unharmed, except for her pride. Impressing the leaders at this exhibition was of utmost importance to Sabrena.

Levan landed at the other side of the courtyard, indecisive about what to do next.

Summoning portals would be a bad idea, can't control them. I don't want to torch her, don't think that can be healed.

The water on the ground evaporated back into the air in a dense fog obscuring his view.

Lightning spreads through water. Perhaps a static touch can incapacitate her.

Levan's hands and staff sparked with energy as his eyes darted around searching for the incoming attack, and listening, though the fog seemed to dampen the sound of her approach as well.

A wave of water washed back in across his feet, rising as it rushed forward, and Levan saw the shadow approaching in time to wade out of her path. Sabrena rode the crest of the wave with a lance of ice extending from her wand, which barely missed impaling him.

He reached out his arcing staff to contact her shoulder, and was stunned when the electricity retreated from the water and could only move back through him. The jolting shock caused him to be thrown back and drop his staff.

"Hahaha!" Sabrena laughed as Levan recovered his staff and stood back up. "These are pure waters, which even lightning cannot pass! Where is your candle, fire-boy? Haha, I will douse you!"

She rose high on a wave surge, the top of which was freezing into a massive iceberg beneath her.

Levan tried to move but found the water frozen around his feet. He hesitated again. He was no longer sure he could hurt her, and didn't want to find out. He gripped his staff tightly and braced for the impact as the huge spinning chunk of ice loomed overhead.

At last the wave fell and inundated him. He was pounded to the ground and swiftly encased in a glassy mountain of crystal-clear ice.

Vixor muffled a giggle. "So much for your prodigy."

"He is not attacking her." Tosgan shook his head in disapproval. "It is only his first duel. He will learn—but look, he is not finished yet."

Levan had exhaled just enough to form a small cavity at his face into which he could speak spells, and though he could only wiggle his fingers a tiny bit, it was enough to bring forth a weak flame. This melted a slightly greater area for movement but gushed water in and was extinguished and he was forced to reach upward to breathe. He found he could not summon flame in this thick, airless liquid, and his other magics were surely not powerful enough to break it.

He imagined himself being carried away by the medics before long, and tried to reassure himself that they would revive him. But he was all alone in a prison of ice and his limbs were going numb.

What if they couldn't get to me in time? Can one really be healed from drowning? What if they just bury us and make up lies about where we went?

As the waters crept up to choke him, he uttered in desperation the word which Sabrena had taught him, along with something a wizard might use to create a campfire.

"**Ignus Perpetua…**Burn—Forever!"

Within the iceberg, a piercing light erupted from the jewel atop Levan's staff and set it ablaze. Wild magical energy poured like a whirlpool into that place. The extreme heat of the burning staff vaporized the water inside so quickly that the steam exploded the outer layers of ice with great force, causing Sabrena, who was still standing high atop the mountain of ice, to be thrown further upward and lose hold of her wand. Not that she needed it to use magic, but perhaps to affect a strong enough water spell to prevent injury from such a long fall.

Levan picked himself up from the shattered ice and stumbled over a few steps, testing his footing, bracing with a wide stance and wafting a bit of aerial assistance upward to slow her fall and finally catch her before she hit the ground.

"See, I will not hurt you." Levan smiled as he cradled her.

"Put me down!" She yelped and wriggled as he set her on her feet. "Gods, you *idiot*! Why would you use it here? Yep, here they come."

Tosgan and the other teachers were yelling and signaling "Stop, stop!" "The match is over!" as they ran towards them. "What *was* that, Levan!?"

Sabrena gave Levan a look that was meant to say: "You better lie, for both our sake."

The first of the group rushing in from the sidelines stopped at a glowing fissure in the ground where the staff had fallen. It melted through the top soil and was slowly sinking deeper, still burning brightly.

"Levan, what have you done!?" Tosgan panted, after a sprint ahead of the others.

"Ah, just a campfire, you know." It was true for the first word anyway. "I don't know how it got that hot. Sorry about the staff."

Tosgan laughed mirthfully. "No, it's quite alright. You are truly my greatest apprentice. Lie to them, not to me." He glanced back over his shoulder as the old sages representing the king's council made their way over to them with some difficulty on the broken terrain.

"Don't move! Don't go anywhere!" Oslan, secret member of the Hidden Hand shouted as he scrambled toward them.

Vixor was the last to realize it and the first to say it. "He—he used forbidden magic! This is Permanence, the word of the Second Seal!" He called out as he started running toward them. "The penalty is death! Call the guards!"

"No!" Tosgan growled at him. "Don't you see his potential!?"

"As a weapon?" Oslan, interrupted argumentatively, "Yes. How much bloodshed do you require? He must be confined and studied!"

"In your jails? Or your library basement? What would the Hidden Hand want with him, hm?" Tosgan sneered with disdain. "Yes, I know all your little secrets, Oslan."

"Why would I be associated with some gang of street thugs? You must be mad." Oslan shot back for the sake of those that were close enough to hear, and didn't already know.

Four armored guards appeared at the gate to the courtyard and began to move in.

Belina had just relinquished Non to the jailer and happened to notice through a high window the scene unfolding behind the wizard's school. She rushed down to the courtyard, her personal guards trailing behind, struggling to keep up.

"Hold on, there!" She shouted as the guards approached to arrest them. "What is the meaning of this?"

"My lady, this wizard has been witnessed using the sealed magics." Vixor indicated Levan.

"Oh, *him*." Belina scowled at him and then Sabrena. "I thought they came for you."

"I wouldn't want your help if they did!" Sabrena scoffed.

"You need to go home, Mom and Dad are worried sick!" Belina chided her.

"Ugh, they know I won't be back until they change. Can I go now?" Sabrena scanned the group in annoyance.

"Yes, have a rest, we'll send for you later." Tosgan

dismissed her.

"Wait, wait!" Belina ran to meet her sister near the eastern gate, and they spoke in a hushed tone. "Is this that spell again—the one the servant boy used? You taught it to him?"

"I needed it, it saved both our lives." Sabrena sighed scornfully. "Why would you keep such secrets hidden away? I suppose you'll have him executed like Edward."

"No," Belina whispered, "we need him...will you be on the field with the others tomorrow?"

"Of course."

"You'd better not get yourself hurt," Belina began as Sabrena turned to walk away. "I'm sending Jags and Wade to look out for you, along with their squads."

"Remind them to keep their distance." Sabrena's voice trailed off as she rounded the building out of sight.

Belina returned to the wizards. They were now surrounded by soldiers, many of the same just back from the skirmish underground who weren't close enough to do any fighting, and were itching to use their weapons. Spears were brandished on every robed figure there, including Vixor who was pleading that he was the one who called them.

"No one resist, we are taking this one." Belina declared as she approached Levan and was handed a set of shackles.

"Resist? I wouldn't dream of it." A grin crept across Tosgan's face. "We all trust in the king's judgment."

Levan was considering that he should express some sort of protest when his hat was knocked off and his head covered in the dark shroud of the condemned as he was quickly rushed away.

＊ ＊ ＊

The jailor and palace guards led Non into the council chamber, occupied only by the monarch and his masked advisor.

"My liege, I am honored to be granted an audience." Non smirked mischievously.

Fahfren stood and scrutinized the captive. "I remember you. The pauper boy, living in the sewers, son of a witch, but without magical talent, no more than a petty thief."

"You flatter me, my lord." Non replied facetiously. "But we are not here to discuss our humble origins, are we?"

"—The time has come for us put aside our differences and join forces. I am offering a pardon to you and all of your organization in exchange for your cooperation."

"In what capacity?" Non asked, if only to illicit information from his inquisitor.

"The Mountain Maker will prove my legitimacy, and win me this war." The king's words sounded certain that he believed it. "Bring it to me, and I will remake this kingdom, and we will share in the power and glory."

"Of course, the old blade will find its way to you I'm sure." Non chuckled.

A singing arrow whistled in the distance outside.

Non's image only wavered slightly to the onlookers as time slowed to an imperceptible crawl. Unnoticed by all, he used the guard's key to unfasten his shackles and took a single great stride which propelled him forth nearly anywhere he wanted to go in an instant. His most reliable associate Garath had left the door open to his balcony overlooking Garden Street and the note on the table as expected. He returned with a satisfied smirk.

"It seems Tor Veldgar is already ahead of you." Non said as he reassumed his captive bonds. "He has a map of the old city. And an unusually strong dwarf."

"The dwarf will survive long enough to show us

the way." The masked minister stepped forth and rasped, "What of the elf, Unadel?"

"She has been dispatched to escort the linguist Rotocles, an emissary to the Kinari lands."

"That is as planned," the king replied, "Rotocles is our man, he will carry out the mission."

"But the elf may yet cause us problems." The masked man warned. "She is said to be the most cunning rogue alive."

Non raised an eyebrow in intrigue. "We shall have to see about that. I myself am a pacifist, but I believe my associate can make your problems disappear with a single arrow..."

✳ ✳ ✳

Unadel and Rotocles trudged through a desolate marsh approaching the great forest spanning the northern reaches of Lorestian. To the elves it was Avalia, their primordial homeland and birthplace of their race. The humans called it the Dread Wood for its dark and haunting appearance, and the dangerous beasts and wild spirits that were supposed to lurk within (a story encouraged by the elven forest-dwellers, who preferred to be left alone).

"Gah!" Rotocles groaned as he smacked his arm, missing a large biting insect. "Couldn't we have taken a better route—and some horses?"

"The roads are not safe, and horses cannot traverse the forest." Unadel curtly reminded the scholar. "Hurry up, and *keep quiet.*"

"I'm trying..."

Rotocles was woefully out of place in the wilderness. He was quickly fatigued from travel on foot, having to jog to keep up with the elf's walking pace as she glanced back at him impatiently. He wasn't going on this journey for Veldgar's peace treaty, or the king's odd request. What drove him was the prospect of being fully immersed in the fascinating culture which the captured invader had given him a glimpse of. He had tried to ask his elven guide about herself and her people, but she only seemed to get more irritated each time she had to tell him to be silent.

Unadel paused at the forest's edge, peering in, then whispering to Rotocles. "Come. Stay close."

Mysterious lights twinkled in the distant shadows, always appearing just at the edge of view, and blinking out before they could be focused on. Unadel pulled strips of bark and leaves from the trees as she went, folding and attaching them to one another, then turning to the bewildered Rotocles and fastening the pieces to his robe.

"What is this? What are you doing?" He thought he was whispering quietly enough but she implored his silence.

"Shh...this will keep your scent from the meat-eaters. Do not speak. Raise your arms."

Unadel lowered a hollow tree trunk onto his torso, his arms coming out through the holes in the sides.

"Really? Come now, is this completely necessary? I look preposterous." Rotocles protested, but was silenced with a steely glare. He sighed and continued to follow.

Suddenly Unadel stopped, gesturing for him to halt as she scanned the area. The forest was still and quiet as far as Rotocles was aware, having no idea they were now surrounded.

"What do you want?" She called out gruffly to the trees.

Melodic voices whispered and chimed back as the forest elves peeked out from behind the foliage. "You've brought a human here? Haha...he looks ridiculous, but at least you've managed to conceal that smell." More mischievous giggles echoed from the shadows.

"See, I told you I look silly! This—" Rotocles quipped, but was muzzled by one of Unadel's gloved hands.

"We do not come to exploit the forest," Unadel replied indignantly, "we are merely passing through. Have your games elsewhere."

"But it is not only you that passes through this day." One voice warned, while another wondered. "Her eye, does it see?"

"I know we are being tracked. I have not lost my senses."

"He is quite mad..." the chant was whispered like wind through the leaves, "...quite mad, yes...and what manner of bow has he...how very unsportsmanly."

"Enough!" Unadel barked with scorn. "I should have known you would be of no help! We continue on our own."

The voices faded into the forest, laughing and whispering, "Who is we...? Watch and see..."

"Come, quickly." Unadel pulled Rotocles forward, but halted after only a few paces. "Wait. Stand very still."

The stalker had stopped moving, but his scent, though masked with moss and roots, was very close, and the trees hummed in reaction to his presence.

The arrow made no sound as it flew like a ghostly streak of lightning and stuck into the tree in front of Unadel. She had sensed it only as it contacted her skin, drawing a single drop of blood from the skin on her neck as she narrowly evaded a pierced windpipe.

This is no ordinary assassin.

Unadel pulled a length of chain from her waist as she scanned the forest to the south, preparing for the next attack. Spotting the flicker of movement from a thicket of shrubs when the next arrow was fired, she spun the cord in a wide vertical orbit, deflecting the needle-like projectile upward into the canopy before it could strike Rotocles. In the next instant, the weighted blade on Unadel's chain whipped forth and eviscerated the shrub where the shot came from, pulling it halfway back to her on her recoil and revealing no person there, only an old bow within a tangle of spider webs.

Has he fled? No. What a peculiar trap.

As the elf took a cautious step closer, the bow suddenly disappeared as it was pulled away into the underbrush. Then she detected the tiny, nearly transparent threads strung about the branches all around.

Another arrow streaked out of the canopy from the right, and was parried in the same way, then another from behind which Unadel nearly had to dive to catch. Somehow arrows were coming from all directions, making the job of defending the linguist's life a great difficulty.

"Ah!" Unadel yelled as her arm was grazed by one of the translucent arrows, then growled to Rotocles, "Just stand still."

She leapt up to stand on the scholar's shoulders, extending a second chain weapon in her other hand, and whirling them around in intertwining helixes, the chains forming a barrier around them, shattering incoming arrows from all sides.

She caught sight of the human archer briefly during this flurry. He was covered in leaves and moss, gliding between branches and latching onto a tree trunk to nock an arrow and pluck the bowstring, which was connected to the network of webs strung between the trees and notched with arrows in such a way that several would fire at once in a rain of projectiles from all directions.

Still spinning the chains around them as the missiles flew in and were deflected away, snapping limbs and ripping chunks of bark from the trees, Unadel noticed the forest begin to react to the damage. The leaves rustled overhead, and all manner of biting, stinging insects and arachnids crept out from their burrows and fallen logs. Crickets and bullfrogs began croaking and chirping in a rising cacophony as the carpet of vermin swarmed toward them and the hanging vines and branches seemed to grow into horrific clawed hands reaching down to snatch them away.

The arrow shots had stopped and Unadel hopped back to the ground as Rotocles shook off a venomous snake that was slithering up his leg with a disgusted shudder.

"It's time to go." With a final glance around the perimeter, Unadel put her hand at the linguist's back and pushed him in the correct direction. "Run!"

While his quarry bolted away through the forest, the branch Garath held had excreted a thick, sticky sap, covering his arm. He had to use all the strength of his other arm to pull free from the dark ooze while a colony of fire ants swarmed across the sap unimpeded, covering him in burning bites. Thorny blooming vines began to twirl up his legs and entangle him, while a gang of enraged hornets stung and buzzed around his head. He hacked, swatted and brushed them off as he fled the scene.

He had missed his mark, and his targets had escaped for now, but it only sparked a festering personal determination to demonstrate his superiority before killing this impudent elf.

* * *

Levan's mind was nearly paralyzed in dread as he was abducted. Never before was he aware of his free will being taken away, and his spirit reacted strongly to it. For most of his life the world had been a kind place. He knew of injustice, but only in the past few days had he personally confronted it, and it began to create a tough callous and a slowly simmering rage within him.

There he sat, powerless, gagged, bound and blinded by the black hood in an enclosed carriage. It creaked and rumbled down rough roads, drawn by a pair of heavy draft horses whose iron shoes pounded loudly ahead through some shouts and commotion outside. They rode for a long time without interruption but for the occasional jarring dip into a rut in the road. Only at length did he realize that there was someone inside the carriage with him, and the fear of what was to happen became more immediate.

The young wizard's foot had briefly contacted her sabaton, and Belina sensed him tensing up. She removed the hood from her wide-eyed, terrified captive and spoke to him.

"Don't worry, we're all on the same side here. You are not to be executed, so long as you cooperate. You and I have a chance at redemption in defense of our kingdom. I have had to put aside my proclivities about fielding untested mages of such a young age, my own sister among them. This may be our only chance to push the invader back off our shores, lest they pour across the land in an endless wave, from whence none of our people could hide or escape."

Levan mumbled an indecipherable question into the strap over his mouth. The copper-haired woman reached across to grasp the buckle holding it in place.

"If I take this off, will you be calm and speak peacefully with me?"

He nodded emphatically in affirmation, and Belina removed the gag.

"Sabrena is coming with us?" Levan repeated his question.

"Yes, in the carriage just behind us."

"Where are we going?"

The coach came to sudden stop and Belina stood to exit. "See for yourself."

She unlocked Levan's shackles and they stepped outside.

The greater part of Lorestian's army surrounded the convoy of armored wagons in a disorganized circle after ending their march. The sight was unsettling to the young wizard. He had never been among such a great gathering of people, and these seemed to all be giants of men, steel sentinels clad in their shining plate mail, who could trample over him without even noticing.

The soldiers knew where their cohorts and leaders were, but even the officers could not help crowding around the lead carriage to observe the new commander and her conduct on the battlefield.

"Where is Kaden?" Belina called out, trying to see over the shoulders of the men around her, "MOVE!" She shouted as she pushed them out of the way, but still didn't make it very far, forgetting for a moment that she was the army leader, until her voice rang out even louder in annoyance, "FORM RANKS!"

Immediately the soldiers fanned out from the huddle into rows, and stood at attention, but the hushed, excited murmurs continued.

"Lieutenant Kaden!" She called again, and the young man approached her. "Set up our command post at the top of the hill. We'll dispatch scouts to recon the east and west fronts, but I want them back before the last units have taken position."

"Yes, ma'am."

As Kaden hurried off to carry out his orders, some sort of lewd joke involving the beautiful new commander, the battlefield and the bedroom, caused the teller and his surrounding comrades to erupt in a fit of laughter. They quieted as Belina drew near, thinking she had not heard where it came from, but she immediately stepped up to the red-faced soldier who had said it.

"A true knight shows dignity and respect," She snarled at him, "give me your sword."

The soldier handed over his weapon and Belina gave it to the standard-bearer for that unit, bringing back the flags to the shocked and embarrassed man. The flag carriers were usually young cadets who would raise colored banners at the front of each brigade to signify various maneuvers and formations, as spoken commands would not be heard above the clamor of battle. It was a dangerous but crucial assignment, and each soldier was taught to pick up and bear the flag if the banner man in front of him fell (an occurrence which was commonplace enough to be expected).

"You won't be needing this." She took the white pennant which signified surrender or retreat, and burned it on one of the torch posts which staked out their staging area.

This new commander was not one for speeches, but her actions were seen by all, and now they took her seriously, and were ready to follow her into battle.

At the crest of a rocky hill, a canvas tent had been assembled for the planning of the assault. Belina beckoned the four young wizards gathered by the caravans to follow her to it. At the precipice they could see the northern shore and the modest port town of Agypto spread out before it. The roads appeared to be barricaded but no enemy troops could be seen from that distance.

Inside the command tent, Kaden had set up a table, unfurled the map of the area, and poured a bag of pebbles onto it from the local ground, the beads of clear glass from which Agypto's famous glassware was crafted. These represented the army units. Then from his pocket he produced four colored stones and handed them to Belina who named them as she placed them in four equally-spaced quadrants on the map, starting on the western shore.

"Red, Levan. Blue, Sabrena. Green, Kalvas. Grey..." She paused looking at the short, stocky boy with disheveled hair and bits of mud encrusted on his face.

"Umber."

"Right. Grey to the east." Belina said as she placed the rock on the map.

Sabrena stepped forward to the table and disagreed condescendingly. "No." She took the blue bead and switched its position with Levan's red, closest to the shoreline. "All that water and you wouldn't put me near it? Do you know *anything* about magic?"

Belina blinked her irritation away for the moment and continued. "Each of you will be supported by an infantry brigade, swords and spears." She spread the clear beads in a diamond shape surrounding the blue stone.

"Are you *serious*!?" Sabrena was incredulous, "I don't need all this!" She dashed the soldier beads onto the ground in frustration.

"We have to work together here, I won't risk you being cut down!" Belina yelled angrily at her sister, "I have seen how dangerous their weapons are, you have no idea!"

"These people are all *dead* if you send them there!" Sabrena was now screaming even louder. "What fool put you in charge!?"

Belina sighed, "Get her out of here." She gave the stern command to the two sentry guards who gingerly pulled the enraged girl out of the tent as she hurled more spiteful words back.

"She's right though," Levan calmly explained, "we can't have anyone in front of us. I think the knights would be most effective in an inverted cone flanking me, like this." He rearranged the glass beads in a wedge formation behind the red stone. "Sabrena can take the western beach alone, her backup should be kept far from the water for their own safety, protecting her right side." He moved a line of beads south and east of the blue stone."

Belina hesitated with a grimace, but relented. "… You'd better be right, kid."

"Trust me, she can hold her own." Levan turned to Kalvas and Umber. "Can you two place troops where they won't be in danger from your magic?"

Kalvas moved his green stone to the eastern shore. "I want to be by the ocean too. The winds are righteous there. And I'll need plenty of breathing room." He moved the jumble of beads around him away from the coast. Belina spread them in a long line southward to enclose the town.

"Hmm," Umber contemplated a moment, then lined up his contingent in rows to his sides, "the ground will become impassable as I advance."

"Interesting…" Belina studied the map, moving the grey rock behind the main line and sliding it side to side, "why not make a line behind us when we've moved ahead, that no surprise attack could happen from the rear?"

"I can do that." Umber nodded.

"Excellent." Belina looked up at them with a grave expression. "Listen, we expect the dock area to be the Kinari headquarters, and for them to fight to the death for it. I am telling you now, and you must warn my sister, do not approach their machines. Destroy them from afar or give them a wide berth."

"I will destroy the machines," Levan began, "I have seen the despicable things myself. But I…I am no killer."

Belina was about to explain again how all of this was necessary when a scout in leather armor entered the tent and waited to be acknowledged before speaking. "Lady Belina, the city's perimeter is clear, no enemy forces were sighted."

"Again they hide…ugh…" Belina shook her head, "this is not honorable warfare. No matter. By fury of nature and force of will, we shall purge the invaders from our midst. Let the battle for Agypto begin."

❉ ❉ ❉

"These toads do bleed, and feel pain, like a man, or sprite. So we will give them a swift death!" Ranser raised his weapons covered in toad blood to the cheers of the sprites.

"Hmm," Yagi played skeptical to counter his bravado, "how so?"

"With these." Ranser plucked a skyshroom from the ground and held it up like a shield, the stalk couched under his arm. "We cannot be swallowed if we hold on to some skyshrooms like Jaeger did." Ranser handed the mushroom to a sprite named Clovis, who was then obscured (and protected) from toes to hair feathers. "Take these, the star leaf." He cut a long thorny leaf from a nearby plant and rolled the spines inward to make a strong and sharp spear. As he wrapped the spear with thin strips of grass to hold it together, Clovis called out from behind the mushroom.

"Um, sir—it's too heavy—" The sprite grunted as he lost his grip on the stalk and fell to ground with it, which prompted some giggles from some of the onlookers.

Ranser helped him to his feet. "Let's see...hold this." Ranser stood the mushroom up behind Clovis and had him hold the rim of the cap while he fastened the stalk to his back with the tough grass fronds, then handed him the leaf spear. "And this. Now you're ready for battle! Can you show the others?"

"Yes, sir!" Clovis affirmed and hurried off, beaming with excitement to show his friends, and equip them similarly.

Yagi and Ranser were striding through the sprite encampment organizing and arming the fighters when Ranser stepped on one of the smaller skyshrooms.

"So this is the stuff that you hunt big game with." He said, observing the gooey pulp on his shoe. "Perhaps it can work if we coat our spears in it."

"Hm, yes," Yagi agreed, "but we'll need to crush many of them. You there, smash these skyshrooms!"

A group of sprites took up rocks and twigs and began bashing the clump of blue mushrooms into the ground as others, by Yagi's direction, brought them the makeshift spears, dipped them in the poisonous pulp, and stacked them to the side.

One of the sprites, Baelfred, was swinging his club down when he slipped and fell into the trough of crushed sky-shrooms, instantly shrinking to half of his already tiny size. The other sprites were at first unable to help him get out, due to their debilitating fits of laughter, but eventually they lifted him out of the pit, and even Baelfred found it rather amusing after the fact.

Suddenly, the forest shook in the downdraft of a robin landing in the sprite village with a shrill caw.

"Bird!" Someone shouted out, and most of the sprites scurried into hiding, while some of the hunters who had their spears ready stayed to thwart it.

A sprite stood up from her perch on the towering bird's back and waved. "Hey, everyone! It's me!"

"Jade!" Yagi yelled up at her, "What are you doing? Get down from there!"

"It's okay, I spoke to them!" Jade called back. "The birds have come to help us reclaim our lands!"

Then another piercing shriek came from above before an even bigger feathered creature landed beside the first.

"HAWK!"

At this alarm, the few brave sprites who stood defending lost their nerve, dropped their spears and bolted into the brush in a panic. An eagle had snatched up a sprite before, and the tale had spread through the village invoking a deep fear of them.

"Don't worry everyone," Jade shouted as she slid down the side of the robin to the ground, "they won't hurt us!"

The other sprites peeked out sheepishly from the grass forest.

The eagle ruffled its gold-tinged feathers and made a high-pitched squawk.

"The birds say they have seen the imbalance caused by the toads, that they do not belong here. The mice and worms will not survive the season." Jade explained as she walked over to Yagi and Ranser. "Now is the time to drive them out."

Yagi glared skeptically at the young maiden. "It said all that? Are you sure about this?"

"Yes!" Jade responded insistently. "I've always known how to listen to the animals. Almost anything with a face talks like us, in a way. The bug's scent thing I can't figure out, but I think I will someday."

The robin chirped, to which Jade turned and nodded.

"She saw a fleet of crickets on its way through the meadow," she translated, "it will be passing us soon."

"That will be the perfect time to attack." Yagi stated with growing confidence in the entire matter.

Then the eagle cawed again and lowered its head.

"Oh. You'll be his rider." Jade said to Ranser. "Just hold on to the neck feathers. Tightly."

Hesitantly, Ranser approached the giant bird, and could see the light of intelligence in its huge eye as it followed him. Or perhaps it was a gleam of predatory instinct, driven by hunger. Fortunately, the bird of prey did not impale with its spear-like talons, or crush him in its beak as he climbed up its neck and onto its back. Jade re-mounted the robin as well.

"Try to surround them on the ground, keep your back to the forest!" Ranser yelled as the hawk's wings began to flap. "I'll aim for the Toad King from above!"

"Good luck!" Yagi called up to them.

"You too! Make ready, friends! Today we fly to victory!" Ranser's voice faded out as the birds rose into the sky.

CHAPTER 14 WINGS OF VICTORY

The eagle soared to such a height that Ranser could see the ocean beyond the forest for a moment before they dived down toward the red mushrooms.   The fleet of insects flitted through the grass to the clearing, hunter sprites riding atop them shouting their war cries as the fight began.

Bulbous masses leapt from the brush with gaping mouths to snatch the grasshoppers out of the air as they fell like raindrops all around. Some were caught and swallowed, but their riders were able to crawl out of the mouths of the shrinking toads thanks to their skyshroom protection.

Emerging from the grasses, the sprite army charged forward with a valorous yell, bristling with leafy spears. They bowled over the first few shrunken toads, flipping them on their backs and finishing them off without any casualties. But they began to take losses when the full-sized creatures hopped down from the towering mushrooms, crushing many sprites underfoot.

The ant army poured out from the sides behind them and harried the toads that dropped in, but were also being smashed and swallowed in large numbers.

Ranser caught sight of the largest toad as they neared the ground, sitting atop the highest mushroom. A large metallic ring engraved with a dragon symbol and a blue jewel sat atop the Toad King's head like a crown.

When the eagle began to rear up from its dive, he leapt from its back and dropped down toward the bloodshroom's pinnacle. The surface was covered in a slippery slime and he had to stab his dagger into the mushroom cap to keep from sliding off. The Toad King's eyes gazed down at him as he struggled to pull himself up. Then the creature turned away and flipped one of its long, webbed feet backward to brush him off the edge. The slimy leg battered Ranser back with terrible force, causing him to lose his grip and fall.

He landed on the cap below and his dagger went tumbling down further, leaving him weaponless as another toad pounced down on him from above. He was pinned to the ground by its ponderous weight and the viscous ooze dripping from it covered his head, threatening to drown him.

A flash of movement darted by below as the agile robin flew past. Jade caught the falling dagger and coaxed the bird upward. The sprite maiden dropped from her feathered steed with a bestial scream and fell perfectly on-target, sinking the steel blade deep into the head of the toad looming over Ranser. She wiped the slime from his face and helped to pull Ranser out from under the dead toad.

"Thanks!" Ranser coughed up some slime as he pulled the dagger out.

"Come on, don't be toad food! Let's get 'em!" Jade shouted with excitement as she leapt off the platform and was scooped up with a whoosh by the robin.

A mangled toad body fell from the sky as the eagle released its talons, and dived back down toward the melee. It was easy prey for him, except for the big one which would be too heavy to snatch, but the things would not die without a few ripping bites from his beak, and the taste was awful. The noxious blood and slime burned down his throat and his vision began to blur. His next target hopped out of the way and he clawed at the air before rising back up. Ranser caught hold of his tail feathers on the ascent and the bird flapped awkwardly, becoming disoriented from the toxins it had ingested.

Jade flew around the battlefield, firing skyshroom arrows from her bow down at the toads who had not already been shrunk. The clearing was littered with dead ants and sprites, but their comrades fought on bravely, swarming on the overturned amphibians with maniacal zeal. Yet the toads still sprang from the thicket with fervor, crushing and biting, withering away the sprite's forces far more quickly than their own.

Ranser landed again on the Toad King's perch, and dived out of the way as its tongue lashed out at him. He pounced on the massive creature and stabbed into its side, but it was not enough to stop it. Then the bloodshroom cap shuddered violently as another toad jumped up to it and shot out its tongue, catching Ranser's leg in its sticky grasp. With great effort he was able to clutch the dagger and prevent being pulled into its maw. But as he was stretched out and fighting to keep his hold on the knife, the Toad King's tongue extended from the side of its mouth and stuck firmly on his back. The dagger wrenched free from the toad's carapace and he was suspended in the air for a moment between the two creatures, until the smaller one released its hold and he was pulled in and gobbled up by the Toad King.

"Oh, no!" Jade cried out in despair as she saw Ranser disappear into the Toad King's craw, and flew up to shoot arrows at it, which glanced off harmlessly. Then a shadow darkened the sky, and the robin had to dodge out of the way to avoid the gargantuan thing that descended near them.

Ranser had kicked and flailed in a vain struggle but was relentlessly pulled down into the suffocating stomach of the toad. Just as his air ran out, a gigantic tooth punched through the flesh, opening a wide hole through which he toppled out onto the mushroom cap. When he looked up he saw the familiar grey coat of his old companion high above.

"Rune!" Ranser cheered and laughed. "You finally found me, and not a moment too soon! Good boy!"

The dog thrashed the Toad King in its jaws, then dropped it on its back amid the clearing, where a victorious shout rose up from the sprite army. The toads seemed to lose their fervor with the death of the patriarch, and hopped away across the field, abandoning their bloodshroom kingdom.

The old sprite Yagi picked up the fallen dagger from the ground and swung it like an axe at the stalk of a young bloodshroom. He took a piece from its cap, ate it and began growing taller. As Ranser hopped down the terraces, he saw all the sprite warriors gathered around, beaming joyously as they grew back to their original height.

"This is a day we will never forget." Yagi handed Ranser a piece of the red mushroom with a smile. "You have awakened the hero in us all, helped us reclaim our home, become a legend to our people forevermore. The one who wore that ring no longer protects the land. We will be with you when the time comes to reclaim *your* kingdom. Farewell, brave prince!"

Ranser gradually grew back to his normal stature while chewing the sweet fungus. Rune's tail wagged excitedly and when Ranser knelt to hug him, he noticed the Toad King's crown hanging from the dog's tooth. He took the ring that bore his family's crest, wiped it dry and slid it onto his finger.

A tiny voice called up to him. Jade waved frantically from the base of the bloodshrooms. "Safe travels Ranser! I hope I can be part of more of your adventures someday!"

"I hope so too. Thanks for watching my back."

"Any time! It seems you will face even bigger foes in your journey. This will even the odds!" Jade held up the bloodshroom for Ranser to take.

"My humble gratitude to you all. I know now, no one can make their way in this world alone. Keep each other well. Goodbye my friends."

Ranser stood up with a new appreciation for his world and all the creatures great and small that lived within it. He pushed the floating cloud onward and continued solemnly on his way to the north coast.

"We're almost there. Just a little further."

* * *

A few townspeople saw, but no one would remember another robed figure entering the library, nor did anyone notice the mask he wore.

Oslan was transfixed in his study of the seven seals again. The old tales were obscure and archaic, but he now had a firm grasp of what the artifacts were. A book, a ring, a scroll, a crown, an armlet, an orb, and some sort of bear figurine. The sword depicted at the top of the circle was still a mystery. A recently uncovered dwarven text appeared to refer to it, but their records were so rare, only a few pages of their writing had ever been found, and no one remained alive who could understand their ancient language. Thus, he wracked his brain on the meanings of the strange markings on these stone tablets. It seemed they spoke of the sleeping goddess at the center of the world as the Life Stone, but this also referred to the sword with a prefix.

"The Heart of the Life Stone? Is that what they called it?" The old sage muttered to himself, unaware someone had entered the room.

The masked man placed his hand upon Oslan's shoulder, startling him from his trance. "Greetings, faithful librarian."

"Oh! Ah...lord minister, I was not expecting you. What is the occasion?"

"Non and the King have requested a reading from the Tome of Records. I require the key." The voice from behind the mask was somehow familiar.

Oslan was hesitant. "You know it is risky to open, correct? It is kept in confinement for a reason."

"Of course. But this is the time of our kingdom's

greatest need, and who are we to deny our leader?"

"Ah, indeed." Oslan produced the key and handed it over apprehensively. "It is up the stairs on the—"

"I know where it is. Thank you, wise teacher. We will have it returned for safekeeping by tomorrow. And may your quest for further knowledge be fruitful."

Oslan watched with unease as the king's minister exited with the book.

That was the easy part. He knew Non would not allow himself to be imprisoned, but there would be other opportunities to corner him. As he walked to his next destination, he stopped a pair of guards on patrol.

"You two, follow me. The king requires your enforcement of his will."

The soldiers exchanged a wide-eyed look and quickly affirmed their compliance. "Yes, sir."

With silent but nervous obedience, they trailed the robed figure down the path to the temple of Agartha.

The clergy and worshippers within followed the trio with their eyes as they traversed the chapel, but no one said a word until they stepped upon the dais and past the altar. The masked man approached the ornate door at the back of the cathedral, and noticed the guards had stopped advancing.

"What are you doing? I said follow me!"

"Uhh...we c-can't..."

"I'm sorry, sir. Agartha will strike us dead if we enter without permission."

"You cowards. Get out of my sight." The king's advisor snarled scornfully.

"Please, you mustn't...no one is to enter there but the high priest." One of the clerics protested, but made no move to stop him. The cold mask turned to glare at him, and the priest took a step back.

"Fools. Your relics and traditions are a lie. This world is ours for the taking. Behold the breaking of your beliefs."

The congregation gasped and averted their gaze as he threw open the doors, but most could not contain their curiosity and looked in as he entered.

The room was walled in white marble, lined with red and gold tapestries, and divided in the center by a crimson carpet. A golden statue of the angelic goddess Agartha stood above the wide altar at the far end. And there rested the thing he had come for, the sacred scroll known as the Vimanticon.

The high priest Herodus interrupted his ceremony unexpectedly. He turned to face the infiltrator with an expression of surprise turning to outrage. "What is the meaning of this!?"

"I've come for the scroll. Stand aside, old man."

"Be gone from this place now! The Vimanticon must never leave this room. I protect it with my life!"

"I expected as much. How unfortunate for you." The masked mage continued walking forth as he cast his death spell. "Compelled cadaver, you choose to join my army of the dead! **Avara cadavera!**"

Herodus planted his staff steadfastly in the floor and conjured a translucent wall of protection.

Claws of dark violet energy sprang from the attacker's hand, slowing as they met the barrier, but could not be stopped. The infernal tendrils raked across the priest's body, clutching at his throat and stabbing into his eyes until he could maintain his defense no more and succumbed to the overwhelming onslaught. Collapsing to the floor, his skin withered and his muscles shrank as he struggled for breath. With a cruel laugh, the dark wizard removed his mask, and the high priest gasped his final words.

"You—! How could you betray us!? You are deceived...you will never gain what you seek..."

"Clearly it is *you* who are deceived. Agartha is with *me*." He reached down to touch a finger to the forehead of his victim before he finally expired.

Donning his mask again, he took up the heavy

scroll and approached the side of the golden statue. The temple had been entirely vacated by then, so no one saw him touch the statue's wing at the fourth feather, causing it to swing open and reveal a dark, descending passageway. The statue slid back into place as he stepped inside.

Spiraling deep into the bedrock, the tunnel filled with the chill air of the caverns, whispering of forgotten secrets and wailing with the cries of lost souls. At the bottom, the ancient sunken city revealed itself, and a voice spoke to him as he crossed the narrow bridge to the stone circle crested by carven wide-spread wings.

Agartha's otherworldly voice echoed in his mind . "You know...the one who brings about my return will gain my eternal blessing, and remain among the living forevermore."

"I know. It is I."

The stone platform was segmented in seven pieces, each engraved with a depiction of the relics that once were there, so long ago. The masked man took from his bag the objects he had brought. He placed the Tome of Records upon the bottom-right slab with the book carved on it, then the Vimanticon at the lower-left, and finally, the crystal-eyed bear doll at the section containing the bear-head symbol.

"I have set the last three seals on their course directly to you, my goddess." The cultist whispered with fanatic excitement.

The ethereal voice spoke again.

"You have done well, my loyal servant. I have begun to awaken from this endless dream. Very soon the circle will be complete."

* * *

The ivory spire of the lighthouse stood in silent vigil, perched on the clifftop overlooking the northern sea and the port of Agypto to the west. Unadel and Rotocles hurried down the hill beside it, descending to the shore. There they came to a great gaping cave which opened up between the bone jaws of some gigantic fossilized beast. A sailing vessel was moored and hidden within.

The sailors there were impatiently waiting to embark as the captain and first mate argued about the delay in departure.

"The crew is afraid, sir. Afraid the invaders will discover us at any moment, and that bad weather is coming. We must go now, if ever." The first mate pleaded in vain.

"We wait for the king's envoy. There are more than enough supplies, have patience."

"Why do we need this scholar from the city?"

"I've told you, he is the only one who can speak their language. Without him our mission is for naught. Think more of the future of our kingdom, a chance at lasting peace, and less of your own coinpurse."

"He has surely met his end on the road. Let's just deliver our cargo and be done with it!"

"Look. They've arrived." The captain grinned smugly.

The first mate scowled down at the pair ascending the rocky ramp, and whispered back, "Oh no, please tell me we're not bringing an elf—"

"No, I am merely delivering my cargo." Unadel sneered in response to the comment she was not meant to hear as they reached the gangplank. "He's your problem now."

Embarrassed, the first mate turned away and boarded the boat.

The captain chuckled happily, eager to get back on the sea. "Departure time right away then. All right men, aweigh anchor, shove off!"

The ship meandered out into the surf as Unadel exited the cavern and began to climb the hill back toward the city. But something caught her eye through one of the windows of the lighthouse, and she paused to observe.

Rotocles had begun complaining immediately as the trip began. His robe was soaked and he requested a change of clothing. The first mate brought him to his cabin and supplied a dry and waterproof outfit, and begrudgingly carried out the scholar's request to hang his robe up on the mast to dry.

One of the sailors had taken the robe down, put it on, and began mocking the guest's finicky complaints, and dancing around for the others, lifting the robe like a skirt. The sailors roared in fits of laughter until he suddenly froze, and looked down in shock at the arrow that had pierced his chest from behind. The stricken mariner's last action was to turn around to see his killer, but no one was there.

Of course, his aim was impeccable, but now, looking out through the low window of the lighthouse, Garath could see that this was not his intended target. The sailors scrambled below deck as someone shouted from the shore.

The arrow flying out to the ship told Unadel that the tenacious marksman had tracked them there, and that he might still carry out his intended assassination if given the chance. She yelled to distract his attention, sprinting to the base of the lighthouse and flinging open the door there.

Above and across from her, she saw the human archer Garath ascending the spiral stairway in long strides, while readying his bow to fire down on her. A pair of arrows zinged toward her neck and torso, and Unadel whipped out her chains to knock them away just in time.

More arrows rained down, and she spun the chains around her as she flipped across the wide expanse of open air between the spans of stairs to get below him and thus obstruct his line of fire. The light from the windows shaded as he moved past them, allowing her to gauge his position as they both ascended toward the top.

The bowman was shooting arrows into the wooden beams of the structure above, but the purpose was unclear until Unadel had climbed the two levels up to where he had been. There the path was blocked by a mass of webs emanating from the arrows stuck fast into the logs. She tried slashing them away with her blades but they could not be cut in any timely manner. Garath loosed another volley down, crossing the other lines and sticking into the beam behind her, forming a narrow cocoon which trapped the elf within and prevented her from swinging her chains in defense.

She saw the archer notch the next arrow with satisfaction, both knowing it would be the one that would finally hit her. In that same moment, a flock of white birds took wing and flew up out of a window, as if to show her the way.

Unadel leapt to the opening in the wall above and strained to pull herself up. Garath let the arrow fly and it struck its mark just as the elf disappeared out of the window, burying itself in the back of her calf.

The wooden rooftop was within reach, and Unadel had slung a hooked chain up to grasp it as the arrowhead pierced her leg. It made climbing more difficult, but she was able, and the pain was bearable until Garath began to pull on the other end of the line attached to the arrow. Ripping through the flesh, blood poured down the arrow shaft, and she screamed in torturous agony as she was pulled down the chain back toward the window. At the end of her line, she gave a final yank against the tension and the barbed missile tore out the remainder of its hold on the elf's leg.

Unadel pulled herself up to the edge of the rooftop where she saw Garath at the pinnacle, clinging to the flag pole atop it, aiming his bow out at the ship, still close to shore.

The shot hit the ship's mast and he attached the web line to the jutting spire. He took hold of the ghostly cord and began to slide down toward the ship just as Unadel mounted the rooftop.

The elven hooked chain lashed up, coiling around Garath's ankle and pulling him back down. He crashed through the brittle planks of the roof near Unadel, and they both fell to the round platform below.

The pyreflies sealed within the great glass cylinder at the center of the platform pulsed their light excitedly as Garath rolled backwards while readying an arrow to finish his opponent off. Unable to regain his footing as the elf tugged at his foot, the archer pointed his arrow at her head and pulled back the string with his free leg.

Unadel whipped forth her bladed chain, ensnaring the arm that held the bowstring, and pulled with all her strength. The honed edges glided through the unprotected wrist, separating the hand from the archer's arm, and the arrow veered to the side.

His final shot, the only one Garath had ever missed, shattered part of the glassy beacon, releasing the pyreflies and destabilizing the entire structure. Huge sections of broken glass tumbled down, smashing through the old wooden platform, causing it to give way beneath them. Unadel was able to hook a line to the roof to save herself as Garath plummeted to the ground floor far below, and jagged chunks of glass and timber rained down atop him.

The unbreakable tether still held the ship in place, and Unadel needed to know if Rotocles had been killed. She crawled to the summit of the tower and looped the hooked chain at her belt around the line, then pushed off toward the sea.

Rotocles had placed the small vial of dark glass upon a table in the ship cabin as he put on the new clothes, and it rolled off onto the floor. It was still intact when he picked it up, examining it with an itching curiosity. He thought he should know what all this was for, why the king's faceless advisor had felt this little jar was so important to bring to the Kinari land. So he pulled out the stopper just to take a peek, and immediately fell to the floor in a deep sleep.

The tiny illusionist giggled with madness as he pranced around the ship full of snoozing humans, and one unconscious elf hanging from the tall mast.

* * *

Tor held a torch aloft as he followed Avus down into the maze of subterranean tunnels. After several seemingly-random turns without checking the map, he wondered if the dwarf might be lost. Of course, this was not the case. Even though Avus had never used this particular passage, he could find the way with his eyes closed. The sound of the running water echoing from the walls and the heat of the air would tell him which paths led to the aquifer, even if he had never been there.

The brickwork of the sewer tunnels ended in a narrow crevasse in the rough bedrock wall, and the passage continued into the caverns beyond. As they went, the way would constrict to tiny cracks in the wall, which they crawled and slid through. What to Avus was like a hallway, but with better grip, was for Tor a crushing, scraping, painful ordeal, and he would have been stuck several times without the dwarf's help.

However, once they came to a high ledge, Tor was able to climb it with ease and pull Avus up.

There, the path split in two. The steep descent to the right was the more direct route, but a curious warmth and odd resonance emanated from the corridor to the left, which also led down to the Deep River Hall. Avus decided to take this route and ascertain the source of the disturbance along the way.

The hall turned and opened to a gaping pit spanned by a long stone bridge. At the other end, a blanket of steam rolled across the ceiling of the adjoining corridor and rushed upward into the darkness. As they crossed the precarious span, the steam cloud became denser, obscuring a faint glow in the depths of the chasm.

Avus paused on the ledge, peering down through

the mist quizzically. "It appears to be a torch. Under the water. And on fire."

"What? How?" Tor tried in vain to see what the dwarf did through the blasting torrent of water vapor.

"I'm not sure, but I would bet Levan had something to do with this. That kid should really stop throwing his things down here." Avus checked the other side of the bridge, then said, "At least the water level is lower. It should make the dive survivable."

"That's a relief." Tor chuckled nervously as they continued on.

Not far away, a forlorn pauper scavenged in the canals of those same tunnels.

* * *

Ward's stomach growled as he waded through the muck, frustrated at the prospect of another day without food. He hadn't found anything of value all day, aside from the armor and weapon of the fresh guardsman's corpse, but possessing or attempting to sell any of those items would only bring swift imprisonment or death on the spot, so he left them undisturbed. Not that he was above robbery, or even murder if it suited his needs and the odds were in his favor. And so he would surely have ambushed that man in the silken cloak who happened by, if not for the dwarf escorting him. Instead, he crouched in the shadows and sat very still as they passed.

In his twenty-two miserable years, most of it spent in the sewers scavenging like a rat, barely sustaining his existence from day to day, he had sent ten souls to Agartha, and felt nothing while doing so. He was more animal than man by then, endlessly searching, driven only by self-preservation, and an insatiable hunger. Long forgotten were the memories from a time when he could feel true emotion like a real person. Here in the darkness and filth, he and his victims were merely empty shells, and he had always been a monster.

Wandering on, Ward stopped when his foot fell on a submerged object. He pulled up the unusual bowl of dark metal and examined it. Having lived on the fringes of society so long, he had no way of knowing that this was a Kinari war helm, only that it was not a piece of the city guard armor, and would likely be worth something. The skull inside, however, would be of no value, and thus was discarded unceremoniously.

Torchlight flickered in the distance and pushed away the shadows as a robed figure drew near. A middle-aged man, unarmed and alone in the tunnels appeared to be easy prey. And he held what looked like a large, black gemstone in his hand.

Ward began to move toward a side passage where he could hide until the opportune moment, but found his feet ensnared. A skeletal arm emerged from the murky stream, clutching his leg as he struggled desperately to escape, and the tunnel filled with diabolical laughter.

The hooded man came to him and placed a hand upon Ward's shoulder, thumb pressed at hollow of his neck in a half-friendly, half-threatening embrace. A dead-eyed and expressionless porcelain mask mirrored Ward's cold gaze.

"Ward...thank Agartha I've finally found you. Are you hungry? Eat." The masked man released his grasp and handed the pauper a roll of bread stuffed with meat, somehow still warm and fragrant, as if freshly-baked. Ward devoured it greedily as his captor continued. "I was there that day, when your father perished in the caverns..." Ward's chewing paused momentarily, then resumed. "...we found it, the great treasure horde in the ancient city below...such riches, we could all have had our own castles. But Veldgar betrayed us. He cut the rope as your father climbed up, leaving him to his doom. He told me to find you, and give you this, that it would make you remember." He held up a white flower. "And to look after Reva."

"Reva..."

The sweet scent washed over him, and Ward remembered his little sister, drenched and filthy, plucking white blossoms from their mother's corpse in the ruins of their collapsed home. "Mother says they are best in bunches of three." His face streamed with tears as he gasped for breath, feeling for the first time since that day.

"That man you saw with the dwarf, he is Tor Veldgar, sent by his father to claim what would have been ours, if not for his treachery."

"Veldgar!" Ward's face twisted in a grimace of fury.

"For we are long in our years and cannot make the trek ourselves. But you know these tunnels better than anyone. You will be the one to find them, pounce on them in the dark, reclaim the life that was owed and taken from you both."

The bone hand released him, and Ward stalked off into the tunnel with a murderous gleam in his eye, dropping the Kinari helmet upon the causeway.

The masked man picked up the black headpiece and regarded it momentarily while another sinister idea coalesced in his demented mind, and he cackled in self-satisfaction as he turned to leave.

CHAPTER 15 SECRET WEAPONS

The air was charged with anticipation. A chill sea breeze shuddered the war banners as ominous storm clouds gathered on the horizon. Fanned out around the city of Agypto, the army held their positions and awaited orders. Some were fearful, others impatient. The scout's horses stamped and neighed nervously.

At last Belina pointed her sword forth to the city, and an indistinct call echoed across the plain as the flags changed to signal advance.

Levan's stomach fluttered, his heart seemed to pound in his throat, and his limbs tingled with energy as he marched at the front of the army, glancing to the other wizards and wondering if they felt the same trepidation. Of course, they did not. Only he and Belina had the slightest idea what they could be facing.

Umber had called up his rocky armor, becoming an imposing giant of stone, which distracted some of the soldiers with awe. His great strides shook the ground as he bounded and rolled into a great round boulder, shattering the land behind the army lines in a pair of long slashes, leaving only a narrow patch of intact ground on the river edge near the western shore, an avenue for scouts to run messages. He was slightly bored with the limitations he was given, unable to simply barrel through and smash everything.

Nearby, Kalvas approached the coastal wall, swirling

the air into a frenzy, and the waves crashed and sprayed in the rising cyclone. The wind began ripping away the spiked barricade, hurling sharp debris in all directions. Some of his supporting infantrymen were hit, but the distance was acceptable, their armor was effective, and no one was hurt. He continued building the storm's raging fury, relishing in having a sandbox to play in, an opportunity to truly test himself.

Across the beach, Sabrena found the wall to be sturdier than it looked. To her annoyance, submerging it in sea water and smashing an icy fist into it did very little damage. But when she sharpened her staff into a spear of ice she was able to punch a hole through the timber planks, then enlarge it to a massive frozen cone which ripped the barrier in half and rolled off into the ocean.

Levan projected a small glowing orb from his hand which exploded in a thunderous shockwave, shattering the blockade before him. He smiled to himself. The fireball was perfectly tuned, powerful enough to break the wall, but concentrated just to the point that it would not damage the adjacent buildings which might contain living souls. He threw another fireball off to the side, and willed a gust of wind to deflect its path into the barricade ahead of Belina's regiment.

From the air, Kalvas saw Levan take down the two barriers. He shook his head in chagrin and muttered to himself, "Show-off."

Belina moved cautiously through the breach, flanked by defenders with tall shields. The high windows near the tops of the weathered stone buildings seemed to glower down on them like hollow eyes frozen in shocked horror. Reaching the first intersection, the only movement in the streets was a tumbleweed being blown out to sea.

The soldier Jagus was having the worst day of his life. His anxiety about the coming battle had led him to drink far too much the previous evening, and his body was a torturous burden to drag out of his tent that morning, only to find he had lost his sword sometime in the night.

In his frantic search to find it he had scrambled around the camp without boots and broken a toe on a rock. Finally he resigned to borrow one of the less-reliable army swords (with a loose crossguard), and hurriedly limped to fill his place in the ranks.

Being the last to take position, he was subjected to the biting jeers of his squadmates about his cowardice and stupidity until the assault finally began. When everyone drew their weapons around him, Jagus did the same, but the pommel fell from the top of his sword, the hilt slid off, and he pulled up only a hollow handle. The hapless soldier was trying desperately to reattach it and keep in step when a heavy impact at his chest knocked him back, and swiftly blinked him out of his misfortunate incarnation.

Kaden saw the dark crossbow bolt fly from the high window and slam into Jagus' cuirass. From within his armor, sparks and flames erupted, charring and pulverizing the man's body. The advancing lines wavered, as those who had witnessed the complete ineffectiveness of their armor were visibly shaken. Before cohesion was entirely lost, Kaden moved to the intersection where he could see the other commanders and called out to them as more arrows flew by, "Archers in the windows! Take cover, clear the buildings!"

Near Levan, the soldiers began bashing in the doors and attempting to enter the stone structures, but the portal was blocked by a pile of rubble, wooden racks and benches. When the man at the front had kicked in enough of the door to push through, he was violently repelled by a shot from within, and the troops behind him were showered with the searing hot metallic fragments that exploded out of his back.

They could see their enemies now, a handful of dark-armored men within the building. Several more soldiers zealously rushed forward to gain entry and engage them, but were similarly stricken and fell in the cluttered threshold.

"Wizard!" One of the squad commanders shouted

in Levan's direction, "Raze this hold!"

Levan hesitated, shaking his head. He had seen the cowering family with children in that building, had they not?

"Destroy it!" The angry commander called out again as more of his men fell in the alleyway.

"No!" Levan called back, "There are people inside!"

"Agh! Useless knave!" The officer yelled just before he was pierced with by a crossbow shot from the window and dropped to the ground.

Levan's mind raced to find a less destructive solution. Fire was out of the question. Anything altering the structure would endanger the innocents within. The high windows were their main advantage, where the archers were raining down death with impunity. The wind had gathered drifts of sand along the north-facing walls.

The wizard knelt and picked up a handful of dust, then tossed pinches of it up to the window holes, and condensed the mist in the air to cover the embrasures, forming several overlapping muddy shutters across the building's façade which congealed into rocky barriers, preventing further shots from above. With the last of the dust, Levan formed a stone shield which floated in front of him as he followed the few soldiers who had finally been able to enter the building.

Three crossbowmen stood atop the towering wooden scaffolding, which rose to a walkway along the high windows near the ceiling. Two of the soldiers were hit by the deadly bolts as they charged up the ramps, then the Kinari dropped their crossbows and drew their swords to fight at close range.

Levan rushed to the craftsman's wife and children in the corner of the room, being watched over by a tall, heavily-armored Kinari soldier.

The foreign warrior swung his massive two-handed sword down in a powerful chop which would have cleaved Levan's torso in two if it had not been blocked by the magical shield of stone, becoming wedged in the top of it.

When the swordsman pressed his thumb into the crossguard, the protruding circular end of the blade detached and fired out at great speed. Even if he had expected it, the sharp ring of steel flew too quickly to be evaded, slicing across the top of Levan's shoulder and deflecting off the wall behind him with a blast of sparks.

The wizard touched the remaining double-pronged tip of the sword, radiating energy into it until the entire weapon began to glow red with heat, and the warrior released his grasp on it. Levan then pushed the shield forward into his attacker, knocking him to the ground.

One of the children yelped as the Kinari warrior grabbed his leg and brought up a knife from his belt. But before he could raise it to strike, his arm was impaled and pinned to the floor by the spear of a knight in a shimmering cape. The young boy recoiled as the wounded Kinari squirmed in pain on the floor, and the knight kicked the dagger away.

Suddenly another Kinari appeared from his hiding place in the livestock pen and fired his crossbow into the knight's back. The spearman was jolted forward but stayed on his feet as the arrow deflected off the dragon-skin cloak. He took up his spear, wheeling around and hurling it through the ribcage of the ambushing archer.

Smoke began to fill the room as the flames spread to the wooden rafters from the fire started in the hay-pile by the last Kinari crossbow shot.

Levan assessed the cowering family, offering them a hand to stand up. "Are you alright? Can you walk?"

"Yes, but my husband..." The woman fretted breathlessly, "at the workshop. We must go to him."

"The streets are not safe, I don't know if I can protect you." Levan cast a troubled glance at the billowing smoke cloud above.

"Wrap yourselves in this and follow us." The spearman removed his cloak, unfurling it to its full length, long enough to fully cover the craftsman's wife and children. The scaly hide glistened in the light as they huddled under it, stepping out into the chaotic battlefield that was once their peaceful town.

Belina kicked her adversary with such force that he crashed through the door and fell out onto the road. She leapt from the building and landed astride the fallen warrior, sinking her sword into his heart.

Kaden and his men had just reached that alleyway, and he rushed to her aid, though she needed none.

"This one's clear." Belina motioned to the house behind her. "We need to regroup and update our tactics. We will set up a forward base in that forge over there." She pointed to the large building at the end of the street, where a plume of smoke drifted up from the chimney. "I'm going for the western entrance."

"I'll head to the east then. We can attack from both sides."

Belina nodded her approval.

Kaden's troops filled the street to the right while Belina's moved left, but she turned around at the sound of panicked cries.

Entering the crossroads at the southeast corner of the workshop, the young lieutenant Kaden and the fifty men nearest him were suddenly launched into the air as the stone square of road lifted up and flew high into the sky. The section of street beneath them disintegrated in the air and they screamed back to the ground. Kaden struck the corner of a building on his way down, crushing his insides, and his own bones left him breathless as he expired on the ground.

A few landed with pained groans, still alive, in the crater below. And as the stones rained back down on them, some fast movement could be seen in the dusty depression as several bizarre, spindly black-legged machines skittered across the rubble toward the survivors.

Rising up from their collapsed positions beneath the road, these monstrous contraptions were taller than a man, with eight long legs like a metallic spider, and a huge circular saw blade where the body should be. They were drawn to the warm breath of the dying men, standing over them and lowering the whirling blade down to grind through their armor.

The saw spiders climbed out all sides of the crater, blades spinning furiously. The legs retracted into sharp prongs on the sides as the blade touched the ground edge-on, and sent it zooming forth into the crowd of gathered troops like an errant wagon wheel, kicking up sparks and gravel as it went. The relentless revolving blade tended to catch hold of armor at the shoulders or head, pulling its wearer down as it rolled over them and wrenching off the helmet, exposing the back of the neck to its thrashing metal teeth.

At the other end of the street, the saw spider reversed direction and tore through the ranks of troops as it transformed its shape in mid-roll. They tried to part in the middle, but the legs shot out from one side, turning the blade flat and cutting men down at the waist in a wide swath.

When it reached the edge of the crater again, it sprang back, landing on the shoulders of one of the knights and dropping the heavy spinning guillotine down onto his head. The man's horrified scream was cut short, and before his collapsing body had reached the ground, the machine leapt from him and latched on to another helpless victim, who quickly suffered the same grisly fate. Buzzing and flying through the air like a giant mosquito, the dark metallic creature glistened and dripped with blood as it pounced upon and butchered the beleaguered soldiers one by one.

The life of the soldiers of Lorestian was being splattered across the coral-stone buildings and streets in each direction.

To the south, the saw spider went spinning down the street, cutting down several men until it came to a sudden stop beneath the crushing, rocky fist of the wizard Umber in his hulking stone giant form. The shattered blade crumbled to the ground as he lifted the mangled heap of metal and pulled off the wildly twitching legs, then discarded it when it ceased to move.

A hail of crossbow fire fell on Umber from above. Many of the bolts were deflected or absorbed by his earthen armor, but one tiny fragment of searing hot metal found its way through to his leg, embedding itself just beneath the skin.

The stone golem roared in fury as it rammed the wall of the house they were shooting from, and proceeded to sunder the building to rubble to get to them.

The unwilling Kinari recruit, Zoku, had never wanted to be there. He was content as a simple farmer until he was conscripted, taken away from his home, and trained on a ship to fight in a war he did not understand in some faraway place. He thought perhaps his odds of survival would have been better had he tried to escape into the wilds and be an outlaw rather than go with them. Now there was nowhere left to flee as he saw his death come through the wall beneath him and the scaffolding he was standing on collapse at the foot of this enraged, unstoppable juggernaut. His last moments were spent frantically, foolishly attempting to reload his weapon before he was crushed into, and became one with the ground.

The accompanying enlisted men held out longer, but were ultimately flattened when the north wall collapsed, along with the furniture-maker who lived there, but was not part of the fighting.

The saw spiders spun out to the north and east, meeting few obstacles on their path out to the edge of town and on to the beach.

Kalvas saw it slam through the wall in the distance and skip across the dunes towards him. Fingers of lightning flickered down to it and the whirling disk stumbled and dug into the dry sand. Its legs extended, and it emerged to continue running forward, staggering when stricken by the crackling electricity and being lifted up by the furious wind. Tumbling into the vortex around him, Kalvas could see the grooves in the blade where it was coming apart as it turned white-hot and spun ever faster with each charged bolt.

These strange new objects, neither of magic, nor of life, were completely unknown to the young wizard only a few seconds before, as was the case for nearly everyone who encountered them that day. He could neither predict nor control the awkward thing's movement and reactions even as it rose in a wobbling spiral around the sandy whirlwind, which itself was an unstable and unpredictable result of his alteration of air currents. He rolled the dice every time he used this chaotic magic, and today, by chance, fate turned up his number.

The machine shattered in a violent explosion as the blade fragmented into blazing-hot, dagger-like shards and flew out in a steep-angled ring, part of which happened to intersect with the upper body of the young wizard. Clutching the metallic shard buried in his chest, Kalvas fell from the sky and the winds gradually calmed.

The soldiers rushed to the eastern shore where the wizard had fallen. The boy was still and lifeless, but no threat remained. They pulled his body onto a cart and took him back to the south, where the other dead and wounded were.

Across the beach, another saw spider was speeding toward Sabrena. Mystified and disgruntled, she squinted and gaped at the peculiar weapon that was moving toward her. Whatever it was, it looked dangerous and it shouldn't get any closer. The surf swelled and trotted up the shore at Sabrena's beckoning, covering the machine in a cold, rolling wave. The waters were much more powerful and abundant here at the sea, but took a bit longer to freeze. The wave washed back, leaving the saw spider immobilized in a gleaming sheet of ice.

In an intersection of the city streets, she glimpsed her sister Belina shouting orders while having to dive out of the path of another of those spinning monstrosities as soldiers were being cut down around her, and Sabrena hurried to reinforce them.

"Take the forge!" Belina shouted as the whirling blade rolled past again, shredding the spears that were thrust into it. Glancing down the street, she noticed Sabrena running in her direction. The stones of the crossroad she was about to enter were tampered-with, depressed in the middle and raised at the corners, like the one Kaden had stepped on. "No, st—!" She called out, but the screeching mechanical roar drowned out the sound as the deadly wheel slashed down the street again.

"Sabrena!" Levan gasped as he saw Sabrena sprinting toward the carnage, and he ran to catch up with her.

Levan did try to discern what Belina was yelling at them, but the clamor was too loud, and the commands always seemed to be unintelligible anyway. Sabrena kept running, so Levan did as well, the craftsman's family following behind him.

Then came the unsettling feeling of the ground shifting and rising up beneath them. The craftsman's family collapsed to their knees with a cry of terror, and the two wizards struggled to remain standing as they all ascended into the air. The mortar between the cobblestones began to separate underfoot, and their upward acceleration tapered off.

Levan could feel the fall coming, unsure he could prevent it for himself, much less the other four people nearby, but he had to try. A bubble of heat produced a swift convection, drawing up air and moisture to condense beneath them in a thick white cloud. To Levan's surprise, the cloud held their weight, lowering them safely back to the ground, and Sabrena stepped off, moving again toward the embattled commander on the next street.

Belina dodged the spinning blade and struck it with her sword in passing, causing it to lose balance and swerve into the edge of the workshop building. It stood up and sprang into the air, landing directly atop Belina's shoulders, clinching its claws in an unbreakable grip. The blade fell toward her helmet, but she was able to raise her shield overhead to block it before it split her skull.

The scattering sparks from the upheld shield were snuffed out when Sabrena created an orb of water around the machine, halting its movement as the liquid solidified, and it fell to the ground encased in a block of ice.

Belina's crest, frayed and dented, bounced and rolled across the street as she took it off and threw it away. She turned to her younger sister with a furious scowl. "What were you doing!? I told you to stop, not to go that way! Are you deaf or insubordinate!?"

"I am not one of your dogs of war!" Sabrena shouted back angrily, "How dare you condescend me when I've just saved your life!?"

"While endangering many more! You've broken ranks and left the western front open to the enemy!"

"There's not even anyone down there!"

As the two fiery-tempered sisters' screaming match continued, Levan noticed the strangely-agile spider-like creature scuttling across a nearby rooftop.

"Umm, this may not be the safest place to stand." He called back over his shoulder, still tracking the unnaturally animated contraption stalking above, but his warning was unheard.

Honing in on its target, the spider leapt down with its claws splayed out. Allies and civilians were too close to unleash any overly-destructive spells. In order to create some distance between him and his subject, he spoke the syllables he remembered from his battle with Merton.

"Ah de fua!"

The words created a cone of sonic resonance emanating from his mouth, and a concussive shockwave that blasted the machine into the air. The wizard hurled three fireballs up in quick succession to converge on it, exploding in a thunderous crash and a rain of broken metal pieces.

The jarring boom interrupted the argument, and they all then became aware of the saw spiders creeping in on the rooftops around them.

"We should go." Levan's suggestion was obvious, but seemed to spur them into action just as a fusillade of arrows zinged from the windows. A few soldiers were hit from behind and fell. One bolt struck the craftsman's wife, and she stumbled forward. but the projectile bounced harmlessly off the dragon skin-cloak on her back.

"This way!" Belina took off toward the door of the workshop where the heroic spearman had just made his entry.

Undaunted as squadrons of his comrades fell around him, the solitary knight charged onward.

At the largest structure in town, Dane pressed his back to the wall as he pushed the bolts from the door's hinges with his spear and pried it from the entryway to fall into the street. As expected, a scatter of arrows flew out from within. One low-angled shot revealed the position of an archer near the doorway. This would be his first target.

Dane stepped into the threshold and launched himself forward in a spinning dive. The attack connected directly at the opponent's center of mass, and even his formidable armor could not stand against the force of this strike. The spearhead tore through the Kinari archer's abdomen, and they fell to the floor beside each other.

A few paces away, another Kinari solder realized there wasn't enough time to reload. He dropped his crossbow and drew his sword to execute the prone attacker.

Still on his back, Dane swept his spear in a wide arc to topple the nearby archer, and pounced to impale and finish him off. The spear's end broke off on the stone floor, leaving him weaponless before the final enemy.

The last armed occupier of this large building was the best marksman of the squad. Standing on the walkway high above, he had readied his crossbow to end the threat from this over-confident barbarian. A loud explosion outside twitched his finger, unseating the bolt from its proper firing position. In the moment he took to notch it back into place,

Dane picked up a hammer from a nearby table and flung it up, striking the end of the crossbow. The taut string whipped back with dreadful force as the impact snapped the cocked bow arm, and the jagged broken end of it lodged in the Kinari warrior's neck. Mortally wounded by his own mechanical weapon, the consummate soldier's last thoughts were of the flimsy nature of the bow's crosspiece, and at that moment, somewhere far away, the same thought occurred to a weapon-maker, who sprang from his bed to draw up the new, sturdier design.

Some of the townspeople of Agypto were cheering their liberator as Belina and the others arrived at the doorway, while the rest were still too frightened to celebrate. Belina ordered the soldiers outside to re-hang the door as they entered.

"Naren!" Rique, the town's master glass-crafter called out in exasperated relief as he rushed to hug his wife and children entering behind the red-haired lady knight. "Are you alright? What is this?" Rique surveyed the glimmering hide they were wrapped in.

"It is the knight's cloak." Naren explained with tearful eyes, "It protected us. We owe him our lives, and the wizards as well."

"As do all of us here, our legends and songs will never forget you." Rique said, handing the cloak back to Dane and shook their hands in introduction. "I am Rique, the glass-crafter."

The spearman raised his dented visor to show his battle-scarred face. "Dane Karikaius. I need no songs, only the service of a blacksmith. Is there one among us?"

"Yes, most of Agypto's artisans have been gathered here since the Kinari came, forced to craft and repair these strange weapons they use." Rique pointed to the roaring fireplace surrounded by tools, logging saws, and disassembled weapons. "You will find Hregar the metalworker and his apprentices there, by the forge."

Belina was busy securing the building, organizing

the troops to remove the dead and bring in the wounded for treatment.

Sabrena gave Levan a concerned look. "You're hurt." She lightly touched his shoulder where the robe was sliced and saturated with blood. "This wound needs treatment."

"It's nothing." Levan dismissed it with a glance, having forgotten about the cut in the excitement of battle. Only now did it begin to buzz with pain. "I can heal it with my salve." He checked his belt and back and realized his pack was missing. "Ah, I must have left it back at the school."

"Just let me clean it." Sabrena clasped her hand over his shoulder, and a cool moisture emanated from it, stopping the bleeding, purifying the wound and numbing the pain.

"Sabrena, I..." Levan's words were cut off by the agonized groan of a soldier being carried to a nearby table, and the shout from his carrier.

"Medic! He's bleeding out!"

Sabrena rushed to him and promptly staunched the bleeding of his severed leg which stained her clothes as yet more casualties were brought in. She cleaned and sealed the wounds of those that could be saved, but she was not accustomed to all the blood and carnage. The horror of it took its toll on her psyche, draining the color from her face and forcing her to look away and sit down, lest she faint.

Levan had followed Rique to the warm glow of the forge, where some peculiar sheets of curved glass flared in the reflection of sunlight from the windows.

"What are these?" The wizard inquired, inspecting the glass pieces.

"The Kinari have us making them, for what purpose is unknown." Rique replied with a shrug.

"They look like spectacle lenses." Levan remarked curiously.

"Reading glasses for giants!" One of the glassworker chuckled.

"They must have crafted a tremendous one of these somewhere." Rique said, indicating a stone trough sloping down and out of the building. "Wherever this canal leads, we've been pouring glass into it for over a week."

A man atop a ladder shouted down, "Crucible's ready to go! Pour?"

"No," Rique called back, "extrude for bottles, we need more water stores for the soldiers."

The man on the ladder descended to the ground. He slid open a panel at the bottom of the tall cylinder, and a glowing rod of molten glass slowly emanated from it. Rique stretched it out and cut off several lengths with long iron shears, passing them down the production table to his assistants who repeated his next procedure. The master glass-crafter lifted the glowing shaft up over a flaming pit and attached it to an axle which revolved as he pressed a pedal beneath the table. Then he inserted a sectioned hollow rod into the end, took a deep breath and blew into it. The liquid glass expanded into a bubble as it spun around, gradually becoming transparent as it was placed aside and cooled.

Suddenly the ground tremored and one of the sentries on the high platform shouted in alarm. "What in t—Belina! You'd better come see this!"

Levan and Dane followed Belina, rushing up the wooden ramp to the lookout spot. Through the window they saw the wide, paved expanse of the plaza near the docks crumbling as it was pushed upward by some huge object rising up from below. Gaping in awe and horror, they looked on as an enormous convex pane of glass lifted up from the ground by a monstrous machine emerging from the crater below it, taller than the surrounding buildings, with many long metallic arms which held more shields of reflective glass.

From the east, the wizard Umber appeared in his rocky shell, smashing the ground with his steps as he bounded toward the towering machine.

The giant lens gathered the sunlight into a narrow

beam down onto the many-armed machine, which reflected it forward and focused on the charging wizard moving toward it. Smoke and flame erupted from the focal point of this searing ray of light, and molten rock dripped down as it scathed Umber's stony shell and burned through his chest. The wizard stopped moving and collapsed to the ground in a smoldering heap of lava and rubble.

"No!" Levan gasped in despair as he watched his classmate die. There seemed to be no defense against this terrible new weapon.

When the soldiers at the front moved to retrieve the fallen wizard, a salvo of tar-filled jars flew from the dock area and fell all around them, exploding with sticky, flaming ooze. The distant catapults kept firing these projectiles into the city, enflaming the streets and setting ablaze the buildings they landed in.

"Fall back!" Belina shouted through the window. She turned to the workshop, anxiously seeking a solution. In the corner of the room, a pile of wooden beams was strangely familiar to her. "The hurling machines—we can build our own and return fire at them!" She hurried down to ground level and brought several troops to begin assembling the parts of the catapult as well as she could remember from the battle at Hollow Dale.

"The dragon-hide resists all heat." Dane remarked with determination. "The blacksmith is fusing it to my armor. I will take on that big one, when my lance is repaired."

"Attacking an iron giant with a pinprick?" Belina chided the idea, "A simple spear will never stop it. There must be something else..." She turned to the woodworker assisting with the catapult. "Have we any oil or pitch to enflame our ammunition?"

"Ah, our lamp oil is imported. It ran dry days ago." The man wore a worried frown.

"Mere stones cannot destroy these things..." Belina sighed, beginning to consider contingency plans for a tactical retreat.

Two soldiers carried in the green-robed wizard with the shard of steel in his chest and placed him on a table near Levan and Sabrena.

"Kalvas! Oh no..." Sabrena sobbed in anguish, knowing he was beyond recovery. "Even magic will not save us. It is hopeless."

"Gah!!" Levan pounded his fist on the table in frustration.

Just then, a flaming jar exploded on the rooftop overhead, scattering fire through the water-catchment and dripping burning pitch into the workshop, to the distress of the occupants within.

"Sabrena! Extinguish it!" Belina called out as the timbers of the roof began to catch fire.

The water wizard formed a thick mist which rose up to quench the sputtering flames, and crystallized into a barrier over the holes in the ceiling, protecting those within for the time being.

Levan looked to the frightened civilians, his dead classmate, and the despondent, grief-stricken living one. The bleakness of the situation was like a heavy weight on his shoulders, compelling him to take action. And the fiery bombardment gave him a seemingly brilliant idea.

"Fire in a bottle..." Levan whispered to himself, moving back to the glass makers. "May I try?"

Rique handed him the air pipe. The wizard breathed his magical words into the revolving jar while scratching a circular symbol onto it with a solidified glass rod. Sabrena sensed the powerful energy spike, and turned to watch with an apprehensive gaze. The glass-crafters observed with amazement as the molten bulb expanded around a swirling crimson cloud, which remained within even after it was pulled off the spindle and sealed.

Levan was unsure of this concept, and even more aware than anyone how dangerous it was. "Step back!" He called to the glass-makers, backing away from the glowing vessel sitting on the production table, half-expecting it to erupt in a fountain of flame.

The people nearby exchanged nervous glances, and whispered to each other, "What is he doing?" "He will destroy us all!" "No, trust the wizards, they are our only hope." "Wizard? He's just a kid…"

But the jar remained intact. Cautiously Levan stepped forward and picked it up. The glass was warm to the touch. The shimmering plasma gleamed in his eyes as he held it up, peering through the roiling smoke within, and assured him of his mastery of this element.

"Here is your ammunition." Levan spoke gravely as he presented the glassy orb to Belina. "With this, the power of wizard fire is yours. Use it wisely, and handle it with great care. When this glass is broken, it will unleash an irresistable destruction upon them."

"Good." Belina nodded in approval. "Perhaps this can turn the tide. The delivery mechanism will take some time to assemble. Can you make more?"

"Channeling this magic is a perilous feat." Levan's face was already pale and dripping with perspiration. "But I will try. Let us hope your aim is true."

A soldier burst through the door from the alley-way beside the workshop where they were carrying the first pieces of the catapult out, groaning in pain. Acrid smoke wisped up from the charred stump where his arm once was. "That monster—it is coming—!" He gasped in horror before passing out.

When Belina went to shut the door, she saw the towering machine in the distance, sweeping its fearsome beam of light across the streets as it rumbled forward, crashing through and obliterating the stone buildings in its path.

"Ugh, we need to do something about that thing." Belina said to herself, examining the melted armor of the armless soldier with a grimace.

The lancer Dane reappeared before her. "I have our new armor." His plate mail suit was now covered in glimmering dragon scales. "Let me show them our new weapon." He beckoned for the jar of fire.

Belina hesitated. "Your courage is admirable, but to go alone against such a terrible giant—no. I've sent too many men to their deaths today."

"Absolve yourself. Victory is at hand if we but reach out and grasp it. I will not fail." Dane's resolute vow rekindled the tiniest spark of hope, and Belina relinquished the orb to him with a sigh.

"Our hopes are with you, brave knight. Make them wish they had never come here."

Dane stepped out into the blackened, sundered street, clad in shining dragon-skin mail, with his winged spear in one hand and the vessel of fire in the other.

The giant machine's spiked treads were smashing through the building next to the workshop. The deadly ray of light turned its piercing gaze on the lone sentinel, scattering on the shiny dragon scales and illuminating him in a blinding radiance. For a fleeting moment, its scorching beam shone through the slits in Dane's visor, blistering lines across his face before he could raise his arm to block it.

A few more strides put him within throwing range at the base of the pounding, thrashing iron wheel. There he could see inside its structure where a team of men were pulling metallic rods heated from a column of light at the heart of the machine, and manipulating its many extremities with them.

Dane hurled the jar up shouting, "You have wrought your own ruin! Now—*burn!*"

The glassy orb flew up, tumbling end over end toward the center of the monstrous contraption, but was snatched out of the air by one of the long metallic arms just before it reached the main body.

Another arm raised high into the air and dropped

the massive pane of glass it held, which crashed down onto the spearman and shattered as it pummeled him to the ground.

Pinned under a huge chunk of glass, he struggled to pull himself from its ponderous weight as a dreadful saw-bladed appendage descended onto him. The jagged metallic teeth scraped across his right shoulder, unable to cut through the dragon-skin plate, but exposed a section of chain mail beneath and tore through the tendons there. Dane felt only the moist warmth of his escaping blood, however, as his right arm had already been smashed, twisted and rendered numb and useless from the crushing impact of the giant lens. As the whirling blade came down again to finish him off, he finally wrenched himself free and rolled out of the way, recovering his spear in his left hand and rising to his feet.

His right arm hung uselessly at his side, streaming a torrent of blood, and his legs were barely able to support him. Then to his dimming vision came the sight of the intact fire bottle held aloft in one of the great mechanical claws. In a final, desperate burst of strength, he launched the spear skyward. The weapon spiraled perfectly into its target, shattering the engraved bottle and releasing the ferocious power within.

The thunderous shockwave threw the spearman back as a blazing globe of magical flame swelled and rose up, disintegrating and blasting away the structure of the terrible war machine.

The soldiers gave a jubilant cheer at the spectacular explosion.

Levan stopped working the glass, looking up through the windows with a troubled frown at the rising fireball. The walls of the workshop shuddered as a stifling hot wind flooded into the room.

The door opened and Dane was carried in with urgency for treatment. Behind them entered a familiar figure.

"Master Tosgan!" Levan was surprised and relieved to see his wise and powerful mentor here.

"It is good to see you well, Levan. What a battle

this must have been."

"I...the wizards..." Levan began, but Tosgan was in a hurry to reach Belina.

"Come, there will be time for remembrances later."

Belina noticed the elder wizard with a raised eyebrow. "Lord Tosgan. What are you doing here?"

"I bring grave news from the scouts," Tosgan declared forebodingly, "the invaders swell with reinforcements from the west. They've overrun the entire kingdom north of Karikoss, closing in to encircle us here in Agypto. An army at least ten thousand strong approach our position from the south as we speak."

"What!?" Belina exclaimed with incredulity. "I knew their main army had to be hiding somewhere, but so many...we had barely half that number at the beginning of this campaign. But now..." She shook her head in despair, and so the soldiers would not hear, she whispered, "If what you say is true, there can be no egress to the capitol. How could I have made such a foolish mistake? We cannot hope to stand against such a force."

"All is not lost yet." Tosgan reassured her. "This is a defensible area, and I would wager any one of our men against ten of theirs. We may yet snatch victory from the jaws of defeat."

Levan began to have a dreadful realization, compelling him to interrupt. "Sir, did you say they've taken the lands west of the Imperial Way?"

"West and east of it, the enemy marauds unchecked." Tosgan confirmed.

"Oh no, that means..." Levan's heart raced and rose to his throat, choking his words, "I must go." He departed immediately without explanation, to the bewilderment of most of them.

CHAPTER 16 EDGE OF THE AFTERLIFE

Tor and Avus leapt from one toppled spire of stone to the next, making their way to the bottom of the Deep River Hall. The river was now a meager stream which disappeared into a fissure worn smooth by the current, barely the width of a man. The standing stone in the middle of the stream had something wrapped around it just below the water line.

"It has a rope anchored already." Avus said, climbing down onto the rock and pulling the rope up from the water. "It's old." He held the frayed end in his hand long before expected; it did not even reach to the hole. "And far too short."

"This should be long enough." Tor produced a coil of climbing rope from his pack and tossed Avus a length of it.

"Let's hope so."

With Tor's help, Avus looped the anchor around the standing stone and secured it with a strong dwarven knot, then approached the fissure.

"A deep lake lies below. We will have to leave our weapons here. Hold your breath and swim that way." The dwarf pointed back toward Karikoss. "Are you ready?"

"As much as I'll ever be."

"Heh, just remember, this was your idea." With that, Avus clutched the rope and dropped into the fissure.

"I know." Tor nodded to himself, gripping the rope to descend. He shook away the inner voice that told him he should not be there, took a deep breath and hopped into the watery portal.

Avus had stopped himself at the end of the rope with the bottom still far below, mustering all his strength to grip the slippery cord and swing out of the waterfall to try to alert Tor, but it was too late. Tor slid down swiftly, crashing into Avus, and they both went tumbling off the rope as they plummeted into what seemed to be a bottomless pit.

At last they met the calm, warm waters of the submerged passage below, and plunged far into the depths.

Tor had held his breath but was completely disoriented and did not know which way to swim. Fortunately, a sunray shone through a skylight somewhere in the distance, and, when he looked up, he could see the dwarf paddling above him. He swam upward, but hesitated a moment to look back when a shadow passed through the water behind him. As his breath ran out, Tor frantically rushed upward to where Avus had his head out of the water in a tiny air pocket.

Tor sputtered as he broke the surface and struggled to tread the water. "There's someone else down there!"

"He's on his own—! Swim toward the light—!" Avus took a gulp of air and submerged again.

Tor followed, but looked back to the spot where he saw the sinking body. On the cavern floor, the sunbeam illuminated a pile of bones, the arm holding a severed rope in its death-grip. He hurried upward to the light, his limbs growing weak, lungs burning and clinching ever tighter, and just as he could hold his breath no longer, the stony ceiling opened up, and his feet reached solid ground.

Avus helped pull Tor up out of the water and they both collapsed on the embankment, choking and coughing.

"I'm sure I saw someone down there." Tor said, catching his breath.

"The eyes play tricks in places like these." Avus stood and offered his hand. "Think no more of it. We have a destination to reach."

A crack in the ground high above blinked and

shuddered like a twinkling star as it was obscured by the wheels of a passing carriage, a brief reminder of the surface world, so close yet so far away.

The water's edge met a great funnel of jagged stone rising upward, whose steep edges made for a difficult and precarious climb, and a fall to the bottom would have been the end of either of them. After several slips and scrapes, they reached the top of the ledge and entered the next chamber.

"Wow!" Tor and Avus gasped in amazement as the scene came into view.

A deep violet radiance shone from scattered patches of glowshrooms, permeating the vast cavern and revealing the ruins of an ancient city sprawled out below.

"Look at it...how could they build all of this down here?" Tor marveled at the scene.

Avus wore a grim scowl as he pointed to the great chasm that slashed across the landscape. "The heart of the Scar was right beneath us this whole time. The old city sank into the abyss."

The ancient buildings tilted inward toward the rift, frozen in a slide down to be devoured in the endless darkness. And at its head, amongst the shattered ruins of a castle, the Great Scar jutted up huge horn-like spires of rock which reached to the cavern ceiling. As they looked, a thin sunbeam moved across the castle courtyard in the distance, illuminating a brilliant crystal in the shape of a sword, and a pillar of light rose up from it.

"I think we've found your sword."

A piercing radiance shone just below the Mountain Maker, and they strained to see the movement in the halo around it. But in a short time the sunlight moved past it, and the ring of light and the sword disappeared as if they were a mirage.

"Amazing!" Tor whispered, astonished. "This is even more incredible than the legends told."

Avus was puzzled and worried. He had seen

slightly more than his companion had in that courtyard.

Why…it couldn't be…have we really been told so many lies? I must be seeing things too.

"Let's get down there!" Tor's eager phrase broke the dwarf's befuddled stupor.

Avus kept his speculation to himself as he followed Tor, clinging to the cliff side and probing for footholds on which to descend. When they had reached a safe height, they dropped off the rock wall onto the sloping, broken ground and proceeded into the ancient subterranean city.

Ash and rubble crackled underfoot as they passed between a pair of ruined buildings, and the fissures in the fractured terrace spouted jets of warm steam sporadically around them. Avus sensed the movement up ahead and pulled Tor to the side, narrowly avoiding the creature's awareness.

"Scarlings…" Avus grunted with contempt. "We need something to defend ourselves."

"There!" Tor pointed to a twisted metallic fence further down the slope, where a sword in its scabbard was tangled among the bars and some skeletal remains. He cautiously edged down toward the spiky fence. "I can reach it." And he did, but as he tried to yank the strap from the fencepost, his feet lost their grip on the steeply-sloped street and he slid down toward the gaping pit. Tor caught the sword's sheath and hung precariously from it, the thin leather baldric the only thing stopping him from plummeting to the depths.

While Tor struggled to climb back up, and Avus rushed to his aid, a small black shadow skittered across the broken fence. The creature took the leather strap in its claws and pulled, then bit into it, severing Tor's lifeline and dropping him down the slope. The clawed shadow chittered in delight as Tor slid downward, and Avus gasped in despair.

The sword and scabbard spun off to the side, coming to rest on the outside wall of the lowest structure, a building half-swallowed and leaning over the chasm's rim. And there Tor caught the edge of the wall just before falling into the endless darkness.

Avus breathed a sigh of relief as Tor pulled himself up onto the wall, but then realized he was not out of danger yet. He saw the dark bodies of three scarlings crawling up from the windows of the building, two ahead of Tor and one below. The dwarf wrenched one of the spear-like fence-posts from its housing and bounded across the gap, running across the steep slope as he slid downward.

As the monster rose up before him, Tor unsheathed the longsword and whirled it from hand to hand, judging its weight and balance. It was light and easy to wield. The first scarling lowered its horned shoulders and charged at him with unnatural speed. The footing was unreliable anywhere but at the wedge where the ground and wall met, there was nowhere to go but up. So he leapt over the scarling, slashing at its head as it went beneath him and stopped just short of the edge.

The second dark hulk was now just ahead, raising a massive stone club overhead. Tor slammed the sword's pommel into the back of the scarling behind him, knocking it off the precipice into the pit, then thrust the blade into the chest of the one in front. It should have been a mortal blow, but the monstrous fiend's attack was not prevented or even slowed. The heavy mace of rocky crystal slammed through Tor's attempted block and battered him to the ground.

As Tor pushed himself up with an agonized groan, Avus saw the third scarling crawling up from below, reaching up finish off the defenseless warrior from behind. The dwarf landed on the platform just in time to stab the makeshift spear down into the climbing scarling's neck before it could attack, then kicked it deeper into the wound, causing the creature to lose its grip and plummet into the chasm.

The club-wielding scarling dribbled green glowing blood from its chest, but continued to advance, stepping past the dropped sword and preventing its recovery as it readied its weapon to crush the kneeling man.

As the club rose again, Avus sprinted up and across the sloping wall, moving around Tor to the side and above the scarling. He sprang from the wall and clenched its head in his arm, bringing the ferocious brute down on its back as he fell.

Tor took the opportunity to pick up the longsword at his feet and plunge the blade into its skull from the soft point beneath the jaw. After it stopped moving, a ghostly voice seemed to rise from the fallen scarling.

"Thank you for releasing me, my king. I had forgotten what humans looked like."

Avus and Tor searched in bewilderment for the source of the sound, but saw no one. "Who are you?"

"Me?" The disembodied voice seemed to ponder a moment. "I suppose I—don't remember. I don't remember my name, but I think I was human. Right? I mean, before I was that thing?"

"Surely, how else could you speak with us?" Avus mused rhetorically, still thinking this might be some sort of prank.

"Yes, that's it! I was human! Like this?" The phantom manifested a faint, luminous haze which formed into the ghostly image of a man, a copy of Tor. "Is this what I looked like?"

"No, that's not right." Tor frowned, slightly disturbed by the likeness. "That's me. What mystery is this?"

"Mystery..." The apparition repeated as its form began to dissipate.

The ethereal mist transformed into a jumble of distorted faces, some silently moaning in despair, some twisted in rage. Spectral whispers seemed to creep in with a cold draft of air. "Kill them...drink their blood...wear their skin...become men again..."

As Tor and Avus stepped back in horror, the spirit they had spoken to before rematerialized into the ghost of a man whose face was a featureless blur, and rebuked the others. "No! Stop it! This is not the way, our king has returned to save us!"

"Wha—" Tor's shocked expression lingered on his face as he began to understand. "There are others like you?"

"The spirits of the dead." The ghost replied with a sigh of pity. "Can you not see them? They are all around us, wandering endlessly, we forget the world of the living, those precious fleeting moments of life and love, the warm light of… the sun! I remember it! The day the shining sword and the false sun came. I went into the light and was reborn. I had a body again, but I…had become a monster. How many ages have I searched for a way out of this prison, this hellish nightmare? Yet here I remain, surrounded by maddened creatures who kill every chance we could have of…of watching over our children as they live out their lives."

The spirit seemed to weep, and Tor told it, "We will find the way out. Come with us."

"Bah!" Avus growled in disgust, "Trust the ghost of a scarling at your own peril, I will slay all of your kind that cross my path!"

"Good." The spirit replied, "They cannot harm anyone for a long time until they find their way back to the light. I just hope that you can bring an end to all of this."

"Very well." Tor said, cleaning the glowing blood from the sword and sheathing it. "What shall we call you?"

"Ah…" The phantom hesitated, and Tor filled the pause with his introduction.

"I am Tor Veldgar. This is Avus."

"Of Deepstone." The dwarf added gruffly.

"Until I remember" Replied the ghost, "…I am Mystery."

CHAPTER 17 ASHES OF DESPAIR

Kneeling on his magical cloud, the wind at his back whisked Levan away to the countryside of his childhood, past the old familiar road stretching to the city, over the hills to the west where the little village had once been hidden.

It was a secret no more. Smoke lingered in the air from the smoldering ruins of the razed hamlet.

Levan floated to where Undra's house had stood.

There in the ashes, the charred body of Mimora was unmistakable. He expected to hear her voice as he stepped nearer.

Oh son, you're filthy. Why don't you wash up for supper?

Only cold, silent desolation met him.

Mother, what have I done? All of my choices were mistakes. I am not a beacon. I have only led us to ruin. Mama...say something...what am I to do without you?

But suddenly, inexplicably, without resolution, she was gone, and no more could be said.

He wished to melt into the ground, but could not.

This is the end. The one who made my name is no more. None remain who know me.

Perched atop the rubble, the hollow eyes of a dark iron Kinari helmet glared at him.

Strangers from another land...how could you? I can never forgive this.

Buried beneath the cindered rubble, the charred, blackened handle of the old grain scythe met his grasp.

My name is Death, the reaper of souls. I will have my revenge.

The cloud reformed beneath him as he stood, darkened as his robes with the soot and ash of desecrated innocence. His eyes enflamed with burning rage, and the black cloud on which he stood crackled and sparked with furious energy as he flew off to the north toward the Kinari army approaching Agypto.

* * *

"This way!" Mystery beckoned to the skewed doorway of a toppled house spanning the great height of the sheer rock face between the levels of the fractured terrace. "Quickly, they are coming!"

Tor and Avus ran up a beam from the shattered wall and leapt to the remains of the collapsed stairs. They rushed to the end of the sloping balcony where a window exited onto the upper terrace.

Tor reached down to help Avus climb out, but met a strong resistance from below. A scarling had grasped his leg, drawing blood with its powerful claws and pulling back at him. A swarm of the mindless dark creatures poured into the dilapidated building and scrambled up toward them. Avus kicked at it fiercely and was at last able to pull free from its grip, toppling out onto the ancient broken street.

Nearby, an ancient mattock lie on the ground, its wooden handle fluted and pitted with age, its teeth thickly encrusted in mottled patina. Avus heaved its final swing down onto monster climbing out of the window. The rotted haft split as the head impacted the scarling's skull, dropping it back to the bottom. But a ceaseless stream of its ilk clamored up behind it, and would rapidly overwhelm them if allowed to make their way out.

Standing fast at the portal while the creatures clawed at him, Avus set himself against the structural timbers and pressed forward, gaining strength with each slashing wound he endured. The last beams holding up the house gave way from the foundation, and the weight of the walls accelerated the crashing cascade. The entire building slid off its perch and crumbled down the cliff in a heap of rubble below, leaving the scarlings no avenue of pursuit.

"That takes care of that." Avus turned away from the edge, catching his breath.

Tor was confounded. "W-what—are you injured?" He noticed the bleeding cuts across the dwarf's limbs, but Avus dismissed it.

"I've suffered worse. Let's keep moving. Look, we're nearly there."

The old castle courtyard was strewn with broken statues and crumbling monolithic towers wrought with exquisite carvings which hinted at the splendor of this place in its earlier age.

From a tiny hole in the ground far above, a narrow beam of sunlight slowly moved across the stone circle which made up center of the courtyard, upon which sat a few small objects which held no immediate relevance to either of them.

Avus thought he had seen that child's toy somewhere before, but even if he had recalled, it would not have made sense to him, and no progress would be made.

"Where is the sword? It was here…" Tor wondered aloud.

"This place…" Mystery whispered with a growing clarity, "I remember—I was alive here! Ah!" The ghost seemed to fall to his knees before a dark stain on the stone, clutching his head as the pain of failure and betrayal wracked him.

"Mister E?" Avus studied the ghost quizzically. "What is the matter?"

"The one who is bringing the seals back…my old

companion…my murderer! My blood is on these stones! It was our ancestor's sword, the Heart of the Life Stone! Tor, my son!" The ghost's face became that of Anderjar Veldgar, his wide-eyed gaze filled with stark realization and anguished terror.

"Father!?"

"We should never have come here! The circle is not complete!"

Avus heard the young girl's distant scream piercing through the cavern then.

Imola had been made to hide in the dust trap beneath the fireplace when the attackers came, but the grate at the bottom had rusted and its fastenings pulled free, dropping her onto the pile of ash and luminous fungus in the tunnel below. She had picked up a glowshroom for light as she wandered to find a way out. A clawed shadow had found her and chased after her. She screamed as it scratched at her heels. She hadn't noticed the tunnel end abruptly and went tumbling down a rocky embankment.

Avus saw the girl fall, and the sinewy little creature creeping out toward her. Though the fall was a short one, only inflicting a few scrapes and bruises, the clawed shadow was dangerous, and he rushed to her aid. When he reached her side, he picked up Immola in one arm and a large stone in the other, stepping on the black ribbon–like creature to immobilize it, and dropping the heavy rock to entomb it beneath.

"Are you all right?" Avus placed her back on the ground.

"Augh, I'm okay. I got lost. I'm so glad you found me, Mister dwarf!" Imola hugged him, looking over his shoulder. "Is that Ranser over there? Where's Levan?"

"We need to get you out of—" Avus was interrupted by a brilliant light radiating from the courtyard and the sight of someone sneaking up behind Tor. "Tor!!"

The tiny sunray streaming down had reached the apex of the stone circle, illuminating the clear crystalline sword and the center of the ring in front of it erupted in a blinding disk of light.

The ghost of Anderjar Veldgar was forced to the ground, and cried out as he was pulled into the circle of light, "My son, remember me!"

Tor moved to the sword, and the ground trembled as he grasped it. "I will take you out of this place with me, Father! At last the time has come to reclaim our k —!"

His words were cut short as the green-jeweled dagger entered his back.

"No!" Avus was too far away to do anything but shield Immola's eyes as Tor collapsed to the ground., and Ward drew the blade from Tor's back.

The light faded away.

Then came the army of scarlings from beyond the courtyard, their eyes gleaming with ravenous malice.

Ward stood up serenely and made no struggle as the monsters swarmed over the castle grounds, battering him down and tearing him apart.

Still more of the hideous wretches emerged from the tunnel whereby Imola had arrived, their eternal hunger driving them madly forth to snuff out the life that tarried in their dark domain.

"I *will* bring you to safety, Imola," Avus vowed, "on my back, hold tight."

With Imola clinging to his back, Avus pushed himself as fast as he had ever run in the only direction not blocked by a horde of scarlings. He sensed an opening to the surface this way.

Without slowing down at all as he leapt down a few giant steps, Avus came to the edge of a great dark chasm. The scarlings moved with unnatural speed, closing in behind them. It seemed to be the end of his options, but he would not let despair claim him. There had to be a way.

Then he saw it.

Beyond a gap in the rocky crag beside them, a long rope bridge traversed the chasm, disappearing into the darkness in the distance. Avus scaled the rock face to find a suitable foothold, then dived across to the platform where the bridge began.

Scarlings were dropping down from above and moving in from the sides just behind them as Avus bolted across the teetering, swaying span.

The faintest glow of waning daylight filtered through above as the endpoint came into view, a tiny ledge just large enough to stand on, and atop it a massive round boulder to which the bridge was anchored.

The pursuing monstrosities were upon them as they reached the ledge and the bulbous face of the immense rock. It was too high to climb. Avus took hold of Imola and launched her up to the top of it just as the scarlings clawed at his back.

"Go! Get out of here!" He called up to the girl as the dark creatures scrambled over him and began climbing up the boulder after her.

"I can't reach! It's too far!" Immola was just out of reach of the next ledge and the way out.

There was no time to plan or think, there was only the singular course of action. There could be no impossibility. Even this greatest of stones could not refuse his vow.

He stooped, bent his knees, spread his arms and lifted the colossal boulder up high enough that Immola was able to ascend the ledge just before the scarlings could take her.

In the next moment all sensation had left him. A sublime tranquility soothed all of his pain and worries, and projected him upward to see the true scope of his journey. NuMoon's face smiled on him, and he knew he had at last earned his redemption.

When the boulder fell, it crushed the meager ledge on which it had stood, and it, the dwarf, the bridge and all the scarlings upon it plummeted down into the depths of the Great Scar.

"Oh no—!" Imola sobbed, peering over the edge into the endless abyss.

A bat squeaked as it fluttered past her and out of the cave. She noticed the movement around her then as hundreds of clawed shadows crawled in along the walls, and she turned to run toward the exit.

The creatures formed a skittering carpet of bodies across the walls and floor as they pursued their prey, but were halted at the edge of the sun's light as the young girl reached the exit.

The cave opened at the middle of a high sea cliff. There was nowhere to go. So she sat on the edge, admiring her first view of the ocean while the writhing mass of monsters behind her crept ever closer as the sun sank into the horizon.

Shrieking frantically, the cave bat landed in a nearby field. The mouse Jade had been talking to scampered away.

"Whoa, whoa, slow down." Jade tried to calm the overly-excited bat so she could understand his message. "There's a female *what* in a cave?" The bat squeaked again, flapping his wings. "*Man-child*? Oh, a little girl. Well that's no good. Let's go then!"

Jade climbed onto the back of the cave bat, flying north to the sea at full speed.

Just as the sun disappeared in the distance, Jade saw the girl at the mouth of the cave and took aim with her bow.

Imola barely felt the skyshroom arrow pluck her arm. She reached across to scratch the slight itch it made before she slumped over asleep, and shrank down to sprite size. They landed beside her as the shadows closed in. Jade hoisted Imola up onto the bat and they departed again, back toward the safety of the sprite village.

"Hi Ranser!" Jade called out as she flew over the hill, but he seemed not to hear.

Ranser nearly swatted a bat out of the air as it flitted past his head.

He reached the shoreline near the lighthouse as the sun's final glow faded out.

The sea washed its soothing whisper upon his feet, returning Ranser to the fondest of his childhood memories.

Here we are again. The beginning of another great journey.

With a heavy heart he pushed Jofon on the cloud out to sea.

Goodbye, Father.

✻ ✻ ✻

As night fell, the Kinari army marched with determination toward the port town, spreading out to surround the area, but their advance was halted at the deep ditch made by Umber before the battle.

Then the black storm cloud appeared on the hill above them, pulsing with crimson strokes of lightning.

Tosgan stood with Belina on the edge of the city. He watched with pride and awe as Levan descended on their adversaries, uttering the songs of destruction with dreadful wrath.

Howling winds spiraled down from the sky, coalescing into a pair of dark funnel clouds, arcing furious blood-red bolts of energy. Swirling up with sheets of flame as The Destroyer swung his scythe, the twin vortexes blasted forth, ripping through the Kinari ranks with devastating ferocity.

The ground heaved and quaked violently, splitting open in long branching fissures which swallowed up lines of terrified soldiers on both sides of the ditch, along with some of the outlying buildings of Agypto.

The last cohesive Kinari unit charged desperately at the dark wizard, and valorous though they were, they fell just the same.

When he swung his scythe again, a great crescent of flame slashed across the landscape, incinerating the armor and flesh of the charging veterans. Hundreds of flaming skeletons collapsed to the ground before him, and the assault was at an end.

As Tosgan made his way across the fractured land, a bright flash and globe of fire erupted on the ship just offshore, and he noticed the figure standing atop the lighthouse in the distance.

"It's Non!" Tosgan called out, running toward Levan and the lighthouse. "He has stolen your jars of flame, and used them to kill your friends and family! Levan, you must stop him! Trap him now at the lighthouse!"

To Ranser, the ship floating in the bay meant nothing until the tiny point of light floated down to it and exploded with incredible force. Only then in the light of the fireball did he see the familiar form thrown from the mast, and, tangled in the crow's nest, sink into the churning waters.

"Unadel!" He gasped as he waded into the sea, then swam with fervor out toward the wreckage.

The metallic braces and the anchor still burned as they sank into the depths, setting the water alight with an eerie glow, and silhouetting the motionless elf being dragged to the bottom by the iron-ringed lookout perch.

Ranser dived toward her, his lungs screaming for air, and the waters tightening their stranglehold on him as he swam ever deeper.

It was too far. The ocean crushed the breath from him and he writhed in agony as his vision faded.

Then something glided through the water to embrace him. It was Felegrin, the fish girl he had met at the Shadow's Rest. She breathed life into him, invigorating his muscles to make the final dive toward Unadel who now rested at the sea floor.

Struggling to free the elf's leg from the iron bars, Ranser beckoned Felegrin to try to give her breath. She breathed into Unadel's mouth, but to no effect, and shook her head in disappointment.

At last Ranser pulled Unadel free, and swam toward the surface.

The disturbance had uncovered something long hidden in the silt at the bottom, which glowed with an ethereal halo. Felegrin picked up the jeweled crown which she felt belonged to Ranser, and followed him back to shore.

Ranser carried Unadel's lifeless body up the beach, and placed her at the roots of an old tree there, falling to his knees in lament.

He tried to wipe the sand from her face as he choked with devastated tears of guilt

"Why...am I powerless to save anyone?"

"You can still save the ones you love." The voice of Titanos spoke to Ranser from the darkened sea. "Find the Heart of the Life Stone within the cave before you, and they will be with you again. Let Nea's sacrifice not be in vain."

Felegrin approached as Ranser stood. "King of the land, Titanos has chosen you." She placed the crown on his head, and knelt at his feet. "Long live the king."

The path to his destiny lay before him. Fearless as ever, Ranser entered the cave beneath the lighthouse alone.

Non had watched with satisfaction as the fireball consumed the ship, and knew that the world had come a bit closer to balance now that the mad wizard Chazriel was no more.

He descended the spiral stair to the bottom where Garath lay trapped and dying beneath the rubble.

"Non—help me, my friend..."

"Who are we to intervene in the course of fate? You have done your part, take solace in that. As always, the pieces have fallen perfectly into place, so to speak."

"Don't leave me to die like this!" Garath's agonized plea went unheeded as Non turned to leave, "You monster! Curse you!"

"All journeys must come to an end. Farewell."

When Non opened the door and exited the lighthouse, he was surrounded by a horde of identical figures draped in ash-darkened robes. He recognized the boy Levan.

"So it is today? Heh..." Non chuckled slightly in amusement. "As good a day as any."

In unison, the multitude of mirror images of Levan reached out a palm toward Non.

In an instant, Non grasped the throat of the wizard and ripped it downward. The black robe crumpled to the ground, empty. His body became a blur as he moved around the circle, dissipating the mirages one-by-one in a blinding flurry of speed.

A cylindrical wall of flame rose up and dispersed the illusory figures as it drew inward, trapping Non in an ever-shrinking circle within. He ceased his movement and stood still in the center, at last resigned to his own fate.

"Fascinating..."

The column of fire converged on him, and when it receded, his ashes blew out to sea and all that remained of Non was the armlet he had worn.

Behind Levan, Tosgan looked on from a nearby hilltop. A few Kinari soldiers had found their way to him, and pressed in around the elderly scholar. With his back to the cliff, Tosgan held forth his arm and suspended one of the Kinari in the air, strangling the warrior in an invisible grasp.

Another soldier pointed his sword and fired the circular end of it at the wizard, striking his hand and causing him to drop the obsidian orb he held, and the man who was lifted fell back to the ground.

The dark orb rolled down the hill to Levan's feet. He picked it up and moved to return it to his mentor, now surrounded and standing on the very edge of the cliff, but the Kinari soldiers stood in his way.

Suddenly, unexpectedly, he felt life's fragile threads woven between his fingers, assuring his mastery of mortality. Life and death were effortless to create for him now.

"Be gone."

The assailing Kinari squad disintegrated into dust as Levan waved them away.

Beneath Tosgan's feet, the ground crumbled and Levan caught him before he fell from the cliff.

The orb pulsed with energy in Levan's hand, and he found he was able to move into Tosgan's memories.

There he saw the carriage, escorted by a squadron of the king's men, arriving at the little village hidden in the hills north of Karikoss. The masked wizard emerged from the coach and spoke to the squad leader.

"Encircle this village, burn it to the ground. Let none escape."

"No." The soldier replied sternly, scowling with anger. "You would murder our own people? This is not the king's will! Men, execute this traitor!"

The squad leader drew his sword and slashed at the wizard's head, but he stepped backward and the glancing blow only shattered the upper part of his mask.

"Insolent swine…" Tosgan growled, removing the broken mask, "you *will* obey me, even in death."

A dark energy cast forth from Tosgan's orb and seeped into the man's flesh, turning it into a sickly gray pallor. His heart ceased and he fell to the ground.

A moment later, the fallen soldier's corpse stirred and rose again, dragging its sword over to his nearest companion and cutting him down. The others sank their blades into the being that was once their commander, but could not stop him. As they fell, they then stood back up and turned on each other again, until the entire unit was converted into the hideous walking dead.

They then set about slaughtering the villagers as Tosgan dropped the Kinari helmet and went about torching the buildings.

At Undra's house he found Mimora, whose death would bring about the transformation of his disciple, and the creation of his own personal army.

Undra took up a kitchen knife and attacked the first zombified soldier that entered, while Mimora pushed away the other with the old grain scythe, then reared back and swung it with all her strength. Even though it had been years since she had harvested grain, the implement was as natural as ever to use.

To Tosgan's surprise, his minion's head went rolling across the floor as it was lopped off by the long blade of the farm tool. But it made no difference.

Mimora flailed in vain as she was levitated above the ground, and the dead soldier's sword flew up to impale her.

Stunned with this terrible realization, Levan was unable to react as Tosgan took the orb from him.

"I trusted you—!"

Tosgan raised the black sphere aloft as he moved around Levan toward the lighthouse, his eyes set on Non's armlet. The massacred army littering the land reanimated all around them, their thousands of charred skeletal hands covering Levan, pulling him to the ground and preventing his pursuit.

"I'll kill you!!" Levan screamed as he struggled against the mass of undead limbs pinning him down.

Tosgan was but a few steps away from claiming the source of Non's power when Levan became engulfed in light and burst out of his bonds, launching upward into the sky. A moment of darkness passed before he came streaking down through the clouds, trailing flames like a falling meteor. As he landed, the air ignited around him in a roaring shockwave, blasting away the lighthouse tower, and hurling Tosgan off the cliff into the sea below. Levan's foot rested on the jeweled armlet, and he reached down to claim it.

Felegrin was floating beneath the water just off-shore when another flaming body plunged into it nearby. Like the crown she'd found on the bottom, the orb in his hand shimmered with the same strange glow, the power of the gods. She felt he had taken it from Ranser, and went to return it to him. But as she drew near, the man's eyes suddenly opened, and he grasped the arm reaching toward him. Darkness and death flashed in her mind like a fleeting nightmare, and she recoiled in horror, swimming away.

The boy held more of the seals, and had gone to find Agartha.

Tosgan smiled, pulling himself from the cold, lapping waves, burned and bleeding, savoring the delicious pain as he limped forth into the sea cave.

The great gaping maw of the fossilized ancient dragon seemed to welcome him, and proclaim their mastery over death.

"Heed my call, old one." Tosgan raised the orb as he stood before the tall fangs jutting from the rock. "Arise. Let us walk the path to immortality together."

The cave rumbled as the ancient bones stirred and the giant skeletal dragon shattered its stony bonds. It lowered its hollow skull to peer at the necromancer who had awakened it.

"The false king lies before us. With the crown and ring he holds, not even the fire-maker can stop us."

To Sabrena, poised at the outskirts of Agypto, the battle on the hilltop was appalling, intolerable. She could not stand to see another of her classmates die. "This must end."

Belina's call for her to stop was unheeded as she rushed up toward the cliff. The commander crossed the ravine with the army at her back, following after her wayward sister, and they clashed with the horde of living dead on the other side.

Sabrena became encased in ice as she ran, the

multitude of burned skeletons closing in around her. She blasted the animated corpses with a frigid wave as her staff became a long icy spear, and she thrust it forth, shattering their bodies into tiny pieces. The moist ocean air became a haze of frost around her, and the ice spread across the ground as she ran, freezing the cadavers in place. Their swords and spears fell from all sides glancing harmlessly off her magical armor as she advanced without hesitation through the throng, leaving them solidified as frozen statues in her wake.

Did Levan raise these wretched souls to fight again? Why had he killed our own soldiers?

Levan had disappeared from the cliff top when she arrived. Looking down, she saw him entering the cave below. Sabrena created a ramp of ice to quickly slide down to the shore, but again Levan was nowhere to be seen. She was drawn inexorably into the cave. To save him? To stop him? She knew not why, only that she must be there.

CHAPTER 18
AWAKENING

Clinging to a narrow shelf of rock high on the cavern wall, Ranser made his way across the expanse of the bottomless chasm and leapt to roll down a steep embankment onto the upper terrace of the ancient sunken city.

When he stood, he was surrounded by a mass of hulking dark-skinned monstrosities with glowing eyes. He drew his only weapon, a small knife, and prepared to defend himself. But the creatures did not attack. The light of the crown showed their true forms, as they had been in life, reviving their memories of who they were. They knelt before him and a ghostly voice spoke from among them.

"Our king, long have we been lost without you, dreaming of this day, when we can finally be set free. The Heart of the Life Stone is just ahead, in the castle courtyard. It is Nea's promise that we will return to the ones we love, always."

"Set free?" Ranser frowned with skepticism. So many things had come to be other than what they seemed. "There must be a hundred exits from this cave. Walk out and set yourself free."

"Impossible, we are held captive by—AH!" The speaker was silenced as he was crushed under the skeletal claw of a gigantic dragon of bone and stone dropping out of the darkness and crashing down in their midst.

The great beast swept its spiny tail across, smashing through the old buildings and hurling away a wide swath of the scarlings that charged on it.

A cloud of ghostly blue flame billowed from its mouth and spread along the ground before it. The scarlings caught in this carpet of ghost fire sank into it as they were melted into dark puddles that flowed along the channels of the cobblestone streets.

Ranser narrowly escaped this same fate as he kicked off a wall to spring up and catch hold of the edge of a high window while the cloud poured across the ground below.

The dragon's breath washed past as Ranser clung to the side of the house. He was considering climbing up through the window, or dropping back down, when the colossal jaws of the bone dragon ripped through the house in a single vicious bite, demolishing the entire structure but for the small section of wall on which Ranser hung.

The cave wall to his side was not climbable, overhanging the building and preventing the remains of the structure from collapse. The ledge dropped off precipitously on the other side and behind him. There was no place left to go.

With his back to the sundered wall, Ranser peeked out and noticed a robed man standing atop the fossil dragon as it recoiled for another chomp to finish him off. He rolled out of the way just as the massive teeth pulverized the thick stone wall, then dived to catch hold of one of the horns on its head.

While the beast thrashed and swung its long neck out over the pit in an attempt to remove him, Ranser glimpsed another figure appear on the dragon's spine.

"A dark spirit is upon *your* back."

Tosgan turned to face the ominous presence and cast forth his necrotic tendrils as quickly as he could. But his pupil now possessed the armlet which contained the forbidden magic to control the flow of time, and he knew it was futile.

Levan instantly appeared behind him again, swinging his scythe upward to rip through Tosgan's back.

"No—I was to become immortal—!" Tosgan

choked up his final words as he clutched the blood-soaked blade impaled through his torso.

Levan wrenched the dark orb from his mentor's hand and the fossil dragon became a lifeless pile of bones once again, collapsing where it had stood.

"Levan!" Ranser gasped.

The wizard turned to meet his gaze, then immediately vanished.

Time stood still. Levan was far beyond the morality or remorse he would have had in his past as he took the crown and ring from the immobilized boy he had called his friend.

Moving to the circular stone plaza, Levan placed the last unclaimed seals upon their altars. Time returned to normal as he removed the armlet and set it into place.

Shouts echoed through the cave. Ranser looked up to see a red-haired wizard create a bridge of ice across the chasm and slide down it, followed by another red-haired woman in a battle-scarred suit of armor, and a large contingent of soldiers behind her.

As the troops moved across to survey the terraces, the sorceress stopped at the body of her old teacher. "Master Tosgan...who has done this?" She turned to Ranser. "You?"

"No, it was Levan. He is—not himself."

"Where has he gone?" Sabrena demanded.

"I don't know, he disappeared."

"Lady Belina!" A soldier shouted with urgency from the ledge above, "Someone has stolen the Vimanticon, and the crown jewels! The culprit is there, in the fortress ahead!"

"Don't let him escape!" Belina called as she took off toward the ramp to the higher level.

"It's Levan!" Sabrena yelled, running in the same direction. "Stay back, you fools!"

Ranser rushed to follow the rest of them to the top terrace where he saw Levan standing at the front of the ancient castle.

The nearest soldiers charged toward the wizard, while others closed in on the sacred relics.

Levan's face was distorted in agonized rage. The orb in his hand jolted with a flash, like a lightning bolt rippling through a still lake. The furious dark energy arced from his fingertip, pouncing from one knight to the next, helmet to shoulder. Those with breath in their lungs at that moment could only scream for an instant as the current incinerated their nervous systems and they fell in a wave and cloud of foul smoke before the dark sorcerer.

"Levan, *no*! What are you doing!?" Sabrena cried in anguish, unable to understand what could drive him to this.

"Halt! Take cover!" Belina shouted the order, but Sabrena continued to advance, and she caught her younger sister's arm as she passed. "*Don't*!"

"Someone has to stop him!" Sabrena yanked free from the grasp and strode into the courtyard.

Levan lowered the final seal to complete the circle. As he placed the orb into its socket, the cavern erupted in radiance, luminous chains shattered from each of the seals, great wings of light spread out and the hand of Agartha reached up to touch him.

A droplet of light shattered through the plane of darkness, plummeting through the quintessence. Its wings formed as it fell through the glassy barrier of the circular green and blue world held atop the surface of Nea. Agartha found her body to be much the same as the primitive people that resided therein.

The elves and dwarves were at harmony with the world. They lived long lives, keeping their traditions, true knowledge of the mother goddess and the protector god, and chose their moment to transition to new forms of life, replenishing the elemental forces of nature. They needed nothing more, and thus fled from this new visitor.

The humans were different. Theirs was a short

physical life, but their wisdom and power lived on in spirits that kept watch over their descendants.

Agartha learned the history and secrets of the world through these spirits, and with each she kept near her, she found her knowledge and power grew. But without their ancestral spirits to guide them, the people in time became afraid of dying, and felt a longing for some greater meaning beyond the endless cycle of time, life and death that was their reality. Agartha wove a myth that fulfilled their need, and exalted herself as their deity.

Humans had lost their way, following and becoming like the being that had also been removed from its source of creation. They turned their tools of progress and enlightenment into weapons, and wars spread across the land, creating yet more disembodied souls upon which Agartha fed. They burned and chopped away the forests for their arrows and forts, and dug deep scars in ground for their wells and mines, coaxing the land to bend to their will, filling the air with smoke of the flames of war, and cries of anguished suffering.

The elven spirit trees were found at last, and Agartha's power grew immensely from their harvesting. The elves made a great sacrifice to Titanos, pleading for his aid. As Agartha watched over her flock from the clouds, the protector god of the sky and sea appeared, and he created the word which manifested the cosmic thunderbolt, striking Agartha down, burying her beneath the land. But the spirits she had gathered around her kept her from destruction.

The seven who had seen Titanos then came to understand the folly they had been led to, and were given the sacred words of power which commanded the forces of nature, time, life and death, meant to overcome the insidious invader.

Agartha's followers dug deep to her resting place, and could hear her commands once more. Hidden from the wrath of Titanos, they built a great citadel around her, and mined the depths, seeking out the source of the dwarves' power.

When they began to cut into the Life Stone, the dwarves called out to Nea. Their mother goddess permitted them to take her heart, the purest of crystals, and forge from it the greatest of weapons. And in the hollow from whence it was taken, a human child was found. The dwarves raised him in secret, the one who was meant to use the weapon to finally purge the evil that had overtaken their world.

An age of chaos and bloodshed came as humankind made war with the elves and dwarves, until at last the followers of Agartha were driven out from their hidden fortress.

The seven wizards and the man who was born of the Life Stone gathered around Agartha's resting place before the sunken citadel. Each of them held an object they treasured in life, into which their spirits would enter, to remind the generations never to let this happen again. Only when the spells had been spoken, to freeze Agartha in time, trap her in an endless dream, recapture the spirits of those she held captive, and recover the lost memories of their ancestors, could she finally be destroyed with the Heart of the Life Stone. The six wizard's bodies disappeared as they uttered the sacred words, but the seventh did not.

Agartha whispered a devious deception to the holder of the final seal, the orb of volcanic glass. She promised him eternal power and endless life. The wizard turned on the warrior who held the sword aloft, prepared to drive it into Agartha's head. A great fissure opened in the ground where the crystal blade missed its mark, sinking into the stone just above Agartha as the warrior was pierced through the back by the wizard's treacherous dagger.

Before the seals could be reversed, and Agartha returned to her full power, the objects imbued with the wizard's spirits flew upward, bursting out of the cave into the sky, and sought out their descendants across the land, entrusting them with their magic, that they might someday complete the circle.

Agartha was bound by six chains, and could only whisper in the dark, but still she held the souls of the dead captive, twisting their memories and turning them into vile monsters. The cult of Agartha was reborn as the holder of the orb sought out the other seals for the next five hundred years.

Levan found himself in a splendid garden with a magnificent gilded tower in the distance, and happy, laughing people all around. The familiar faces greeted him, smiling in adoration as they saw him. From the resplendent tower emerged a sublimely beautiful winged angel, her flowing robe and golden hair shining with divine light, and she walked hand-in-hand with another person.

It was Levan's mother, Mimora. Her face beamed joyously, but she did not speak.

"At last, the light has returned." The Radiant One smiled in praise of him. "Together we can thrive in blissful eternity, our own world, free of suffering and death, if only you take the final step." She pointed a finger to Ranser who was running toward them, but slowed as if moving underwater. The vivid foliage of the garden withered and turned black around him as he approached. "The one who would destroy us draws near. Call your glorious flame! Free him from his confusion, let him join us here in our garden!"

"Kill Ranser? I...couldn't..."

"You *must!*" The images of the multitude of soldiers Levan had killed appeared around them, their faces silently pleading. "For all these souls you've liberated, make this one last sacrifice! We beg of you!"

"No!"

"Foolish mortal!" Agartha roared in fury, her face sinking inward to a hollow, darkened recess.

The sky was devoured by a serpent of embers, and as it struck forth, the gilded tower behind Agartha shattered and crumbled down, the garden turned dark and the bright spirits surrounding them transformed into hideous, bloodthirsty scarlings.

The angel now held the blade of a flaming sword across Mimora's neck. "You doom us all! This is your last chance to save your mother!"

Levan's lifelong reverence for the goddess tempered with the pain of losing his mother and clashed with his realization that Agartha was not the savior that she seemed, the guilt of causing so much death, and the innocence of his friend. A tempest of conflict raged in his mind, bringing hesitation to the casting of his spell. "**Ultima Ignus**..."

Rushing up the incline just behind Belina and Ranser, Sabrena saw the fiery mist swirl up in Levan's hand as he prepared to incinerate them, his eyes clouded with anguished strife.

"Levan, stop!" She cried in desperation, but to no avail. Reluctant though she was, she knew what must be done. "**Perpetua crystallum...glacia!**"

The cave's copious moisture condensed and poured down on Levan, crystallizing into an indestructible pillar of ice around him.

The ground tremored and the sunken city began to fracture along the lines of the seven seals.

Blindingly intense light flooded the cavern as Agartha took on a giant, faceless angelic form and ascended to the surface, shattering though the cave's ceiling in a deluge of crushed stone. Trailing behind her, a shimmering chain still clung to her leg, emanating from the orb held in the frozen wizard's hand.

The world quaked violently, splitting the courtyard in a web of widening fissures, and into these cracks fell the seals which once held her.

As the crystalline sword began to slide into the yawning chasm, Ranser bounded across the crumbling platform, diving to catch it. From the darkness below, a benign, maternal entity reached up to him, seeming to hand him the sword, and prevent him from falling into the depths.

"Take my hand!" Belina reached down to pull

Ranser to safety.

She then noticed Sabrena had fainted behind her, and hurried to hoist her sister up across her shoulder.

Ranser returned to Rune and commanded him, "Find the way out!" The surface soil on the trail left by Tosgan was easily trackable, and the dog barked assuringly at the tunnel beyond the courtyard. "This way!" Ranser beckoned, and Belina carried Sabrena after him, across the stone bridge into the concealed shaft spiraling up to the temple.

A thick rope hung at the top of the stairwell before a wall of hewn stones, which slid away when Ranser pulled at the rope.

The temple was a sundered ruin, much of the ceilings collapsed, through which the floating light in the distance could be seen, the false sun turning the night to day. A gaping hole punched through the center of the cathedral, and they moved around the rim of it with cautious haste.

Exiting onto the temple grounds, they saw Agartha hovering across the plateau into the city, and the buried dead arose in her wake. The reanimated bones of former generations shed the tatters of their burial cloths as they clawed their way to the surface, and dripped with mud as they shambled from all corners of the graveyard to close in around the one who held the shining sword.

Rune growled nervously while Ranser and Belina brandished their weapons in preparation for what seemed would be a hopeless fight.

Thousands of skeletal arms reached in from all sides to strangle the life from them.

Ranser swung the sword in a wide arc, and its luminance flared brilliantly as the power of the legendary weapon revealed itself. The Life Stone's Heart became a gigantic blade of light, annihilating the multitude of risen skeletons as it swept across the graveyard.

The ancestral souls gathered around Ranser, rejoicing in the arrival of their liberator, and pointing the way, along the magical golden chain, to the false sun which he was meant to destroy.

The ill-fated blood of Ranser's forefathers compelled his pursuit of Agartha toward the lower end of the city, diverging from Belina who carried her comatose sister onward to their family estate.

As Belina reached the manor, an exasperated soldier ended his dash to confront her. "Lady Belina—the enemy —they've reached the northern gate."

"Bring all of our archers to the battlement, arrows aflame."

"The horsemen are ready. Shall we send them forth behind the barrage?" The apprehensive officer suggested, presuming the new commander needed advice on traditional tactics.

"No, save the horses. Hold at the gatehouse and fight on foot should the wall be breached."

"But—"

"Do as I say! Now go!" Belina snapped impatiently as she reached the opulent mansion door.

"Yes m'lady." The officer rushed off toward the north gate, even more worried than he had been.

The guard pulled back the tall door and greeted Belina with a bow as she entered.

"Belina!" Her mother gasped, rushing to the portal of the entry hall. "What's happened?"

"She expended her strength to save us from the fire wizard." Belina explained solemnly as she laid Sabrena on a padded couch.

"Oh my baby Brena," their mother sobbed as she knelt, touching Sabrena's pale face, "please wake up!"

"She will be fine, just let her rest."

"They said we are not to leave," her father wore a vexed frown, "what's going on out there?"

"The city is under attack."

"Oh, heavens no," her mother wailed inconsolably,

"please stay with us."

Belina turned to leave. "I must go to lead the defense. Stay indoors, keep yourselves safe."

The bombardment began as Belina rushed to the rampart. Fifty flaming iron spheres were launched from the powerful Kinari catapults, soaring over the walls like a shower of falling stars.

From the height of the castle tower, the king looked down with dread at the sprawling army on his doorstep. Never had he felt so powerless and alone, and his inability to handle a crisis was evident in his panicked expression of despair as he turned to his accompanying pair of royal guards.

"Find my minister! Find Oslan! Find anyone!" The king ordered frantically. The guards hesitated but complied without a word.

Turning back to the window where the light hovered across the city, he muttered a desperate and futile prayer. "Agartha, please save us..."

But alas, the end of Fahfren's reign was already hurtling through the sky toward him. His eyes widened in horror as the fiery orb flew in, smashing through the tower wall and exploding within.

The bombs rained down on the city like a hail of meteors with devastating force.

Great stone columns crashed down as a shattering shell ripped the library in half, blocking Ranser's path with a wall of flaming rubble.

Just below, the captured Kinari soldier regained his senses from the dazing impact and scrambled up the wreckage of his shattered enclosure. But before making his escape, Wrexon stopped at the sound of a pained groan.

"Oslan!" Wrexon lifted away the heavy broken bookshelf which fell on the old sage whom he had grown fond of in his time at the library. Long daggers of splintered wood were embedded deeply into Oslan's body, and bled profusely from these mortal wounds as he took his final breaths to speak to Wrexon.

"Agartha has awakened…she has enslaved and deceived us all…"

"Yes." Wrexon replied somberly in his own language. "My people have come to banish this false god."

"Impossible…" Oslan choked forth the words. "Only the shining sword can destroy her. The Kinari are needlessly killing innocents. Please trust me, help us bring an end to this war."

"I will trust your wisdom, my friend." Wrexon sighed as Oslan's breath ceased.

The next wave of explosive projectiles tore through the Fafhren manor just as Sabrena was waking up. The dark iron orb set the roof ablaze as it plummeted down through the floor, disappearing into the darkness of the great cavern below.

Sabrena's parents moved to the edge of the crumbling crater as it consumed the gilded statues and antique suits of armor within their treasure vault.

"The jewels, save the jewels!" Sabrena's mother cried as her husband struggled to pull a heavy chest away from the growing chasm.

Appalled at the scene taking place, Sabrena stood and moved to the pit. "We have to get out of here!"

"Not without our family's treasure, we are ruined without it!"

"We will be alive! It means nothing if we die here! Leave it!" Sabrena shouted desperately over the crashing din as the building crumbled around them.

But her father would not relinquish the chest. The flaming timbers of the roof toppled down as their home collapsed beneath the barrage.

Sabrena was only able to dive in desperation to jaunt her mother away from a crushing death. The fleeting sight of her father falling into the darkness in a shower of jewels seared a perpetual scar into her memory.

Wrexon's flight was fraught with the greatest of peril. Any Kinari would be slain on sight, he carried no weapon, and the chances of escaping the besieged city and convincing his commanders to halt the attack seemed almost beyond probability. More alone than ever he felt as he sprinted through a narrow alley toward the high end of city, his heart surging with imminent dread as he checked each intersection from both sides before dashing through. Soldiers seemed to be marching through every main thoroughfare but not noticing him, so he hoped.

Wrexon checked the next crossing and found it clear. But as he launched himself into it he was immediately met by a hard wall of steel, and he stumbled and fell to the ground.

A tall, elaborately armored soldier stood over him, pointing the end of a sword blade at his neck.

They were both amazed to see each other.

How has a Kinari without gear entered the city?

They use women as soldiers here?

"Lady Belina!" an ambitious young officer named Martellus called out as he ran up the street. "The royal guards report the king has fallen! We are leaderless!"

Just then another bombardment fell from the Kinari catapults, exploding the nearby buildings and covering the area in rubble.

Martellus coughed up the stone dust as he lifted himself from the wreckage, pleading again for the dire fate of the kingdom. "My lady—we are finished—the archers are taking heavy losses on the walls—we cannot hold any longer!"

Belina stood up, shaking off the rubble and regaining her senses. "They cannot yet breach the moat, we still have time!"

Wrexon rolled out of the avalanche of stones nearby, his face swollen with bruises and dripping with blood from various lesions.

"A-a Kinari! Kill it!" The officer stammered as he fumbled for his weapon among the disarray of shattered construction materials.

"Wait," Wrexon's pained groan halted the sword and stone from striking him, "I have Oslan's final words. Hear me. Kinari army has come to kill Agartha, but only the one with the shining sword can harm her. I must bring an end to this battle if he is to have a chance."

"And how would you accomplish that?" Belina inquired warily. "Are you one of their leaders?"

"I am but a common soldier, and a captive here. I know not if they will believe me, but I must try." Wrexon pleaded.

"You'd never make it past the lines, unless..." Belina paused to consider.

The officer interjected incredulously. "Why are we speaking with an enemy combatant? They are not to be truste—" His protest was interrupted by something rising out of the wreckage very near him.

A crushed and twisted man with a distorted skull and missing body parts lurched forth, knocking Martellus to the ground, clutching and biting at his neck.

He was already bitten and turning pale from shock when Belina kicked the cannibal off him and brandished her sword in warning. But the creature was no longer human, beyond pain or fear as it continued advancing to attack Belina even when being impaled by her blade. She pulled her sword from the heart-piercing thrust and heaved it in a low and level arc, slicing through the mid-section of the reanimated man and separating the torso from the legs.

Yet the monstrous body continued to crawl toward her in a frenzied bloodlust. The next stroke of Belina's blade took its head off, but still it did not stop moving, the jaw gnawing away and the arms still crawling until she severed one of them, and the risen corpse was reduced to a scatter of body parts, still flailing madly but no longer able to attack.

The young officer Martellus had been unconscious on the ground until he began to stir and get back up with the same dead eyes of his killer. More soldiers and civilians appeared in the streets in varying states of injury and decay, from seemingly unharmed to entirely fleshless skeletons, all moving toward Belina and Wrexon.

"Damn you, Agartha." Belina muttered under her breath. "Come, follow me!"

Belina dashed off to the north, detouring around a crowded alley between two fractured buildings, making her way to the high gate. She hailed the sentries in the murder holes above as she picked up a fallen shield and handed it to Wrexon. "Open the gate! Lower the drawbridge!"

The sentry hesitantly moved to comply, but the thought of being overrun by a fanatical army stopped him from carrying out this bewildering order.

"Our last line of defense—will she really let it fall so easily?"

"You heard the commander, just do it!" Another soldier took the rod from the first and pried loose the catch, unwinding the great chain and lowering the bridge down to span the moat.

In the next moment it was not the foreign invaders that broke in but a swarm of the living corpses of their own comrades and countrymen filling the room and devouring the unprepared archers. Thus they were unable to lower the portcullis to stem the flow of the undead pouring across the drawbridge behind Belina and Wrexon.

Ahead, the black, beetle-like army of spikes, spears and siege machines bristled with aggression, while behind, a crowd of unkillable cannibals rushed madly toward them. Arrows flew from both sides, one from the Kinari side was deflected by Belina's shield while others struck the mangled monstrosities to little effect.

The beleaguered army leader slung her shield upon her back and turned to face away from the Kinari archers just as the undead creatures reached them. She hacked away an encroaching arm as Wrexon bashed another with his shield, pushing it off the bridge for the long fall into the moat.

The Kinari engineer finished turning his catapult's crank down to its flattest trajectory and released the projectile. Just as the two reached the end of the drawbridge, the huge flaming orb flew over Belina's head and crashed through the wooden planks, shattering the bridge and dropping the teeming mass into the chasm below.

Belina was nearly among them as she was taking her last step to the other side and her leg was grasped by a falling skeleton. But Wrexon caught her arm and struggled to pull up the weight. The boney grip would not relent from kicking at it repeatedly, so Belina reached down and unlatched her calf armor, letting it fall, along with her sword and the creature which had held her.

Arrows continued to fly at them on the other side of the moat, but ceased at last the third time Wrexon shouted to them in his own language.

As the two approached the Kinari front line, a mounted warrior came forward with whom Wrexon spoke briefly. The Kinari commander raised his eyes to the glowing light of Agartha moving across the mountaintop, then spoke a final word.

Wrexon turned to Belina. "It is done. The attack is halted."

Belina gazed back at her ravaged city. "It's up to you now, Ranser."

Harley Aguilar

CHAPTER 19 THE SEVEN SEALS REUNITED

Sprinting through the bloodied street, Ranser avoided the ravenous risen corpses where he could, but when he could not, he swept them from his path, the blade of light flashing out and burning them out of existence. Dodging and leaping piles of rubble, Ranser and Rune pursued the floating light across the mountain city.

When he reached the causeway he could see Agartha still flying away, but now facing back toward him. The shining goddess raised her giant sword and it hovered in the air above her, becoming seven swords which spun in a halo around her.

You are my creation. How dare you oppose me?

The giant blades shot forth and converged on Ranser, and he leapt back as they smashed through the thick bridge of stone just ahead of him. The arches of the causeway crumbled in on themselves and the entire structure began to collapse.

In the avalanche of ancient stone columns, Ranser landed near the base of the partially collapsed causeway. A wide slab of stone wedged above him, preventing his demise.

"Rune!" Ranser reached out in anguish as he watched his companion plummet into the depths of the canyon.

He was pinned to the ground by an enormous weight, the crystalline sword just out of his reach. All of his desperate efforts to escape achieved nothing.

This can't be how it ends.

An ant crawling across the stone paused to waggle its antennae at him before moving on. This brought him to recall the gift he'd been given from the sprites. If only he could reach his pocket.

He twisted his arm and compressed it against the jagged rock, straining to clutch the two red mushrooms between two fingers. The grip was precarious, and he dropped one of the stalks of fungus, but was able to reach to his mouth and swallow the other.

The rocky cage pressed in on him as his body grew in size, until he was able to reach his weapon. The sword blazed with light as it melted through the thick chunks of masonry and he was able to regain his footing.

Above his head, Ranser saw the ethereal golden chain to which Agartha was bound, and dived to take hold if it. The winged creature rushed upwards, slamming him into the cliffside above the city. Ranser's grip held, and he pulled himself up by the chain to the edge of the plateau.

The true sun's rising light had begun reaching up to dissolve the stars behind The Great Deciever as the boy and the towering goddess faced each other.

Streaking in from the sky, the ancient objects which were used to bind Agartha in ages past formed a circle surrounding Ranser. As they landed, the spirits which embodied them stood, emboldening him with the forgotten power of his own people, and the vengeful wrath of countless captive souls. The ancients dissipated into revolving specks of light as Ranser continued his pursuit of the false goddess.

The words of the collective will spoke through him. "This is our world, you cannot take it. For all that have been lost, we will banish you!"

Agartha spread her enormous wings, blocking out

the sun and scattering an array of glittering plumage. These feathers flew back in toward her as she plucked the strings of a gilded harp. From each note launched a shining missile which pierced the rocky, frosted ground in all directions with the force of a furious barrage of comets.

Yet before the flurry of feather arrows could fall on Ranser, a ghostly armored knight materialized before him, crested with a familiar crown and a great shield. From all sides the feather arrows dove in, but they could not penetrate the defense of the brigade of spiritual knights which appeared around them with their shields interlocking.

Agartha continued to fly across the plateau at great speed, but only one-seventh faster than the boy who was surrounded and propelled by the spirits of the ancients.

The mountains reached in to create a narrow pass ahead, a place where ancient ruins still spoke of long-forgotten history. Agartha waved her arm as she flew beyond it, and a great wall of ice rose up to block the way.

A wisp of light floated ahead of Ranser, and the image of the sacred scroll erupted into a cone of flame, taking on the figure of an immolated man rushing toward the wall of ice in a blazing streak of energy. As the fiery one drew near, the wall of ice began to weep, then crackle and explode as he rammed into it.

Yet beyond the hole in this wall had gathered countless multitudes of brittle ancient bones, held together by the growing power of The False Sun.

It was then that the bear appeared at the breach. Its fierce roar ricocheted in a visible shockwave, bouncing between the narrow walls, concentrating their waves into a rising and resonating crescendo which shattered the bones of the undead host.

Ranser strode atop a mountain of bones, into the rising sun which now became wreathed in a whirling circle of giant swords.

The blades began revolving ever quicker around

the winged disc of light and then flew out, high into the sky where the air was no more. A flaming aura surrounded the hundred colossal metallic spires as they slashed the sky back toward the ground, pushing the haze of battle away in their meteoric fall.

Ranser was alone and defenseless until the heat of the burning blades was on his face.

A speck of light materialized into a bejeweled armlet, and there appeared a hooded man wearing it. In the next instant, the still master reached upward and halted time, pointing all the swords to land in the shape of a blooming flower around them. As he let time revert to normal, he lifted Ranser by the heels and launched him upward past the blasting impact of the enormous blades. The ground erupted in destruction below as Ranser found himself flying through the air.

Above, Agartha's ring of light was silhouetted by a growing spot on the sun behind her. The approaching orb shimmered with its own steely glow, heralding an unstoppable, crushing death.

As the hero soared forth, a luminescent torus of energy materialized below him. From the shining signet ring sprang a monstrous toad, leaping from the top of the wall of swords to boost Ranser's jump.

A shimmering flame grew and fell with incredible speed above as Agartha called down the immortal wanderers.

The comet ripped through the sky, setting it ablaze with light until it was swallowed by the gaping jaws of the giant toad. The heavenly stone drove the ancestral spirit creature a short way into the ground by Nea's reckoning, but to Ranser it made the world appear to explode, shattering the ground beneath him in a fiery shockwave.

The Tome of Records then activated, and beneath Ranser appeared a massive green insect springing upward. The wings of Merton's mantis propelled them out of the main blast of scorching ejecta and high into the air.

Approaching the cloud layer, Ranser was inundated by a punishing storm of hail and lightning. The carapace of the mantis transferred the electric energy to its furiously beating wings, which dispersed the arcs of lightning out and down to the peaks of the mountains around them.

As they rose through the mist, a volley of gigantic icy spears rushed in, only to be slashed away by the swift claws of the mantis and the shining sword of the sailor boy. At last the flying insect sprang in a burst of speed to launch Ranser upward before fading out of sight.

The light of Agartha bathed the tops of the clouds as they punched through them. For a moment they floated in a sublime and peaceful overworld. There, the spectral chain went taut, ensnaring the winged disk of light from rising furthermore.

The faces of the fallen flashed before Ranser's eyes, Jofon, Tor, Undra, Mimora and countless others he could not name.

Strike now, end this tyranny.

From the ground, those left alive saw the endless ray of divine light slashing across the heavens to meet the shimmering globe of the second sun.

The shadows of the mountains fled away as the Heart of the Life Stone blazed out from its crystalline blade, splitting the clouds and cleaving through the body of the false goddess.

The city of Karikoss and the army gathered outside shielded their eyes as the sky erupted in a blinding flash of energy. When they could see again, the haze had parted to show two great wings, disintegrating as they drifted apart from each other in a shower of feathers and light around the boy who fell from the sky.

As Ranser plummeted down, the risen dead collapsed, and the fighting in the city ceased.

When the physical remains of their forebears returned to the ground, the spirits that had embodied them rose up from it, free at last from their imprisonment below.

The faint image of Sabrena's father embraced his family as they wept with joy. Ward held Reva's hand as they gazed into the sky, and she smiled up at him. And all across the land, the spirits gathered around their descendants and those they knew in life.

Reunited with their ancestors, the living would come to know that death was not the end, and they would continue their journey with purpose, assured that their knowledge and memories were never lost.

* * *

Avus awoke to a dog licking his face.

Rune yapped excitedly as the dwarf sat up on the bank of the river just above its confluence with the sea, shaking the grogginess from his head.

"Ho, that was some fall. Heh, how'd you get here?" He rubbed Rune's furry coat.

The dog barked insistently at him. "Wake up! It's time to save them!"

"Yes, I'm fine. What is it?"

The animal dashed off in the direction of the treeline. When Avus arrived, he recognized the body lying there, and she awoke when he said her name.

"Unadel!"

She sat up with a gasp. "What happened? Did the ship survive?"

"I don't know, I'm sorry."

"Where is Tor?" Unadel demanded, clutching his shoulder.

"He—has finished his quest." Avus could not bring himself to tell her yet.

"So he'll be back in the city with the others."

"Yes, perhaps he is."

"Then we must return now." Unadel stood shakily.

"Yes. Let us return."

They began to climb the hill overland when Rune demanded their attention. He barked at them and the cave nearby, running to it and back.

"What is your problem, dog?" The dwarf's rhetorical question was answered by the elf.

"He wants to return to his master. He thinks we're going the wrong way."

"Ranser's in there?" Avus pointed to the gaping cave near the shore.

Rune barked as if confirming it.

"Well, back to the cave it is." Avus turned to Unadel. "Maybe you'd fare better taking the forest route."

"Hah, you'd have no chance without an elf and a climbing rope. I owe the little sailor a favor anyway. Let's go."

✶ ✶ ✶

"Atheras Opteros, arise, awaken, your journey is not yet finished, return to us, **Vitalitas**."

The moment Sabrena began the spell, Ranser's eyes began to open, and by the end of it he was able to speak to the group of friends he saw surrounding him.

"It is finished. Have I died?"

Avus laughed joyously as the others celebrated. "Haha, no, you are not dead. Though I'm not sure how long you'd have lasted in that canyon if Unadel and I hadn't found you."

The one-eyed elf was there too, and she spoke solemnly to him. "We had no idea what you did for us. For me. The false sun is no more, the world is returning to balance."

"I could not have done it without you all."

A voice came to Ranser, somehow familiar, as if from some deep corner of his memory. "I knew there was a powerful destiny for that child I set out to sea so long ago." The face of Anderjar, his true father smiled benignly down at him.

"Father?"

Materializing from the morning's early light, the ghostly image of the sailor Jofon smiled upon the resplendant warrior king Anderjar. "Reunitin' you two has taken longer than expected, but finally, here we are."

"Jofon! How are you here?"

"No longer are we held under Agartha's spell. We are eternal, may it never be forgotten again."

"Our ancestors have returned." Sabrena beamed with joy as the image of her father appeared beside her. "In time, with their help, we will come to learn again all that we once knew."

From Boden's Rock, high above the ruined city, Ranser surveyed the remains of the kingdom.

"What do we do now?" Ranser implored his family from the other side.

"That is for you to decide now, brother." Tor replied with all the optimism of the departed.

Observing the carnage below at length, Ranser came to his conclusion. "We rebuild it. Not as a fortress to keep others out, but as a palace to welcome all."

"They will call you king." Tor assured him.

"I would not accept such a title." Ranser's head shook as if to fling the temptation of power away, though it never crossed his mind to be so ambitious. "A friend taught me that our fates are equal. We cannot rule others. Nor are we our true selves if we are not sovereign. I would rather help everyone make their own kingdom."

"As it should be." Anderjar stepped forth to place a hand upon Ranser's shoulder. "But we may not convince them all in our lifetime. Behold, a new battle begins on our doorstep." The spirit pointed to the restless army across the chasm. "If we can persevere, within the fires of this conflict, our differences as men will soon dissolve, and we will return to the harmony that was once the song of our world."

Ranser vowed "I will see it done, in this incarnation or the next. Nea and Titanos are with us. Yet it will take more than blind luck and faith to fix all of this."

"You will learn to fight on the land," Unadel appeared on the ledge beside him, "and in the shadows. The forests cry their outrage more than ever. We must be prepared for what is to come. I am with you."

"I will always be thankful of you, Unadel."

A pair of reptilian wings momentarily obscured the sun before descending to the plateau in a gust of wind.

Unadel snapped into stance to slay the flying serpent, but Ranser stopped her as a voice came from behind the wings.

"Hey Ranser! Look who I learned to talk to now!" Jade giggled as she stepped off the winged serpent. She stood nearly as tall as Ranser now.

"What—!?" Unadel looked on, perplexed but still on guard.

"Amazing. So the little dragons really can be your friends?" Ranser asked, eyeing the strange, hovering creature with fascination.

"Ah no, not really, they're not very smart or nice but—oh! I forgot." Jade fumbled in her pocket and turned around to toss a fuzzy morsel of food at the snake, which snatched it up and promptly flew away, uninterested in her gratitude. "Thanks for the ride..."

"You've been eating well." Ranser smiled at her. "I seem to remember you being much shorter."

"Heh, umm....the animals showed me which ones were the best Sunshrooms so I ate those to become big. I wanted to be human-sized so I could...umm, ha..." Jade stammered and looked away to find her answer. "Help you talk to animals too, and fly around like we used to and win this war coming up!"

"Fly around?" Unadel interjected argumentatively. "Has this giant pixie been sprinkling you with her dust?"

"I'm not a pixie! Pixies have clear wi—" Jade's face lit up with excitement. "OH YEAH, LOOK! My wings are growing back!" She turned to wiggle her short, vestigial irridescent wings.

"Wow. I'm so happy for you, Jade." Ranser chuckled at the infantile wonderment of the sprites. (She would forget about her wings soon and get just as excited when she remembered again.) "And of course I look forward to flying with you again. But perhaps the war is over. Agartha is vanquished, the Kinari have no more purpose here."

"The raccoons say another war is coming." Jade replied with certainty. "Something is going way wrong down there. When the humans start fighting again, we have to fight too."

A large fish appeared to tumble down the waterfall and splash into the pool nearby. Another familiar face rose up from the water.

"Ranser! I've found you!" Her melodic voice seemed to lilt like a siren's song from beneath the waves.

"Who is this now?" Unadel muttered, uneasy at the growing crowd, but also struggling to remember why she felt she knew the shimmering scaled face of this merfolk maiden.

"Felegrin!" Ranser strode to the water's edge to embrace her. "I never got to thank you for saving my life!"

"I knew it was worth the scorn of my people when I swam to the top of this mountain and saw what has become of your kingdom. None of them has ever gone so far from the sea, nor cared for the woes of the land-dwellers." Felegrin gazed sorrowfully into Ranser's eyes. "I wish to save you once more. Give you gills to soar through the ether in endless tranquility. A peaceful existence. No more fighting."

Unadel scoffed in disdain. "So that's your answer

when things go wrong, just swim away? Ranser, you're not going with her, not even for a moment."

"Uhh!?" Jade exclaimed her incredulity. "You are *not* taking Ranser!" She yanked his right arm away from Felegrin's. "Get your slimy tentacles off him!"

"He's the only one that can reunite the kingdom, we need him here!" Unadel was now shouting as she pulled on his other arm.

"Stop!" Ranser commanded with exasperated dismay. "Listen, the challenges ahead are too many to be at odds. The four of us have taken a leap out of all we once knew, into an uncertain future, and because of this we are reunited with our ancestors. There may still be fighting to do, but we have a chance to begin again, to learn again, a better way. I hope it will be with your help."

"Hey, Ranser!" A gruff shout echoed up from the slope below.

As they turned to look, a clearly exhausted dwarf was bounding up the mountainside, sweating and panting as he climbed up to the ledge.

"Glad to see you, Avus!" Ranser called back as he reached down to help his friend up.

"Thanks!" Avus wiped the sweat from his brow as he caught his breath. "Chasing these kids around while I'm trying to patch a wall has worn me right out."

"Kids?" Ranser grinned curiously.

"So many lost their parents," The dwarf's brow furrowed with heartache as he spoke, "Imola, Reva, my entire spelunking class. I could not leave them to their fate. I'm turning the old ruined chapel into an orphanage and schoolhouse. My adventuring days are done. That's why I'm glad I saw you up here, you being king now and all, do you think you could do an old buddy a favor and send some...uh...troops or food to help us get this thing started?"

"I'm not going to be king." Ranser replied in an optimistic tone. "That order will be up to whoever is in charge of the army I suppose, but I'll help however I can."

"That would be Fahfren's niece, Belina." Unadel added.

"Oh, yep," Avus recalled the lady knight aloud, "the fire-head. I need to talk to her."

"I like that idea." The mermaid Felegrin spoke up. "The orphanage. I want to help. Your children are stuck on the ground, they can't go far. It will be easy."

"You need food?" Jade's eyes twinkled joyfully. "I can make a boar grow taller than a tree if you guys can find a way to take it down!"

Unadel nodded thoughtfully. "We may want to find that spearman Dane, the one who fought at Agypto."

"And that ice-girl."

"Sabrena."

"Right."

"We'll need her help as well." Ranser affirmed with renewed optimism. "There is much work to be done, a new world to be built."

"Hehey! let's make it happen!" Avus cheered.

Felegrin dived away into the waterfall, Jade called an eagle, soaring up into the sky, and Unadel vaulted off the cliff, catching tree limbs with her chains and spinning around them to disappear into the forest below.

Avus looked at Ranser and uttered the obvious assessment of the situation: "Well, I guess we're walking."

"Race you to the bottom."

They sprinted down the mountain to begin rebuilding a new peace.

It was not to last.

* * *

Deep in the dark and silent underworld, a tiny fissure grew into a splintering crack in the glassy surface of a pillar of ice. A pair of burning eyes opened up within.

Betrayed and buried, yet I will not be silenced. Forget me at your own peril.

CPSIA information can be obtained
at www.ICGtesting.com
Printed in the USA
LVHW031621220219
608477LV00003B/290/P

9 781794 491076